Praise for

The Old Testament stories of [...]
The Story of Ahinoam. Mesu Andrews's depiction of the courageous woman who became David's wife shows us that God has a purpose for everyone, no matter how unconventional our past. Wonderful!

Angela Hunt, Christy Award–winning author of THE EMISSARIES

Unexpected plot twists, empathetic characters, and well-researched biblical history make this an exceptional work of Scripture-based fiction.

Publishers Weekly starred review of *Of Fire and Lions*

With fascinating insight into biblical history as well as the human heart, this story will capture your attention until the last page.

Tessa Afshar, award-winning author on *Miriam*

With skillful prose, impeccable research, and a clear devotion to the biblical account of Israel's Exodus from Egypt, Mesu Andrews depicts these Old Testament men and women with a sparkling clarity, never shying away from what makes them relatable human beings—the failings, triumphs, and yearnings that are timeless.

Lori Benton, Christy Award–winning author on *Miriam*

The novel is full of intense drama, palace intrigue, and bouts of frenetic action. A superbly satisfying and inspiring story of an ancient prodigal son. Highly recommended.

Historical Novel Society on *Isaiah's Legacy*

With deftness and deep insight, she brings her characters to vivid life. Well-researched and richly presented, this latest offering is a literary feast!

Laura Frantz, Christy Award–winning author on *In Feast of Famine*

Mesu Andrews has pieced together Scripture's truths with historical supposition through her masterful, research-based writing and captured the spiritual climate of those ancient days.

Mesu Andrews takes a biblical tale of great tragedy and skillfully weaves beauty and love amid the loss. Job's story brought vividly to life!

BRAVE

KING DAVID'S BRIDES

—

ONE

BRAVE

THE STORY *of* AHINOAM

MESU ANDREWS

BETHANYHOUSE

a division of Baker Publishing Group
Minneapolis, Minnesota

© 2024 by Mesu Andrews

Published by Bethany House Publishers
Minneapolis, Minnesota
BethanyHouse.com

Bethany House Publishers is a division of
Baker Publishing Group, Grand Rapids, Michigan

Printed in the United States of America

Library of Congress Cataloging-in-Publication Data
Name: Andrews, Mesu, author.
Title: Brave: The Story of Ahinoam / Mesu Andrews.
Other titles: Story of Ahinoam Description: Minneapolis, Minnesota: Bethany House,
    a division of Baker Publishing Group, 2024. | Series: King David's Brides; 1
Identifiers: LCCN 2024006097 | ISBN 9780764242618 (paperback) | ISBN
    9780764243981 (casebound) | ISBN 9781493448081 (e-book)
Subjects: LCGFT: Christian fiction. | Novels.
Classification: LCC PS3601.N55274 B73 2024 | DDC 813/.6—dc23/eng/20240216
LC record available at https://lccn.loc.gov/2024006097

Scriptures taken from the Holy Bible, New International Version®, NIV®. Copyright © 1973, 1978, 1984, 2011 by Biblica, Inc.® Used by permission of Zondervan. All rights reserved worldwide. www.zondervan.com. The "NIV" and "New International Version" are trademarks registered in the United States Patent and Trademark Office by Biblica, Inc.®

This is a work of historical reconstruction; the appearances of certain historical figures are therefore inevitable. All other characters, however, are products of the author's imagination, and any resemblance to actual persons, living or dead, is coincidental.

Cover design by Peter Gloege, LOOK Design Studio

Baker Publishing Group publications use paper produced from sustainable forestry practices and postconsumer waste whenever possible.

24 25 26 27 28 29 30   7 6 5 4 3 2 1

To Sherril Odom

You started out as a follower on social media, joined several launch teams, then worked hard to earn your CMS certification and volunteered to edit my short stories. You have been friend, brainstormer, and life-saving-in-a-pinch-last-minute editor on this project. "Thank you" just wasn't enough.

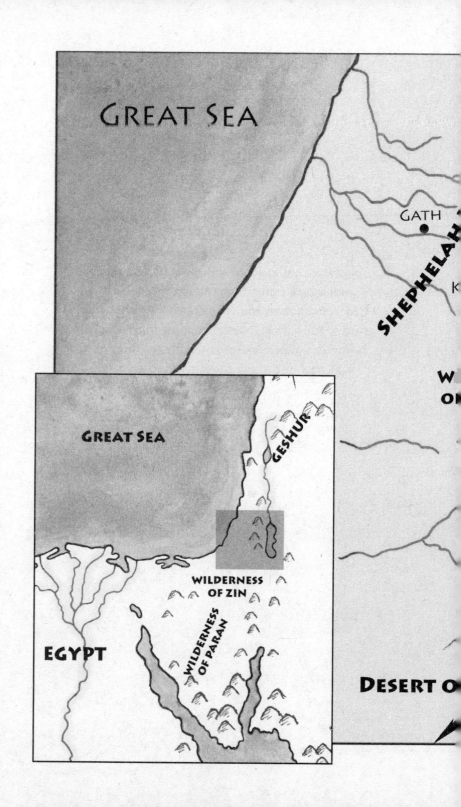

GREAT SEA

GATH

SHEPHELAH

K

W
O

GREAT SEA

GESHUR

WILDERNESS
OF ZIN

WILDERNESS
OF PARAN

EGYPT

DESERT O

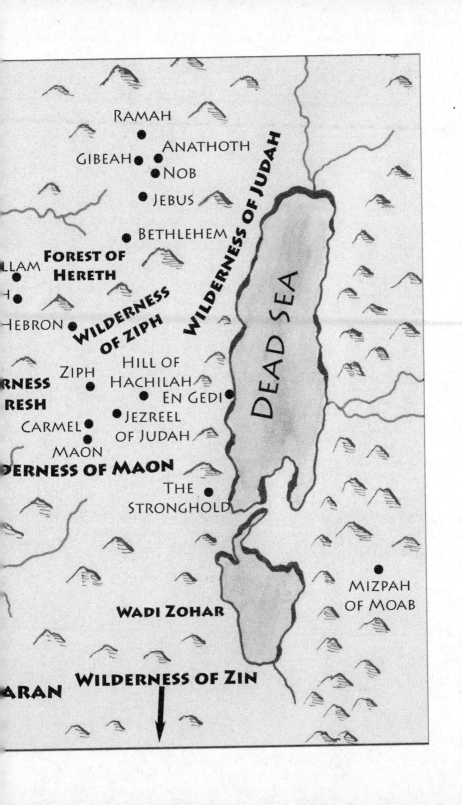

CHARACTER LIST

Abiathar—David's personal priest

Abigal—David's half sister

Abigail—Nabal's widow; David's wife

Abishai—David's nephew; Zeruiah's son; Commander of the Three

Abner—Saul's general

Ahimelek—High Priest at Nob

Ahimelek—Hittite soldier

Ahinoam—Toren's daughter; David's wife

Amasa—David's nephew; son of Jether and Abigal

Amasai—Kohathite (Tribe of Levi); one of David's Mighty Men

Asahel—David's nephew; Zeruiah's son; one of David's Mighty Men

Attai—a Gadite who joined David's army at the stronghold

David—son of Jesse, anointed as Israel's next king while Saul
    remains on the throne

Eglah—daughter of Moabite maidservant (Keyalah)

Eleazar—one of David's Mighty Men; a member of the Three with
    Shammah and Abishai

Elhanan—one of David's Mighty Men; son of Dodo, from Bethlehem

Eliab—son of Jesse; David's oldest brother

Eliphelet—one of David's Mighty Men; son of Ahasbai, the
    Maacathite (ties him to Achish)

Gad the Seer—a prophet

(Old) Jeremiah—a Gadite who joined David's army at the stronghold

Jesse—David's father (abba)

Jether—Ishmaelite; husband of David's half sister Abigal

Joab—David's nephew; Zeruiah's son; Commander of David's army

Jonadab—David's nephew; Shimea's son

Jonathan—Shammah's (the warrior's) son

Jonathan—King Saul's crown prince; David's best friend

Keyalah—maidservant from Moab

Michal—Saul's daughter; David's first wife

Miriam—(fictional name) one of Abigail's maids

(Old) Miriam—friend of Toren's and Ahinoam's from Jezreel

Nabal—wealthy Judean landowner; Abigail's first husband

Nitzevet—David's mother (ima)

Orpah—(fictional name) one of Abigail's maids

Ozem—Jesse's sixth-born son; David's troublesome brother

Paltiel—Michal's second husband

Samuel—a priest and prophet who anointed Israel's first and
    second kings

Saul—first king of Israel

Shammah—one of the Three

Shimea (biblical spelling also: Shimeah, Shammah)—Jesse's third-born
    son

Toren—Ahinoam's father

Uriah—a Hittite; one of David's Mighty Men

Zeruiah—David's half sister; mother of Joab, Abishai, and Asahel

NOTE TO READER

> [God said to David through His prophet Nathan,]
> *"The Lord declares to you that the Lord himself will establish a house for you."*
>
> *2 Samuel 7:11*

David is one of my favorite Bible heroes. He slew a giant with a sling, a stone, and a faith bigger than Israel's army. When King Saul accused him falsely and chased him into the wilderness, David could have taken his revenge but remained obedient to Yahweh and chose mercy instead. The decision meant years of hardship for David and his loyal followers. While Saul passionately pursued David, David passionately pursued God. Though scholars debate how many years David evaded Israel's mad king, all agree that many of David's most gut-wrenching psalms were written while he and his misfit army were fugitives in Judah's wilderness.

In the pages of *Brave: The Story of Ahinoam* (KING DAVID'S BRIDES 1), I use the foundational truth of Scripture, historical research, and creative fiction to build a story about the first of David's wives listed in 2 Samuel 3:2–5. The six women who bore his first six sons in Hebron established the foundation of David's household. If

13

you'd like to read the biblical truth about David's background with King Saul and life with Ahinoam and Abigail before reading my compilation of truth, facts, and fiction, you'll find the truth alone in 1 Samuel 13–26.

Ahinoam, Abigail, Maakah, Haggith, Abital, and Eglah each had a role to play, though only Abigail's story is fleshed out in Scripture. David's love of multiple wives may assault our modern sensibilities, but please remember that ancient Israel was a very different time and culture. More importantly, keep in mind that though David and his wives may have been surprised each time David added a bride, Yahweh was *never* surprised! From the creation of time, God knew Jesus would rise from "the Root of Jesse" and be called "the Son of David," and He chose each of the six women named in 2 Samuel 3:2–5 to become David's brides.

In the following pages, you'll meet Ahinoam and Abigail, the first two wives listed among King David's brides in Hebron. But this is Ahinoam's story. In the Bible, she's mentioned six times, and in each reference she's defined only as a Jezreelite, referring to her Judean hometown of Jezreel (Joshua 15:56). Though I found little historical information about Ahinoam, she has become one of the most intriguing characters I've ever written because of her (fictional) heritage as a Kenite. I hope you'll enjoy the biblical history woven into the story with that tidbit of creative fiction.

Come with me to ancient Israel and meet David's *brave* bride.

PART I

When Saul realized that the LORD was with David and that his daughter Michal loved David, Saul became still more afraid of him, and he remained his enemy the rest of his days.

1 Samuel 18:28–29

PROLOGUE

DAVID

Michal, David's wife, warned him, "If you don't run for your life tonight, tomorrow you'll be killed."

1 Samuel 19:11

Elul (September) 1018 BC
Saul's 34th Year of Reign;
7 Years after David's Anointing
Gibeah of Benjamin

With Saul's ever-tightening grip on his spear, my hopes of remaining in his family plummeted. My focus now was staying alive. He only brought his spear to a feast when his mind was tormented, and I brought my lyre as both weapon and shield. Tonight's strumming had been in vain, unable to silence the chaos behind his eyes.

Which were now fixed on me.

The feast was small. Some might consider it intimate if they weren't privy to the underlying tension. Princess Michal was the only royal offspring officially invited and I the only son by marriage. Michal's ima, Queen Ahinoam, sat on her daughter's right. Across the low cedar table, perched on newly stuffed Tyrian-purple cushions, were the king and his concubine, Rizpah. She nursed her newborn son and cast invisible daggers at the queen. Ahinoam met her stare with a shield of integrity honed by almost sixty years as Saul's wife. The king ignored the war between his women and continued glaring at me.

Michal, however, had never walked away from a fight.

"You witch!" she hissed at Rizpah, then sheltered her ima's shoulders like a hen brooding over chicks. She'd been so focused on protecting her ima, she hadn't seemed to notice her abba's wild eyes.

I continued strumming. *Calm now. Breathe. Show no fear.* From my periphery, I noted his royal guards, alert and wary. I'd been their captain until Saul promoted me to a commander of thousands in the army, hoping the Philistines would kill me so he wouldn't have to.

Michal scooted toward me and lifted a hand to cover her whisper. "I'm going to escort Ima back to her chamber. She need not endure this humiliation."

I nodded, maintaining both the rhythm and tune. When she turned to go, however, I stopped playing only long enough to pull her close and whisper, "Why were you surprised when my regiment arrived this evening? Didn't you receive my message?" I released her, resumed playing, and locked eyes again with the king.

Michal cast a wary glance at her abba before lifting her hand again and whispering, "I think Abba blocked your reports to Gibeah months ago. We only received military messengers about Abba's and Jonathan's victories. Word about your success came from traveling merchants."

When she drew away, Saul began rolling his spear. His eyes narrowed. The moment felt eerily similar to years ago, the first time he'd thrown his spear at me. That evening, our troops had marched into Gibeah to the welcoming song, "Saul has slain his thousands but David his tens of thousands." Later that night, he'd tried to pin me to the wall with his spear. Last year, we'd returned home to similar accolades, and the next day Saul issued an order to every commander for my execution. Thankfully, my comrades were too stunned to obey, and Jonathan's quick intercession saved my life.

Saul's mind was miraculously restored when he vowed to never lay a hand on me. He became the welcoming abba he'd been after I killed Goliath, as were Michal's brothers, her sister, and their families. Last winter, I learned what it meant to be included in Saul's family, and I'd fallen in love with my beautiful, vibrant, royal wife. We'd prayed unceasingly that the Lord would open her womb before I left for war last spring. He hadn't. *Yahweh, what lies ahead for us if her abba tries to kill me again?*

I'd allowed my attention to lag while reminiscing, and my fingertips were numb from strumming. When I noted Saul's neck and cheeks had grown rosy, I sat up straighter. Strummed harder. Checking my path of escape with quick glances, I noted Michal whispering something to her ima. *Please, Lord, don't let anyone else be harmed when Saul aims at me.* I should have known something was amiss when only my regiment was summoned back to Gibeah and then quickly dismissed to their homes in Judah. *Oh, how I wish you were here, Jonathan, my friend and brother.* Perhaps he could have soothed his abba's fury.

Maybe a quiet song would help. "I cry aloud to the LORD; I lift up my voice to the LORD for mercy . . ." Saul's agitation seemed to intensify at the mention of Yahweh, so I resumed the tune without words.

The sudden awareness of battle descended, and everything around me slowed to a step-by-step progression. *Yahweh, protect me with Your strength and speed.* Saul's nostrils flared. His breathing hitched. His right hand drew back with the spear and his left hand stretched toward me—his target. Perfect throwing form.

"Michal!" Throwing my lyre aside, I lunged toward her as the spear's sickening thud pierced the wall above my head. Scuttling to my feet, I slid both hands beneath my wife's arms and pulled her with me toward the only doorway. An unearthly howl joined Queen Ahinoam's shriek behind us and turned Michal's head.

"Keep running!" I urged her, escaping the palace and skirting the shadowy edges of the main courtyard. "He won't hurt her. Only me."

We passed the stables, ran through the vineyard, and finally reached the small two-story house Saul had given us as a wedding gift. Michal's sister, Merab, lived in the house on the east with her family, and one of their brothers and his family lived in a house on the west. Oil lamps glowed in their windows, but all was quiet at this late hour. We slipped into our home, barred the door, and lit a single lamp.

"You must leave!" Michal said, shaking as she held the lamp. "Go now!"

"Go where?" I combed fingers through my hair, pacing, then tightened both hands into fists. "Your abba may have already stationed men at the city gates to kill me."

The lamplight showed all color draining from Michal's cheeks. "If you ever loved me, David, you must leave Gibeah tonight."

Halted by the rawness of her challenge, I gawked at her. *If I ever loved her?* "Have I given you reason to doubt?"

"No, I only meant . . ." She released a huff and studied her jeweled sandals. "I only meant you must leave tonight." The lamp sputtered. Or was it Michal's trembling hand on the clay vessel that made the wall shadows dance?

I took the lamp from her and placed it on a nearby table, then wrapped my arms around the only woman I'd ever loved. Resting my cheek on her head, I spoke gently but with as much resolve as I could muster on a night filled with so much uncertainty.

"You know I've never felt worthy of a king's daughter, Michal. I was a shepherd boy, raised by my abba's chief shepherd and a widowed sister with three boys of her own. When your abba proposed our marriage, I soon discovered he'd set your bride price at one hundred Philistine foreskins in hopes that I'd be killed while collecting them. Our match wasn't exactly fertile soil for true love, but I have well and truly loved you as Yahweh's gift to me." Sliding my hands beneath her hair, I looked deeply into her eyes. "Though we've only spent a few months of our two-year marriage together, Michal bat Saul, let there never be any doubt that my love for you is real." I leaned down to taste the sweetness of her lips, dreading another departure.

"David." She pressed against my chest and stepped back, eyes averted. "Please, you must go now."

"Are you in such a hurry to be rid of me?" The question came out sharper than intended.

"If you don't leave now, you'll be dead by morning!" The fire in her eyes glistened in unshed tears. "I can't bear it, David. Go. Please."

"Come with me." I reached for her, but she pulled away, avoiding my touch.

"No, I can't leave Ima." Again, she examined her sandals. "Besides, how can I stay with you when you don't know where you'll go?"

Her sensible reply felt more like a rebuke, and old insecurities stirred in the dregs of my heart. What if Jonathan couldn't reason with his abba this time? Would Princess Michal choose a shepherd husband over her royal family? *Yahweh, might this be the last time I see my wife?*

Overwhelmed by the possibility, I held out one hand. "Michal, look at me." Slowly, reluctantly, she lifted her eyes to meet mine. "I'm leaving tonight. Right now. But I'll need your help. Your abba may have posted men at the city gates, so you'll need to lower me from our bedroom window to the path outside the city."

Already shaking her head, she protested, "I can't. Abba will know I helped you and—"

"He won't." I bounced my waiting hand, and she finally placed both henna-painted hands in mine. I lifted them to my lips while holding her gaze, trying to infuse her with the assurance I felt from Yahweh. "When I fail to report for duty in the morning, your abba will summon you. Simply tell him that you woke to an empty bed, that I must have slipped away in the night while you were sleeping."

Searching my eyes, she paused. "I think I can do that," she said finally, voice quavering.

"I know you can, Michal. And I'll come back to you as soon as—" When? What could I promise? Pressing a kiss to her forehead, I inhaled the faint scent of her juniper-scented oil and said, "I'll come back when your abba's torment is no more." *Yahweh, let it be soon.*

When David had fled and made his escape, he went to Samuel at Ramah . . .

So Saul went to Naioth at Ramah. But the Spirit of God came even on him, and he walked along prophesying . . . Then David fled from Naioth at Ramah and went to Jonathan and asked, "What have I done? What is my crime? How have I wronged your father, that he is trying to kill me?"

1 Samuel 19:18, 23; 20:1

Six Days Later

I made a third line on the boulder, marking day three since I'd returned from Ramah. Then I crouched lower behind the Stone of Ezel. The irony of my hiding place brought a wry smile to my cold face, so I pulled the lamb's-wool cloak Samuel had given me tighter around my shoulders.

I'd escaped Ramah and returned to the Stone of Ezel—the Rock of Departure—as a memorial to my old life, knowing I could never return to Gibeah or my wife. When I arrived, Jonathan had been waiting—not for me but simply obeying a nudge in his spirit for early morning archery practice. We fell into each other's arms in the exact location where, a year earlier, he'd successfully reasoned away his abba's intentions to murder me. Having known nothing about his abba's attempts on my life, Jonathan had left me beside the Rock of Departure, hoping he could once again reason with his abba and restore my position of favor.

But I knew it was a fool's errand. I tried to explain that this time was different. "You didn't see the hatred in his eyes when he hurled that spear, and I never thought he'd send assassins into the heart of Samuel's camp."

"But Abba saw how Yahweh protected you, sending His Spirit to prophesy through his own assassins. Even Abba was overtaken and prophesied. How could his heart not be changed?" Jonathan had proposed I remain at the Stone of Ezel, leaving my seat at the royal table empty for the New Moon celebration. "I'll explain your absence," he said, "and Abba's response will reveal his heart toward you. I'll return in three days with the truth."

He'd provided enough food for my three-day wait and promised to return with both good news and a little archery competition. *Thank You, Yahweh, for the love of my brother Jonathan.*

I heard the thunk of a bowstring's release. Then a bronze-tipped arrow pierced dew-sodden earth ten paces east of my hiding place. Two more shots fired in rapid succession, landing in a neat arc. A servant boy's delighted laughter split the morning silence and grew louder as his footsteps came closer. I shifted my position around the boulder to be sure I was completely unseen.

Holding my breath, I listened for the carefully worded message Jonathan and I had arranged. If he said, *"The arrows are beside you, boy. Bring them back,"* I could return to Michal and enjoy another quiet winter. During my three-day wait, I'd tried to convince myself it was possible.

"Isn't the arrow beyond you?" Jonathan shouted instead.

My blood ran cold, hearing the coded words that proved Saul still wanted me dead and I could never return to Gibeah.

"Hurry! Go quickly!" Jonathan added. "Don't stop until you reach the arrows!"

"Master?" The boy's voice was too close, just on the other side of my boulder. Heavy footsteps pounded the earth, and I knew Jonathan was running toward him.

"Master, are you well?" Fear laced the boy's tone. "Have I displeased you?"

An intimidating warrior thirty years my senior, Jonathan halted at the boulder, cleared his throat, and spit. "Take the arrows and my weapons back to the palace." Metal clanged against metal. Why would he relinquish his weapons? Jonathan was always armed for battle. "Tell Ima I'll return before midday."

"Yes, Master." The boy retreated with a lumbering gait.

"Run!" Jonathan shouted the impatient command. After two heartbeats, my friend whispered, "Stay hidden, David, until I tell you it's safe."

Safe? Emotion tightened my throat. *How will I ever be safe? Where can I go that's beyond Saul's reach?* I pressed the heels of my hands against my eyes, paralyzing fear warring with dreamlike memories. Only last week, I'd led a thousand men to victory over the Philistines. Israelites lined the streets to welcome me home with pride, and my beautiful wife welcomed me with warm kisses. Must I now slither away like a viper to its hole? Saul's unjust hatred stirred despair to fury, until a hand suddenly clamped onto my shoulder. Startled, my battle instincts roared to life. I bolted to my feet, dagger drawn.

"No weapons, brother." Jonathan stepped back, hands lifted. "See? You never need fear me."

Instantly, regret warred with shame, and then I realized how well he knew me. "You relinquished your weapons because you knew I'd react first and think later." I sheathed my dagger.

"I relinquished my weapons because you're Israel's fiercest warrior, who fights with reflex and instinct. Yahweh gave us those keen reflexes and battle instincts to survive." Jonathan let his hands fall to his sides. "I needed them two days ago when Abba hurled his spear at me."

"He intends to kill you now?"

Jonathan shook his head but with little conviction. "Everyone is in danger when Abba is tormented, but he's only determined to kill you."

"Why, Jonathan?" I pulled at my hair, choosing anger over despair, and released a war cry before turning back to the one man on earth I could trust. "Tell me if you know!"

Eyes full of tenderness, he said, "I believe Abba knows Samuel anointed you as Israel's next king."

I couldn't have been more shocked if he'd produced a purple donkey. "How—" My mouth was suddenly too dry to speak.

Only my family had been present seven years ago when Samuel had come to Bethlehem and summoned me from Abba's sheep pastures to pour over my head the horn full of sacred oil. My brothers hated me and Abba barely acknowledged me as his son, but none would benefit by betraying my secret. They'd only put the whole family in danger by revealing that Israel's great prophet had anointed Israel's next king while Saul still occupied the throne.

"Don't look so surprised." The glimmer of mischief in Jonathan's eyes almost made me smile. "I've suspected it since the day you killed Goliath."

"When did you know for sure?"

"Just now." The mischief faded. "And you were right, David. Abba won't stop until he kills you."

Hearing the ungarnished truth from his lips was like a cudgel to the gut. I stumbled to my knees, bowing to kiss the feet of my prince. My brother. He helped me stand and embraced me so tightly, I could barely breathe. Or maybe it was my weeping that stole my breath. The honor of Jonathan's friendship salved my wounded heart. Israel's valiant prince had knowingly befriended a shepherd boy whom God chose to inherit the throne his abba fought to keep. Yahweh had drawn us together through our insatiable thirst for Him, making Jonathan my earthly protector since the day our God helped me slay Goliath.

"You are God's greatest gift to me," I choked out on a sob.

"And you to me, little brother. We'll see each other again. I vow it."

The declaration, meant to comfort, instead hit like a lightning strike of loss. "Michal!" I pushed him away. "I must see her. Is she safe? Can you get her out of the city? Does she know—"

"She's living in the palace now." My friend averted his eyes, then turned and kicked a small stone.

The air between us went suddenly cold. "What are you not telling me?"

Without turning to face me, he said, "There were two more empty seats at the New Moon festival. Abba hurled a spear at me for defending your absence but made no fuss about Ima's and Michal's unoccupied cushions. So, I visited Ima. She said Michal had been honored with the second-finest chamber in the palace harem. I then sent my spies to discover why Abba would bestow such an honor on my spoiled little sister."

Spoiled little sister. Saul had always indulged Michal, but why would Jonathan send spies? "Why not just ask Michal about her new chamber? I'm sure your Abba is bribing her with finery because he thinks she knows where I am."

"No, David." Jonathan whirled around, fury in his eyes. "She betrayed you and gave Abba a reason to charge you with treason."

"Treason? That's impossible."

"After Michal helped you escape, Abba's men found an idol with goat's hair in your bed. It was obvious she put it there to trick them."

"Idolatry isn't treason in your family," I said, "and she probably got the idol from your ima." My friend winced, and I knew I'd hurt him. "I've talked to Michal about the idols. Forbidden it, Jonathan. She said she'd stopped."

"It's worse than the idol, David." Jonathan's calm sigh sent a shiver of dread up my spine. "The guards took Michal to the throne room, and Abba questioned her."

"I begged her to come with me, but—"

"My little sister loves no one more than herself, David. She'll never leave Gibeah or relinquish comfort or status for anyone." He placed a hand on my shoulder. "Michal testified before Abba's royal council that you threatened to kill her if she didn't help you escape. . . . Threatening a member of the king's family is treason, punishable by death."

"I didn't." Shrugging off his hand, I stepped back. "I would never . . ."

"I know, David. And anyone who knows Michal also realizes what she's like."

Anyone who knows Michal. The words sent shards of pain through my mind, shredding logic, draining hope. I bent to cradle my throbbing head and released a guttural sound.

Jonathan hovered over me. "I know the sting of betrayal, brother. Abba kept all this from me."

"You know betrayal?" I shot to my feet. "By a wife with whom you've covenanted before God to become one flesh? To share your life? At least your abba and brothers never refused to acknowledge you as their own."

He circled the back of my neck and pressed his forehead against mine. "Yes, I know betrayal," he said through clenched teeth. "The betrayal of an abba and family whose disobedience cost me Israel's throne and their continued disobedience that makes me alone in my faith every day. You were my gift, David, the spring of water in my desert that my sister has taken from me by giving Abba a reason to kill you. Our love is deeper than any woman's because it was a gift from Yahweh, and I'll never betray you as your wife did."

Releasing me, he lifted his chin and stood like the warrior I'd fought beside in battle. "I'll never lead Israel's troops to you, my brother, but you must hide somewhere that no other tracker in Israel can find you. Abba has recalled the whole army to search for the traitor David ben Jesse, and he will not stop until you're found."

Dazed and shattered, I could barely whisper the words, "Thank you, brother." We renewed our covenant together, wept until our eyes were dry, and parted with no idea when or if we'd meet again.

ONE

AHINOAM

This is the inheritance of the tribe of Judah, according to its clans . . .
In the hill country . . . Maon, Carmel, Ziph, Juttah, Jezreel, Jokdeam,
Zanoah.

Joshua 15:20, 48, 55–57

Two Weeks Later
Jezreel of Judah

Eager to begin our day of gashing figs, Abba and I had already broken our fast by the time the sun peeked over the horizon.

We had only a few trees on our modest farm, but the second harvest—the more plentiful but less tasty—would sustain us for winter. Gashing the unripe fruit would speed their ripening during the next few days so that we could time our harvest to rest on Sabbath.

"Don't forget to wrap your hands, girl," Abba shouted over his shoulder.

"Yes, Abba." He often forgot I was a twenty-one-year-old unmarried woman, not the five-year-old child he'd raised after Ima absconded with an Amalekite soldier. "Are *your* hands properly protected?" I grinned, anticipating his growl.

Since he was walking three paces ahead, I couldn't decipher his mumble but noticed the cloth-covered hands with which he adjusted his leather belt. Even his work-hardened skin needed protection from the unripe figs' irritating sap.

Repositioning the curved gashing blades in his leather belt, he also checked his flint knife. He then slipped his hand behind his back for the third time to touch his two hidden daggers. He'd seemed unsettled all morning. Was he concerned our increase in Israelite customers would somehow leak word to the Philistines about our bronze weapons? Abba and I had followed the traditions of our Kenite ancestors and continued metalsmithing—the Kenite name meant *smith*—even after we'd moved to Jezreel, and the Philistines forbade metal sharpening in Israel.

Though we'd fled the Amalekite city seven years ago and I'd been weak from the journey, I still remembered Abba's impassioned speech to Jezreel's elders. *"From the time Israel left Egypt until their arrival in Canaan, we Kenites have lived as your reciprocal allies and protectors. Your King Saul warned us before attacking the Amalekite city where my daughter and I lived. We fled and were saved, but your King Saul disobeyed Yahweh's command to completely destroy the Amalekites. Now the Amalekites hate all Kenites for colluding with Israel. If you allow my daughter and I to live peacefully among you, we'll supply you with bronze weapons and will arm you to fight when foreign raiders come to rob your harvests."*

Abba became an instant hero in Jezreel of Judah, and we found even more favor when they discovered we and our ancestors were faithful to Yahweh. True acceptance came, however, when the Jezreelites learned it was my distant *savta* Jael who killed the Canaanite commander Sisera by driving a tent peg through his head. Abba warned everyone that I showed the same fire and resourcefulness, which was why he'd never taught me to spin or weave.

"Don't lag behind, girl!" Abba groused. "If you climb the trees this slowly, I'm sure to best you today." Competition always motivated me, so I hurried to catch up and linked my arm with his.

He looked down with a begrudging smile. "Stay close today. Understand?" Before I could ask why, he turned his gaze forward. "Yesterday was a good Sabbath. You'll return to Old Miriam's house tonight and stay with her. I'll take first watch in the grove."

"Please no, Abba. We spent all Sabbath with the old widow." I released his arm. I was too old to pout, but I still didn't want to spend a night alone with the woman. "I listened to her stories until my head throbbed. And she talks constantly about finding me a husband. She always wants me to help her grind grain or sort lentils or some other boring—"

"Enough." His hard stare sobered me. Why was he so grouchy today? "Someday you'll need a husband to protect you, and you'll need to know those household skills."

The familiar fire leapt to my cheeks. "I'll never need a husband, and my daggers will protect us."

He shook his head and mumbled again.

I pulled him to a stop. "You've always said if I can mumble angry words, I should have the courage to speak them aloud."

"Don't use my words against me." His stony glare could have sharpened a blade. "Life isn't like figs, Ahinoam. We can gash figs and force them to ripen in our time, but we can't make life conform to a predictable harvest of our desires. What if life gashes *us* unexpectedly? What if I'm taken from you? Hmm? Today? Tomorrow?"

"Stop!" I stomped my foot, a childish response, but at least his tirade ended.

The deep creases softened between his bushy brows. "Nomy." He tilted his head with the pet name, and I thought my heart would fall out of my chest. I was more used to his tirades than tenderness. "Haven't you noticed how many daggers we've sold during the past month?"

"I thought more people had become aware of your skill, and the extra sales helped pay the overdue rent on the farm. Why is it a bad thing to sell more—"

"Amalekites are raiding in Judah."

"Amalekites?" I whispered as if they might hear. "Are you sure? Raiders come every year. Philistines. Geshurites."

"Only Amalekites—" Abba's eyes slid shut. "Only Amalekites are so cruel to the living and so . . . *uniquely* dishonor the dead."

I dropped my gaze, unwilling to show him my fear. Memories of living in a tent outside their city sent a shiver through me. Thinking of their violence stirred terrifying thoughts. "Abba?" My head jerked up. "If more people have purchased our daggers, how long before the Amalekites know we're in Jezreel? How long before they find *me*?"

Saul's attack seven years ago on Amalek's capital had likely saved my life. Days before, an Amalekite soldier came to collect the weapons Abba sharpened for him. Though I always hid in the tent from soldiers, this one glimpsed my retreat and demanded I show myself. I was only fourteen, wore no lotions or braids in my hair, but he leered at me like a wolf drools over a lamb. The man left his weapons as my bride price, despite Abba's attempts to dissuade him. We knew how Amalekites treated women, but we had no choice but to accept.

Will I be another life ruined by Amalekites because King Saul disobeyed Yahweh's command to destroy them?

"As I said . . ." Abba placed his arm around my shoulders, nudging me toward our small fig grove. "I'll keep watch over the ripening figs, and you'll stay with Old Miriam at night."

I didn't dare argue, but Abba would not be alone in this grove tonight. I'd sneak out of a window after the widow fell asleep. "I'm coming to you, Abba, if there's a raid."

"Make sure Old Miriam is safe first, and then come."

I stopped again, shrugging his arm from my shoulders. "No! I'm staying with you in our house. We have a plan in place, and it's a good one."

"If you stay at Miriam's home, you'll hear the shofar's nine blasts. Make sure Miriam is hidden, then come to me. *This* is the new plan, daughter." He adjusted his leather belt. "I've trained you well, Ahinoam. Don't be a silly woman."

My cheeks warmed at the censure. He resumed his short-legged strides toward the trees, and I dutifully followed. A million questions reeled through my mind. We'd already worked through a plan with Old Miriam. She knew where to hide. Why must I stay with her at all? Did he think the Amalekites rode slow mules that would wait on me to run from house to house before ransacking our little farm and stealing our tools and supplies?

Now that the awful reality of a raid was more than a possibility, I needed clearer direction. "If they come too quickly, am I to stay and protect Old Miriam or run home and protect—"

"*You.*" Eyes remaining forward, he added, "At all costs, I command you to protect *yourself.*"

Throat clogged with fear and unspoken questions, I said no more until we reached the first row of trees. Abba handed me a climbing rope and kept a second one for himself. With a steadying sigh, he slung the hemp rope around the tree, fastened both ends to his leather belt, and slid the belt beneath his backside. He placed a sandaled foot on the tree trunk and turned to me with a glint in his eye. "Ready to climb?"

Danger forgotten, I mirrored his position. Muscles taut, I grinned at the man who was my whole world. "Are *you* ready to be humbled by a woman?"

He threw his head back and laughed. The deep, resonant boom burst out of him with joyful abandon and sent birds to flight. This was the abba who had raised me, the abba who shrieked with joy when I threw a dagger and hit the target's center. This was the abba who chose to raise a daughter rather than marry again. And his daughter would forever honor the many sacrifices he'd made.

His laughter suddenly ceased. I turned and saw his countenance fall, his eyes widen. Before a question formed on my lips, the ground beneath me trembled—and I knew before any shofar sounded.

"Get to the house, Ahinoam!"

My fingers fumbled to dislodge the climbing rope that held me captive to the tree. Finally releasing it from my belt, I caught up with Abba and matched his gait stride for stride. Jezreel's watchmen finally sounded the *t'ruah*, warning of attack with nine short blasts. We reached our courtyard gate, heard faraway screams. Like a long-forgotten nightmare come to life.

"Hide! Now!" Abba pushed me through our curtained doorway. Tools thudded onto a goatskin on the packed dirt floor while I hurried to the far corner of our single room and skidded to my knees. Metal clanged behind me as Abba added our irreplaceable forge hammers, small anvil, and best whetstones to the goatskin bundle. My fingers shook as I removed the two sideboards beneath his elevated mattress and heard Abba's hurried footsteps behind me.

"Get in, girl!" He nudged me into the small, dark space and then shoved our smithing supplies toward my feet. His eyes met mine. "Not a word," he said. "No matter what you see or hear. Now hold the boards in place so I can close you in."

"Abba, I—"

"The boards!"

I replaced the sideboards over the opening, and Abba pounded them into place with his fist. With one hand I covered a sob, and with the other I clutched the dagger in my belt. Should the Amalekites discover me, they'd receive an unwelcome greeting.

TWO

Saul went to the city of Amalek and set an ambush in the ravine. Then he said to the Kenites, "Go away, leave the Amalekites so that I do not destroy you along with them; for you showed kindness to all the Israelites when they came up out of Egypt."

So the Kenites moved away from the Amalekites.

1 Samuel 15:5–6

I peered through the crack between two boards and saw Abba reposition the daggers behind his back.

Yahweh, I beg You, protect the only family I have.

For the thousandth time, I lamented King Saul's disobedience that led to this moment. Every life lost in an Amalekite raid surely weighed like an avalanche on the king's shoulders. Or did it? Some still thought Yahweh merciless for commanding Israel to completely destroy the nations of Canaan when Joshua led Israel. Granted, it would have been horrific. Hundreds of thousands—perhaps millions—would have died. Instead, God's people showed mercy and hoarded treasure. Now, the screams of my Jezreelite neighbors testified that more generations of men, women, and children would die for Israel's disobedience. How many could have been saved if Saul had destroyed the Amalekites?

The sound of hoofbeats arrived at our door. With one hand on his daggers, Abba raised his other hand in greeting and strolled through our curtained doorway. I wanted to burst from my hiding place and let my daggers fly, but he'd taught me better during my first hunting lesson. *The rabbit that runs gets boiled in a pot.*

The curtain closed behind him, hiding Abba from view. "I greet you, valiant men of Amalek," he said. "Take whatever you like. If you had waited another week, I would have harvested all my figs for you."

Abba's tight chuckle preceded the sounds of scuffling, grunting, and then several sickening thuds. Angry shouting quickly followed. Foreign words. In all the time we'd lived among them, Abba never taught me their language. I knew only Aramaic—the language of trade—and Hebrew, the language of our God and His people.

Abba stumbled through the doorway, blood dripping from his eyebrow, nose, and mouth. He fell on the packed-dirt floor, rolled on his back, and lifted both hands in surrender as a man knelt astride him. The man held one of Abba's daggers at his throat and shouted in his foreign tongue.

Abba calmly answered.

A slow, terrifying smile curved the man's lips, and he stood. What had Abba said to gain his freedom?

When two more raiders entered, the first man pointed at Abba, and the two men promptly helped him stand. The first man was obviously their leader.

Abba bowed politely to the chieftain, a smile affixed on his bloodied face when he straightened.

Surprisingly, the Amalekite commander returned his bow. How had Abba won such favor? When the chieftain and his men turned to leave, Abba shouted in their language. Their leader turned, brows lifted in challenge. He examined Abba's dagger—still in his hand—admiring it with a chuckle.

Abba shouted again and extended his hand, clearly demanding his dagger be returned.

Abba, no! Let him take the dagger and leave!

To my astonishment, rather than growing angry, the Amalekite laughed. Then, quicker than a viper's strike, the blade slashed across Abba's extended palm.

I stifled a gasp. Abba seemed stunned for a moment. When he reached to cradle his hand, an equally quick move sent a small knife from his sleeve, past the chieftain's head, and into the doorframe—barely missing the man's right ear.

The chieftain's eyes were as round as our wooden plates. Abba extended his hand again, the wound now dripping blood onto the floor. He repeated his demand in their foreign tongue—calmly this time.

The chieftain grinned, chuckled, and then broke into a full-bellied laugh. As his laughter ebbed, he locked eyes with Abba and pressed the dagger into the gaping wound.

Abba didn't even wince.

The chieftain's cheek twitched before he offered another bow and motioned his two soldiers outside. Abba stood in the doorway, holding the curtain open. I saw five wounded Amalekites in our courtyard, each holding one of Abba's daggers, inspecting it, comparing it with another. Their chieftain strode toward them, barked out an order, and each soldier threw his dagger into the dust before mounting his stallion and riding away.

Abba stood at the doorway, watching. "Remain hidden," he whispered while bandaging his wound with the cloth we thought would protect from fig sap. I ached to help him but obeyed.

Other raiders passed our home with terrifying war cries. Still Abba stood in the doorway, and I waited. Just when I thought it was safe, more raiders would pass by, shrieking and urging their horses toward the next farm or village. Grateful we'd been spared, I could think only of Old Miriam. I wished I could have protected her. Our tools could have been replaced, but the old woman had been kind to us from the first day we arrived. *Yahweh, please protect our friend.*

When the only sounds were the wails of mourners, Abba crossed the room and knelt beside his bed. "It's safe now." He pried away the sideboards with his dagger while I pushed from inside.

Relief propelled me with such force, I knocked him onto his back as my arms circled his neck. Then I sat beside him, sobbing. He hated tears.

I kept my head down to hide my weakness. "What did you say to make them leave? Will they return?"

"Now that the Amalekites know where I am, they'll always return." He tipped my chin up. "Their king holds me captive with a secret."

"A secret? What secret?"

"Many years ago, I took something precious from the Ammonites' king."

"You stole something?" Abba was the most honorable man I knew.

"I took something—someone—that wasn't his and returned her to her family." The furrows between his brows deepened. "The Ammonites captured a Judean woman, and because of her beauty, King Nahash made her his concubine. The woman's husband was part of a Judean rebel clan that purchased weapons on a regular basis to protect their homes from raids. He purchased so many daggers that we became friends. So when his wife was taken, he asked me to help rescue her. But it took months to form a plan. By the time we saved her, she'd borne King Nahash a daughter and was pregnant with his second child. Somehow, the Amalekite king discovered I'd been part of the woman's rescue. With that knowledge, he branded me his Amalekite slave."

"You mean those awful scars on your back?"

He nodded. "The sign of the ox was meant to remind me that I would forever wear the yoke of Amalek's king. I would obey him without question or complaint, or he would turn me over to King Nahash and the Ammonites. I was sure Yahweh had delivered me from the Amalekite's yoke when He commanded Saul to destroy them." His eyes blazed. "But Saul's disobedience will cost lives for generations."

I swallowed the dread rising in my throat. "What do we do?"

He stood and grinned down at me. "Thankfully, the chieftain was impressed with my dagger throwing today, so I offered to train his men."

"You can't train our enemies!"

"I told him I'd train his men if he left me in peace for a week to harvest my figs." He winked and added, "We won't be here when they return."

"What do you mean?"

Offering his uninjured hand, he launched me to my feet and hurried toward the wall pegs, grabbing both his shoulder bag and mine. "Collect only what you can carry." He tossed a bag to me. "A tunic, your sleeping mat, a little food—but take all six of your daggers. After we're sure Old Miriam is safe, we're off to find the renegade David ben Jesse."

I felt the blood draining from my face. Everyone in Judah knew King Saul had put a bounty on his son-in-law's head. "Can we trust a man who threatens to harm his wife? He sounds like a coward to me."

"The prophet Samuel anointed Jesse's son as Israel's *true* king, and I've heard men are flocking to him like birds flying south in winter."

"But what kind of men, Abba? Bandits? Criminals?"

He paused his packing, his eyes alight with excitement. "*Peculiar* people, Ahinoam, like you and me—people who others underestimated because of our heritage or appearance but who Yahweh chose because we have passion like David ben Jesse."

Our needs were few, so we each packed an extra tunic, a thin reed mat, a forge hammer, one whetstone each, and then stuffed a little hard cheese and nuts around them. We'd roast a quail or desert hare along the way. Abba carried a second bag with our small anvil and walked through our doorway without a word.

I slung the bag over my shoulder and followed, but hesitated at our courtyard gate for a final glance at our home. Though it was only a humble, rented farmhouse, those stone walls felt like a palace after having spent my first fourteen years in a Bedouin tent. My seven years in Jezreel with Abba had been the happiest of my existence. The sorrow of leaving our home and friends settled into my bones.

I closed the gate and caught up with Abba. "Will we ever return?" The continued sound of mourners' wails beckoned us to the town's main road, and my hands instinctively brushed the hilt of each dagger on my belt. I'd always walked in Toren the Kenite's mighty shadow but within the safety of Jezreel, I was known. My peculiarities accepted. Even celebrated. Could I feel safe without a home?

"I don't know, my girl." His voice quaked. He cleared his throat and wiped his nose. I knew he needed quiet.

We walked past our fig trees, heavy with nearly ripe fruit. "Will someone harvest our figs? What will the Amalekites do to the Jezreelites when they return and find us gone?"

"Yahweh will care for our figs and our friends, Ahinoam."

His faith proved true when we found Old Miriam tucked safely away behind the false wall Abba had built in the lean-to where her two goats were housed. The Amalekites had taken the livestock but overlooked the real treasure.

"You must find her a husband, Toren!" the old woman shouted as we waved good-bye.

"You hide from those pagans and let me raise my daughter!" he shouted back. Walking faster, he wiped his nose with his sleeve. He was grieving, too, in his way.

Abba set the pace, remaining on the worn path that joined Judah's hill country villages. With every step, I became more certain that an entanglement with David ben Jesse would be a mistake. As Abba slowed to climb a rocky incline, I ventured to say, "If our ancestors have always maintained peace with Israel and its leaders, why would we follow a known fugitive and make ourselves fugitives by association?"

Abba ignored the query until he reached the crest of the rise, then he stood over me like a king declaring an edict. "The Kenites fight tyranny in Israel and remain faithful to Yahweh. King Saul has become the tyrant and is no longer faithful to the Most High God, so we will find and follow the new king Samuel has anointed."

"How will we find him if King Saul's men can't?"

"Don't be ridiculous, Ahinoam. Who is the army's best tracker?"

"Prince Jonathan." Everyone knew that.

"Who is David's best friend?"

The answer dawned, but I wouldn't give him the satisfaction of answering aloud.

He grinned at his victory. "As long as Prince Jonathan is tracking his best friend, Saul won't find David."

"The king can't be so dull that he'd allow his son to deceive him. Surely he'll employ Israel's second-best tracker."

"*You*, daughter, are Israel's second-best tracker." Abba wiggled his eyebrows and resumed his determined march. "We'll start in Bethlehem, Jesse's home, and gain information along the way. So stay alert."

I lagged behind, wishing to spend no more words on a futile argument. We were deep into the desert hills by the time we reached Maon at dusk. Abba requested hospitality from Nabal, a wealthy landowner and descendant of Joshua's spying comrade Caleb, but Nabal was nothing like his courageous ancestor. He refused us water and food, even though he'd grown wealthy and fat on the land of his inheritance. We were well on our way north to Carmel when we heard a donkey trotting behind us.

"Wait!" a servant shouted. "I have food, bedding, and water!" He hurried toward us, tugging the donkey's halter. The man wrestled the donkey closer and then bowed to Abba. "My mistress, Abigail, must often make reparations for her husband's breach of hospitality, my lord. Please accept not only the provisions but also the donkey for any offense you may have suffered." The man straightened to face us, and I noted a telling bulge at his side, hidden by his fine cloak.

Abba and I shared a knowing glance, proving he'd noticed the hidden weapon, too. "Please extend our thanks to Mistress Abigail," Abba said. He stepped closer to the man and added, "Might you or anyone in your household know if David ben Jesse is hiding somewhere in these hills?"

The servant's face instantly paled. "I know nothing about the traitor. My master is loyal to King Saul."

Abba stepped closer, and the man stepped back. "Your master is loyal, but are you? I see a dagger in your waist belt. Did King Saul give it to you, or is that blade one of the weapons I produced for Jesse ben Obed to arm his Judean militia?"

The servant's eyes widened. "Are you T—" He stepped back again. "Are you the Kenite whose identity we protect with our lives?"

Abba gave a single nod. "My daughter and I are searching for David ben Jesse to join his supporters."

The servant looked at me for the first time and made no effort to hide a sneer. "A woman shouldn't cut her hair or wear a man's short robe."

Abba inhaled a deep breath while color rose from his neck to his face. "And a servant with a single dagger should never insult my daughter, who wields six blades." He nodded at me, which was his signaled permission to display Eve, my favorite dagger.

Before the servant could gasp, I'd already drawn my bone-handled blade. Spinning the hilt in my palm, I tipped it, then tossed it into the last rays of sunlight and caught it behind my back. The man gulped audibly as I slid Eve back into her sheath.

"The Bethlehemite Jesse ben Obed and his family traveled this way yesterday." He was suddenly very cooperative. "Mistress Abigail gave them gifts like those I've given you. They were on their way to Adullam Cave."

I began examining footprints along the path and any broken branches on trees or bushes along the way that might have indicated they left the main road.

"Did Jesse say if they planned to meet David at Adullam?" Abba continued, probing the servant's memory.

I interrupted. "The road between Maon and Carmel is too busy, Abba. There's no way to be sure if these footprints are normal traffic or Jesse's family group."

"Master Jesse's whole family was with him," the servant added. "His wife, sons, their wives, and children. They were all quite concerned when they received word that David was hiding in the cave after he escaped from the Philistines at Gath."

"Gath?" I didn't even try to hide my disdain. "Abba, do you really want to join a fugitive who has ties with the Philistines of Gath?"

"He *escaped* Gath." The servant's sneer was back. "And barely, from the reports we heard."

"All right." Abba scrubbed his bearded chin. "Adullam Cave. Northwest of Keilah, yes?"

"Yes, but—" The man glanced around, then drew close to whisper, "Make sure my master doesn't discover it. He'd betray Yahweh's anointed to maintain favor with Israel's mad king."

Why would this slave defy his master and his king for a traitor?

"Thank you," Abba said. "May Yahweh bless you and your mistress for this kindness." He took the donkey's reins, clucked his tongue, and started walking.

The servant eyed me from head to toe. "If you ever wish to

marry, you should spend more time tending yourself and less time playing with daggers."

"Ahinoam!" Abba shouted. "Come. *Now*." He didn't even bother to turn.

But his command stayed my hand, though it was already on Eve's hilt. Obedient but humiliated, I left the presumptuous man with the last word and released my frustration on my lifelong protector. "I was only going to frighten him. You know I'd never harm anyone."

"We're not in Jezreel, Nomy." He halted the gray donkey and looked at me with the kind of tenderness that cut deeper than any blade. "That man trusted us with the location of David ben Jesse and showed us kindness with these gifts."

"He insulted me, Abba. Is that kindness?"

"It was ignorance. Give people a chance to know your heart so they can discover your beauty."

Beauty? I would have laughed if I hadn't been so stunned. No one, including Abba, had ever called me beautiful. When men came to purchase weapons, I remained in the house or with my back bent over the forge in our barn. Those in Jezreel had known me since I was as thin as a palm tree and no more shapely. I met very few strangers and needed no friends. "Why must everything change?" I whispered. "Why can't we simply wait a few weeks and go back to our farm?"

"You're talking like a silly woman. I've taught you better." He waved away my words, then Abba and our new traveling companion headed north.

I followed, silent and sullen, returning my favorite dagger to its sheath. I'd named all six, but Eve was my first and the one always ready to defend me. She was also the first to sin and regret, often drawn with my impulsive anger and fear. Or, like today, my humiliation. Eve had caused some serious consequences in my life like the Great Mother Eve's sin in the Garden had cursed the earth and every human descended from her. But Yahweh hadn't forsaken Eve when she'd sinned. He promised that her Seed would defeat the conniving serpent that tricked and belittled her. Perhaps someday Yahweh would use my Eve to conquer the serpents within me.

As darkness fell, Abba led the donkey to a roadside cave where we could rest overnight. The tasty treats from Nabal's wife brightened our mood: two waterskins, roasted grain, fresh bread, pressed figs, and raisin cakes. We reminisced fondly of Old Miriam's Sabbath meals and fell into exhausted slumber.

When morning dawned, Abba rose and left the cave to tend to his private needs while I packed our sleeping mats and readied the donkey for travel. I took my turn behind the bushes and caught up with him on the road. It was unusual that he began traveling without breaking our fast, but I knew better than to question him. He was as ferocious as a bear in the mornings.

Before the sun rose overhead, we passed the city of Ziph, and the smell of roasting meat from their market made my mouth water. Abba finally reached into his shoulder bag for a crust of bread. I followed his example, wondering what thoughts kept him so thoroughly wrapped in silence. By midday, I was panting and sweating; my stomach growled, and I no longer mused about his thoughts. "Let's rest in the shade of that outcropping."

Without acknowledgment, Abba veered right. A scraggly acacia spread its branches near the rocks but only provided a small circle of shade. Abba placed the donkey between us in the tight space.

"I'd rather you beat me than punish me with silence."

His head snapped up, eyes ablaze. "I'd never strike you, nor will any other man while I have breath."

Any other man? I tried to lighten the mood between us. "No other man would touch me when Toren the Kenite is my protector."

Without a glimmer of humor, he said, "You must marry, Ahinoam. I've been wrong to keep you to myself." He turned away but not before I glimpsed his trembling lips. "You were embarrassed by the servant's comments, which means I should have allowed Miriam to teach you more womanly things."

"No!" My emphatic reply spooked the donkey. We both needed to stroke her neck so she'd settle. I continued a quieter protest. "Abba, I've never wanted to marry. Though I was young when Ima left, I remember how unhappy you both were, and her betrayal nearly broke you."

"I had no idea you remembered." He bowed his head. "I'm sorry, Nomy."

"I don't need an apology. I was happy after Ima left. You loved me well, Abba, and proved every day that a man—or woman—could be whole and happy without marriage."

Abba placed his callused hand on my cheek. "But Yahweh said it's not good for man to be alone."

"Yahweh never said that about a woman."

He chuckled and dropped his hand. "Marriage can be God's richest blessing. I hate that your parents modeled the opposite."

"You've given me a good life and sound advice—like when you said life wasn't as predictable as a fig harvest. The Amalekite raid proved it. You've given me something more reliable than a husband. You've given me a trade—metalsmithing—that will provide for me as long as women chop vegetables and men fight wars."

He still studied me with that worried-parent look. "You sound very logical and brave, but you were still embarrassed by the servant's comments."

"I'm being logical and brave because you've taught me not to be a *silly woman*."

He pursed his lips. "I'm sorry I've made those two words a single label. You are an intelligent, beautiful woman, and there's nothing wrong with wanting people to see that."

"I just want life to be as it was." But the quaver in my tone betrayed me. I looked down, hiding the emotion. Abba was right. Something inside had withered with shame when the servant condemned my hair and robe. Why?

My reasons for short hair and a shortened robe were practical. Logical. I kept my hair clipped to shoulder length and pulled back with a leather string to ensure it didn't catch a spark or fall forward into smelting fires. I wore a man's-style shorter robe to move freely during training exercises and while forging weapons. But my robe extended past my knees and halfway down my shins, which was much longer than a man's fighting tunic. And I wore laced sandals up to my knees that helped cover my exposed legs. No one in Jezreel protested. I'd worn the same attire since I was a child.

But that was in Jezreel.

"You and I are . . ." He seemed to be searching for words. "We're *unique*, Ahinoam, but evidently Yahweh chose David ben Jesse because he is also special. He isn't Jesse's oldest or strongest son, but he has great passion for God—or so I've heard. I think you also have that peculiar passion that pleases Yahweh, Nomy." Abba's large knuckle lodged under my chin and nudged it upward, forcing me to face the truth in his eyes. "And I should tell you more often that you're capable and *beautiful*."

His final word pierced me like a dagger. I pulled away and reached for the donkey's reins. "Let's go. If your directions are accurate, we might reach Adullam Cave by dusk."

We continued our travel in silence, this time by my choice. Shortly after leaving our shady respite, we passed Hebron, one of the six cities of refuge set apart by Joshua after Israel's conquest of Canaan. Though its walls had originally sheltered only Levite guards and unintentional murderers, Hebron now thrived with more diversity. Though it still served as a city of refuge, its Levite population had become an elite group of warrior priests, who fought at God's command on behalf of those who couldn't fight for themselves.

After passing the large city, we reached the final peak of Judah's hill country and looked down on the *shephelah* as the sun began sinking in the west. Today's wordless trek had started with foul moods and tepid hearts, but determination and tenderness had carried us farther west than I'd ever traveled. Abba searched in his pack for cheese and dried meat, sharing the quick nourishment with me as we coaxed the stubborn donkey with grass he'd plucked from the roadside.

Another walled city loomed in the distance. "Should we lodge there for the night?" My voice was a mere croak after so little water and sparse words.

"We won't stop at Keilah. Adullam isn't far."

My legs ached and thighs burned. Though we now traversed the easier terrain of a rocky plain, my hands and knees were still bloodied from a tumble I'd taken after we left Carmel. I watched the sun slowly descend while Abba looked right and left, seeming uncertain about our direction. I'd seen few footprints on the road since we passed the city of Keilah, and the sun would soon be a mere glow on the western horizon.

"Are you sure this is the way to Adullam?" I'd rather risk Abba's wrath than meet a hungry jackal.

"I'm sure." He continued walking.

I'd stared at the back of his head and the donkey's backside all day. I was thirsty. Hungry. Tired. Scared. I wanted more than two words of assurance.

"You're sure? Sure of what?" I halted, both fists on my hips. "Following a traitor or finding a cave you haven't seen in decades?"

Abba stopped and turned slowly. "If you have questions, daughter, ask them before we arrive at Adullam."

"Oh, I have questions! Are you sure David ben Jesse won't betray us to the Amalekites? When were you at the Adullam Cave? You've said his abba, Jesse, is your friend, but why has he never come to

Jezreel? I don't remember him visiting Amalek. When have you ever gone to Bethlehem? Why would a man you haven't seen in years trust you now?"

Abba drew one hand down his face, smearing travel dust. "Jesse will trust me because it was his wife, Nitzevet, who I rescued from the Ammonite king." His weary eyes met mine. "Jesse is a good man. He received Nitzevet back into his home and raised the Ammonite's children as his own."

"Why am I twenty-one harvests old and never heard this story?"

"Jesse's drive to rescue his wife consumed him for nearly two years. Though he was grateful to me for saving Nitzevet, our friendship was a reminder that she had needed saving. After his wife returned, Jesse's shame of having allowed her to be ravaged by another man stared him in the face every time he looked at the Ammonite's children."

"Oh, Abba." Though I pitied Jesse and his family, I pitied us more. We'd just spent two days chasing Abba's grander days. "What makes you think a man who shut you out of his life years ago will allow you in now—especially when his son is in danger?"

His spine stiffened, and he stood over me like a tower. "Jesse ben Obed is a man who honors Yahweh and pays his debts. It's said Samuel passed over seven of Jesse's sons to anoint David, the youngest, as Israel's new king. Jesse had only three sons when we saved his wife, so Jesse sired five more boys after Nitzevet returned, including Yahweh's anointed." He crossed his arms with a smirk. "Jesse would never forget the man who helped save those boys' ima."

Was he taking credit for Jesse's sons? "How many years since you've spoken to him, Abba?"

The smirk left, and he dropped his hands to his side. "Thirty-three years."

"He won't even recognize you after so long."

"He will, Ahinoam! And he will trust me." As if punctuating the fervent declaration, arrows rained from a hill above us and landed near Abba's feet.

I ducked behind the donkey, searching the hilltop. "Abba? I don't think Jesse remembers you."

THREE

DAVID

David left Gath and escaped to the cave of Adullam. When his brothers and his father's household heard about it, they went down to him there. All those who were in distress or in debt or discontented gathered around him, and he became their commander.

About four hundred men were with him.

1 Samuel 22:1–2

Adullam Cave

Joab rushed into the cave where I sat at Ima's side. "Intruders." My nephew's clipped whisper showed his usual urgency. "Two men—a scrawny young one and a bulky old. They bring a donkey with supplies. The archers halted them."

Archers? I released a weary sigh. Why not send a scout to ask their intentions?

"Well done, my son." My sister Zeruiah encouraged her son. She sat opposite me, tending our ailing ima, but looked up from her ministrations to give me a scolding look. "You've made my son your general. The least you could do is thank him for protecting you." She'd been more ima than sister all my life.

To appease my bossy sister, I said, "Thank you, Joab." His

51

shoulders sagged, and I felt a stab of conscience. "Truly, I appreciate your caution. What have you learned about our visitors?"

"Nothing yet. I thought you'd want to question them yourself."

"That's very thoughtful, my love." Vered, Joab's wife, peeked around a few baskets.

Zerry gave her a stern look, sending her daughter-in-law back into the raucous area where my nephews' wives and children had remained since unpacking their meager possessions.

"You wonder why my wife doesn't like you?" Joab groused at his ima.

"Hmm." I rubbed my forehead, hiding my frustration. Though relieved that my family had arrived yesterday, safe from Saul's repercussions—at least for now—the clan of Jesse brought with it a unique set of challenges. Despite the tension between us, I was still responsible to protect them because I was responsible for making them Saul's target. Had King Achish willingly shielded me in Gath, Saul wouldn't have dared pursue me—by bargain or battle. My family would have been safe.

I mused about what might have been and watched Abba and my brothers, who stood at the cave's opening, argue in coarse whispers. I would never have seen my squabbling, annoying, opinionated family again if not for Eliphelet, King Achish's nephew, who also needed to escape Gath. *Thank You, Yahweh, for all You do that I don't understand—like bringing my family here.* I still didn't know how Abba heard I was hiding at Adullam Cave. He'd led the whole family to safety—even though Ima was ill—before I could send men to fetch them.

"Her fever is getting worse. That's why I don't want Vered and the children to see her." My sister placed a fresh damp cloth on Ima's forehead. Her eyes didn't even flutter. Zerry glanced over my shoulder, nodding toward Abba and our brothers. "They'll listen to you if you insist Ima's too weak to travel," she said in a whisper.

"The travel from Bethlehem to Adullam was hard enough. How will she survive a weeklong journey to Moab?"

"We don't have a week, Zerry. We must reach Moab in five days—at most—or Saul's trackers will find us."

"And you're sure Moab's king will offer sanctuary?" Joab asked, looming over us.

I shot to my feet and announced loudly enough for everyone to hear, "I'm grateful you came when you heard of my narrow escape from Gath. I realize you've left your homes, and you're likely frightened, so let me assure you. I'm no longer the mischievous shepherd boy you remember. It's been six years since I lived among you. I was trained by Saul himself and fought at his side. I know how he thinks and how his enemies think. I'm a soldier and Yahweh's anointed king, so you must trust me—as I trust Yahweh—to keep us safe."

Then I turned to Joab but still spoke so all could hear. "The Moabite king will give us sanctuary because the Gadites he often hires as his mercenaries have now joined my four hundred loyal followers. They will advocate on our behalf when we arrive at Mizpah, and the Lord will protect my family as He's protected me."

"And you'll promise him a portion of Jesse ben Obed's sheep." Abba marched toward us, my brothers trailing behind him. He glanced down at Ima, then at Zerry. "How is my wife?"

"She's not well, Abba."

"Do you have all the herbs you need?" His words were clipped as they always were when speaking to Zerry.

"Yes, Abba." She bowed her head.

"She'll be fine." He returned his focus to me. "And offer the Moabite king a percentage of the wool from each shearing while we remain in Moab." Stabbing my chest with his finger, he added, "You'll pay me back in silver when you sit on Israel's throne."

And the fifth commandment God gave to Moses: You will honor your abba and ima so that you may live long in the Land Yahweh is giving you. "Thank you for your generosity," I said. Joab fell in step beside me. "Let's go meet our visitors." I needed fresh air.

As we walked down the narrow path, I heard one of my soldiers exclaim, "That's a girl?"

Joab's brothers, Abishai and Asahel, waited for us on the precipice overlooking the visitors.

Abishai chuckled. "It wasn't a scrawny man. It's a woman in disguise."

My abba and brothers had followed and crowded around us to look below. "She could pass for a man," said Eliab, the oldest of my brothers and most like Abba.

I ignored their ridicule and scanned the jutting rocks that surrounded Adullam Hill. At least fifty of my men waited in strategic positions, arrows nocked and ready.

The older of the two newcomers shouted toward our promontory perch. "We've heard Yahweh anointed David, the youngest son of Jesse ben Obed, to rule as Israel's new king. I am Toren the Kenite and this is my daughter, Ahinoam. We wish to provide Yahweh's army with the finest bronze weapons."

"Toren?" Abba shouted over the ridge. "Is it really you?"

"Jesse!" The man's features brightened. "You old dog! Wait there. We'll come up." Seeming to forget he'd been halted by skilled archers, Toren passed off the donkey to his daughter and began bounding up the narrow footpath. The daughter followed, warily eyeing my warriors.

"Have you ever seen a homelier woman?" My brother Ozem elbowed Raddai. The two were nearest my age but still boys in men's bodies, even after living more than thirty harvests.

"Quiet." I silenced their snickering and then hurried to catch up with Abba, who was almost giddy as he walked down the path. Keeping my voice low, I asked, "Is this the same Kenite who supplies Judah's rebels with weapons?"

He waved the comment away. "Yes, yes. But don't worry. I send a representative from another clan to purchase the rebel weapons for Clan Jesse, so our involvement doesn't trace back to you."

"Trace back to . . . Abba, are you saying my family is among the rebels trying to undermine the king's throne?" No wonder Saul thought me a traitor!

His abrupt halt silenced me. "I remained true to King Saul at Gilgal when others deserted him for fear of the gathering Philistines. I watched his impatient burnt offering and heard Samuel's rebuke, promising a new king for Israel who would follow Yahweh without question. After that, Saul changed. He fought scared and refused to help the tribes too far from his home in Gibeah. So when your ima was captured by the Ammonites, my king refused to intervene, but Toren and the rebels helped me bring her home." He scanned the misfit army that had gathered around us and pointed at Toren, who was now five paces away. "These are the men who will follow Yahweh's new king, David. Welcome them."

Without awaiting my answer, he turned and opened his arms to the Kenite—an embrace like I'd never seen my abba offer. Kenites were well known for smithing and could be of great benefit to our camp, but the rebels always seemed too radical to honor Yahweh. *Lord, must my whole army be as crazy as the king who chases me?*

Joab and his two brothers joined me, each carrying a torch, and offered me one, as well. Dusk was quickly turning to darkness.

"Seeing you healthy and strong gladdens my heart." The Kenite released Abba and perused my nephews, as well as my brothers who had joined us. "I heard you had eight sons, Jesse, but I see nine fine warriors, six with your fiery red hair!" He patted Abba's back with the force of a forge hammer and seemed oblivious to his verbal misstep.

Abba had only seven sons now. One of my brothers was killed by a Philistine in battle, and my red hair had been the contentious proof that Ima had been faithful during the year Abba shunned her.

Such was the fodder provided by Clan Jesse for Bethlehem's gossip-mongers.

"Only my sons inherited my red hair." Abba continued their reunion, disregarding any introduction of Zerry's sons.

Toren's daughter arrived with the donkey, looking as uncertain as I felt. She stood aloof with an alertness hinting at battle skill. Abba may have trusted this Kenite to rescue Ima decades ago, but could he still be trusted? While the two old men continued to reminisce, my annoyance piqued. Abba had publicly acknowledged his red-haired sons but ignored my nephews—dark-haired and dark-eyed like Ima and Zerry—who had served alongside me in his pastures, repeatedly risking their lives to protect our family's flocks. Now, he disrespected my whole army by welcoming a man and a sharp-eyed woman who could be Saul's spies.

"These men are Jesse's grandsons," I said, motioning toward my nephews. "They're the sons of the little girl you rescued with my ima from the Ammonites." When every eye fell on me, an awkward pause ushered Toren the Kenite into my presence. I withered a little. He was at least a head taller than me, hairy like a bear, and brawny like Joab. Yet his eyes were kind, his furrowed brow more pensive than disapproving.

"Have I offended you somehow, my king?" He seemed sincere. Truly curious.

Another pang of conscience held my tongue. I'd reacted more like Bethlehem's rejected boy than God's anointed king. In all my life, I'd never seen Abba respond as warmly to anyone as he had to Toren. "No. I wanted you to meet the men who are alive today because of your courage." I sent silent repentance heavenward and introduced my nephews. "This is Joab, Abishai, and Asahel."

Abba grasped Toren's hand. "You always seem to arrive when my family needs rescue. How did you know we were going to Moab tomorrow?"

"Moab? I had no idea, but I'm afraid this time, my friend, we must rescue each other."

Joab shot me a wary look as if to say, *Now the deceptive story from Saul's spy.* My eldest nephew saw everyone and everything as a threat, which is part of the reason I chose him as my general.

"The Amalekites found me in Jezreel," the Kenite was saying. "They want my daughter and my weapons, and I will give them neither." He turned to me. "Even if we must go to Moab to serve our new king." He bent to one knee and lowered his head.

His daughter remained standing, her cheeks and neck mottled with red splotches. Was she nervous? Angry?

She was a mystery I had no need to solve. "Rise, Toren. Ceremony means little in a wilderness kingdom. Our camp could certainly use its own metalsmith, and I'm grateful for your heroic rescue of my ima and sisters."

"Sisters?" His bushy gray brows shot up. "Your ima had only one daughter and was still with child when I delivered her to Bethlehem. I'm happy to hear she brought a second daughter into your household, Jesse." He turned to coax his own daughter nearer, completely missing the sneer on Abba's face.

Toren's shy daughter shook her head and stood her ground. Six paces away, she remained behind their donkey. She grew more intriguing when I recognized her perfect defensive position aided her disguise. Two men traveling would have attracted little attention.

"My daughter, Ahinoam, is the center of my world," Toren continued. "She can sharpen a blade to split a hair and throws a dagger quicker than I." He beamed with pride, despite the heckling that came from my warriors.

What Israelite ever praised a daughter? Our abba reminded my sisters daily that they were offspring of a foreigner and should praise Yahweh for bringing them into his honorable home.

Another inner pang of conscience. This one felt like Zerry flicking my ear when I'd disobeyed as a boy—hurting my pride more than my body. Had the Lord just flicked my heart for criticizing my family? The thought grated. *But they've wronged me, Lord, and keep doing wrong!* His only response came in peaceful silence, and an instant realization that the offense was mine to forgive. I must change how I responded, even if my family never changed.

"No women will touch any weapon in our camp." Joab stepped toward Toren, his tone also full of challenge.

You see, Lord? I argued with my new resolve. How would I deal with rude family members and lead my army well?

"My daughter isn't an ordinary woman." The Kenite leveled his gaze at my general.

"That much is clear."

"You will speak of her with respect, or we'll have trouble." Before Toren took a step toward Joab, I blocked his advance.

"There will be no trouble." I pushed him back with my free hand and heard the whiz of a dagger fly past my left ear. The torch in my left hand lurched. Sparks flew. I secured my grip on the torch shaft while my nephews surrounded me. Others shouted, but I could only gawk at the bone-handled dagger embedded less than two finger-widths above my hand on the torch's narrow shaft. None of my men could have made that throw—nor would they have tried!

"Forgive her, my king!" Toren hovered over his daughter, pleading. A handful of my men created an arc around them, daggers and spears drawn as if ready to pounce. "I'm telling you," he said, "if she'd meant it, my king, you would be harmed."

That was her defense? I chuckled. There was nothing false in this man. "I believe you, Toren, but your daughter owes me an apology."

The Kenite rose slowly, and his eyes flitted from Joab to Abba, as if he might engage his old friend's influence. To his credit, he examined Joab instead. Short—like me—my nephew had the stature and temperament of a bull. The Kenite then turned to me. "Ahinoam will apologize to you, my lord, but shouldn't your ignorant nephew also apologize to her?"

I liked this man more every moment. "My ignorant nephew will be your general if you remain in my camp."

"My king, did Yahweh approve of him as your general?"

"Abba!" his daughter scolded.

I grinned at the pair, touched by their mutual protectiveness. In the years since I'd fought and killed Goliath, I'd led thousands of Israelite troops into battle and become confident in reading men's character. Toren was a good man. Women, however, had been my downfall—Michal's betrayal proving how woefully deficient I was in judging their motives and true feelings.

With a beleaguered sigh, I proposed my terms. "Toren the Kenite, I ask only two things of those who follow me: loyalty and honesty."

"As I serve Yahweh, I serve his anointed—until my dying breath." He slammed his fist over his heart. I acknowledged his vow with a grateful nod, hoping someday we'd be friends.

"Ahinoam . . ." He nudged her forward. "Your apology to our king."

"First," I said, returning her dagger from the torch, "Joab owes you a public apology because he insulted you publicly."

"No." She shot a burning glare at him. "A general doesn't apologize to a soldier."

A soldier? Joab's insult was wrong, but he was right that a woman would never train with weapons in my camp. "Ahinoam, your throwing accuracy is impeccable, but surely you realize I can't allow a woman to live like a soldier among my men."

"She'll help me with Ima." My sister's voice split the night air. Zerry marched toward us as if *she* were my general. "I can't care for Ima by myself all the way to Moab. Who better to help than a dagger-wielding young woman who dresses like a soldier? She can both help me with Ima's personal needs and be our protector."

"Has Ima improved?" I asked.

"She woke and took a little broth." Waving me aside, she jabbed both fists at her hips and said to Toren, "Who are you? And why would you drag your daughter into the wilderness to live with my brother's soldiers?"

Toren broke into a smile brighter than our torches. "You're her, aren't you?"

"I'm who?" Zerry looked at me. "You've added another crazy one to this bunch?"

"I'm the man who fed you candied dates all the way from Rabbah to Bethlehem."

Zerry's hands fell to her sides, and she turned to offer Toren a rare smile. "I remember little about the rescue, but I remember those dates. Will you come inside? I'm sure Ima would like to thank you again, too." She pushed through her sons and led Toren toward the cave.

Joab shrugged. "I'd like to hear the story, as well." He swatted his brothers, coaxing them to follow. Abba and my brothers fell in step behind them.

I was left with the dagger-wielding woman who seemed unsure what to do next.

I reached for the donkey's reins. "Let me help." She retreated and reached behind her back. "No, no," I whispered. "Don't pull another dagger." I glanced around to be sure my men hadn't seen. They had already returned to preparations for tomorrow's journey.

I heard Ahinoam's shallow breathing and made sure I moved slowly so as not to frighten her again. Her eyes blinked fast, flitting side to side. The poor woman was terrified. And why wouldn't she be? *Lord, be her strength.*

"Ahinoam, I'm sorry we've given you such a poor welcome, but our lives are at stake. I now live with the certainty that anyone can betray me."

She stepped behind her donkey. "Just show me where I can find a little grass so she won't stop at every green shrub on tomorrow's journey." She stroked the donkey's neck, which seemed to help calm them both.

I lifted fingers to my lips, whistling the call to my inner circle. The same sound echoed from nearby. Within three heartbeats, Eliphelet appeared beside me. "How can I help?"

Ahinoam's jaw dropped. "He's a Philistine!"

"Was it the accent or the armor that gave me away?" my friend teased.

I swatted him. This woman wasn't in the mood for his humor. "Graze her donkey with the others, and have it packed by sunrise for the journey to Moab."

"I'd rather prepare my own pack animal." Ahinoam held tightly to its reins.

Afraid or not, this woman—like my family—needed to trust my commands. "And I'd rather be in Gibeah, Ahinoam, enjoying a peaceful winter with a faithful wife. But other people's choices have a way of changing our plans, don't they?" I extended my open hand toward the startled woman, waiting for her to willingly give me the reins.

After a moment's pause, she placed the leather straps across my palm. "Abba says we can't make life conform to our schedule, like we plan harvest by gashing figs to ripen before Sabbath." She looked up, her eyes meeting mine. "People have changed my plan, too, *King* David. So, I trust only my abba and Yahweh. Not you." She lifted one brow. "Not yet."

FOUR

AHINOAM

From there David went to Mizpah in Moab and said to the king of Moab, "Would you let my father and mother come and stay with you until I learn what God will do for me?" So he left them with the king of Moab, and they stayed with him as long as David was in the stronghold.

1 Samuel 22:3–4

Bul (October)
Three Weeks Later
Moab, Palace of Mizpah

"You've made another knot in your thread." Zeruiah snatched the whirling spindle and wool from my hand. "How many times must I—"

"Zerry." Mistress Nitzevet's gentle censure silenced my gruff teacher.

Seated on my stool, head bowed, I tried for the fourth time this morning to calm my breathing. *Yahweh, why must I be so different than other women?* Already today, I'd failed at mending, embroidering, weaving, and now spinning.

I would have much rather stayed in the rough-hewn tower on

Mizpah's southern city border. When we'd climbed the steep grade to Moab's capital, two great towers greeted us—one a luxurious palace with fanciful architecture and engravings, and the other David called a stronghold. It seemed to touch the clouds but was unadorned. That day he'd gone directly to Moab's throne room, accompanied by his eleven Gadite mercenaries and three fierce nephews. When they returned to our waiting army with the news that Moab's king would willingly provide sanctuary, David had thrust Goliath's sword toward the heavens and the whole army raised a shout.

If only I could have marched with Abba and David's men up the rugged, plateaued mountain to the right of the city nestled in Mizpah's valley. The towering stronghold had many visible caves for adequate housing and would be ideal to defend against any spies or assassins that King Saul might dispatch. Alas, Abba ordered me to follow the women of David's family into the palace to the left of the valley. I was now a prisoner of luxury in a chamber with Mistress Nitzevet and Zeruiah, on the top-floor palace hallway where the noisy wives and children of King David's army were forgotten. Nitzevet and Zeruiah lived separately from the other wives in their family. Though the children loved and respected their Savta Nitzevet, Vered—Joab's wife—ruled the other women with her false kindness and curt tone. After sixteen days of silence from the stronghold, I would either find a way to see Abba or die trying.

Zeruiah plopped down on the floor in front of me. I kept my head bowed, but she pushed aside my shoulder-length hair and peered into the hiding place my hair created. "You must forgive me," she said. "I'm accustomed to correcting three stubborn sons. They pretend not to hear unless I shout. Unfortunately, I've started shouting at everyone—including my daughters-in-law—which is one of the reasons they hate me." She tucked one side of my dark brown hair behind my ear. "I could promise to be softer, but it won't work. I am who I am, Ahinoam. But I want to be your friend."

Emotion ricocheted in my chest like a stone off a tree. "You want—" I could more easily withstand her complaints than compassion. Zeruiah's gruffness reminded me of how Abba and I bantered, making me miss him more. Was I a prisoner? No. I was a grown woman, and there was no lock on our door. I darted from the stool and toward the door.

Somehow, David's sister arrived before me. "I said I was sorry! You can't leave, Ahinoam. David gave strict instructions—"

"He's not my king—yet."

"He's Yahweh's choice." She moved away from the door and folded her arms. "Will you disobey the king Samuel has anointed? You see how poorly that turned out for King Saul."

I tamped down a grin. "You are brutal, Zeruiah bat Jesse, but I was raised by Toren the Kenite and know Yahweh is compassionate and gracious. He's slow to anger, abounding in love and faithfulness." I ducked left, then lunged right for the door—just as our maid came charging into the chamber. The door's edge slammed against my forehead, which made cymbals ring in my ears.

"Oh, Mistress Ahinoam!" the woman screeched after somehow steadying every morsel and dish on her tray. "Forgive me, I—"

Zeruiah gripped my shoulders, staring at my forehead. "You've already got a knot bigger than any you made this morning." She nudged me toward my bed. "I told you there would be consequences for disobedience. Did you listen? No, you did not."

I touched my throbbing forehead and drew in a quick breath. *Ouch!* Maybe Zeruiah did have a direct connection to the Almighty. During our five-day journey to Moab, Abba and I both helped care for Mistress Nitzevet and discovered even illness dared not defy David's older sister. By the time our caravan entered Moab's capital, Mistress Nitzevet was taking nourishment and playing with her grandchildren.

Abba had seemed smitten with Zeruiah. Though she'd been only a little girl when he rescued her, and he a very young man, David's sister was now a formidable woman. He, too, was convinced Yahweh would delay a sunrise if Zeruiah asked it of Him.

"You'll sit on your bed and enjoy the nice meal Keyalah prepared." Zeruiah pressed down on my shoulders, and I obeyed.

The maid moved our low table and Mistress Nitzevet's stool closer to my bed. Keyalah, too, was now quick to obey Zeruiah after their encounter on our first morning in Moab. I was still sleeping soundly on my elevated, wool-stuffed mattress when Zeruiah shouted, "You'll never empty my waste pot!"

On my feet, dagger drawn, I sliced the sheer linen curtain around my bed and faced the whimpering maid. She alternated glances between David's sister and me, then addressed the more frightening one—Zeruiah. "If the palace steward hears of my slacking, he'll refuse to pay me or replace me with a slave."

"Who's going to tell him?" Zeruiah grabbed the pot from her. "And if you touch my waste pot again, I'll empty it on your head." She turned to gather Mistress Nitzevet's waste pot and added, "In this chamber, we empty our own foulness, we'll help you tidy our chamber, and then you'll join us for every meal you serve. There's no need for one woman to do the tasks four could do in a blink." That's when I realized Zeruiah was much like our unripe figs before gashing—all hard exterior with a sweet, tender middle.

"You look dazed." Zeruiah leaned over me now, staring into my eyes.

"I was running away because I need to see Abba, but I'd still like to be your friend."

"Good! No harm done." A mischievous grin curved her lips. "Except to your poor head." She busied herself with the next task, which was another thing I admired about David's sister. Unlike the women I'd met in Jezreel, Zeruiah didn't let petty arguments fester or hold grudges. She did, however, enjoy the gossip our maid brought every day with our meals. Whenever I asked Keyalah for news about David's men in the stronghold, she looked at me askance and returned to similar stories and juicy rumors like I heard from women at Jezreel's central well.

My head was now throbbing, but even that couldn't distract me from missing Abba. "Any word from the stronghold?" I asked, though I knew what to expect.

She waved a dismissive hand. "I'm sure your men are doing what men do." I accepted the plate she'd filled with raisins, nuts, and a piece of warm bread slathered with soft cheese. She cupped my chin and examined my head. "Forgive me for barging in like that, Mistress Ahinoam. I'll bring honey and aloe to treat your head when I come with this evening's meal." She returned to the stool Zeruiah had placed beside the table for her, and they entered the world of women I neither cared about nor wanted to join. My eyelids felt heavy, and I let them droop, conjuring my next attempt to escape.

"You can tell your gossipmongers to mind their own business!" Zeruiah's angry tone snagged my attention.

"Forgive me, I meant no harm." Keyalah struggled to her feet, but Mistress Nitzevet stopped her flight with a gentle hand.

"My daughter is very protective," she said. "Sit down, my friend, and I'll tell you the story of my son's birth." The elegance with which David's ima moved and spoke was like that of royalty.

Keyalah resumed her place, casting a wary glance at Zeruiah, whose silence proved her displeasure. I, too, had heard the rumor that Jesse had refused David as his son for a time but hadn't dared ask. I tried not to appear too eager to hear but rolled to my side at the edge of my bed.

"David *is* Jesse's son, regardless of the rumors you may have heard," Nitzevet began. "But the rumors are also true Jesse put me away for a time, and it was during that separation when David was conceived."

Keyalah gave Zeruiah a sideways glance before asking, "How could you conceive if—"

"Because my ima is a resourceful woman," Zeruiah proudly declared.

Nitzevet ducked her chin, but I noted her wry grin. She didn't seem at all ashamed of David's beginnings. "The story begins when I was taken captive by Nahash, the Ammonite king, and made his concubine," Nitzevet began. "My husband and Ahinoam's abba heroically rescued me, but only after Zeruiah was born and I was already carrying the Ammonite's second daughter I later named Abigal."

Now I understood why Zeruiah was defensive. Jesse must have put Nitzevet away years after her captivity because of her daughters. By the way he treated everyone—including his family—he'd already proven during our journey to Moab that he wasn't the honorable man Abba had described.

"Eleven years after my rescue," Nitzevet continued, "Bethlehem was raided again, this time by Ishmaelites, and they took Abigal. Jesse was so distraught. He believed both raids were Yahweh's extreme judgment on his family for mixing foreign blood—his great-savta Ruth's Moabite heritage—with a pure Israelite lineage."

"Which is ridiculous," Zeruiah grumbled, "because everyone lauds Savta Ruth and *Saba* Boaz's victorious story."

"Zerry." Her ima's single-word rebuke silenced her, then she returned her attention to Keyalah. "As I said, my husband was distraught and not thinking clearly. He resigned his duties as Bethlehem's elder, provided me with a small home outside the city, and planned to take my maid to his bed for comfort." Keyalah's eyes widened, but to her credit, she remained silent.

Nitzevet shifted on her cushion, seeming uncomfortable for the first time. "On the night Jesse planned to take her, my maid and I changed places—like our matriarchs Leah and Rachel tricked

Jacob on their wedding night. This time, however, I returned to my little house before Jesse realized he'd slept with me. When my belly began to swell a few months later, tongues wagged. When Jesse publicly accused me of adultery, I explained what my maid and I had done. The elders, who could have followed the Law and had me stoned, decided I deserved mercy. Though my life was spared, all of Bethlehem—including my older sons—shunned me. However, when David was born with his abba's red hair, no one could deny his true parentage." She pursed her lips and lifted her brow as if reaching the end of her tale.

I finally understood why her sons' wives and their children avoided this lovely woman. "Did your husband apologize?" I blurted.

"You've met my abba." Zeruiah scoffed. "What do you think? I was relegated to a second maid after Abigal was taken and Ima was banished. When Ima returned home, Abba *forgave* her for the shame she brought on our house, but he wanted nothing to do with David. As soon as my youngest brother was old enough to carry a stick, he was sent to the pastures and raised by our chief shepherd."

"Zeruiah," Nitzevet said, head bowed, "you make your abba sound like Leviathan. He's suffered much in his lifetime." An awkward silence settled between them.

Zeruiah's eyes met mine, and understanding passed between us. The wounds of those years had never fully healed, and the scars left this family badly misshapen.

Keyalah reached for another piece of bread and spread more cheese on it. "Every family has its difficulties. The latest harem rumor is that the king's third wife put urine in the queen's juniper oil." Nitzevet and Zeruiah broke into peals of laughter, tension shattered by the maid's quick tongue.

I rolled onto my back. My head ached, but not as much as I yearned for our lives in Jezreel. At least there I knew where I belonged. Now I didn't belong anywhere, not with these women, nor with Abba in a stronghold of soldiers. I *definitely* didn't belong with Zeruiah's daughters-in-law—Vered, Raya, and Dalit—and their noisy children next door. They'd only visited us once, which was enough. Vered was meaner than a cornered viper, so Raya obeyed her without question. Dalit was pregnant, due to deliver any day, and looked like a cushion with too much stuffing. She appeared constantly on the verge of tears and barely spoke.

"Come, Ahinoam," Mistress Nitzevet called. "You can watch me embroider."

I sat up. My head swam a little. The others had finished their meal, and Keyalah was pulling the door closed behind her. "Thank you, mistress, but I think I'll rest awhile." I lay down again. I needed to rest, but I needed to see Abba more. Perhaps when Mistress Nitzevet and Zeruiah settled down for their after-midday rest, I would again muster the courage to venture an escape.

I woke to a quiet chamber—except for Mistress Nitzevet's snoring—and noticed through my sheer linen that Zeruiah was also asleep. Scooting off the bed, I searched beneath the mattress for my leather belt and daggers. I'd hidden them after Zeruiah disposed of my short robe and high-laced sandals. She'd insisted I wear the new robe and jeweled sandals waiting for us in the palace chamber so we wouldn't offend our Moabite hosts. She would likely have given my daggers away, too, had I not hidden them.

While tying my leather belt, the soft linen robe caught in my knot. I could barely silence my frustration. Leaving the chamber might have been the worst idea I'd ever had. How could I—an unmarried, foreign woman—walk alone through Moab's capital with six daggers?

Spying Zeruiah's headscarf and shawl hanging by the door, I slipped into my stiff new sandals and borrowed the scarf and shawl woven with the wide blue-and-crimson stripes of Jesse's family. When I lifted the metal latch, it clicked so loudly I was certain it echoed two floors down into the throne room.

Eyes closed, I waited for Zeruiah to bark a command. But there was only silence. Relief gave me courage to pull open the door. The leather hinges groaned. Had there ever been a noisier exit? Grateful, for once in my life, for my small stature, I slid through an opening no wider than a donkey's head into freedom.

I glanced both ways down the curved corridor and paused. Children's playful laughter came from chambers on our right and left. I hurried down the hall, thankful to be free from their world even for a while. Hopefully, the two women who had at least attempted to welcome me wouldn't be too angry when I returned.

Following the hallway, I remembered the first day's trek from the throne room to our top-floor chamber of the palace watchtower. We'd climbed two flights of curved stairs, passing the royal harem's level to reach our own lofty perch. The balcony in our chamber had offered necessary fresh air, but I needed more than mountain scenery to settle my heart.

"I need *you*, Abba." My whisper echoed against the rock walls of the stairway. Even the scrape of my leather-soled sandals sounded louder than usual in the tight space. I rolled my feet to lessen the sound as I passed the harem doorway, ducking beneath the barred window where eunuchs guarded the king's living treasures. Continuing my descent, I passed another barred window on the royal level, which housed the king's throne room and living quarters and was also heavily guarded. Having successfully escaped the top three levels, I descended into the bowels of Moab's royal fortress. No longer did scented oils fill the stairwell but rather stale sweat mingled with food scraps and baking bread.

I paused to cover my nose with the headscarf and heard hushed voices below.

A woman's voice whispered, "Did you hear someone?"

I held my breath.

After a short silence, a man answered, "You're just nervous."

"I am nervous," the woman said. "Why kill the women? Why not make them servants or—"

A strangling noise suspended the woman's suggestion. "David shouldn't have come into Mizpah's throne room thinking we would protect his family because he carried a giant sword and his great-grandmother once lived here." The man scoffed. "David ben Jesse should have fought his own battles in Israel. We will teach him how Moab deals with cowards. Must I teach you the same lesson and find another chambermaid for David's women?"

Keyalah? The woman we'd shared our meals with?

"I'll do it," she said with a raspy cough. "Just don't hurt my daughter."

"Do what you're told, and she'll be fine!"

I covered a horrified gasp as receding footsteps beat the awful truth into reality. A door slammed shut, and the awful silence felt like a shroud. What if the assassin was on his way to kill David? Did they plan to attack David's whole army? Abba was in danger, too!

I pressed my back against the cold stone wall. *Yahweh, give me wisdom.* It was well after midday, and our traitorous servant would soon collect our meal from the palace kitchen. Could I intercept the maid before she delivered our evening meal? She had been afraid for her daughter. I would promise David's protection in return for information on the assassin and his plan, then she could take me to the stronghold. Whether it was Yahweh's wisdom or my own desperation, the spontaneous plan was my only hope.

Sounds of clanging knives and servants' chatter filled the stairwell, so I continued down the steps to the lowest, packed-dirt level and saw two closed doors. Through a barred window in each, I glimpsed a kitchen courtyard beyond one—the source of the spoiled food odor—and a hallway behind the other, likely leading to the clamor I heard.

Had Keyalah returned to her kitchen duties or gone outside to the courtyard and possibly into the city? *Yahweh, which do I choose?* Both doors were weathered but stout, and each had a metal latch. Before I could decide, the handle lifted on the door nearest me. I slipped into a shadowy corner and watched as a woman's backside appeared, pushing open the door. Backing out farther, she swung around toward the stairs with a silver tray balanced on each hand. The trays, laden with food, pitchers, and dishes, completely blocked her face, but I recognized a small tear in Keyalah's robe.

Yahweh, You answered my prayer!

Before I could plan my approach, a furry creature skittered over my foot. I tried to stifle my squeal, but the noise startled Keyalah.

She jumped. Whirled. Both trays tilted. I grabbed one. She lurched for the other, but all the bread, nuts, and goat cheese plummeted to the floor with a ghastly splat. Triumphantly balancing the tray with a pitcher and two bowls of yogurt, I offered a sheepish "Sorry." The maid stared at my dagger belt, now visible since Zeruiah's shawl had fallen to the floor.

"You were listening in the stairwell," she whispered, then lunged toward the door for escape. A male voice shrieked her name, and she stiffened like a statue. I shoved the tray into her hands and hid behind the door when it swung open.

"Forgive me, Cook," Keyalah said. "I tripped and—"

"You clumsy ox! That wasted food will be your wages. Deliver the wine while I prepare a replacement tray." He slammed the door behind him, leaving me alone with a woman who had just proved her loyalty.

"Thank you, Keyalah," I whispered. "And yes, I heard your conversation in the stairwell."

Her tear-filled eyes glistened in the torchlight. "They'll kill my daughter if I don't obey."

"But if you help us, King David will protect you both. Prove loyal to him, and he'll be kind to you." I hoped it would be true. "He's been kind to me, even after I threw my dagger at his torch. Simply lead me to the stronghold across the valley, and tell him everything you know."

"I can't. If Bezeel finds out . . ." She shook her head. "I've heard how he tortures traitors."

"Please, Keyalah. Please." I grasped her wrist.

She stared down at my daggers again. "Are you a spy? Is that why you can't embroider? Why should I trust you?"

If she hadn't been so afraid, I would have laughed. "I'm much better handling daggers than a bone needle." I released her and stepped back, hoping to reassure her.

She lowered her head. I waited, wondering if she was praying, which was actually a good idea. *Yahweh, give this woman courage to help me. And work in David's heart to protect her and her daughter—though she'd been willing to betray us.*

"I'll do it," Keyalah said. She set aside the tray. When I started toward the courtyard door, she grabbed my arm. "No, no. You can't walk through the city with those things." Pointing at my daggers, she added, "People will already wonder why a proper lady would be seen with a raggedy maid. We need not stir more suspicion."

After giving myself a mental shake at being called a "proper lady," I wrapped Zeruiah's shawl around my shoulders. Keyalah nodded approvingly and led us through the courtyard, where we escaped unnoticed through the servants' entrance. We cleared the city gates and traveled alone on a narrow dirt path.

Since Keyalah wore no head covering, I assumed she wasn't married. "Are you a widow?" I asked. When she offered no reply, I thought she hadn't heard, so I repeated the question.

She whirled on me. "Will my answer change your promise to protect my daughter?"

"No, Keyalah. I'm sorry, I—"

She turned and continued walking. She didn't need to explain.

Perhaps after hearing my story she'd realize I wasn't a *proper* lady and would be more willing to share about her life. On our way to Moab, I'd heard a few disheartening whispers about David from some men in his army. Perhaps the troubled past of Yahweh's anointed king helped him truly *see* distressed people who other leaders ignored. Abba had been right to follow him. *But will he see and protect this frightened woman too?*

FIVE

DAVID

The prophet Gad said to David, "Do not stay in the stronghold. Go into the land of Judah."

1 Samuel 22:5

I stood at the mouth of the stronghold's uppermost cave, watching rain clouds clear and listening to the rushing mountain wadis calm to a trickle. My men and I were safe from winter floods in the middle and upper caves, but I'd denied permission for anyone to venture into the city or to visit family at Mizpah's palace.

Toren had paced like a prowling beast, worrying about his dagger-wielding daughter, until Abba challenged him to a sharpening contest with the two whetstones the Kenite brought along. The old friends had been sharpening daggers, knives, and short swords every day since. The Kenite lived with my family and me in the stronghold's highest level, in a single, expansive cave that gave us privacy but also space for the two distant friends to reconnect. I'd never heard Abba laugh so much or speak so freely as he did with Toren the Kenite. *Yahweh, have you sent me an angel to prove Abba has a heart?*

I cradled the lyre in my right arm and pressed my cheek atop

75

the wooden frame, tuning each string by tightening or loosening its clamp until a full strum produced the perfect sound. The process used to annoy Michal. She never understood how I could block out everything and everyone else with a lyre in my hands. My voice became like the ladder in our patriarch Jacob's dream—a ladder between the heavens and this earthly existence. All fear and despair fell away. Whatever darkness encompassed me slowly turned to light. Whatever snare had entrapped me, the bonds were loosed, and my inner being burst free, dragging my reality into the undeniable truth of Yahweh's sovereignty and goodness. I once thought only Jonathan understood, but when Zerry arrived at Adullam Cave with my childhood lyre, I'd never felt such gratitude. She knew I'd need it for these uncertain days.

How long, O LORD? Will you forget me forever? How long will my enemy be exalted over me?

We arrived in Moab to the king's warm welcome—too warm. Something about his overly accommodating manner had raised a warning shofar in my inner being, but where else could we go? When I mentioned my suspicions to my nephews Abishai and Asahel, they ignored my concerns and said I'd been too long at war to appreciate peace. When I mentioned my nagging feelings to Joab, however, he sent the Gadites to begin scouting the territory. These skilled mercenaries scaled the mountains with the agility of goats and the swiftness of ibex.

Consider and answer me, O LORD . . .

Humming the tune, waiting for more words, I watched the loyal men on the level below me. They'd become good friends during our two weeks in Moab. Training together. Cooking together. Learning to trust one another.

I have trusted in Your steadfast love, O LORD, and my heart will rejoice in your salvation. I will sing to You for you have dealt bountifully to me.

"You didn't even notice I've been watching you." Joab plopped down, startling me. "With such poor battle instincts, it's a wonder you collected those Philistine foreskins for Michal's bride price." He chewed a piece of dried meat, smacking his lips like a camel chewing cud.

I was in no mood for teasing. "Never again speak her name to me."

His playful demeanor shifted to the caring friend he'd been since we were boys. "Why won't you tell me what really happened? I can't believe Michal would say you threatened her. Let me take a small contingent, sneak into the Gibeah palace, and bring her here to Moab so you can question her."

He was crazy enough to try. "Someday I'll tell you everything, Joab, but not now. And no more questions. Tell your brothers and mine not to speak of her to me."

"As you command, lord king." He pounded his fist over his heart on the leather breastpiece.

"I'm not Israel's king yet." I grinned at his overexuberant response.

"You were *my* king the moment Yahweh chose you to rule." He offered his hand, and we locked wrists, draining all tension between us.

Though he hadn't witnessed Samuel's anointing, I'd run to the pastures after the prophet left Bethlehem to tell Joab first. He'd been my closest confidant and was the best warrior to command my army. "How were this morning's drills?"

"Spear and javelin skills are improving," he said. "Archers need work, and you'll need to personally instruct the slingers if you want them to match your accuracy."

"Why can't you teach them? You're almost as accurate. I'm busy training the men to shepherd our flocks."

He lifted an eyebrow, accompanied by a mischievous grin. "I'm your best warrior in all other weapons. If the men think I'm perfect in slinging, too, why would they need you?"

"Get out of my sight!" I laughed, shoving him toward his afternoon duties. But his nudge to spend more time with the men was effective. I set aside my lyre and followed my eldest nephew down the path to the second level of caves, where Abishai and Asahel waited.

Zerry's sons were exhausted. I'd given each one authority over a hundred soldiers, and they'd assigned lieutenants over contingents of twenty. I'd winnowed out the remaining hundred men to personally train as shepherds, also dividing them into groups of twenty under the leadership of an under-shepherd. I still knew many of the sheep and goats by name in the large flock Abba brought with the family from Bethlehem and was, perhaps, a little overprotective. But the animals would be our source of provision and trade during our indefinite stay in Moab. My nephews and I had worked hard to train our ragtag army into a semblance of disciplined soldiers who followed orders and hit every target in their sights.

The shofar's *t'kiyah* blast drew our attention. Too early for its typical pronouncement of changing guards, the only other occasion for the single long blast was to affirm God's sovereignty over a weighty decision—but I was the only one who would issue such an order. My nephews and their lieutenants mustered their men on the large plateau while Abba and Toren hurried down the path from our upper cave. My shepherds were scattered over the mountains, and each answered the t'kiyah with a single sustained blast, assuring all was well with our flocks. Joab's conscientious shouting at our men to straighten their formations proved nothing was amiss with the army.

Joab stood in front of me and said over his shoulder, "Isn't that Gad the Seer, and Israelite soldiers with . . . is that Ima?"

"That's Ahinoam!" Toren pointed down the switchback path leading to the stronghold.

Toren was right. His daughter was wearing Zerry's scarf. "And she's brought a Moabite woman to our stronghold. Do you recognize any of Saul's soldiers, Toren?" Though I liked this man immensely, and his faith seemed as real as the mountain on which we stood, the arrival of Israelite soldiers piqued my suspicions about everyone. "Do you or your daughter know Samuel or any seer at Ramah or Naioth?" He paused, seeming puzzled by my question, so I asked another. "Why would your daughter bring Israelite soldiers to our stronghold, Toren?"

The man's eyes narrowed. "Perhaps you should look more closely, my lord. It's Gad who seems to be leading Saul's soldiers to this stronghold. My daughter's arm is linked with a Moabite woman, whom I've never seen before." He placed his hand on my shoulder, his features softening. "Take courage, my lord. Remember, your watchmen sounded the t'kiyah, not the warning t'ruah. Perhaps the seer brings a timely message for you from Yahweh himself."

I wanted to believe him, this good and faithful man. "Remain behind me, Toren, until we learn why Gad has come with strangers from Ramah and your daughter escorts a foreign woman into our midst."

"Of course, my lord."

My gut said Toren and his daughter were loyal to me, but Saul was a brilliant strategist. He could have recruited Gad to infiltrate my camp and win my trust. Though Gad had been one of my favorite students at Samuel's prophets' camp, if I trusted too easily, I'd risk the lives of five hundred men.

As the visitors continued to wind up the muddy, serpentine path, the whole plateau fell silent, shields lifted and weapons in hand. Some of my men held daggers, others cudgels, still others were armed with whittled sticks serving as makeshift spears. Joab, Abishai, and Asahel stood like sentries in front of me. Abba and my brothers huddled behind me, having refused military assignments.

Joab seemed anxious and shouted, "Lieutenants to the ready!" Each of my nephews' five lieutenants shifted into a secondary row of protection in front of their captains, forming a wall like towering cedars in front of me.

Frustration surged, as I knew the newcomers neared, and I shouted, "A king must be protected but not blinded by his guards!" Pushing through my front line, I spoke as I approached the intruders, "What brings you to our stronghold unannounced?" I met Gad's placid features, but before he could speak, I saw the terrible bruise on Ahinoam's forehead. Fury rose at the realization that the Israelites had forced her to escort them. I locked eyes with their captain. "How dare you harm this woman!"

Ahinoam halted my hand on my sword. "My lord, no! I ran into a door." Her hand lingered on my arm, and she looked up at me, our faces barely a handbreadth apart.

"A door?" I was momentarily captured by the fullness of her lips.

"Yes, my lord," she whispered. With my other hand, I reached up to touch the bruise.

But she lurched away, nudging the Moabite woman forward. "I've come with our chambermaid, Keyalah. An assassin named Bezeel threatened to kill Keyalah and her daughter if she didn't help in his conspiracy to attack this stronghold and kill your women and children in the palace."

"How would a chambermaid come by such information?" The Moabite withered under my scrutiny. My brothers shouted panicked threats at the poor woman. Thankfully, my nephews restrained them and contained their own fear and fury against our deceptive hosts.

The maid hid behind Ahinoam and spoke in a trembling voice. "I told you he wouldn't help me."

The Israelite captain beside Gad moved forward and nodded respectfully. "*King* David, may I speak?" His voice boomed like a trumpet over the noise.

I granted permission.

"We are men from Benjamin and Judah—from Saul's standing army—among those sent to Naioth at Ramah to kill you. When Yahweh's Spirit overwhelmed us, and we could do nothing but lay naked and prophesy, we knew you were God's chosen king for Israel. We've come to serve you with our voices and our swords." He bowed to one knee and his men did the same. "Our lives belong to Yahweh and King David."

Joab stood beside me, his brows drawn together. "It's a trap. Saul has somehow discovered our location and sent his best warriors with a prophet you trust to infiltrate our ranks."

He was right about one thing. I did trust Gad. He'd been the most encouraging of Samuel's students when I fled to the prophets' camp. But could I trust Saul's assassins—even after Yahweh's Spirit had overwhelmed them in Naioth? The Spirit had also caused Saul to prophesy, but he was still intent on killing me. How could I be sure these men's hearts were true? *Yahweh, only You can search their hearts.*

I held their captain's gaze. He never flinched. No sign of wavering. "If you have come in peace to help me, then join me. If you have come to betray me, may Yahweh Himself reveal it and judge you."

The man shot to his feet, inhaling a deep breath, and released a spontaneous chorus.

> "We are yours, David!
> We are with you, son of Jesse!
> Success, success to you,
> and success to those who help you,
> for your God will help you."

Recognizing the practiced cadence of a priestly gift, I blinked back tears. "You're a Kohathite."

"I am, my king. My name is Amasai." We locked wrists. "I often admired your psalms when I heard you play for King Saul."

"How lovely for you both," Ahinoam said, nudging the distraught maid toward me. "Did you hear what I said? An attack on this stronghold and your family in the palace is imminent. I promised

Keyalah you would protect her and her daughter if she told you everything about the Moabites' plan."

Toren's daughter wasn't a lamb in need of protection. She was a lioness protecting those in her pride. "I heard you, and I believe the threat is real." Leaving Ahinoam shocked, I turned to the maid and said, "I suspect if we hear from Yahweh's seer, I might not need you to speak—though I appreciate your courage and will send a contingent of men with you to extract your daughter from the city before we leave Mizpah tonight."

"Aren't you even going to hear what she has to say?" Ahinoam's left eyebrow, shaped with a natural arch as if Yahweh created her to challenge, was all fire and vinegar—so much like Zeruiah.

"The Lord God of Israel says do not remain in this stronghold. Rather, return to Judah and the land over which you will one day rule." Gad spoke so all my men could hear, then bowed his head. I knew no more words would come. Yahweh spoke short messages to Gad. Urgent ones.

Turning to the maid, I offered my hand, palm up, hoping to reassure her of my intention to embrace and protect. "What is your daughter's name, Keyalah?"

She seemed startled by the question. "Eglah. She's all I have in the world, my lord."

"I understand. We'll make sure she's safe. Can you tell us about the conspirators' plan?"

"I was to add hemlock to the porridge bowls for the women and children in the palace tomorrow morning. Bezeel would deliver the news of their deaths and escort you and your family to the palace to collect their bod—" She swallowed audibly, glancing at the angry men behind me.

"Look at me," I said. "You were very brave to come to me with this information. No one will harm you or your daughter. What was the plan after our women ate the poisoned porridge?"

"While you and the officers in your family were collecting their dead from the palace, Bezeel's contingent of assassins would attack your stronghold of unsuspecting soldiers."

"I have one more question for you, Keyalah." She nodded, seeming almost eager now to help. "Did the king sanction this plan, or was Bezeel acting with a rebel faction of Moabite soldiers?"

"Bezeel only acts under the king's orders, my lord."

Another betrayer. I sniffed back instant fury and lowered my head to keep from frightening the poor woman. First, Abba rejected me. Then Saul falsely accused me. My own wife betrayed me. Now a foreign king pretends friendship but conspires to kill my whole family. *Why, Lord? Am I so unworthy of love or respect? How can I rule a nation when no one remains loyal?* Feeling the impossible weight of my invisible crown, I bent to one knee and lowered my head. *Yahweh, how can I take my family back to Israel where more will betray, and Saul could harm them?*

"David." Joab placed his hand on my back. "Speak to your men. They must hear from their king."

I squeezed my eyes closed. How could I speak? *Adonai Elohim, I'm a prisoner of pain and fear, brought low by those who hate me. They're too strong for me, Lord. Rescue me so I can once again honor You with praise.*

Someone crouched beside me. "I can't imagine the responsibility you feel." Startled by Ahinoam's voice, I looked into her big doe eyes. "You're not alone, my lord. Yahweh has given you a warrior-musician-priest. I've seen El Shaddai's hand at work from the moment I walked down the palace steps to when Yahweh helped me find Keyalah and then gave her courage to entrust her only child to your protection. I had no idea who Gad was or why he'd come to Moab. He and the Israelite soldiers were waiting when Keyalah and I reached the base of the stronghold's path. They said Yahweh had commanded them to escort us. What more evidence of God's faithfulness do we need?" She glanced up at Toren. "And it all started because I missed my abba." Without another word, she left my side and rushed into his arms.

I watched their happy reunion and realized that not everyone betrays. The Kenites had certainly been an unexpected gift from the Giver of Life.

The Moabite maid stood alone, her eyes flitting from one of my warriors to another. "Keyalah," I said, drawing her attention. "I'm sending some of these men to accompany you into the city. They'll escort you and your daughter back here to the stronghold."

"What then?" Her chin quaked. "I'm hired labor, my lord, not a slave, but Bezeel has contacts in every Moabite village. He'll hunt me for this betrayal."

"You and your daughter are coming with us to Israel."

Ahinoam stepped from her abba's embrace. "Thank you, my lord."

Bolstered by the approval of Toren's feisty daughter, I scanned my warriors' expectant faces—those who had proven faithful and those newly arrived. "Amasai, you and your men will accompany the maid to fetch her daughter. Joab will assign a skilled contingent to extract our family from the palace. The rest of you, prepare to leave Moab after sunset. We go quietly under cover of darkness and travel through the night. If Moab's king wants a war, he'll pursue us, and we'll be ready. If he was merely tired of our presence, he'll wake and be relieved to see us gone."

Amasai, the newly arrived singing priest, raised his short sword and booming voice. "Yahweh's king back to Yahweh's Land!"

SIX

AHINOAM

Though my father and mother forsake me, the Lord will receive me.

Psalm 27:10

Four Days Later
Moabite Wilderness, East of Dead Sea

David and his captains chose a very different route for our return journey to Judah than the well-traveled paths and trade routes we'd taken east. Asahel and the Gadite scouts under his command had remained in the Moabite mountains behind us, and for our first two days of travel, Abishai and two other skilled soldiers were also missing. David assigned the new guards—those who had once served among Saul's special forces—to protect Keyalah and her teenaged daughter, Eglah, as we traveled. Still, the poor woman constantly looked over her shoulder. She barely ate and barely slept, certain Bezeel would find her and Eglah.

I traveled with Nitzevet and Zeruiah, who never left Keyalah's side. David and Joab took turns leading the caravan, then the other would shift to oversee the rear guard. Abba stayed with Jesse's clan, which followed the maid's protection team—a position in the caravan that some in the family said David meant as blatant disrespect. I tried to ignore their pettiness and focus on Eglah. She seemed to be bright, with an inquisitive mind, stopping to inspect the various desert plants and unusual rock formations. Her wide, dark eyes seemed to take in every detail of our surroundings. Though she hadn't spoken a word since she left Moab, she'd stolen Mistress Nitzevet's heart.

Sunrise broke after our fourth night's travel, and a subdued celebration began at the back of the caravan. Applause, then a few whistles. Despite the joyful sounds, Keyalah's guards tightened formation around her and Eglah. David looked my way. "Guard Ima and Zeruiah while I investigate."

"I will." Drawing both Adam and Eve, my favorite daggers, I was ready to throw. A sense of pride welled within that he would trust me to help protect his ima and beloved sister. *Thank You, Yahweh, for granting me favor.*

In less than ten heartbeats, the sea of celebration parted, and Joab ushered forward his younger brother Abishai, along with the two men he'd taken with him for the special assignment. Zeruiah rushed past me, shouting, "Abishai ben Ahitub, what took so long? You give your ima a hug right now!" The tallest of her sons lifted her off her feet with a tight squeeze. He set her feet on the ground, and she hugged the two other men who had accompanied him, Ahimelech and Uriah, Hittites who had been Abishai's best friends as children in Bethlehem.

"Is it done?" David asked Abishai.

The grin on his nephew's face forecasted the news. "It's done. Neither Bezeel nor his assassins will ever hunt Mistress Keyalah or her daughter again. And, as you commanded, since Amasai's contingent was seen escorting her through town, we left a piece of their clothing, too, as if Saul sent his assassin squad to Moab to kill Bezeel and his men. Since no one witnessed our nighttime departure, they won't know Amasai's men left with us, and Moab's king should have no quarrel with David ben Jesse."

A cheer rose from all five hundred soldiers following Yahweh's anointed king. But David raised his hands, bouncing them on the air for silence. "All right, yes, we're safe, but Saul will have even more of a quarrel with us now. We must still stay off trade roads where merchants might report our location."

David looked west, and a smile softened the tension his features had shown for days. Every head turned to see the morning sun sparkling on the calm, salty Dead Sea. "Choose your campsite. Get some sleep. At nightfall we cross the Great Tongue into Judah!" He pumped his fist in the air, a silent celebration that others mimicked as they dispersed onto the shore of the briny sea.

Everyone sought out shade to set up our simple tents. Nitzevet, Zeruiah, Keyalah, Eglah, and I continued to live separately from Zeruiah's brothers' wives, her daughters-in-law, and their children. My abba, Jesse, and his sons created the barrier between the two camps of women. Vered ruled one camp, Zeruiah the other. Neither initiated conversations with the exception of Nitzevet's occasional request to see her grandchildren and great-grandchildren. The family relationships seemed odd to me, but I'd never experienced generational ties of my own. Though my savta Jael was larger than life in my mind, she'd died long before I was born.

The family tension did, however, make camp setup predictable. Zeruiah, Keyalah, and I took turns carrying Mistress Nitzevet's shoulder bag and setting up her private stick-and-blanket tent. We also flanked Nitzevet through the mountains as our guards held torches aloft, supporting her through every pass and outcropping. When we reached the Dead Sea's sandy shore, we searched our packs for whatever dried meat and nuts remained.

"How much farther can we go without more supplies?" Nitzevet asked, her voice quaking. "Is there a town nearby?" When angry voices at the back of the caravan drowned out the bleating of our flocks, Nitzevet turned to see the commotion. Her face paled. "Oh, Jesse."

"Why must he always complain?" Zeruiah's tone held none of Nitzevet's forbearance. "Is David like Moses? Can he provide water from a rock?"

Ignoring her daughter's challenge, Nitzevet turned to the maid. "I'm feeling a little tired, Keyalah. I'd like to rest while Jesse decides whether we cross during daylight or wait and continue our travel tonight."

Zeruiah mumbled, "Yahweh help us if Abba makes the decision."

"Enough, Zerry." Nitzevet's rebuke was as quick and deadly as a thrown dagger. She then offered a hand to her maid. "Could you help me to the tent?"

"Of course, mistress." Keyalah grasped Nitzevet's hand and shot a scolding glance at Zeruiah. Eglah had already prepared their tents.

Tears glistened in Zeruiah's eyes. "Come, Ahinoam. Let's set our tent closer to David's and pray Abba doesn't force him into a decision we'll all regret."

Grabbing my pack, I followed, stomach rumbling and tongue sticking to the roof of my mouth. We'd found a spring on our first day of travel but had to ration water when we'd found none yesterday. When I'd overheard David tell Joab he planned for our whole army to hide from Saul in Judah's wilderness, my palms had grown sweaty with fear.

I had relived my first wilderness journey, when Abba and I escaped Saul's attack on the Amalekites, and we'd walked two days to Jezreel without water. Abba was strong, but I was only fourteen and near death when Old Miriam found us at the city's central well. She nursed me back to health—and reminded me of it every time we went to the well together. Thoughts of Jezreel brought to mind its plentiful orchards, vineyards, and fields, making my stomach rumble again, and worse—stirring my hunger for home.

Zeruiah and I approached David's family and heard Jesse ask, "How can you provide for five hundred people in the desert?"

"Yahweh will provide," David answered calmly. "Look how He's already protected us."

"Our packs are empty!" Jesse turned his shoulder bag inside out. "*My* clan is crossing the Great Tongue into Judah *now*, and we're taking my flocks with us."

Had his idea not been so deadly, I might have laughed at how Jesse slurred when he spoke the name of the narrow land bridge. From the mountain heights, the Great Tongue did, indeed, look like the Moabite shore stuck out its thin tongue and licked Israel's eastern shore, but Jesse's speech proved his tongue was as swollen as mine. How could he hope to make that crossing in the glaring sun and then wander into the unforgiving wilderness on the other side?

"Abba, if you'll just be patient." David maintained a calm respect I'm not sure I could have mustered. "I've sent the Gadites to scout for springs. We must fill our waterskins before crossing into the wilderness on the other side."

"My clan isn't resting another day in Moabite territory," Jesse rattled on. "We'll find springs within Judah's borders, and my flocks will provide for food until we reach Bethlehem. My family will not continue to starve on grass and nuts!"

As if launched from a sling, Zeruiah marched to David's side. "We aren't starving! And if you and my stubborn brothers had listened when the soldiers raised in desert towns trained us how to find berries and edible wildflowers and grasses, you wouldn't be so grumpy right now." David's family had scoffed at the wilderness foraging and called the fruit of our labors *animal fodder*. However, when David's best archers returned from a hunt, and we roasted six wild goats, Jesse's clan shoved to the front of the line, taking more than their portion.

His men, hearing the commotion, had meandered over and surrounded him—men from the tribes of Judah, Levi, Benjamin, Dan,

Ephraim, Issachar, Gad, Manasseh, along with a Philistine, two Hittites, and an Ammonite.

Rather than haughty, David looked at his abba with something more like disappointment. "Listen to the bleating of your unsettled flocks." Though the animals were at the rear of the caravan, their desperate cries were as loud as a shout. "Those animals are as thirsty as we are."

"Then why not cross now?" Jesse shot back. "Reach En Gedi sooner!"

"Look at those animals!" Frustration crept into David's tone. "A hundred men can barely keep them from drinking the briny water that would kill them. How will you, with only my six brothers and their wives, keep five hundred animals from drinking their death?"

Every eye turned to watch the flocks, mad with desire, leaping over one another and ramming their shepherds to reach the very thing that would do them harm. Wasn't Jesse himself acting like his thirsty flock, wild with impatience and panic that could place his family in danger if David conceded?

I eyed Abba, who stood beside his old friend, stone-faced and silent. My abba's joy had ebbed since the escape from Moab, and he'd placed his tent far away from Jesse and the family during rest days. "May I speak?" he asked David.

The king nodded permission.

Abba turned to his longtime friend, features softening. "Listen to me, Jesse. Stay with your son and his army. Tomorrow, after we're all safely across the Tongue, we'll kiss Judah's shore, march to En Gedi, and bathe in its pools. Give yourself a few days at the oasis, and then decide if you'll return to Bethlehem or remain under David's protection. Hmm? What do you say?"

Jesse leaned forward, barely a handbreadth between them. "I say you should stay out of my family's decisions."

"It's a *military* decision, Saba." Joab moved to David's side and folded his arms. "David is Yahweh's anointed and leads by Yahweh's command. *Everyone* will obey Yahweh's king."

Jesse drew breath to argue but when thirty warriors stepped forward to flank King David, his abba swallowed the protest.

Zeruiah reached for my hand and whispered, "Victory."

"I found a spring, my lord!" one of the Gadites shouted from an outcropping above.

A cheer arose, the sound reverberating in my chest, making the relief more palpable. David directed more men to help the shepherds herd the sheep toward the water. The other Gadites came from every direction, joining their fellow scout with the sure-footedness of the ibexes we'd seen yesterday.

Again, David lifted his hands to quiet the celebration. "Let the flocks drink first, then fill your waterskins. Find some shade and sleep for the day." As the crowd began to disperse, he lowered his voice and whispered, "Abba, you were willing to feed the family with your flocks on the way to Bethlehem. Are you willing to feed my men from your flock tonight?"

The soldiers who heard David's question waited to hear the answer. Jesse glanced at his sons as if hoping one of them might refuse for him. They, however, scanned the waiting soldiers and then coaxed their abba with a nod.

With narrowed eyes, Jesse spat, "Fine, but only ten sheep." He turned on his heel, kicking sand as he stomped away. Ten sheep would provide delicious meat, though little more than a few bites for each person.

"Thank you, Abba!" David called out behind him. Undeterred, Yahweh's anointed jogged away. When he reached the shepherds, his whistling and tongue-clucking called the flock to quench their thirst. His brothers and their wives were already bickering about who got which shady spot. I had no doubt Vered would soon win the battle.

Zeruiah and I returned to the shady spot where Keyalah had already set up the simple shelter she and her daughter shared and Nitzevet's small tent. All three had already disappeared into their tents. David's sister and I stepped off ten paces—far enough to avoid Nitzevet's snoring—and set up the tent we shared. Anchoring our walking sticks in the sand near a boulder, we hoisted a blanket over them. I removed my dagger belt and shoved it into my shoulder bag, then crawled into the tent after Zeruiah. Lying on our sides, we faced each other, heads pillowed on bent arms. I closed my eyes, since her silence usually meant she was ready to sleep.

"I'm as different from Jesse's clan as my black silky hair is from their coarse red curls." Her whisper held a slight tremor. "Ima questions Keyalah and says she's enamored with Ruth's foreign heritage, but I think she loves me *despite* my Ammonite blood. Abba—I mean, *Jesse*—he's never shown anything but disdain for foreign—" She rolled over, her back to me, letting quiet sniffing prove her tears. "I thought our time in Moab would draw Ima and me closer as we celebrated Ruth's heritage together. I feel like she's replaced me with Keyalah—a new Moabite daughter."

"Oh, Zeruiah." I placed a hand on her shoulder but had no idea what to say. "Maybe you could demand more time with your grandchildren? Maybe tell Joab to put a bridle on his wife or have your sons tell their wives to treat you with more kindness?"

She choked out a laugh and peered over her shoulder. "You really don't know anything about relationships, do you?"

I covered a giggle. "It's that obvious?"

She lifted on one elbow to face me. "Why don't you call me Zerry? Maybe I'll feel like I have a real friend."

"I'd like that, *Zerry*." We both lay on our backs, staring up at the apex of our shelter. "What do friends talk about?"

"They trust each other with secrets they don't tell anyone else."

"You would trust me?"

"You saved our lives in Moab, Ahinoam. David trusts you to protect Ima and me. Of course I trust you."

"I trust you, too, Zerry." I paused, thinking of what I might share. "Abba calls me Nomy. That's a secret no one knows."

"All right, Nomy. I'm going to trust you with a secret only David and I share." She released a quick sigh. "When I was tending Ima at Adullam Cave, David confided things to me that Samuel told him while hiding from Saul in Ramah. Years ago, when Samuel came to our house to anoint David—"

"Did you witness the anointing?" The hair on my arms stood at attention.

"Yes, but at first Ima and I only listened from the adjoining room. When Samuel came to Bethlehem, he announced that he'd come to make a sacrifice. Then he entered our house and told Abba to call my brothers, one at a time, to pass before him. That's when Ima and I suspected the public sacrifice might have been an excuse to find Israel's next king among the faithful tribe of Judah. But Samuel refused Eliab, my oldest brother, saying, 'The Lord hasn't chosen this one.' Then he refused the other six."

"Wait, did you say he refused seven brothers?" I rose on one elbow. "Why have I met only six brothers?"

"We had another brother between Ozem and David, but we don't speak the name of the dead. He was killed fighting Philistines."

I lay back while she continued, "After Samuel had refused the others, he asked Abba if he had more sons." She released a little huff. "I was ready to charge into the room if Abba denied David's existence. Jesse ben Obed had exiled David to the fields when he was five years old. Ima and I took him meals every day, and the shepherds treated him as their own. But Abba never included him in family celebrations."

"How could . . ." My words died when I thought about how harshly Jesse still treated David—and Zerry. "Forgive me. Go on."

"Abba commanded Ima and me to prepare a meal for the prophet while we waited for a messenger to fetch David. But Samuel said no one would sit down until the matter was settled. Ima and I were serving the men wine when David arrived. Samuel gasped and ran to him as if reuniting with an old friend. Then he pressed on David's shoulders, forcing him to kneel, and emptied his entire horn of scented oil over his head. I'll never forget David's laughter, the oil dripping off his hair, his eyebrows, and the little whiskers on his top lip and jaw. He wasn't even old enough to grow a beard yet."

Her soft chuckle squeezed my heart, and I, too, fought tears.

"Without another word, the prophet left our home, completed the public sacrifice he'd announced as his purpose for coming, then left Bethlehem. David hadn't spoken to him again until he fled from Saul. That's when Samuel told David what Yahweh whispered to him the first time he glimpsed my short, red-haired little brother."

"Tell me," I almost squealed.

"Yahweh said, 'I don't judge by outward appearances. I see a man's heart. This is the one I chose when Saul disobeyed at Michmash. I sought out David because he seeks My heart.'" She turned to face me. "Think about the timing, Nomy. God declared He'd chosen David when Saul disobeyed Him at Michmash."

"How could—" I suddenly caught her excitement. "That battle was fought before David was born!"

"Yes! *Before* David's humiliating birth. Before Abba rejected him. Before he killed a giant. Before David did or experienced anything bad or good, God chose my red-haired, freckle-faced brother to become Israel's next king."

"Do you know what that means, Zerry?" I sat up. "If Yahweh formed David in the womb for His good purpose—despite the difficulties surrounding his birth—couldn't the same God also use your difficult birth circumstance for His good plan? Because He sees every heart, Zeruiah bat Jesse, and yours seeks after Him, too."

She stared at me, dumbfounded. "I . . . I'd never considered that Yahweh might see *me*." She rolled over quickly, back facing me again. "Thank you, Nomy. I must think on that awhile."

I lay down beside her, trying to settle myself as the camp sounds quieted. Exhaustion warred with the thrill of revelation. Yahweh was real. Not only had He proven Himself repeatedly on our journey, but Samuel's revelation proved more than existence. *You know us before birth, LORD!*

Though I'd questioned Abba's decision to join David ben Jesse's army many times, somehow the realization that Yahweh had chosen David before his birth gave me confidence to follow him anywhere— even into Judah's wilderness with five hundred hungry warriors.

SEVEN

AHINOAM

The Lord is the stronghold of my life—of whom shall I be afraid?

Psalm 27:1

I woke with a start but wasn't sure why. I shivered, though the air felt heavy. The camp was still quiet, so I scooted out of our shelter and gazed into an overcast sky. A few men walked along the salty shore. Lambs from Jesse's flock roasted near the sea. Clouds shrouded the sun, making it hard to determine the exact time. A mood darker than dusk lingered over us as it often did when David's abba and brothers publicly displayed their disrespect.

I looked down and found two full waterskins laid beside our tent and three more propped against Nitzevet's and Keyalah's shelters. The foreboding eased. The giver could have been any number of thoughtful men. Abba. Zeruiah's—rather, *Zerry's*—sons. Even David himself had sometimes performed such simple acts of kindness, which meant his soldiers had begun mimicking his thoughtfulness.

Sheep and goats now grazed contentedly on the hillside. No more wild bleating and frantic dashes toward danger. Their shepherds reclined under nearby shade, ever watchful. Scanning the sea's odd-shaped salt formations, I noticed Abba standing alone, watching me. Or was he waiting for Zerry to wake? He'd been especially attentive to David's lovely sister—not protective as he'd been with Old Miriam, but rather awkward and overly . . . nice. He lifted his hand in a timid wave and turned away. Clearly, he wasn't waiting to talk to me.

I felt a moment of panic at the thought of Abba flirting with my new friend. He was at least twenty harvests older than Zerry. The thought of them together—*oh no!*

Needing a distraction, I snagged my traveling pack, slung it over my shoulder, and started up the hillside. I climbed over rocks and ignored the dark clouds. Spying a copse of trees at the top of a distant hill, I stopped long enough to get my dagger belt out of my bag and cinched to my waist. It had been too long since I'd felt the smooth release of a practice throw, and those trees would provide perfect targets. I carefully scaled a rocky ledge and hugged the mountainside on another narrow path, then finally arrived atop a plateau.

Bodies lay everywhere.

I stumbled back, halted by a boulder, and reminded myself to breathe. Our soldiers lay sleeping, but the sight was too similar to what could be reality if Saul's army attacked.

Hands tightening on my dagger hilts, determination hardened into resolve. Though I treasured Zerry's friendship and appreciated the household skills Nitzevet had tried to teach me, I was a metalsmith. A good one. I threw daggers more accurately than any man in David's army—including Abba—and for the safety of our camp, I needed to convince the next king of Israel that I should fight among his soldiers. My stroll turned into a jog, legs churning toward the copse of trees. I must practice throwing every day. Zerry would support me if I explained what I'd just seen and the yearning in my heart to—

What was that sound?

I stopped near the hill's peak, ducking behind another boulder.

Listening. I heard the strumming of a lyre. A voice. Crouching low, I crept closer and heard singing.

"Lord, *You* will be my stronghold, I need never be afraid."

David? He would make Yahweh his stronghold—a mightier Protector than the mountains of Moab. The words were so brave, but the sorrow in his tone made my heart ache. Today's quarrel with his family had cost him dearly, even as he'd demonstrated venerable control.

"Though an army pursues me, my heart will not fear."

Did Yahweh's chosen king feel fear? Was Israel's greatest champion afraid Moab's army or the king's assassins would catch us?

"Though war may break out against me, even then I will be confident in *You.* I ask one thing from *You,* Lord: only let me dwell in *Your* presence all the days of my life. O Adonai, hide me in *Your* sacred tent."

Yahweh's sacred tent? Was David leading us to the Tabernacle in Nob? Wasn't it less than a day's march from Saul's palace? My breaths came quick and shallow. How could our army of five hundred fight against Saul's hundreds of thousands?

"Then I'll be exalted above my enemies, and at *His* sacred tent I'll sacrifice with joy. Though my abba and ima forsake me, I know You'll always be with me."

Would he risk his life and ours to prove his valor to an abba who despised him and brothers who never accepted him? *Yahweh, please! Give David wisdom! This can't be what You're asking of us.*

David strummed the lyre harder, sang louder. "I am confident of this, O Lord, that I will see *Your* goodness in the land of the living!"

I gasped as a hand gripped my arm. *Joab.* "Never spy on your king!" He dragged me toward the secluded tree, where David stood to meet us.

Tears had washed streaks down his freckled cheeks, making him appear more boy than warrior. "Ahinoam? Is Ima all right?" His concern made my heart seize.

"Yes, she's sleeping. I—" How could I explain my hope to prove trustworthy when Joab had just found me spying? "Are you really taking us to Nob?" I blurted out.

"Why would you think . . . ?" His furrowed brow smoothed. "Oh, the sacred tent I sang about."

I nodded.

"Leave us, nephew."

"It's not . . ." Joab left the obvious unspoken.

"It's not what?" David prodded.

"Not *proper*," I said, "for the next king of Israel to be alone with a woman not his wife or relative." I jerked my arm from Joab's grasp. "No one would even notice I was a woman if Zerry hadn't stolen my short robe and high-laced sandals."

David laughed, but Joab's scowl deepened. "My ima's name is *Zeruiah,* and the anointed king must be beyond reproach, or he could lose his men's respect."

"Your ima instructed me to call her Zerry, General, and if a man's respect for our king is lost because of one meeting with the homely daughter of a Kenite metal worker, that man isn't a soldier worth having."

Joab opened and closed his mouth, but no words came.

"My nephew will stand guard a few paces away," David intervened, "ensuring my reputation and yours, Ahinoam, remain beyond reproach." Then he patted the grass beside him.

Joab mumbled something as he walked away, and I sat a respectable distance from God's anointed king.

"We're not going to Nob," David began. "I will sometimes lead my people into hard places but never into known danger. Yahweh does the same." He pointed in various directions as he rehearsed our journey. "Behind us, the Moabite mountains; below us, the Dead Sea; and beyond it, the Judean wilderness. Yahweh will lead us into the desert—a hard place—because it's safer than dangerous cities on fertile plains."

"The wilderness is safer than a city with plenty of provisions?"

"Wherever there are people and provisions, there also will be King Saul's spies. That's why I've taught our soldiers to graze flocks on barren heights and find streams in the desert. The barrenness strengthens and shapes us into what the Lord wants us to become."

I still wasn't convinced and scanned the landscape to avoid his penetrating gaze. Though I didn't need or even enjoy fine things, I couldn't imagine living in the wilderness for months—or longer—without basic necessities.

"How long must you . . . must *we* . . ." I began as my head turned toward him. His brow was furrowed while studying me. Had I already ruined my chance to serve among his men? "I wasn't complaining, my lord. I'll follow you anywhere."

"I believe you." But his unnerving frown remained. "Saul will never stop chasing me, Ahinoam. I realized it when he sent three contingents to kill me at the prophet's camp in Ramah. Then he came himself. The Lord helped me escape to Gibeah, where Prince Jonathan and I reaffirmed our covenant."

"Your best friend?"

"My brother." His expression softened. "He's more like family than those related by blood."

"The crown prince's loyalty seems rather miraculous considering he should inherit the throne Yahweh gave to you."

"Miraculous is a good word to describe the bond Jonathan and I have. Once Samuel declared Yahweh had taken the throne from Saul at Michmash, Jonathan knew his title of crown prince was in name only. From that day forward, Saul had his spies watching Samuel to kill whoever he might try to anoint as the next king. They never knew about Samuel's journey to Bethlehem." He turned to me with a grin. "Until I confessed it to Jonathan at Gibeah before I fled. We struck a covenant to protect each other and our heirs forever."

"And then you went to Gath?"

"No." David looked away, his features darkening. "That's when I made the first of many mistakes. I went to Nob to ask for help from my friend Ahimelek, the High Priest. When he asked why I was traveling without the troops I usually brought to present offerings, I lied and told him I was on a secret mission. Saul's spy, Doeg the Edomite, was there. I knew he'd hurry to Gibeah with news of my location, so I asked Ahimelek if he had any food or weapons. He gave me day-old showbread and Goliath's sword, which I thought was a sign from the Lord I should escape to Gath. I knew Saul could never reach me in Goliath's hometown." He barked out a cynical laugh. "Gath was my second error. A reckless mistake."

I wasn't sure what to say. He was right. Going to Gath did seem foolish. I shrugged and said, "You almost lost your life, but you gained King Achish's nephew as one of your lieutenants."

Yahweh's anointed king chuckled at my joke, then turned to me, searching my eyes before he whispered, "*Yahweh* is my sacred tent, Ahinoam, not the Tabernacle at Nob. Elohim is my stronghold, not the mountains at Mizpah. Even if family betrays and all others disappoint, I will trust my God to keep His promises."

I swallowed the lump in my throat. "That's the most beautiful thing I've ever heard."

"He's the Rock on which I've stood for much of my life. Now, was there a reason you were looking for me, or did you accidentally stumble on my quiet place?"

"I, uh . . . I'm . . ." As much as I wanted to speak of my future in his army, this wasn't the time. "I needed to clear my head. Thank you, my lord." Bolting to my feet, I offered a quick bow and rushed away.

Hurrying past Joab, I skittered down the rocky hill and toward the shore, where Abba was with Zerry and my other traveling companions, eating the roasted lamb.

Zerry waved me over. "Where were you?" Nitzevet and Keyalah leaned closer to hear.

"I tried to find a spot to practice."

"Practice what?" Eglah asked.

Her ima gave me a sideways glance and answered for me. "Never mind. Ahinoam has many things to practice before she's as proficient at women's tasks as you." It was true. Even a girl five years younger could best me at spinning and embroidery.

With the smell of roasting lamb wafting over the hillside, the rest of David's men descended on the shoreline. The dark clouds grew darker, and daylight died without the official announcement of a visible sunset. A cool mountain breeze swept over the water and sent a chill through me. The lieutenants gathered their contingents of twenty; the shepherds assembled the flock at the rear; and torchbearers lit their pitch-covered clubs before the cookfires were extinguished. The procession was ready to march. David vaulted to the top of a boulder and held a torch aloft.

"Tonight, we cross the Great Tongue and return to the land of Judah. If the water level on the west side has risen higher than our kneecaps, each man will carry at least one of the animals to shore. We care for the flocks, and they'll care for us. Tonight's journey may test our patience and endurance, so give one another grace and work together. When we reach Judah's shore, we'll head south and—"

"South?" Jesse shouted. "Bethlehem is north. We go north!"

Tension rose as David's soldiers closed ranks around his abba and brothers. As quickly as the king had climbed the boulder, he scurried down, weaving through his men toward his family.

Jesse had gathered his sons around him, glancing frantically over the advancing soldiers. "Nitzevet!" he shouted. "Nitzevet, where are you?" His voice quaked, sounding more like a frightened child than a bitter old man.

His plea launched Nitzevet into motion, but Zerry grabbed her arm. "Let Abba suffer for his obstinance, Ima."

Nitzevet removed Zerry's hand from her arm and lifted it to her lips, then strode toward her husband with the dignity of a queen. David's men stepped back, offering a slight bow as she passed. When she linked arms with Jesse, she was the one who spoke to their son. "We will obey and cross the Tongue together, David, but perhaps it's best that your abba leads our clan north to Bethlehem once we arrive in Judah. I have no doubt that Yahweh will lead and protect your army, but our family needs stability, my son. Don't you agree?" Her loving gaze held as much resolve as Jesse's shout.

"All right, Ima. If both you and Abba agree." David hesitated only the length of a deep sigh before he bowed on his knees and lowered his head. "I humbly request that you, my family, would allow us to keep half the flock in our care as continued provision for the five hundred men who have safeguarded them on this journey. As Clan Jesse has so faithfully provided for my brothers who served in Saul's military service, would you now partner with your anointed son to secure Yahweh's promised future?"

"You're a fugitive, not a king," Jesse hissed. "This is no army. You're putting all our lives in danger."

"You've shamed us," Eliab said. David's oldest brother stepped to his abba's side. "When we return to Judah, we'll be the family of a traitor. Who knows if we'll even keep our homes or land."

David bolted to his feet. "Which is the reason it's unwise for you to return to Bethlehem."

Eliab shoved through the family and grasped the arm of Asahel's pregnant wife, putting her on display like a mare at auction. "Would you rather Dalit give birth in a cave? What if Saul attacks while she's in labor? Will your so-called army hide in hyrax holes while she labors alone?"

"Stop this!" David pulled Dalit into a comforting embrace, his face crimson.

Asahel leapt from a rocky height, giving Eliab a shove. "Don't ever touch my wife again!" David transferred her gently to her husband's arms and strode toward Eliab. Though David was at least a head shorter, the older brother recoiled. Joab and Abishai emerged from the faithful, separating their wives from Jesse's clan. Their children—four little boys, two toddlers and a baby in each woman's arms—whimpered softly amid the tension.

David's eyes focused on Jesse. "It doesn't have to be this way."

The wind began to blow, and a sudden downpour pelted my face. Would God Himself step from the clouds to defend His anointed? Gad the Seer stood with David and his nephews, wind whipping his rough-spun robe, long hair, and gnarled beard. The hundreds of other men who had left families and possessions also surrounded God's king.

David shouted over the storm, "Eliab, Abinadab, Shimea, Nethanel, Raddai, and Ozem, escort your wives and children to Bethlehem. They are your responsibility to protect. Jesse ben Obed and Nitzevet bat Adael—Abba and Ima—I will honor you for as long as I live but can only keep you safe when you choose to dwell under my protection. Bethlehem is too near Gibeah of Saul, and if the king was willing to send assassins to Samuel's camp of prophets, he *will* send soldiers to Bethlehem."

"Stop!" Eliab shouted. "You're trying to frighten the women. King Saul would never—"

"He would!" David shouted in reply, eyes wild. "Please, Eliab, endure what's hard to avoid what is truly dangerous."

The two men locked eyes, their fury matching the storm's. After a dozen heartbeats, Eliab turned toward the family. "Let's go! Now!"

"Wait!" Asahel stood between the two groups. He looked at David, tortured with indecision, while his pregnant wife wept in his arms. "I don't want Dalit to give birth in a cave."

"What about Keyalah?" Zerry shouted at David. "You promised her and her daughter protection. Will she stay in the wilderness or go to Bethlehem? And Ahinoam? If the other women go to Bethlehem, must she go, too, and be separated from her abba?"

"Ahinoam stays with me," Abba shouted, leaving no room for argument. Then he turned to Zerry. "And we stay with King David."

The wind and rain began to calm, the night growing still as quickly as the storm had come. "Form ranks!" Joab shouted, giving the captains and lieutenants something to do while Clan Jesse made final decisions.

Zerry left Keyalah, Eglah, Abba, and me to join David and her sons in private conversation. Not long after, David nodded his agreement, and his nephews rejoined their wives.

Zerry marched toward Abba and me. "Toren," she began while still ten paces away, "you and Ahinoam need to be part of my conversation with Keyalah." She walked past us and halted beside the Moabite and her daughter. Before she could speak, however, a wail drew our attention, and Asahel's wife melted in his arms.

"That was expected," Zerry said. "My sons' wives will return to Bethlehem with the family, but my sons will follow Israel's anointed king into the wilderness. After Dalit's child is born, and when it's safe to do so, their wives and children will be free to join us."

"Us?" Abba said with a hopeful lilt.

"I'm getting to that." Zerry focused on Keyalah. "You and your daughter will return to Bethlehem with Ima to help her with household chores as I would normally do."

"But your brother said Bethlehem wasn't safe." Keyalah pulled her daughter close, causing the girl to whimper.

"Stop that!" Zerry said. "Show me your courage! Both of you. The kind of courage that proves a woman alone can survive in this world." Her eyes locked with the maid's until the woman nodded her agreement. Then Zerry pulled both ima and daughter into a ferocious embrace, whispering assurances that somehow stanched their tears. After only a few moments, Keyalah straightened, nodded, and led her daughter toward Nitzevet.

My friend then turned her attention to Abba. "Toren, my brother asks if you are willing to teach others your craft."

He lifted his chin. "I will try to teach others, but Ahinoam stays with me. Kenites have metalworking in their blood. Some things cannot be taught."

I nearly leapt for joy. *Yahweh, have You just added me to David's army?*

Zerry turned to me with a mischievous grin. "Since it would be unseemly for a single young woman to appear in a sea of men, I've offered to accompany you."

"You . . . and me?" I threw my arms around her neck—something I'd never done before—and quietly chuckled. "Are *two* single women in a sea of men more acceptable?"

"I see you approve of the arrangement, Nomy." A grin played at the corners of Abba's lips.

The torchbearers took up their positions, a shofar blew, and we began our exodus from Moab. Keyalah and her daughter still tended Nitzevet but now were positioned between Jesse and David at the back of the procession. Nitzevet spoke calmly but intently to the two men, likely arguing that their son should be given their flock for his legitimate military campaign.

"Abba will never give David half the flock," Zerry said, as if knowing my thoughts. "No matter what Ima says, it will be just like all those years she pleaded to bring him in from the fields and include him in the household." She let out a huff and left Abba and me to join her sons and grandchildren. Evidently, she would cross the Tongue with her family before their good-byes.

With the rain ended and a cool breeze at our backs, I fell in step with Abba. "Are you ready for the wilderness?" he asked.

"More than ready," I said, remembering David's words. "I'm waiting to be strengthened and shaped into what Adonai wants me to become."

His eyebrows lifted with an approving nod. "And I'm ready to strengthen King David's army so he can become Israel's new king."

EIGHT

DAVID

But one son of Ahimelek son of Ahitub, named Abiathar, escaped and fled to join David.

1 Samuel 22:20

Wadi in Southern Judean Wilderness

I stood atop a large outcropping, scanning the 485 men, two women, and one hundred goats Abba had begrudgingly contributed to my "rebel cause"—as he called it.

Four days ago, we'd endured tearful good-byes and painful indifference at the Dead Sea's eastern shore. However, Ima's whisper during our parting embrace brought some comfort. *"Remember, David, a rebel is better than a fugitive in your abba's eyes. He's supported Judah's rebels for thirty years, and he'll support you."* She patted my cheek and hurried off to join the hard man she had honored with her words and deeds through impossible situations.

Yahweh, protect my family, and may I prove as faithful as my ima in forgiveness and honor.

Familiar bitterness still nipped at my heart, so I fought it with the weapon more effective than any blade.

"I love you, Lord, my strength.
The Lord is my rock;
My fortress, my deliverer;
    my God is my rock,
In whom I take refuge."

Giant cliffs rose above while a flash flood raged through a narrow wadi. If we'd tried to cross the Great Tongue four nights later, during last night's storm, we couldn't have turned back and would surely have lost both lives and livestock. When my family went north, I'd led my men farther south and skirted the southern border of the Dead Sea, which meant navigating more wilderness. We'd foraged for food, every bite with the heavy seasoning of my family's disdain.

Despite Ima's pleading, Abba had given me only a hundred goats. Not half the flock. Not sheep. And Eliab had chosen the weakest and sickest among the animals as a final stab at my heart. Every time my mind conjured the family's sneers, I would lift my voice to my deliverer:

"In my distress I called to the Lord for help.
From his temple he heard my voice;
My cry came before him.
The earth trembled;
The mountains shook."

Last night's storm hadn't been a coincidence. Yahweh proved he heard my cries. I had lifted my face to the wind and rain, receiving the stinging drops with shouts of praise. At first, those who huddled in caves and beneath rock ledges remained hidden—perhaps thinking I'd lost all good sense. As I continued to worship with abandon, hands and voice raised, others joined me, emerging from their hiding places. Ahinoam had been the first, laughing and dancing, then Zerry and Toren. The Kohathites joined soon after, their voices echoing over the canyon. We were all drenched to the bone after singing long into the night. This morning, we woke to another day of hunger and hiking but with a joy that was somehow as fierce as last night's storm.

Dragging in a deep breath of rain-washed air, I lifted my voice again.

> "The LORD rescued me.
> From a powerful enemy,
> From my foes too strong for me
> Who confronted me
> In the day of my disaster.
> But the Lord was my support.
> He brought me out into a spacious place;
> He rescued me because he delighted in me."

"Sing louder, my king, so we can praise Adonai with you!" Amasai's booming voice echoed off the canyon walls, coaxing a cheer from the others. How could I ever be melancholy with these brave souls to accompany me through whatever lay ahead?

Raising my voice, I leapt from rock to rock, using my rope when climbing grew treacherous, and kept singing the same choruses again and again.

> "You, Lord, keep my lamp burning;
> My God turns my darkness into light.
> With your help I can advance against a troop;
> With my God I can scale a wall.
> God's way is perfect;
> His word flawless;
> And He shields those who take refuge in him."

By midday, we'd passed Arad, and my men had learned the whole song that replayed in my soul. The wadi had calmed to a gentler flow, so we took shelter in the canyon, and our shepherds led the goats to drink. Several men commented on the motley animals, but I reminded them that Elohim, Creator of heaven and earth, could multiply our flock as He'd done for Jacob's speckled-and-spotted animals when Laban had cheated him. We simply needed to trust the Lord and humbly receive my family's gift as from the Lord. Truth be told, I, too, had wanted to slap Eliab's triumphant grin off his face. *Lord, forgive my bitterness and change my heart.* The decision to forgive took only a moment, but healing from the pain would require Yahweh's constant help.

"David! My lord!" A shout came from the north.

Every man rose. The sound of unsheathing blades sang louder than the water's quiet trickle.

The repeated caw of a jackdaw proved the visitor was our own Gadite. When he drew nearer, he shouted, "King Saul attacked Nob!"

I heard nothing else and ran toward him, then realized a second man lagged behind our fleet-footed scout. I recognized the second man's priestly robes, and his face was a younger version of Ahimelek, the High Priest I knew well. Why would a priest leave his duties? Dread slowed my advance, but duty pushed me forward.

The priest stumbled into my arms, sobbing. "They're dead. All dead."

I fell to the ground, cradling him like a child. "What happened?"

He could only groan. I rocked with him, weeping.

The scout stood over us and whispered, "This is Abiathar, my lord, son of Ahimelek, Nob's High Priest. Doeg the Edomite reported to King Saul that Ahimelek gave you food and Goliath's sword. The king ordered Abner and his men to execute the priests. They refused, but the Edomite was eager to obey. He killed every man, woman, and child in Nob, my king. Abiathar is the only survivor."

"No! No!" My own wail split the air, and I pulled away from

the young priest I'd wronged so deeply. "I never should have asked Ahimelek for help."

Abiathar lifted his tear-streaked face. "You've done nothing wrong, my lord. King Saul is mad. He even accused Prince Jonathan of conspiring—"

"Prince Jonathan?" I shot to my feet. "Did the king harm—"

"No, my lord! The soldiers would never harm the prince. The king sent his son away so he couldn't save my family. Upon his return to Gibeah, Prince Jonathan found me hiding in a cave. I told him what Doeg had done. He threatened to kill Doeg, but King Saul protected the Edomite and rewarded him with an estate in Anathoth. Then he ordered Jonathan to bury the bodies in Nob as punishment for conspiring with you. The prince kept me hidden and took me to Nob, allowing me to help anoint my family's bodies and bury them. Then I went to Samuel, who inquired of the Lord and told me where to find you."

Someone shouted, "Which family in Anathoth lost their estate to that murderer?"

Abiathar's eyes flitted like a caged bird's at the ruffians pressing around us. My whole army had gathered.

"It's all right," I said. "You're safe here. Whose estate did Saul steal and offer to Doeg?"

"I don't know the name," Abiathar said. "Only that it belonged to one of the king's relatives, and the man was angry that he was forced to relinquish his property to a murderer of priests."

Fury stirred in my chest. "Don't worry, my friend. Doeg the Edomite won't keep that land for long." I helped Abiathar stand, and we faced my men together. My three nephews eagerly awaited my command.

"Let me form a contingent," Joab whispered. "We'll slip into Anathoth, kill the Edomite, and return to you before anyone discovers we were in Benjamite territory."

Zerry pushed through the soldiers. "Don't you dare send all three of my sons, David ben Jesse."

"Send me, my lord," Ahinoam begged, standing beside my sister. Something visceral and protective rose up inside. I would never send her into battle.

"Are you insane, woman?" Joab sneered.

Toren stood between my general and his daughter. "Ahinoam could kill six men at a distance quicker than you could fight off ten watchmen, but she doesn't have the stealth and strength required for this mission." He turned to me and inclined his head. "Please forgive my daughter's enthusiasm, my king."

"So . . ." Zerry stood beside Toren like a two-panel wall. "No Ahinoam and no more than two of my sons." She crossed both arms over her chest. "But clearly something must be done about this Edomite."

Did she somehow think I'd chosen her to be my general instead of Joab? I ignored them all and mounted the nearest boulder to address my men. "The priests of Nob have been butchered by the traitorous Edomite Doeg. Before anyone risks his life to repossess the estate Saul awarded Doeg in Anathoth, I must confess that I saw the vermin when I visited Ahimelek at the Tabernacle and thought it likely he would tell Saul."

Fixing my gaze on Abiathar, I said, "I lied to your abba and told him I was there on a secret mission for the king to protect him when Saul questioned him. He could honestly say he didn't know I was fleeing. My lie was meant to save your abba's life as surely as the sacred showbread your abba gave me kept me from starving." Tears burned my throat and blurred my eyes. "I never thought . . ."

Regret strangled me. Abiathar was alone in the world because of Saul's unjustified vengeance. I bowed my head to regain composure and hide my confusion. *Lord, You saved Samuel and the prophets when I went to them for help. Why, all-powerful, all-knowing God, would You let Your faithful priests die?*

113

Abiathar stood at the base of the boulder. "My lord, you often came to present offerings before the Lord. My abba died knowing he served Yahweh well. Prince Jonathan had told him years ago that Samuel anointed you as Israel's true king."

Startled, I felt Jonathan's encouragement even in this dark moment and left my perch to meet the young priest face-to-face. "If you stay with me, you'll never need to be afraid. The man who wants you dead is also trying to kill me, but we'll be safe in the righteous hands of El Shaddai."

He nodded his agreement, and only then did I realize he wore Ahimelek's linen ephod. The hidden pocket behind the breastplate bulged with two barely visible bumps, proving he'd brought a blessing along with the horrible news. "You inherited the office of High Priest upon your abba's death."

Abiathar stood taller, shoulders back. "King Saul chose another High Priest, but I took the extra ephod Abba kept hidden in his chamber—the Urim and Thummim with it—when I left Nob." He pulled out two stones, one black and one white, each the size of a man's thumb, from the pocket behind the twelve colored gems on his chest. "The anointed king of Israel should always know the mind of God before making a big decision, my lord."

"Indeed, Abiathar." I focused on my sister, nephews, and my Kenite friends. "Joab has offered to choose a small contingent to travel north and bring God's judgment down on Doeg's head. We'll inquire of the Lord through the Urim and Thummim if he is to go and let Yahweh determine his course."

"What about your family?" a man shouted. "Will Saul attack them next?"

"Very unlikely," I answered while Abishai reassured Zerry.

"What about our families?" another man called out. Fear scattered through the ranks like sparks rising from a fire.

"Saul's own soldiers refused his order to kill the priests," I shouted over the growing chaos. "And there's been no retribution against Prince Jonathan even after the reigning king accused him of treason. After word spreads about what happened at Nob, Saul will be dancing on the precipice of mutiny. He won't dare risk killing more innocent people—especially if the Lord uses Joab and Yahweh's chosen men to demonstrate his wrath on Doeg."

Still, ripples of dissension moved through the ranks. I heard some say they might return to their homes. The faithful accused them of cowardice.

I pulled Goliath's sword from the giant sheath across my back and pointed it toward heaven. Respectful silence fell over the gathering. "None of you are required to stay. But those who remain must vow to exhibit the faith in Yahweh by which this sword was won. You do not follow me alone. Yahweh is our true leader. We follow him together. If you believe the God of Israel is with us, stay. If you fear he has no plan for me or for your lives, please—I beg you—return to your families." Silence massaged my words into waiting hearts, and only affirming nods returned to me. *Thank You, Yahweh.*

I turned to Abiathar. "How many of Saul's men remain battle-ready near Gibeah?"

"Only his standing army of Benjamites, perhaps three or four hundred. The others have returned to their homes for the winter and won't be mustered again until spring."

"All right," I said. "Cast the lots."

Holding one rock in each hand to display them, he said, "Since I've noticed foreign soldiers in our midst, I'll explain how Yahweh has chosen to speak to Israel's leader since the days of Moses. These stones are called the Urim and Thummim. Yahweh's chosen leader asks a question that has a yes-or-no answer or asks for a verdict to declare innocence or guilt. An upright white stone signifies innocence and, in this case, means Doeg lives. An upright black stone signifies guilt and means Joab chooses men who will carry out Doeg's execution, God's justified punishment for murdering Yahweh's priests."

Abiathar bent to one knee and tossed the stones. They skittered across loose gravel. The black Urim landed upright between two small stones, while the white Thummim lay level on a bed of sand.

Joab led the first cheer, and shouting spread through the ranks. Zerry's face drained of color, though she surprised me with a smile. She knew her eldest son would choose his brothers to accompany him. Ahinoam whispered something to her, which Zerry answered with a quiet but protracted explanation. Toren listened intently, and I assumed my sister was clarifying the process we'd witnessed.

I'd first seen Ahimelek cast lots in the winter after Samuel had anointed me. Until then, I'd only heard legends about the Tabernacle and the High Priest's ephod. King Saul had summoned me to the palace, which was a brisk morning's walk from the holy site. At first, we'd thought he might have heard of my anointing, and the summons was my death sentence. Abba sent me with a donkey and plenty of olive oil, dates, and other gifts, hoping to save our family from slaughter, if not my own worthless life.

However, when I arrived in Gibeah that first winter, the king's steward said he'd heard I was a valiant warrior who also played the lyre. I didn't dare tell him I was barely fifteen, a shepherd, and had only killed bears and lions to protect my flock. My task was to soothe the king's tortured soul with my lyre—nothing else. He said the Lord had sent an evil spirit to torment Saul after he'd disobeyed the prophet Samuel. Then the steward warned me to stay alert, sing softly, and duck if the king threw his spear. For three years, I'd remained in the king's shadow, attending the Tabernacle sacrifices and watching each time he'd asked Ahimelek to cast lots.

I was a nameless, faceless musician in Saul's palace, watching his daily routine and nighttime torture. The king looked through me—

not at me—and each spring, when all kings went to war, I returned to my shepherding duties in Bethlehem.

It was springtime after my third winter of palace service when Abba sent me to the Valley of Elah with food and supplies for my brothers. The Philistines had drawn battle lines against Israel, and I refused to let Goliath shout obscenities against the God of Israel for a forty-first day. I was eighteen when I killed Goliath and Saul learned my name.

Now I wished he could forget it.

"I choose Abishai and Asahel," Joab shouted, shattering my reflections. "Also," he continued, "I'm taking Shammah, Eleazar, and Amasai." The three men who had joined us in Moab stepped forward. They joined my nephews with the soldiers' victory language of shoves, grunts, and cheers.

My sister's quivering chin broke my heart. "Joab is my general," I said, pulling her into my arms. "And it was Abba's chief shepherd who taught us all to fight, so blame him for your sons' battle instincts, not me. Dodo and Abba defended Bethlehem against every enemy raid, and Dodo was the best of them."

"I know." She shoved me away. "I just hate that you've got your very own priest with an ephod, so I can't even win arguments anymore."

I got a smile from her before returning my attention to Abiathar and the men Yahweh had chosen. "Abiathar, what can you tell us that will help my men get into Anathoth, find Doeg, and get back to us safely?"

His eyes widened as if I'd asked him to raise someone from the dead. "I . . . um . . ."

"Anything," Joab said. "Is Doeg married? Does he have children? Will he have an army of guards around him?"

"Yes," Abiathar said. "I mean, I don't know about a wife or children, but while Prince Jonathan and I were in Nob, the men who moved the Tabernacle also took everything of value and complained that the king planned to give it to Doeg. They said the Edomite had already hired bodyguards for his new estate."

"At least we'll have a little fun." Joab playfully shoved Eleazar. "Since you're the only Benjamite among us, you can talk in that funny north Israel accent."

"I have no ack-SENT." Eleazar's drawl proved Joab's choice a wise one.

Amid teasing and laughter, Joab asked me, "Where should we rejoin you after the mission?"

All eyes turned to me, and I suddenly wished Abiathar's lots weren't limited to yes-or-no answers. I searched the expectant faces of my men. They'd left everything to follow me. *Why do You so seldom give long-term plans, Lord? Where do we rest for the winter while Saul is in Gibeah?*

A goat bleated loud and long, stealing my attention. One of my new shepherds led the troubled animal away from the rushing stream toward quieter waters. He held out his staff, letting the animal pass under it as he inspected the noisy beast from head to toe. When the animal started to nibble on a thistle, he gently applied the rod to its nose, guiding it toward a tender green shoot less than two steps away. Warmth flooded my body, and I knew the momentary lesson had been for me.

"David?" Joab stepped closer. "Where should we meet you?"

"The Lord is our Shepherd, Joab." I grinned, knowing he wanted a simple answer, too. "We won't lack anything. He'll make us lie down in green pastures and lead us beside quiet waters. He'll restore our souls and guide us along right paths for the glory of His Name."

My nephew folded his arms with a deep sigh. He hated riddles.

I turned to speak to the larger gathering. "We've walked through this valley and death has overshadowed us, but we will *not* fear evil because Yahweh's presence goes with us. Regardless of where the

Tabernacle goes, Yahweh is our Shepherd. Both His instructive rod and guiding staff will comfort us."

Overwhelmed by God's goodness, I stabbed Goliath's sword into the dirt and lifted my hands toward heaven. "El Shaddai, You will prepare a table for me not far from my enemies. You have anointed my head with oil, and my cup already overflows! Your goodness and mercy will follow me all the days of my life, and I will dwell in Your house forever."

Eyes closed and face upturned to feel the sun's warmth, I felt another bath of Yahweh's peace. Wherever the Lord chose to lead, His presence would go before us and behind us, surrounding us—not in a Tabernacle or atop the holy Ark. No, not even the heavens could contain His glory! Yahweh would dwell among us every day in bold acts of provision, grace, and protection.

"David?" Joab prodded. "Does this mean you haven't yet decided where you want us to meet you?"

I opened my eyes and met the puzzled stares of several hundred men and two very concerned women. "Meet us at the Forest of Hereth," I said. "It's near enough Bethlehem that Asahel can visit his wife—and likely his newborn child—on your return from the mission. From Hereth's position on a hill, we'll see an enemy approach from any direction, and Toren will have plenty of wood to feed a forge and make more weapons."

NINE

AHINOAM

Here now is the man who did not make God his stronghold but trusted
in his great wealth and grew strong by destroying others!

Psalm 52:7

Forest of Hereth

Moving the bronze blade in small circles on my whetstone, I replayed that moment at Moab's stronghold when I'd gripped David's
arm and he'd leaned so close. Had I imagined something more than
protectiveness in his eyes?

I should never have touched his arm. Women didn't touch a man
who wasn't her husband—especially the next king of Israel! But if
he had hastily drawn his sword, the repercussions could have been
devastating. But wasn't staring into his warm brown eyes devastating? Since that day, I'd replayed that moment thousands of times and
ruined three dull flint knives, trying to knap them to a razored edge.

"You're going to warp that blade," Abba grumbled. "If you can't
concentrate on sharpening, go help Zeruiah with women's work."

"I'll concentrate," I barked back. I couldn't face Zerry today. She'd
grown increasingly morose during her sons' absence. As the first

week passed into the second, I'd reminded her, *"Joab said they'd return in one or two weeks."*

Today marked two weeks since the six men left for Anathoth. The rest of us had continued north through Judah's wilderness. Zerry was unusually withdrawn while we traveled. David sent scouts into the Judean towns of Maon, Carmel, Ziph, and Hebron, trading a few of our goats for grain and supplies. After our three-day hike, we arrived at the Forest of Hereth, and David invited Abba, Zerry, and me to join his twenty-man encampment.

The invitation was solely because I was Zerry's charge, and Abba refused to let me out of his sight—wasn't it? Of course it was. Still, I felt honored to be part of the king's inner circle. The others he'd chosen had either known him since childhood or had proven their loyalty during the past two years in Saul's army. David had been the commander of a thousand Israelites, winning every battle with the Philistines—more victories than the king—which was apparently the reason for Saul's jealousy.

Every day, Zerry had awakened in the tent we shared, saying, *"Joab and the boys will return any day now."* And every night, she'd roll onto her mat having lost hope after another day passed without their return. *"They'll be back tomorrow,"* I'd say, then snuff out our single oil lamp. Today, I'd purposely left camp before dawn, unwilling to face her hopefulness.

My stomach rumbled, regretting that I'd missed this morning's goat milk and gruel. I pressed against my belly, silently admitting I regretted abandoning Zerry more. What kind of friend would let her wait alone? *I'm a coward.* But what could I say to bring comfort?

Abba set aside his double-edged blade and rose from his comfortable rock. I turned the blade over and continued with even strokes from heel to point but stole a glimpse to compare his work with mine. His was better, as usual. Abba would always be better at sharpening, no matter how much I concentrated. Despite my imperfections, however, David had organized competitions for the men to win the new daggers we produced.

Yahweh had led David to the perfect location for our winter encampment. The Forest of Hereth provided soft pine for building forge tools and cook fires, as well as the hardwood olive trees for hotter smelting fires and sturdy dagger hilts. Abba added more olive wood to the forge, stoking the heat to smelt more copper and tin, creating the strong bronze blades my family had produced for generations.

"You should talk with her, Nomy." Abba stood beside the forge, his weathered face creased with concern. "Zeruiah was too quiet this morning."

I stopped sharpening. "Why don't *you* talk to her, then? You two have become good friends."

"She needs a woman who can share her feelings, not a gruff old man who always says the wrong thing." He snatched my whetstone and blade. "Off with you. Go!"

I stood but was rooted to the ground. "We've promised David five daggers by tomorrow. We've only finished three." Truly, I would have rather poked my eye with a stick than watch Zerry grieve today.

"I'm sure David cares more about his sister than two more daggers."

His words felt like a stick to the eye, so I finally told him the truth. "I don't know what to say, either."

"She's a frightened ima whose sons mean everything to her."

"I never knew an ima like that."

Abba flinched as if I'd slapped him.

"I didn't mean—"

"I know." He placed a callused hand on my cheek, the tender gesture heaping more guilt on my cowardly heart. "But you have an abba who loves you like Zeruiah loves her sons. Comfort her like you would console me."

I gave a quick nod and rushed away before he saw my misty eyes. After escaping the weaponry clearing, I slowed and quieted my steps to enter the shady copse of pines where our cohort lived like family. Eleven lean-tos circled a central fire and our community supplies. Waterskins, food, and shoulder bags were stored in a wooden receptacle. David had assigned specific jobs to people in each cohort. Zerry prepared our meals and taught designated cooks in other units how to stretch sparse supplies to feed their hungry comrades.

When I reached the area where our tents had been set up, I heard the soft strumming of David's lyre and the perfect harmony of a brother's and sister's song.

"The Lord is my shepherd. I lack no good thing. He makes me lie down in green pastures." The words David recited after Abiathar inquired of the Lord had become a familiar chorus during our tense wait for the six men to return. "Even though I walk through the valley of the shadow of death—"

Zerry's voice broke. David lowered the lyre and slid his arm around her shoulders. When he leaned close, as if to whisper something, he turned just enough to glimpse me looming near the trees. His face lit with a smile, but I wanted to crawl under a rock. How many times would he catch me spying?

David motioned me forward, allaying my fears—and sending my heart into a gallop. "Ahinoam, join us."

Zerry self-consciously wiped her cheeks. I felt like an intruder. "Forgive me, my lord. I should go back to sharpening. I only wanted to check on Ze—"

"Please stay." He stood. "I think Zerry should learn to throw a dagger."

I chuckled despite the sober mood. "I'm afraid Zerry's throwing will resemble my spinning."

She launched to her feet. "You haven't even given me a chance!"

"I saw your attempts to gut a fish, my friend. Did you think Abba took over that task to be polite?"

David covered a grin, and his sister swatted him. "I can admit I'm better at other tasks, but no one has taught me to wield a knife." She glared at her brother. "You've taught all your men to be shepherds. Shouldn't your whole company—including your sister—know how to protect themselves?"

He lifted both hands. "I'm not the one you need to convince." Turning a mischievous grin at me, he said, "It's up to Ahinoam."

Zerry planted both fists on her hips. "Don't expect me to wear a silly belt over my robe like you do."

"It wouldn't look so silly if you hadn't taken my short robe and high-laced sandals!" I lowered my head to hide the rising heat in my cheeks. Did David think I looked silly, too?

With a few purposeful strides, the king was close enough to tip my chin up. "My sister needs a distraction," he whispered. "You're the dearest friend she's ever had. The only one who can stand toe to toe with her harsh words and come away laughing—usually. Don't let one rude comment rattle your fierce heart." His fingers lingered beneath my chin, his eyes lingering too long on mine.

My heart fluttered. I could barely breathe. He tilted his head as if he'd spotted something perplexing inside me, then quickly stepped away. "Begin the lessons today." Now he looked everywhere *except* at me.

"As you wish, my lord." I offered a nervous bow. *What was that?* I'd never curtsied in my life! Had a strange curse befallen us?

Confused, I glanced at Zerry.

She rolled her eyes and retrieved the camp's kitchen knife. "Come on." With her next step came a loud whistle from the northern watch. She cast a pleading look at her brother. "Is it—? Have they—?"

Distant shouts rose to celebration and allowed my heart to beat again.

We ran toward the sound. David raced ahead of us through the forest and toward the clearing. When we reached the north side of camp, his men ushered him to the returning heroes. Zerry and I, breathless and shaking, followed closely. Every cohort gathered, parting like the Red Sea for Zerry to greet her sons and welcome them home. When she saw them at the center of the crowd, Zerry launched herself like a stone from a sling, and they caught her mid-air. David cackled like a hyena, as did most of the men who saw the reunion.

I halted beside Abba, opposite the king and the returning warriors. When Zerry finally released the stranglehold on her sons, she crossed the small divide and stood beside me. David's nephews and the other three victors still celebrated with the king and introduced a stranger they'd brought to Hereth with them. I couldn't hear his name or why he'd been entrusted with our secret location, but I noticed the visitor wore a forced smile. With eyes locked on David and slightly narrowed, he seemed impervious to the emotional reunion that had caused even the most stodgy soldiers to rejoice.

Why would our six best warriors trust this unknown soldier, and why allow him to stand so close to our king? While Asahel recounted the visit in Bethlehem with his newborn son, Eleazar mocked Joab and Abishai for being such ima's boys. Shammah and Amasai added to the heckling, and only Joab stood between the stranger and David's left side—an easy lunge for a dagger's kill strike. Sickening dread rose when I compared the warrior's size with the king's. The stranger towered over Joab and was just as stout, which gave him twice David's bulk. *Surely, Joab has reason to trust him.*

Joab lifted his arms, commanding quiet. "Let me introduce our new comrade, Uzzi the Gibeathite, without whose help we couldn't have completed our mission."

A quiet hum spread through the ranks. Uzzi bowed and kept his head lowered.

"Uzzi helped us escape Anathoth," Joab continued. "He served as one of Prince Jonathan's royal guards and knew some of Doeg's protectors."

Uzzi held his humble bow for the duration of Joab's praise, but his hands began nervously fidgeting at his belt. One hand moved to the front knot while the other slipped behind his back. The hand at his back was hidden by loose folds of his robe.

Like Abba's before he throws.

"You were one of Jonathan's guards?" David stepped around Joab to face Uzzi. "I thought I knew them all, but you don't look familiar."

In that terrible moment, I saw a glint of metal flash at Uzzi's back. Instinct overwhelmed protocol, and my blade flew.

The next thing I registered was David's shock when the dagger fell from Uzzi's hand. Shock turned to horror when he looked at me. A woman too quick with her dagger—surely he thought me an abomination.

The assassin dropped to his knees and fell facedown. Blood pooled. Chaos erupted. Zerry screamed. Her sons surrounded the king.

Joab kicked the enemy onto his back. "Why save our lives then try to kill our king?"

Drowning in blood, he choked out, "Prince . . . Jon . . . should be . . . king . . ." Life fled with a rattled exhale.

"On that we agree." David spit on the dead man. "But God decides, not man." He pulled my dagger from the assassin's chest and looked at me. "How could you do this?"

I felt every eye bore into me like a hornet's sting. My heart pounded so hard, I thought my chest would explode. Looking to Abba, I found him smiling—*smiling*. Zerry's trembling hand covered her mouth. She, too, was horrified at what I'd done—the woman with a silly dagger belt.

Backing away, I bumped into a muscled chest and turned.

"How?" The man's brow furrowed in accusation.

Mind tangled, I pushed past him through a sea of smelly bodies. Shouts chased me like wild dogs. Trembling legs carried me to open space. I spotted an olive grove, pressed harder, and ducked under low-hanging limbs. Sobs burst forth like the great deep, stealing my breath and making my legs weaker. I stumbled toward the largest tree, crashing onto my knees in the dirt. Rocks and twigs cut flesh. I fell forward, peeling more tender skin from my palms. *Pain.* Wilting against the trunk into a whimpering heap, I pulled my robe above my knees and stared at the red blood oozing from my hands and legs. *The same color as Uzzi's, the first man I ever killed.* His empty eyes would forever be seared in my memory.

"Ahinoam?"

David. I lunged to escape but was shaking too violently to stand. Curling on my side, I shrieked, "Leave me alone!" Panic overtook me. I covered my ears and closed my eyes. *Yahweh, make me disappear.*

"Shhh." Gentle hands slid beneath me. Lifted me. "It's all right."

Another wave of panic overwhelmed me. I felt suffocated and pushed against the man's chest. Strong arms pulled me close, held me fast.

"Shh, Ahinoam." His breath whispered against my cheek. "You saved my life."

He understood? I stopped fighting. Stopped breathing.

"The first kill is the worst. Breathe, brave soldier."

Heart pounding, eyes still closed, I pressed my cheek against his chest and surrendered. King David was kind, but he'd never again look at me as he did in Moab. I saved his life, but I'd proven an emotional, silly woman who could never endure the pressures of war.

"What you're experiencing is called battle fury," he whispered. "The shaking and energy lessen as you fight more battles—and take more lives. I still tremble after battle, and I hope it never becomes easy to take a life." His beard tickled my cheek, moving back and forth. "You honor Yahweh to recognize the gravity of taking a life, but you also honor Him by defending the man He's chosen to lead His people."

His understanding was unbearable. "I'm sorry, my lord. I didn't have time to think. I should have let one of your men—"

"Why would you apologize?" He paused, as if waiting for me to look at him, but I kept my cheek pressed against his chest. "Had you not killed Uzzi, my blood would have mingled with his in the dust."

"Don't say that!" I flung my arms around his neck. The image of David even injured made me tremble from head to toe.

When his hand began rubbing circles on my back, the intimacy of our position dawned, and I squirmed against him. He gently set me down and steadied me, supporting my elbow.

"Forgive me, my king." I shook my head, ashamed, but the simple motion made me dizzy.

He reached for me, but I pulled away. "No!" I glared at him. "Why did you say to me, 'How could you do this?' and then pretend you are grateful for my protection?"

"I—" He shook his head, his face reddening and brows drawing together. "I had just seen you make a throw none of my men could have made, Ahinoam. I asked you that because a trained assassin was less than a step in front of me, and you drew, aimed, and threw your dagger quicker than he could thrust his."

"Well, it sounded like—"

His perfect lips quirked into a lopsided grin. "You have no idea how amazing you are, do you?"

My mind had cleared enough to wonder if he'd seen my bare and bloodied knees. *I hugged the king of Israel!* "My lord, please." I couldn't look at him.

"Anyone who saves my life should call me David." He tipped my chin up and offered an achingly tender smile. "Zerry will be even more eager now for you to teach her to throw."

"And I'll willingly do so, my lor—" He lifted a brow, and I remembered. "I mean, *David*." My legs still felt wobbly, but was it because I'd killed an assassin or because the king of Israel had seen my heart—and didn't seem to think me silly after all?

Oh, Yahweh, I've never wanted a man in my life. If I must marry, surely You could provide someone whose goodness doesn't remind me of all my failings.

TEN

DAVID

When David was told, "Look, the Philistines are fighting against Keilah and are looting the threshing floors," he inquired of the Lord, saying, "Shall I go and attack these Philistines?"

1 Samuel 23:1–2

Aviv (March) 1017 BC
Four Months Later

Holding our cohort's Passover lamb in my arms, I sat on a hilltop in the Forest of Hereth, watching the sun fade and dreading twilight. "You are the finest animal I've ever presented to the Lord, Tamim." I laid my cheek against his freshly washed wool. "Thank you for the blood you will shed for our sins this night. Thank you even for my sorrow, the way loving you makes me regret my sin even more." My throat tightened with too much emotion, so the final words came on a prayer. *Yahweh, bless this precious lamb whose blood will cover our sin and whose death will give us life.*

The *shevarim* sounded—three short blasts—signaling the beginning of our Passover Feast. I released the year-old ram Ahinoam had chosen from the provisions Abba sent for my rebel cause. Ozem, the youngest of my older brothers, arrived four days ago with enough perfect lambs, Bethlehem wine, bags of grain, bitter herbs, and sweet grapes for my whole army to celebrate Israel's most sacred remembrance.

"He's softening a little," my brother said with a shrug. *"He might even let me come fight with you."* Though I prayed we never had to fight our brother Israelites, I was both surprised and touched to hear that any of my brothers would want to join me.

I started down the hill toward the small camp I shared with ten others, warmed by the thought that my family in Bethlehem and my whole camp would be gathering at twilight on the fourteenth day of Aviv, as the Law commanded, because of Abba's generous offering. Tamim nibbled at my fingers as we walked. He was as tame as any of my old ewes had been. Ahinoam had named the yearling *Tamim* to emphasize his perfection, then looked at me for approval.

My immediate thought was, *You are perfection, Ahinoam.* I quickly looked away, plagued by the memory of Jonathan's angry words about Michal. *"She betrayed you and gave Abba a reason to charge you with treason."* Ahinoam had simply asked for affirmation of Tamim's name, but I was afraid to give a woman anything.

I had gaped like a fish out of water until Zerry intervened. My sister had grown accustomed to almost four months of my incoherent behavior. Other members of our cohort encouraged Ahinoam's choice of the lamb's name while I silently reprimanded myself.

Why did I lift Ahinoam into my arms in that olive grove? The memory of holding her in my arms, the sincerity in her eyes, the innocence mixed with ferocity—all Ahinoam's genuineness warred with the graven image I'd created of Michal bat Saul.

Halting midstride, I released my frustration on a tree with the butt of my palm. Tamim stopped beside me. I leaned against the tree to calm myself. *Yahweh, please! Help me stop thinking about both women.* For months I'd been trying to push away these feelings—and

131

had pushed Ahinoam away with them. I wasn't even sure *what* my feelings were for her, but I knew they were different than anything I'd felt for Michal.

Whenever Ahinoam was near, my palms grew sweaty. My heart raced. My thoughts grew addled. What I felt for Ahinoam was so much more . . . more . . .

"Baaahhh!" Tamim bleated his impatience.

I chuckled at his timing and vocabulary. "Baaahhh?" I bleated back. "No, my friend. Ahinoam is in no way baaahhh." We resumed our march toward camp, dread slowing my steps.

Tamim had been in our household only four days, but the little ram's antics drew our whole cohort closer. Even Uriah—the unsentimental, grumpy Hittite—had grown to love him. Such was Yahweh's intent when he commanded that we tend to our perfect yearling ram within the household for four days. The shedding of his blood would cost us all.

As Tamim and I neared camp, my stomach clenched. Ahinoam and Toren were helping Zerry prepare the spit.

Ahinoam looked up, seeming to sense our approach, and met me before we reached the gathering area. "This is for . . ." She let the words die, handing me a new dagger. "Abba sharpened it so the cut will be swift and clean. I want to help if you'll allow it." Without ever meeting my eyes, she bent down to scratch Tamim's soft black muzzle. That's when I saw a single tear roll down her cheek.

My hand twitched at my side, begging to wipe it away.

Toren cleared his throat. "I'm at your service, my lord." When had he arrived?

"Of course." Why was I shaking? "Gather around, everyone." I straddled Tamim, keeping him calm between the shelter of my legs. When the other members of our camp were present, I shared a memory Yahweh had called to mind earlier in the day.

"Each year I'd watched my family's Passover celebration from afar as Abba or one of my brothers cut a ram's throat and recited a required prayer of thanks. Though horrified by the lambs' deaths, I still yearned to be included in the household's celebration—especially on my twelfth Passover, when I was to become a man. However, instead of the typical honor of choosing the family's sacrificial lamb, I was again excluded from any participation. Worse, Abba chose my favorite lamb for the sacrifice, and for four days I dreaded the twilight ceremony."

"David, I'm so sorry." Ahinoam's eyes glistened with tears.

Her sympathy, so unexpected and sincere, felt like a warm blanket around my shoulders. "Thank you. But even in my deep sorrow, Yahweh taught me an invaluable lesson. Dodo, our family's chief shepherd—a man dearer to me than any abba—allowed me to choose a lamb for the shepherds' separate Passover celebration. He taught me how to honor the sacrifice, and we'll treat Tamim with the same care and respect Dodo modeled for me on my first Passover as a man and every year in my abba's pastures."

I motioned Zerry forward, took the bowl from her hand, and offered it to Ahinoam. "The one who holds the bowl to catch the blood also gets to whisper comfort and gratitude to the lamb for redeeming our sins. Would you do that for Tamim?"

She nodded, blinking a stream of tears down her cheeks.

To Toren I said, "Would you be willing to lift Tamim's muzzle and stretch his neck? I'll hold him close, and he'll feel only a momentary sting of your razor-sharp blade."

"I'd be honored."

I leaned over our little ram, whispering my own thanks to him before kneeling at his side and securing his middle with my right arm. Tamim bleated nervously, unaccustomed to so many human restrictions.

"What do I say?" Ahinoam's eyes widened with panic. She looked as frightened as Tamim.

I reached for her hand to steady the bowl and felt as if our hearts beat the same rapid rhythm. "Life is in the blood," I said, still looking only at her. "Adam and Eve's sin brought death to us all, and only through the shedding of blood can our lives be redeemed. So when the Death Angel searched out Egypt's firstborns, He *passed over* every Israelite doorway painted with lamb's blood, and all the firstborns of Israel were saved. Today, we remember the great Passover and paint Tamim's blood over the doorposts of our hearts, saving our lives from sin and death so we can live in fellowship with Yahweh." I reached for my dagger.

"Wait!" Ahinoam pleaded. "Shouldn't Abiathar do it? Shouldn't a priest—"

"Ideally, yes." It was an appropriate question, though ill-timed. "All of Israel has gathered for the Passover sacrifice at the Tabernacle since the days of Moses until the Philistines stole the Ark and returned it to Kiriath Jearim. Now Saul has moved the Tabernacle, and many in Israel won't celebrate this feast. Abiathar and I agreed that we should remember God's Law but maintain distance between our cohorts for safety's sake. He believes, as I do, that Yahweh cares more about the heart than outward appearance."

"Samuel told you that, didn't he?"

It felt as if Ahinoam stared directly into my soul. I'd shared Samuel's words with only two people, Jonathan and Zerry, but somehow it seemed right that Ahinoam should know.

Nodding, I spoke through a tight throat. "Samuel simply repeated what Yahweh told him."

"Then on this Passover and every day," she said, "we will seek to please Yahweh with our whole hearts." As tears gathered on her lashes, she whispered, "I'm ready now."

Before she could recant, I made a quick cut. Tamim's truncated bleat came with Ahinoam's startled gasp. She held the bowl in place while I stroked the yearling's side. We whispered our thanks as his legs grew weak. Toren released his head, allowing Ahinoam to support his muzzle with her right hand while holding the bowl with her left. Our comforting words continued as his lifeblood drained out. I lowered him gently to the ground.

Ahinoam covered a sob when the flicker of life faded from his eyes. She looked at me, her pallor reflecting the horror of death.

"It's awful, isn't it?" I croaked. "Sin does this." I glanced up at Toren and held out the special knife he'd made for tonight's event. "Will you help me prepare it for roasting?"

He drew both hands down his face before accepting the knife and sighed. We'd skinned gazelle and roebuck together, but this wasn't a slab of meat. This was our friend.

Ahinoam gave the bowl of blood to her abba. Our sacrifice and redemption. We would hang the lamb's body to fully drain the blood, as the Law of Moses required.

Gently tapping Ahinoam's arm, I stopped her. "Thank you for your help."

She pressed her lips into a smile, nodded, and walked away. My heart seized. She was an incredible woman, but I'd allowed my inner battle to cause awkwardness between us. I must somehow make it right.

"My lord?" Toren waited with the carcass, reminding me of the more pressing need.

Zerry shooed the others toward the spit, where they would help her prepare the meal and begin songs of celebration. When the moon reached its zenith, we'd dip bitter herbs in bowls of salt to commemorate our ancestors' slavery and then celebrate sweet freedom with the wine Abba had provided. Bethlehem's finest vintner had sent a wineskin for each cohort. *I must remember the good things Abba does and be grateful.*

The shofar's sudden t'ruah halted me midstep.

"My lord?" Tension laced Toren's tone in the growing darkness.

"Get a torch," I said, "and meet me in the clearing." Toren left the blood bowl on the ground and quickly returned with the torch. We field-dressed our ram and hung the meat over the bowl in a tree, high enough so scavengers couldn't steal it, then hurried to the clearing where nearly five hundred men waited.

I'd designated thirty as captains, who now crowded around a Gadite scout. During our winter in Hereth, these Mighty Men had established themselves not only as the most skilled warriors but also as courageous leaders with godly intent. Joab was among them and remained the general over the whole army. The five who accompanied him to Anathoth held special honor among the thirty. Asahel was captain of our Gadite scouts since he could keep pace with them in mountain terrain and knew my heart. Abishai, Eleazar, and Shammah comprised the Three, an elite force that completed the most dangerous missions. And my musical warrior priest, Amasai, led my Mighty Men with worship and truth.

"Attai has news from Judah's shephelah plain." Joab nudged the Gadite toward me. "Tell King David what you witnessed."

Attai panted, breathless from his run. "Philistines. Encamped around Keilah. The day after they completed barley harvest. Keilah's people started winnowing. Philistines attacked."

Uneasy chatter rippled through the Mighty. I lifted my fist to signal quiet, then refocused on Attai. "How long till King Saul's army reaches them to help?"

"Israel's army isn't coming." The fury in his eyes ignited mine.

The angry jeers around us wouldn't be silenced. I shouted over them to ask, "How do you know?"

Attai leaned closer. "Because I intercepted one of Keilah's messengers. He said our cowardly king refused to march into Judah's southern plain. He feared the Philistines were trying to draw his troops away from Gibeah, that they might circle north through the Jezreel Valley and attack his palace."

My eyes met Joab's fiery gaze. Jaw set, he offered a barely perceptible nod, and I knew he was with me. Most of the others were still roiling with unfocused fury but would aim at any target I commanded.

"Abiathar!" I scanned the crowd and found the priest and Gad the Seer already rushing toward the fray.

A respectful hush fell over the gathering as both men bowed to one knee before me and looked up. A thousand questions raced through my mind. Were my men ready for a real battle? They'd come to me as tax evaders, malcontents, and rebels with farmers' tools and kitchen knives. Could we defend Keilah against a trained and equipped Philistine army?

The injustice of Keilah's burden outweighed my hesitation. "Prophet of God," I said to Gad, "have you received word from Yahweh that we are to protect the people of Keilah?"

Head bowed, he said, "No, my lord, but you are Yahweh's chosen king. Why not inquire of Him directly through the ephod?" He looked up, his countenance alight. "You don't need a seer, my king, as long as you seek God with your whole heart."

His confidence was encouraging—and terrifying. How much easier it would be to have both a prophet and priest assure me of Yahweh's direction.

Abiathar reached for the lots inside his ephod, but I turned to the scout first. "Battle assessment." I needed to know what we were up against before asking God's counsel.

"At least ten thousand Philistines," Attai said, "with chariots and iron weapons."

Joab shoved him aside. "What is that to the Maker of heaven and earth? We have sheltered in the shadow of Yahweh's wing for four months. Will we repay His faithfulness with cowardice?"

"We feared for our lives every day of those four months" came a lone voice from the ranks.

Before I could discover who spoke, another added, "We're threatened by Israel's own soldiers. Why start a fight with the Philistines, too?"

Fire raced through my veins. "Have you forgotten Yahweh's protection? An assassin ventured into this camp, yet I was untouched!"

"Because of a woman's dagger!" someone shouted.

"And my daggers will follow King David to Keilah!" Ahinoam's petite form shoved through the mountainous men, Toren on her heels.

"We follow David!" he shouted, two paces behind his daughter.

When the Kenites halted before me, I could see only Ahinoam. The thought of her on a battlefield, facing a giant like Goliath, turned my blood to water. I gripped her arm and discreetly leaned close. "You're not fighting."

She jerked away and shouted at the men, "If Yahweh says we fight, I throw my daggers."

Toren added his shout. "If a Kenite trusts Yahweh's protection, why would the bravest of David's warriors hesitate?" While my men bickered among themselves, Toren turned toward his daughter. "You will not fight, but you will guard Zeruiah while Yahweh gives the Philistines into our hands."

"But, Abba, I—"

"A soldier obeys." My words stole her attention, and again I found myself face-to-face with feelings I couldn't ignore or explain. "To disobey is a betrayal, Ahinoam. Please don't ever betray me."

She held my gaze, then nodded and lowered her head.

I lifted my fist overhead, and the bickering settled. "We came to Hereth fully committed to trust Yahweh's corrective rod and guiding staff. That decision has not changed."

Abiathar stood beside me, already holding the Urim and Thummim in his hand. He raised his eyebrows in silent question, and I announced, "We will inquire with the stones. The white Thummim is Yahweh's affirmation that we defend Keilah and its grain. The black Urim forbids us to intervene."

Abiathar raised the stones in trembling hands and prayed. "Yahweh, we offer our lives to serve You and ask You to speak clearly." He cast the lots, and every man leaned forward to see how they would land on a grassy plateau.

God's answer, illumined by torchlight, sent warmth through me. The white Thummim stood straight and tall, propped against a sturdy blade of grass. The black Urim lay flat on a bald patch of dirt.

The yes could not have been clearer.

Five hundred men fell silent. Eyebrows rose. Lips pursed. Eyes averted. Not a single soldier would meet my gaze. I studied each noncommittal face. What had happened to my zealous warriors?

Only Joab returned my determined look, his face growing more crimson as the silence stretched into tension. Ahinoam moved to my side. Though she made no attempt to touch me, her nearness felt like a shield. Protective. Comforting. Secure.

"Will you condemn Saul's cowardice yet somehow justify your own?" Joab shouted.

Uriah the Hittite shouldered his way to the front. "How do we know those rocks aren't merely stones the priest picked up on his journey from Nob?"

I'd known Uriah since he was a boy. He and his brother Ahimelek were purchased as slaves by the Bethlehem vintner to pay their family's debts. The Hittite boys had rejected all gods, but Ahimelek had come to believe Yahweh was real after Abishai had befriended them. Perhaps now was as good a time as any for Yahweh to prove Himself to my nephew's longtime friend.

"What would it take for you to believe, Uriah?" I asked. "How can Yahweh prove the Urim and Thummim are His voice to me?"

All eyes turned toward the largest man among us. "I don't want to know if we're simply going to save Keilah's grain." Uriah smiled, revealing the hole where Abishai's slingshot knocked out a tooth when they were ten. "I want to know if your god can give the whole Philistine army into our hands."

"Of course He can," Ahinoam said, crossing her arms, then looking up at me.

I tried to hide my shock. What had come over her tonight?

She lifted her chin. "Well, He can prove Himself, can't He? Tell me we didn't kill Tamim for no good reason. There is a God who hears and sees and responds to our prayers, isn't there?"

Her passion set my heart aflame, and I shouted at Abiathar, "Throw the stones again."

"But, my lord—" His pallor said the rest. Did Yahweh's priest also doubt God's ability to speak?

Righteous fury spilled out in words I neither planned nor considered before voicing them aloud. "If you cannot trust Yahweh to guide two stones, how will you trust Him to guide our arrows, our javelins, and our spears? If we cannot credit God for months of safety in the forest, how can we trust His provision in the wilderness with danger on every side? If you cannot follow me to fight an enemy who would steal our brother Judeans' grain, then leave me now to wallow in your fear!" My loud shout sent birds to flight and Abiathar to gather the sacred stones.

I waited in silence for deserters to go. Not a single man moved, but I couldn't risk a coward among us. "If you don't believe, then leave. God wants only those who seek hard after Him! Men who willingly protect His chosen people with their last breath." With fire in my veins, I shouted at Abiathar, "Throw the stones, priest!"

He flipped them into the air. No prayer. No ceremony. No hesitation. They landed, and a collective gasp became a cheer. Not only had the white Thummim stood perfectly upright, but it also stood *atop* the Urim without any support at all.

Without thinking, I encircled Ahinoam's waist and flung her in a circle. I released her and did the same with Toren. Zerry appeared at my side, so I flung her in a circle, too. When I placed my sister's feet on the ground, I gripped her hand and reached for Ahinoam's. "You two will stay in the foothills overlooking Keilah until we've gained victory over the Philistines."

"I won't disobey you," Ahinoam said, "but if you'll allow me a little closer, I can throw—"

"No." I held her face between my hands. "You're too important to me—" I pulled away as if her crimson cheeks had burned me. "And too important to Zerry and your abba."

Joab shoved my shoulder. "Don't you agree?"

"Yes, yes, absolutely!" What had I agreed to?

"The king has spoken!" Joab announced. "We'll eat our feast and leave in haste as our ancestors left Egypt, except we go to free God's people in Keilah!"

I turned to join my cohort and was disappointed to see that Zerry and Ahinoam had already gone. Toren waited. His brow lifted, questioning, when he saw me watching the women's departure. Was he being a protective abba, demanding to know my intentions?

I don't know my intentions! My full and true intention was to never let a woman betray me again. But how could I ensure that unless I stayed away from all women forever? I could never stay away from Ahinoam. Zerry was my responsibility, and Ahinoam was her charge. Not to mention, the thought of going a single day without seeing her was like stabbing a red-hot sword into my belly.

Toren took two steps toward me. I wanted to run, but instead blurted, "I'm not sure what to do about your daughter."

He scratched his beard and looked around as if checking who might have heard. "I'm not sure what to do about your sister."

"What?" It was definitely not the reply I'd expected. "What are you talking about?"

His bushy brows drew together. "I assume you're not talking about my daughter's desire to fight."

"It's my desire we need to discuss."

"Well." He cleared his throat and looked over his shoulder again. Coming closer, he said in a low voice almost too quiet to hear, "Your sister is a beautiful, vibrant woman, and though I'm old, I am not yet dead, my king. She seems to enjoy my company, as well, so if you have no objections, I'd like to approach your nephews about a betrothal—after we defeat the Philistines at Keilah, of course."

I had no reply. How had this happened without my notice—or permission?

Toren grinned. "Don't worry, my king. There's been no impropriety between us. Who would dare, with Zeruiah's temper and her sons' battle skills?" He waved away my concerns before I voiced them. "However, with your permission, I'd like to stand guard over Nomy and Zeruiah in the foothills during the battle. I'm not sure I could focus on the battle, not knowing if they were safe."

"Yes, Toren. Thank you."

"Now, what are your intentions toward my daughter?"

"Intentions?"

"Let me say this, my king. She's very similar to Zeruiah in two ways."

"And what are those?"

"In that no man in his right mind would dare venture impropriety with Nomy's temper and an abba who is very good with a blade." He reached behind his back and offered me the dagger—hilt first—that I'd used to sacrifice Tamim. "I made this dagger for you, my king. And if Yahweh made my daughter for you, He will make it clear to us all in His good time."

ELEVEN

AHINOAM

So David and his men went to Keilah, fought the Philistines and car-
ried off their livestock. He inflicted heavy losses on the Philistines and
saved the people of Keilah.

1 Samuel 23:5

Keilah, Judah's Shephelah Plain

I sat on a cushion in the gathering room of our new Keilah home
and sorted lentils for tomorrow's stew, rehearsing memories of the
war I should have fought. I'd imagined hurling daggers at Philistine
soldiers while sheltered behind one of David's big-bodied warriors
and his shield. One of the Thirty could have been my human shield.
He could have fought hand-to-hand, and I would have thrown my
daggers, retrieved, and thrown again, witnessing God's glory and
our victory unfold. Instead, I'd watched the gruesome reality from
the foothills.

We had surprised the enemy at night. The Philistine horses and
chariots were at rest—as were their leaders. Called to arms, a giant
roared into battle shouting, "David ben Jesse, I've come for you!"
His declaration turned my knees to water. I hugged a tree to keep
from falling and searched in vain among thousands on the plain for

the one ruddy, handsome warrior I was trying not to love. *Yahweh, protect your anointed!* Zerry buried her face in Abba's chest, covering her ears to block out the noise. Though horrified by the sounds, smells, and heinous acts of men, I couldn't look away.

They fought through a night lit only by a moon made bright by its Creator. I heard swords clanging, men dying, and David's army calling on the only Name by which men could be saved. Sunrise came, and our men still fought. No more valiant cries. They managed only desperate lunges at a retreating enemy. Two lonely chariots escaped the blood-soaked plain now littered with dead and dying and a deserted Philistine camp.

That was three days ago. The memories still played in my mind as if they were happening in front of me. Here. In this room.

Each morning, our men traipsed outside the city walls to burn Philistine bodies and dead livestock. Smoke shrouded the sun by day, and ash coated every surface of our lives. It tainted the food we ate and the edges of our dreams.

The part most unbearable? David ben Jesse hadn't spoken or even looked at me since we were in Hereth, since he looked into my eyes and begged me not to betray him. *"To disobey is a betrayal, Ahinoam. Please don't ever betray me."*

I shot to my feet, nearly upsetting the bowl of lentils. Did it matter? Zerry had only given me the task to keep me busy. Something I could do without ruining it.

I went to the doorway and drew aside the curtain, peering into the street. Only weary soldiers passed our home, their sandals dragging in the mud. As the sun began to set behind Keilah's western wall, more and more men entered the southern gate.

The city elders had given David a three-room house he shared with Abba, Asahel, Zerry, and me. It was a fine home built into Keilah's southern wall and the largest dwelling Abba and I had ever lived in. The three men slept in a private chamber on one side of the gathering area. Zerry and I shared a chamber on the opposite side. The central room was decorated with embroidered pillows and stocked with plentiful cooking utensils. A baked-brick fireplace vented both smoke and cooking smells through the city's high wall, creating a utilitarian fire for both meal preparation and cozy warmth for the cool spring mornings.

Well, cozy for four of us. David hadn't come home before dark and always left before daylight.

He consumed my every thought. I was tired of it. Letting the curtain fall closed, I released a determined sigh and tried to clear my mind. Zerry was humming one of her brother's tunes, and I almost laughed at the absurdity of it. How could I clear my thoughts of David ben Jesse when every moment was full of him? The people I was with. The place I now lived. The air I breathed was a smoke-filled victory made possible by the God who had chosen him as Israel's next king. Every prayer I prayed was to the God who loved him and had only strengthened the feelings I'd begged to be taken away. *Why, Yahweh? Why must I feel this way about a man I can't have?* I pressed my forehead against the doorframe with a frustrated growl.

"Standing at the doorway won't make him appear," Zerry said tersely.

Three days in this room with Zerry had done nothing to improve my mood. I stiffened, trying to control the words that came out of my mouth. "Is something bothering you, Zerry?"

She huffed and banged the spoon on the pot of stew she'd been stirring. "I think you should be more grateful about our miraculous victory, Nomy. We didn't lose a single man from our army, and only fifteen of Keilah's citizens died, compared to *thousands* of dead Philistines. Yet you've been moping around this house as if you were grieving Toren." She paused. "Or is it David you're grieving?"

I whirled on her. "Why would you say that?"

"It's obvious you and David have feelings for each other." She tilted her head with a sympathetic pout. "My little brother has a complicated heart, Nomy, and when his wife broke it, she made it even more mysterious. Though David has deep feelings, he's not yet ready to share them."

Hearing the words spoken somehow made it real. "And that's why I'll never marry."

Zerry's mouth dropped open. "What did I say to give you that horrible idea?"

"You simply reminded me of what I know."

She didn't seem reassured.

"I don't want the pain that comes with marriage. If I feel like this when David doesn't talk to me for a few days, how would I feel if . . ." I couldn't even finish the thought. "For a year after Ima abandoned us, Abba was like a walking dead man. I saw the same emptiness in the eyes of Keilah's widows when we helped them bury their husbands. I don't want to love like that."

Zerry dropped her spoon, wiped her hands, and left her cook fire. "You listen to me, Ahinoam bat Toren." Marching toward me, she wagged her finger. "You can't run away from the love that expresses the One God in such a beautiful way. He made man and woman to become one flesh so we can appreciate His complex nature. Didn't Yahweh say, '*Let Us make humans in Our image?*' Then He created us as both male and female to become one flesh so we, with our Creator, could then create new life together. The love of a husband and wife, whether it produces a child or not, is unlike any other. So when that love is taken either by death—as it was from me—or by betrayal—as happened to your abba and David—only Yahweh can heal those wounds."

"Was my heart any less wounded when my ima left me, Zerry? Love is love, and the pain is the same no matter who shreds your heart."

"There." She opened her palms as if presenting me with a prize.

"You said it, love is love. The pain is the same. You can't avoid pain by avoiding marriage, Nomy." She lifted one dark eyebrow. "I believe David is avoiding you because he's falling in love with you and is equally afraid of being hurt again. So you should consider how you'll answer him when he finally proposes a betrothal."

"What? No! Zerry, he's already married."

"Is he? How could David ever serve Michal a certificate of divorce?" She didn't even pause for an answer. "He can't."

"Zerry, I don't want to be his wife. I came to fight for him. David is God's anointed. I want him to know I'd lay down my life for him."

"Would you give your life *to* him?" she asked. "If he asked you to become his wife?"

"Don't be ridiculous!" I turned away to hide my burning cheeks.

"Marriage contracts are struck for many reasons, Ahinoam. The one good thing Abba Jesse did for me was arrange my marriage to Ahitub. He was older than Abba, but Ahitub was kinder than any man I knew. I bore him three sons in the five years before he died. Our rowdy sons likely wore him out, but he was happy. His last words were of gratitude for the life we'd lived together. I've not married again because I'm certain I could never again find a man like him." Zerry squeezed my shoulders. "All marriages don't have to bring heartache, my friend."

I shrugged her off without answering and hurried out the door to the sound of expected protests. I couldn't bear more truth from David's knowing sister. Did she have a window into my soul—and David's? She'd read my heart like a scroll. Was she as accurate about his?

Despite the elders' decision to keep women inside the city like caged birds, I hurried toward the south gate. I was tired of waiting for David to talk to me. Tired of pretending to be like other women. I was a descendant of the Kenite she-warrior Jael, the woman who killed a Canaanite general with warm milk and a tent peg to his temple. David needed my dagger-throwing skill, not my love. He needed my loyalty as a soldier, not another swooning maiden. And I needed to be of use. Surely I could find a way to help clear the battlefield and begin the restoration of Keilah's pastures, vines, and orchards.

Greeting Keilah's citizens along the way, my attempts at kindness were met with cool indifference. I passed a few of David's men who were returning from a long day of work outside the wall. Each of them offered a weary smile and greeting. Eliphelet the Philistine even stopped and asked me to sharpen his dagger this evening if I had the time.

"Gladly." I examined the blade, noticing a few chips. "I can help a little, but I'll need to do a fuller repair when we get the forge set up."

"Thank you, mistress," he said. "I'll appreciate whatever sharpening you can do overnight. Your abba can return it to me tomorrow since we've been working together at one of the burn piles."

"Can you tell me which burn pile? I need to find him."

Only a heartbeat's hesitation and a subtle lift of a brow betrayed his surprise. "Go straight out of the south gate about a hundred paces. We were burning mostly livestock today." He offered a quick bow and continued toward the barracks that had been assigned to our men. Keilah's guards had been steadily killed by Philistine night raids during the past five years, so the barracks had been empty and waiting for Yahweh's new king to prove his care for God's people.

I started toward the south gate with a little bounce in my step. *Thank You, Yahweh. I feel a little more like myself again.* I could ask our hardworking soldiers outside the city if they needed me to sharpen their blades in the evenings. Abba could return them each morning. Maybe I just needed more human interaction besides Abba, Zerry, and Asahel.

Dear Asahel. He, too, had been rather withdrawn on the evenings he returned with Abba for our evening meals. Though he was my favorite of Zerry's sons, I was puzzled by David's decision to invite him to live with us. Asahel hadn't been a part of our cohort in Hereth, and when I'd asked Zerry about it, she hadn't seemed to understand the decision, either. Regardless, we were pleased to have Zerry's kindhearted youngest son among us.

A pool of muddy sludge stopped me at the unguarded south entrance. Keilah, like other walled fortresses, was built on a slope so all waste ran downhill through a central drain in the main street. The sludge ran into a ditch, then to a ravine outside the city. For the past three days, so many exhausted soldiers had tromped through Keilah's south gate that the drainage ditch had widened to more of a pool, nearly spanning the entire width of the entrance. After warming a full day in spring sunshine, its contents had cooked to a rank and steamy simmer.

I swallowed the gorge rising in my throat and stepped carefully around the murky sludge. Tiptoeing to my escape, I finally reached solid ground and lifted my head.

Battle images assailed me. The bright red blood and violence in every direction I'd seen three days before had become a putrid, burning wasteland. A different kind of nightmare. Thick smoke and flames rose from more than a dozen pyres. Shrouded figures moved amid the haze, their heads completely covered, leaving only slits to navigate the Sheol victory around them. Why hadn't I brought a scarf to cover my nose and mouth? Or a waterskin to clear my throat? My eyes stung, and I squinted to see the burn pile closest to me.

Is that . . . ? The realization of dead bodies piled as high as the city wall made me retch. *They're still burning bodies?* I wiped my mouth and heard a familiar voice shouting commands nearby. *David.*

Barely able to keep my stinging eyes open, I searched for him amid the awful reality. He was standing by a burn pile only ten paces away, one in which hooves and legs stuck out at every angle. I gasped, the sudden intake of smoke and ash choking me. With every cough and gasp, I drew in more smoke. My chest felt like I'd breathed in fire.

Panicked, I turned to run back into the city but slammed into something. Arms surrounded me, pulling my head back.

"Ahinoam, drink this." Abba held a waterskin to my lips, pouring water into my mouth as I sputtered and choked. The burning sensation eased as the cool liquid trickled down my throat.

"My eyes!" I gasped, unable to open them.

A damp cloth's furious swiping answered my plea. I grasped it to take over the task, but he pushed my hands away and continued mopping and splashing the water until the stinging subsided. Then he pulled me tightly to his chest, and I cried with relief.

"You silly woman." The voice rumbling beneath my cheek was David's, not Abba's. The chest on which I'd pillowed my head was well-muscled and firm. The heart that pounded in rhythm with my own was that of Israel's next king.

"Why aren't you at home with Zerry?" he whispered, soft and husky.

A different sort of panic rose now. How many of his men were watching us? Joab had said the anointed king must be beyond reproach or he could lose his men's respect. I could never be more than a plaything to him. David's men would label me as they did Ima when she fell in love with a soldier. Then Abba and I bore her shame as the Kenite harlot's husband and the harlot's unfortunate child. I could never add to Abba's shame.

I wriggled from David's grasp. "Forgive me, my lord. I won't trouble you further."

Before I could flee, Abba grabbed my arm. "Why didn't you stay with Zeruiah?"

"I wanted to help with—"

"There's nothing for you to do, Nomy. You can't drag bodies or repair broken chariots."

"Go, Toren." David replaced his scarf over his nose and mouth. Only his eyes were visible, but they avoided mine. "It's dusk. Take your daughter home. Get some rest. You've done enough for one day, my friend." He left us without another word.

Abba watched him go and mumbled, "When will you rest, my king?" Then he turned his stern glare on me. "What came over you? You were acting like a silly—"

"I'm not like Ima," I gritted out through a clenched jaw. "I heard you tell Old Miriam that Ima was a silly woman, but I'm not like her, Abba. I don't love any man who gives me fine things. Linen robes. Fancy jewelry. You told Ima to stay with her soldier if he wanted a *silly woman*. And she did, but you didn't want her to go."

"Our lives were better without her, Ahinoam!"

"Then why did you cry when she left?"

He looked as if I'd stabbed him with his own blade. "I didn't."

"I heard you weeping, Abba. It was the only time I've ever heard you cry. After that day, I've lived by two rules: One, I would try to accept any woman who could heal your heart. Though I desperately hoped it wouldn't be Old Miriam."

He grinned. "And your second?"

"I vowed never to let anyone hurt me like Ima hurt you."

His features hardened like granite. "My past is no excuse to ruin your future." He marched past me toward the city. I caught up and matched his strides but didn't dare speak. We'd nearly reached the gate when he said, "The next king of Israel is a good man who is in love with you."

"He's not!" I grabbed his arm, turning him to face me, and accidentally splashed my foot in the south gate's simmering sludge.

Abba looked down at the filth dripping from our robes, then back at me. "The king was right. He told me this morning that you and Zeruiah have been on edge and needed more contact with women to . . . do whatever women do. He's already sent messengers to invite our troops' families to reunite here in Keilah. Some wives and children will arrive as early as tomorrow."

Could this day get any worse? Before I could explain my dismay, I glimpsed a group of Keilahite women gawking at us from inside the city. They pointed and giggled at Abba and me, who stood ankle-deep in sludge. Then they walked away. Abba bowed his head, giving me the perfect example to explain my dread.

"Do you really think I'll feel less awkward in Keilah when families from our own army also begin to mock me?"

He looked up and studied me. Was that pity on his features or merely dusk's shadows? "If you allow people to know you, Ahinoam, some may mock you, but others will love you. It's worth the risk." He kissed my forehead and strode toward home.

Maybe I was a silly woman. Peering down at my dim reflection in the reeking water, I realized I felt more comfortable in this waste pit than in a king's arms. The truth was painfully clear. I didn't belong anywhere. Or with anyone.

Making the short trek home, I grabbed an empty water jar from beside our doorway and went straight to the city's central well. Both Abba and I needed a bath. David would, too. At least now, after witnessing what our men faced outside the city walls, I understood David's need for seclusion to replenish his soul. I'd hear him strumming his lyre and singing God's praise late into the night. Maybe Zerry was wrong, and he wasn't avoiding me at all. Perhaps David simply needed to remember Yahweh's goodness before facing another day of messy blessings.

Thankfully, there was no one at the well when I drew our water. The streets were deserted when I walked home and left my smelly sandals at the door. I tried to ignore Abba's and Zerry's worry-creased foreheads as I passed through the gathering room, slipped into my chamber, and closed the door. I heard their muffled conversation, pleased they'd grown even closer during our winter in Hereth.

I'd often wondered about Zerry's husband and why she'd never remarried. I couldn't imagine her married to an old man. Zerry had been her sons' only parent since she was eighteen harvests old. Still, she'd found her place in the world of women with children and the household skills that filled her day. Even in her uniqueness, Zerry belonged.

The cloying stink on my robe reaffirmed the only place I belonged. Moving to the corner to undress, I placed my belt in my laundry basket and then my robe. I thought to leave my tunic on, but even my sheer undergarment reeked of smoke. Stripped naked, I poured water into a large basin, dipped a rough-spun cloth in wine and salt, and began scrubbing myself. After tossing three dirty water basins out the high window in my chamber, I finally washed my hair with a little salt and vinegar. When I turned my head to reach for a fresh headcloth, a whiff of lingering smoke still clung to my hair.

How could I rid myself of the smell? The memory of saffron oil filling our palace chamber in Moab came rushing back. Zerry had washed Mistress Nitzevet's hair with the sweet-scented oil. The aroma was almost as sweet as their laughter. Surely Zerry would rather I borrow her luxurious oil than fill the gathering room with the stench of smoke.

I searched through her basket of remedies and found the bottle. My friend would happily share a dose of saffron oil if it helped me smile on this dreadful day. I sprinkled a few drops on my palm, rubbed my hands together, and worked the oil through my wet hair. The sweet scent filled the room, washing my senses with an equally sweet peace.

I donned the only other robe I owned after Zerry destroyed my short robe and high-laced sandals, the sky-blue linen provided by our duplicitous hosts at Moab. On our way to Hereth, Abba had traded a new dagger to buy me a full-length woman's woolen robe. When it needed washing, I wore the fancy blue linen only long enough to wash the woolen one. I'd then don my plain woolen robe while still wet rather than endure the humiliation of unwanted luxury.

Tonight, however, as the blue linen slipped over my head and skittered down my freshly washed body, I shuddered at the softness of expensive cloth. Closing my eyes, I breathed in the sheer rapture of being clean.

The oil lamps sputtered, reminding me of David's exact words. *"You silly woman."* Momentary pleasure drained in an instant. Nothing could have wounded me more.

Not true.

He'd spoken words more wounding. *"You're too important to me."* Though I didn't want his love, the words had felt like a pledge. Had he meant to test me? Confuse me? Or had he been toying with me?

Shame burned my cheeks. I'd been such a fool. I would serve God's anointed with my daggers—or not at all.

A timid knock interrupted. "Ahinoam?"

David! My heart slammed against my chest. "Ye—" I coughed. "Yes?"

"May I come in?"

"No, I—"

"Are you dressed?" Zerry barged into our chamber, took one look at me, and opened the door wide. "Asahel, Toren, and I will wait in the gathering room while you two talk."

She left David at the threshold. Staring at me. Jaw slack. Eyes wide. Ash and sweat smeared down his face. "Ahinoam, you look . . . *beautiful.*"

"I . . . um . . . thank you." My voice quaked in tempo with my pounding heart. I couldn't look away. Then I noticed something in his hands. "What's that?" I pointed at what appeared to be a folded robe and sandals.

"They're for you." He extended the offering.

"Why?" I stepped back. I wasn't like Ima. "I don't need gifts."

Lips pursed, his features darkened into a storm. "Consider them replacements for what my sister took from you." He dropped them at the threshold, strode through the gathering area, entered his private chamber, and slammed the door.

Abba, Zerry, and her son exchanged quizzical glances while I knelt to inspect the items David left at my door. When I lifted the garment, I gasped. "A short robe." It was exactly like the one Zerry had taken from me in Moab. The high-laced sandals were also identical to those I'd worn in Jezreel. My throat was too tight to ask for an explanation, so I cast a pleading gaze toward the three intently watching. *Please tell me one of you did this.* Abba and Asahel looked away, confirming how brazenly I'd rebuffed David's kindness.

Zerry explained, "The day after we moved into this house, David asked Keilah's elders which sandal maker and seamstress could prepare the finest quality gifts in the shortest amount of time."

The walls around my heart cracked. I had no words. No more excuses. I closed the chamber door, pressed my back against it, and wept into my new short robe. Regret. Confusion. Hope. Fear. All swirled in a giant knot I had no idea how to untangle.

TWELVE

DAVID

When you are on your beds, search your hearts and be silent . . . In peace
I will lie down and sleep, for you alone, Lord, make me dwell in safety.

Psalm 4:4, 8

Michal stood on the narrow edge of a wadi, flooded into a rushing river by winter rains. As if in a stupor, she walked toward the churning water. Ahinoam stood on the opposite shore, her cries echoing off the canyon walls. "Save her, David!"

From an outcropping above, I shouted at Michal, "Go the other way! You're too close!" But she ignored the warning, and I was too far away to save her. I tried to leap from the rocks but couldn't move. I looked down. My hands and feet were bound by golden chains. Ahinoam was screaming again, and I looked up as Michal stepped into the current. She was swept away. Gone.

I bolted upright on my mattress, panting and soaked with sweat. The woven blanket was wrapped around my arms. Moonlight streamed through a single high window. Toren's snoring sounded strangely like the roaring waters in my dream. Usually, Goliath's empty eyes haunted my nights, leaving little room for other nightmares.

On my right, Asahel lay on his side, facing me. "Another dream?"

"Go back to sleep."

He rolled over, facing the wall.

I pushed to my feet and snatched my short robe from the peg beside the door. The memory of Ahinoam in that blue robe immediately came to mind. I thought she'd be pleased with the short robe I gave her. It was a daring gift. Unconventional—like her. The robe would likely fall to the middle of her calves, showing her ankles. *Scandalous.* I almost grinned, but the sting of last night's encounter sobered me. The woman warrior I'd called friend at Hereth had become timid and unsure in Keilah.

Friend? Conviction twisted my heart. *All right, Yahweh, that's a lie.* My reaction to her terror yesterday proved I felt more than friendship. I'd shoved Toren aside, wiped her eyes, and held her in my arms, which I'd longed to do for weeks. To embrace her publicly had been foolish. Joab would hear of it and recite all the reasons I should have been more circumspect. I'd avoid Joab as I'd avoided Ahinoam.

"Because that's working so well," I huffed before looking over my shoulder. Good. Asahel seemed to be sleeping again.

I sat at the door and laced my sandals, pondering the dream. Michal and Ahinoam, standing on opposite sides of rushing water. It was as if they stood on two sides of a window. Every night since arriving in Keilah, I'd slept deeply, had the same dream, felt the same helplessness, and awakened with the same confusion. *Yahweh, I know You're speaking, but what are You saying?*

Finished lacing my sandals, I strapped on my weapons and grabbed the ash-caked scarves I'd worn for three days. Hopefully we'd finish the battle cleanup before Sabbath and I could burn my scarves and bloodstained robe in the cleansing ceremony.

The elders had been reluctant to follow all the Laws of Moses, especially when it came to giving half the spoils to my soldiers, the other half to Keilah's people, and dividing God's portion among the priests and Levites throughout the towns of Judah. *"I'll willingly* return the home you generously gave me," I'd said, "If anyone is in need. As leaders, we must be the example not only of obedience to God's Law but also of extravagant generosity." Reluctantly, they'd divided the spoils among Keilah's Levites, priests, and townspeople, as well as sending gifts to every city of refuge. Keilah's neglected priesthood had been especially grateful.

Checking my shoulder bag, I found enough nuts, dried meat, and bread left from yesterday to sustain me today. *Thank You, Yahweh. There's always plenty.* When would God's people learn that His provision didn't stop with manna in the wilderness?

My hand froze on the door latch as the familiar heaviness descended on my chest. *When will I learn that lesson, Yahweh?* The food was still in my shoulder bag because I'd had no appetite since we left Hereth. I was weary. Anxious. Tired of death. Tired of being hunted by Saul. Tired of fighting Philistines. Tired of being betrayed by Moabites. By Benjamites. By my own family. I let my forehead fall against the door and closed my eyes. *Please, Yahweh. I can barely manage my own emotions, let alone navigate the questions and conflicts others lay at my feet.*

I opened the door and stumbled over something.

"Oh!" Ahinoam jumped to her feet, facing me.

"Sorry!" we said at the same time in the dim light of a few lamps.

She stared up at me, a delicately lifted brow making her seem vulnerable. Every impulse said, *Kiss her!* True wisdom shouted, *Run!*

"I, um . . ." She looked down, scuffing the toe of her new sandals on the packed-dirt floor. "I wanted to thank you for my robe and sandals."

Now it was too late to run away. She was wearing the garment I'd dropped at her threshold—before running from her like a frightened boy. The tightly woven wool seemed well made and stopped a handbreadth above her perfectly sculpted ankles. The laces of her new sandals crisscrossed up her calves, disappearing under the robe to a place I dared not imagine. *Yahweh, help me!*

Then it dawned on me. "Were you sleeping outside my door?"

Her head snapped up. "Were you trying to sneak away again?" Her lips curved into a playful grin that definitely needed to be kissed.

Before I could answer, my dream flashed in my mind. I saw Ahinoam shouting, *"Help her, David!"*

"Are you all right?" she asked. "You look pale."

"I'm still married," I blurted.

"I know." She stepped back, color rising in her cheeks.

Memories of the dream overwhelmed me. I closed my eyes and saw Michal falling into the dangerous river. *Yahweh, must I tell this to Ahinoam?* As if the dream's continuation was His answer, this time I comprehended a detail in the replaying that I hadn't remembered after waking any of the other mornings.

"Ahinoam," I whispered, "I need to tell you about my dream. Will you sit down with me?"

"Of course." When she turned toward the embroidered pillows, I placed my hand at the small of her back, which felt both reassuring and exhilarating. She chose a cushion, and I chose one across from her.

"I've experienced the same vivid dream all three nights we've been in Keilah," I began. "You and Michal are on opposite banks of a rushing wadi. I'm standing guard on an outcropping above both of you. Michal deliberately enters the raging river, and you shout at me to help her, but I'm bound in place with golden chains."

Her brow furrowed. "David, I'm sorry. That sounds awful."

"I've had the same dream each night since we arrived in Keilah, and I know Yahweh is telling me something. When I woke this morning and found you at my door, I remembered a detail that had escaped me until now."

Wariness shadowed her features. "What did you remember?"

159

A sudden certainty settled over me, dispelling weeks—no, months—of confusion with the single revelation. "You wore the head covering of a married woman, which bore my family's colors—Judah's sky blue with the red stripe of Boaz's clan." I took a steadying breath and added, "You wore it because you were my wife, Ahinoam."

Looking more puzzled than surprised, she said, "But I'm a Kenite, not—"

"I see what you *are*, and I want you to be my wife." I reached for her hand, but she pulled away, lacing her fingers together.

She wasn't ready. Her wide eyes and posture looked like a doe that just heard something unusual and stands utterly still to listen further.

"I won't approach Toren about a betrothal without your permission," I assured her. "But I'd like our friendship to grow." *Until I can convince you to marry me.*

Her shallow breaths proved my bold admission had unsettled her. *Yahweh, only You have ever been able to absorb my unbridled feelings.* To lose her completely would gut me.

"I need to think," she said, bolting to her feet.

Before she could dash to her chamber, I caught her hand. "Wait." But she wouldn't face me. "I'll return at midday. Please don't be frightened by what I've said."

Before I could blink, the tip of her dagger was beneath my chin. "I'm not afraid of you, David ben Jesse." Mischief danced in her eyes. "And I look forward to being friends."

Joy surged through me. *Yes, this woman is a gift from You, Yahweh, and someday she'll be my wife.*

I'd experienced long days in my short life, but every task and all my soldiers seemed to require twice the effort this morning. "Stoke that fire!" I shouted at my men. "If you let the flame dwindle, you'll use kindling from your own barracks!"

Joab, who stood among them, offered a half-hearted "Yes, my lord" and used an extra-long Philistine spear to bank the embers and remaining livestock carcasses to rekindle the flame. He then whispered a conspiratorial comment to his men, waved as he left his lieutenant in charge, and began a determined twenty-pace march toward me. His expression looked much like I remembered Zerry's right before she scolded me.

"Our men are as tired as you are," he said. "It's not their fault you're not sleeping."

"I'm sleeping."

"Three donkeys could carry the bags beneath your eyes."

I chuckled. "That was almost witty."

"I must be at my best." He wiggled his eyebrows. "My wife arrives today."

I stifled an inward groan. Abishai, Uriah, and Ahimelek had gone to Bethlehem to collect our soldiers' wives and families and bring them to Keilah for a short visit. We'd also sent Gadite scouts to the various hometowns and villages of our other soldiers to gather families for long overdue reunions. Despite dreading the arrival of my nephews' wives—mostly Vered and the tension she added—I eagerly anticipated the joy on my men's faces. They sorely needed a boost in morale after such grueling days. *And I'll get to focus on Ahinoam.*

"My lord!" Old Jeremiah ran toward us. Though the oldest among my Gadite scouts, likely well past his sixtieth harvest, he still had the eyes of a hawk and was familiar with every wadi and cave in Israel. "Your nephew and his Hittite friends are in the foothills with the Bethlehem families."

Joab broke into a sprint, and Old J kept pace. Asahel must have seen them running because he dashed like a stag across the plain and would likely beat them both to greet his wife and newborn. I jogged at a leisurely pace, allowing husbands and wives to have their reunions before I greeted friends and family. The Bethlehem caravan emerged from the forested hillside and descended onto the shephelah plain. Abishai escorted his wife, Raya. He, Uriah, and Ahimelek each carried a child on his shoulders. Dalit, Asahel's wife, carried their swaddled infant against her chest. Vered led the other two women, each one holding the reins of a heavily laden donkey.

Abishai was first to spot his two brothers running toward him. The Hittite brothers' heads jerked up a moment later. The three returning warriors placed fingers to their lips and released the shrill, three-toned whistle we'd used as children to signal our arrival in Abba's pastures. Joab ran straight for Vered and scooped her into a twirl. They giggled like children until both were dizzy and stumbling. Uriah lowered Joab's oldest boy off his shoulders so he could join his parents' fun.

Abishai lowered his eldest to the ground. The little one ran directly into my arms. "*Dohd* Daydey!" Zabdi squeezed my neck with surprising strength. "We came to fight da Phi-du-steenz!"

"Let me test your muscles." I coaxed his arm into a warrior's flex and squeezed the four-year-old's bicep. "Now we'll be victorious for sure!"

"Dohd Ozem says he'll join your army when Saba Jesse goes to Paradise."

"What?" I shot a panicked glance at Abishai.

"Zabdi, I told you to let me speak with Dohd David about Saba."

"Sorry, Abba." My nephew's exuberance drained.

I placed his feet on the ground and breathed out. "Tell me."

"Jesse is ill, David." His arm tightened around his wife's shoulder. "Very ill."

"If it's bad, we must prepare Zerry."

All three women avoided my eyes. Abishai looked as if he'd swallowed his dagger sideways. Finally Uriah said, "He won't recover, my lord. Mistress Nitzevet doesn't expect him to live through the summer heat."

My heart seized. I tried to swallow the truth, but my mouth was too dry. Would my last memory of Abba be our hostile good-bye? No—he'd provided the Passover meal for my whole camp. It was his way of making amends, and as an expression of gratitude, I'd returned the new lyre I'd made during our winter in Hereth. Still, I wanted to race to Bethlehem. Would I finally see forgiveness in his eyes?

"Should I go to—"

"No." Abishai's quick answer left no doubt.

Ahimelek quickly added, "The Gadites with us stalked the perimeter of Bethlehem while we gathered the families. Saul had spies watching the city. He would know if you entered Bethlehem, and within a day, the whole city could be just like Nob."

I drew a hand down my face, knowing he was right but begrudging the truth. "Should one of you at least escort Zerry back home to be with Ima?" My nephews exchanged reluctant glances. It was then I realized that all the donkeys were packed for more than a short visit. "I thought I was clear that families were coming for a temporary reunion in Keilah."

Vered marched toward me, hands fisted on her hips. "Zerry told us months ago, when we crossed the Great Tongue, that after Dalit delivered her baby and it was safe to join you, our families would be reunited. Our husbands fought a whole Philistine army for you, David. You live in a walled city with a well and winter provisions. Why wouldn't you welcome your men's families, David? Hmm?"

This is why I dreaded Vered's return. I'd tried reasoning with Vered before and found the effort more damaging—to myself and others—than beneficial. So, ignoring the tired, angry woman, I placed the burden on her husband. "Joab, I will inform Zerry about Abba's ill health while you and your brothers settle our Bethlehem arrivals in a portion of the barracks."

Vered gasped. "My children and I can't live in a barracks with hundreds of soldiers!" The woman who had twirled in her husband's arms now barely held back tears.

"It's a temporary solution," I said more gently, then resumed my instruction to Joab. "After I've spoken to your ima, you and I will meet with Keilah's elders and request housing for the *hundreds* of women and children who are about to descend on this city. I'm sure our kin from Bethlehem aren't the only ones who will wish to remain with their husbands."

Without waiting for opposition or suggestion, I strode toward town, inwardly kicking myself for not giving more thought to housing for my men's families. Of course they'd want to be reunited. Keilah was an opportunity for me to lead well. I must think of both the citizens we'd rescued and my men who had so bravely given up everything to follow me into exile. The Philistines had attacked Keilah in hopes of raiding their grain stores. We'd saved them— and their winter grain. Would the people of Keilah and its elders willingly share their hard-won winter provisions with my soldiers and their families? Or would they show the same stinginess they'd evidenced when I'd enforced the offerings to the priests? *Yahweh, give me wisdom to deal fairly with the people I serve and those who serve me.*

I splashed through the stinking pit at the city's south gate and nearly tore the curtain off our doorway as I entered. Zerry and Ahinoam jumped, spilling the kernels of grain from the hand mills on their laps. Ahinoam smiled at me, and my tongue stuck to the roof of my mouth.

"Something's wrong. What is it?" Zerry asked, studying me. How did she always know?

She lifted her chin. "Say it, David. Whatever it is."

"Abba is ill."

Her hard shell cracked slightly. "How serious?"

Ahinoam moved to Zerry's side, looking almost as pale as my sister.

"Abishai and the Hittites returned with the news. One of them can escort you to Bethlehem tomorrow if you want to see Abba again."

"He's *that* ill?" Surprise flashed across Zerry's features.

I nodded.

A thousand emotions passed between us before Zerry's practiced calm resettled into place. "I said good-bye when we parted at the Dead Sea. My presence would only upset him."

Toren rushed through the curtained doorway. "Joab just told me Jesse is ill." He stood by me but looked directly at my sister. "I would be honored to escort you to Bethlehem. I'm sure your ima needs you at her side while she grieves."

Zerry's chin quivered. "Thank you, Toren, but Ima has Keyalah to comfort her, and my family is right here in this room."

Ahinoam met my gaze, her expression inscrutable. "Do *you* need to see your abba, David?" More unspoken questions screamed from her intense honey-brown eyes. *Is your conscience clear? Will current regrets turn to enduring guilt after your abba's death?*

"I believe the gifts Abba and I exchanged during Passover were the healing balm between us." Crossing the distance between us, I lifted Ahinoam's hand to my lips. "But thank you for asking such a searching question. Only the woman God has chosen to become my wife is brave enough to challenge the dark corners of my heart."

Still boldly holding my gaze, she slipped her hand away. "And only Yahweh can convince me that I—a Kenite maid past her prime—is His choice to be the wife of King David."

PART II

Test me, Lord, and try me, examine my heart and my mind; for I have always been mindful of your unfailing love and have lived in reliance on your faithfulness.

Psalm 26:2–3

THIRTEEN

AHINOAM

Saul was told that David had gone to Keilah, and he said, "God has delivered him into my hands, for David has imprisoned himself by entering a town with gates and bars."

1 Samuel 23:7

Ziv (April) 1016 BC
One Year Later
Keilah

Dawn's dim light shone through the wooden shutters, illuminating a layer of dust and sand on my thin blanket. I swallowed, aware of the blessed silence and the absence of unbearable heat that had come with three days of sirocco desert winds.

Throwing off my blanket, I stretched, imagining the spring colors that would soon explode on the shephelah plain. The cold, dreary winter rains would become a distant memory, and perhaps Keilah's citizens would be more welcoming when they saw what a great benefit David's army and their families could be to the town, rather than the burden we'd been on their grain stores and water supply all winter.

Abba's low chuckle came from the common chamber outside

my door, then Zerry's soft voice in a tone she saved only for him. I bolted to my feet, wrapped my short robe and belt around me, and quickly laced my sandals. Though Abba and Zerry seemed happy to be trapped inside by the windstorm, I was more confused than ever about David's insistence that Yahweh had chosen me to marry Israel's next king.

"It's absurd," I mumbled, folding my blanket. "Absolutely ridiculous." After tidying the chamber, I flung open my door and ran headlong into my confusion.

"Shalom, lovely Ahinoam." David smiled down at me, dressed in his casual linen robe. My knees turned to water—again—though he'd greeted me with the same words every morning since sharing the dream in which I wore the proof of becoming his wife. "I was just coming to knock on your door. Join us." He extended his arm toward Asahel, Zerry, and Abba, who patted the cushion beside him.

Breathe, I reminded myself. "Shalom, everyone." I sat on the proffered pillow, opposite Zerry and her son. She glared at David as he settled beside her. He didn't seem to notice.

"The end of the first sirocco means it's time for sheep shearing," he said.

"And my brother doesn't seem to realize the kind of preparations shearing requires of the women." Zerry's words were taut, clipped. "Every woman in Keilah will be busy ridding her home of the dust the winds blew inside."

David met her hard stare. "Is a clean house more important than our livestock? They endured the heat in their heavy winter wool. There could be more siroccos. Our flocks will be cooler if they're shorn before another storm comes. Plus, we need the wool as soon as possible to replenish Keilah's grain and supplies. The booty we gained from battle wasn't enough to feed our five hundred men and the families that chose to remain."

"You can't simply come out from a three-day seclusion and announce a shearing festival *today*," Zerry protested.

"I'm only trying to help," David replied. "Surely, the elders will see that and—"

"There's already unrest among the Keilahites, David. Nomy and I see the women whispering each morning when we go to the well, but they fall silent when we approach them."

I'd received the same reaction from women all my life, but Zerry had been deeply offended when the same women she'd grieved with and helped bury their husbands shunned her during our harsh, cold winter in their city.

"And let's consider what all married men know to be true." Humor played on Asahel's features. "Whatever Ima is sensing in Keilah's women is a good indicator of what their men are saying at home or in clandestine meetings. If you command all the men in Keilah to help with shearing today, then all the women must be ready to immediately wash the wool, store it, and prepare it for storage or trade." A wide grin made him look more like his handsome uncle. "But look at the positive side. Such a command would likely change Keilah's hidden complaints into open rebellion."

Asahel's lighthearted observation made even David join the laughter.

What no one had mentioned was that spring was also the time kings went to war. Keilah was a jewel on the plain with walled protection, vineyards, groves, and grain fields, and our victory last spring would only last until our enemies mustered their army to fight again. Selling the wool now would mean certain profit and early planting.

"All right, all right," David said as our laughter ebbed. "I hear your counsel, but I'm still responsible for the flock Abba placed in my care. Perhaps when the people of Keilah see the fun we're having, they'll wish to join in today's shearing."

"But, David—"

"Zerry, I'll organize the men for shearing. You must convince the wives of our soldiers that washing and processing the wool can build relationships between them, and that you—not Vered—are the matriarch of my camp. Joab's wife has rained terror on those poor women all winter long. Spring has arrived and with it the warmth of your firm and caring heart."

She sighed with a rueful grin. "You and your silver tongue." Then she looked at me. "Don't think you get to hide in that forge today. You'll stand right beside me when I face Vered, and you'll wash wool with the rest of us."

"Zerry, no." I dropped my head into my hands. Every contact I'd had with our soldiers' women left me more convinced I was unworthy to marry King David.

David's gentle touch coaxed my hands away. He knelt before me, a precocious smile on his handsome face. "When you finally agree to be my wife, not even my sister will be able to command you." He'd stolen my breath twice already this morning.

Abba cleared his throat, and David winked before releasing me. "Yahweh's anointed king has waited almost a year for your answer, Nomy. I've saved my portion of the Philistine spoils to pay your dowry and already prepared the contract." Before I could object, he hurried into his chamber and returned with a scroll.

My mouth went dry. He wouldn't. He didn't. Not yet. Not until I agreed.

"You need only give your approval." Unrolling the *ketubah* before me, he pointed at the document awaiting David's signature, his own already given. "We could sign it today."

"Let's talk about it after the sheep shearing." I leapt to my feet. "Washing wool with the women might be enjoyable." Or at least preferable to Abba's pressure to marry.

"Marriage doesn't have to end in tragedy, Nomy." His features brightened with a mischievous grin. "Don't tarry too long, or I'll wed before you."

"Well!" Zerry scurried to her feet. "Let's get started on the day, hmm?"

Only Asahel seemed to share my surprise at Abba's comment. David gave Abba's shoulder a congratulatory squeeze and then nudged Zerry's startled son out the door to announce the shearing. After three days of seclusion, the men who had risked their lives for King David and spent a winter reunited with their families would happily endure a day of backbreaking work at his command.

Their wives, on the other hand . . .

Zerry and I filled shoulder bags with food in silence, preparing for our long day away from home. Finally, she slammed her bag on the table. "Go ahead and say it."

I chose my words carefully. "I thought you and Abba were content to live as friends."

She hurried to the corner, busying herself with straightening already perfectly stacked food baskets. "I don't know if you'll understand this, Nomy, but true yearning is more than physical. I've missed belonging to someone. The certainty that Ahitub loved me more than anyone else on earth gave me a confidence unlike ever before." She shrugged. "Or since."

"I can't imagine you with more confidence."

She whirled, tossing a piece of day-old bread at me to lighten the mood. Holding each other's gaze, we let the silence speak what words couldn't. Our friendship had grown more comfortable with quiet during the year in Keilah. I'd held her through the pain of Jesse's death and the inevitable guilt of an accusatory heart that told her she should have returned to Bethlehem for a final visit or to comfort her mother.

Though I'd offered reassurance, what had comforted her most was when she, David, and her sons' families gathered on the night they received word of his death to recount *happy* memories of Jesse ben Obed. It was a short evening. However, the best memories were the most recent ones, and there was shalom in knowing he would forever be honored whenever his youngest son's name was spoken as Israel's king, David *ben Jesse*.

"I'm afraid if you marry Abba," I said, finally breaking our silence, "he'll replace me as your best friend." Come to think of it, they'd already started spending more time together—as David and I had. When Abba and I returned from the forge, all five of us ate the evening meal together, but David and I often took evening walks afterward. Sometimes we practiced dagger throwing or checked the flocks.

"I'll always need you," Zerry was saying. "You accept me as I am when other women accuse me of being harsh. Too bossy. Too . . . everything annoying. You understand my good intentions." She sighed. "Not even Ima allowed me to speak unguarded truth. You and Toren seem to know my heart when my words fall short."

"I know you wouldn't intentionally hurt someone." Which led to my second concern. "Marriage means pain, Zerry, and I don't want either you or Abba to be hurt—especially by each other."

"Life is pain, Ahinoam." She reached for my hand. "I never imagined finding a better man than Ahitub, but Toren is a man of honor and integrity." She ducked her chin and grinned. "And he's younger. I won't wear him out as quickly."

"Oh, stop!" I waved off any such talk and grabbed the shoulder bags. "Let's go wash wool."

She giggled like a maiden and snagged my arm. "Tell me the truth, Nomy. What's the real reason you hesitate to marry David?"

Reason? My list was as long as the coastal highway. "I'm not fit to be any man's wife." I shook my head and looked away, knowing if I detailed my unworthiness, she'd try to reassure me.

"Is it because he's already married?"

My head jerked toward her, and I started to answer, but shame strangled me. David's previous marriage was a far more honorable reason than my deep-rooted insecurities. "Princess Michal is a barrier not easily breached." My throat closed around more words. Thinking of David loving another, looking at someone else the way he looked at me . . . I couldn't bear it.

"Nomy, listen to me." She led me to a cushion where we could sit opposite each other. I kept my head bowed, and she began, "I told you David would divorce Michal if he could, but the truth is, I believe they're already divorced in Yahweh's eyes."

I looked up, confused.

"Now that you've witnessed the pain inflicted on David by his blood family, you can appreciate how precious Prince Jonathan became to him as a brother-in-law. He is a true brother in every sense. And right after David killed Goliath, Saul favored David as if he was a true son. But when the evil spirit began tormenting Saul, his familial warmth for David fled, and Saul has considered my brother his enemy since the day he threw his spear at him—twice."

"Twice? Why would David allow Saul the chance to throw his spear a second time?"

"Because my brother is too loyal. He was utterly convinced Saul loved him like an abba and refused to believe another abba would reject him."

"As Jesse had."

Zerry nodded. "After Michal helped him escape, she could have invented a dozen different excuses for her actions. Instead, she chose to testify before her abba's council that David threatened her with murder, which made him a traitor. What Michal did that day wasn't only a wife's betrayal. She shattered David's already-broken heart and ripped away the rest of Saul's family who had loved David as their own. Only Jonathan remains true to him now."

"Oh, Zerry." My chest felt as if a donkey sat on it. "I see now."

"Do you? Do you see the miraculous healing Yahweh has done in my little brother's heart that allowed him to love you? Before all this betrayal, David had an enormous capacity to love and forgive. I've seen Yahweh beginning to restore that heart as my brother moves into his anointing as king. The Thirty have become his new family. Toren, too. But you, Ahinoam, have become the one with whom he shares his heart." Something shadowed her countenance. "But you must realize that as a king, he may have the ability—and necessity—to love more than one wife."

I squeezed my eyes shut. "Enough, Zerry. I'm happy for you and Abba, but who am I to marry a king? And I could never spend my life in a harem."

"All right, all right." She tugged at my hands, pulling me to my feet and toward the door. "Let's focus on what we'll say to Vered."

I gladly followed. Even facing Vered was preferable to more discussion about the man I adored but dared not marry. At least among our warriors' women, I was an anomaly to be avoided—like a three-horned goat—and could easily find seclusion to hum David's praise songs. When the watchman's shofar sounded the shevarim, all of Keilah gathered to hear the news at the central well.

The assembly chattered, seeming eager for fellowship and sunshine. David stood atop the well's surrounding wall and lifted his voice. "Today, my men will celebrate *Hag ha-Gez*, the first shearing, with our flock of sheep and goats! We'll share the firstfruits of our flocks with Keilah's faithful priests, and the profit from the trade of our wool will replenish the city's coffers for what Keilah has so generously shared with us."

Though he paused for applause, there was only awkward silence. "My trained shepherds will set up two sheepfolds at the southwest corner. Divide the sheep from the goats and each flock by color, light-colored and dark-colored. I'll choose the most skilled shearers and would welcome any of Keilah's shepherds or flock owners to join us. I ask only that you keep your flocks in separate sheepfolds and keep record of your personal profits—unless you'd like to include them with ours as an offering to the city." He chuckled, but the humor fell flat.

"How many days will this take?" one man shouted.

"I still have barley in the field," said another. "Why don't your men help with that?"

David scanned the surly crowd. "Your barley is already ruined by the sirocco. If we had worked together to harvest *everyone's* fields—as I suggested to the elders last week—no one would have lost crops. That's why I suggest *every* able-bodied man participate today, helping to gather, shear, and shepherd Keilah's flocks, while every available woman washes and prepares the wool for storage and trade. My sister Zeruiah has organized many such Hag ha-Gez Festivals in Bethlehem, and General Joab would willingly coordinate the private owners' recordkeeping."

Rumblings of discontent rippled through the gathering. Didn't they remember that without David's courage and care they'd all be dead or enslaved to the Philistines? Our warriors had trained Keilah's soldiers during the winter and made them a respectable force. But if David's army left Keilah's men to their grumbling, they could easily become Philistine slaves and their women conquests of the enemy.

"Enough complaints!" David shouted. "Sheep shearing is a celebration, friends. Those who bleat like sheep can go to your barley fields and lament your ruined crop. Those who wish to enjoy this day may demonstrate your shearing skills and join the celebration. My captains will winnow you accordingly. Joab, make it so!"

I'd seldom seen David angry, but his face matched his fiery hair.

Bedlam ensued while Keilah's men and women separated themselves from Joab and Zerry's leadership. David watched intently. His irritation simmered into sadness, and he jumped from the well onto Keilah's main street, as dejected as I'd ever seen him.

With a few long strides, I closed the distance between us. "A good shepherd once sang about using both rod and staff to comfort his sheep. You needed to use the rod just now, but you've comforted with your gentle staff all winter."

"Unfortunately, they don't recognize me as their shepherd." He continued scanning the crowd, speaking so low I could barely hear him. "You and Zerry aren't the only ones who noticed secretive whispers. When I went to check the city's grain silos a few weeks ago, I interrupted a clandestine meeting of elders. They immediately quieted, and when I questioned them, they gave obviously false answers."

Even now, the city elders huddled together, at least ten paces separating them from David's gathered men.

"Perhaps they'll always see us as outsiders," I said.

"We're from the same tribe!" David's outburst garnered everyone's attention and increased the tension.

I ached to entwine my fingers with his for comfort, but such intimacy wouldn't be appropriate, even in private. Instead, I leaned close and whispered, "Perhaps they're still frightened of Saul's repercussions."

David released a slow sigh. "Perhaps, but their rebuff feels like another betrayal—and it stings." He walked away, focused on Joab arguing with a group of Keilahites. David engaged the conflict with calm strength, and I realized anew the burden poured on his head with Samuel's anointing oil.

"Ahinoam! You're with my sons' wives." Zerry pointed toward the three sour-faced women already walking toward the north gate. She snagged my arm as I passed. "You were the only woman I knew Vered can't sway with her cutting comments about David. Listen carefully to Dalit's instructions about washing the wool. Gently submerge and swish. If you handle it too much, you'll ruin it."

Was it too late to help Abba sharpen the shears? I frantically searched for him, but he was nowhere to be found in the sea of faces. Tamping down my dread, I followed the unofficial queens of David's women. They continued toward the nearest wadi, whispering behind cupped hands. Though they probably weren't talking about me—since I wasn't important enough to be despised in their world—I still kept my distance.

I always kept my distance.

Abba and I spent most days at the forge. During last year's cleanup, we'd salvaged both bronze and iron from the Philistine camp. Not only did we collect daggers, swords, lances, spearheads, and axes, but also copper and tin household goods that we could use for trade or to smelt in Keilah's furnace to make more bronze weapons.

The nephews' wives settled beneath a tamarisk tree, content to gossip and wait for the first delivery of dirty wool. I longed to feel a whetstone and blade in my hands. However, I dutifully sat in the shade of the same tree, leaving a few paces between us, and turned my back to gaze across the plain.

The shephelah was beautiful, but I missed Jezreel's rugged hills. Our small farm had been snuggled in a valley with steep inclines on every side. The cities on Judah's level plain were exposed. Naked. Multiple towns and byways displayed their lush fields like a harlot with her lamp in a window. How long would David stay? Surely Saul's spies would venture south as spring war season progressed and discover our location.

I lay back, looking up at the budding branches of the tamarisk, and managed to block out the women's inane chatter for most of the morning. Puffy white clouds drifted across the sky as the sun rose higher and the air grew warmer without even the slightest breeze.

Dozing in and out of consciousness, I heard Vered boldly declare, "David ben Jesse is a fool to think he can demand Keilah's allegiance because he fought one battle on their behalf."

I bolted upright, but before I could turn to upbraid the old battle-axe, I glimpsed Joab approaching with a group of men who carried the first rolls of freshly sheared wool.

"You should have told Joab right away about the messenger," Dalit whispered. "What if it's true?"

I sat as still as a corpse, feeling color drain from my cheeks, barely able to breathe.

"True or not," Vered said, "Yahweh fights for our husbands despite David's poor leadership."

Vered's audacity brought me to my feet. "You ignorant, shameful woman."

She choked on a mocking laugh. "How dare you, a filthy Kenite, call me shameful?"

Joab stepped between us, glaring at me. "You will speak to my wife with respect."

"It's your wife who needs a lesson in respect, *General*. And loyalty." I stepped around him to face a subdued Vered. "Go ahead. Tell your husband what you heard the elders' wives saying about a messenger sent to Gibeah—and the reason you didn't inform him."

Joab whirled toward his wife. She was instantly defensive. "I only heard that an elder sent his personal messenger to Gibeah, but—"

"Vered!"

"It could have been for any reason, Joab."

"When?" He started to grasp her shoulders but clenched his fists midair and forced them back to his sides. "When *exactly* did you hear this conversation, Vered?"

Pale now, she said, "Six days ago."

"Six days?" he shouted, then immediately turned to his men with a guttural roar. They dropped the wool and slammed fists to their chests. "You two, muster the captains at David's house right away. I'll fetch Abiathar." Then he whirled on his wife again. "Vered, I love you more than my own life, but I swear by God Most High if you've brought Saul's wrath down on our heads . . ." He shook from head to toe but gently drew her close and kissed her forehead. "You and the other women must pack everything and immediately leave Keilah with the children."

"What? Why?" She buried her head against his chest. "I'm sorry, Joab. I thought Yahweh would take care of us. Why must we be afraid?"

He looked at me, his expression a war of emotion. "Ahinoam, you should return to David's house with the captains. He'll need you by his side when I tell him." Nudging Vered away, he held her gaze. "Yahweh *will* care for us, but good and loyal men have sacrificed everything to protect David. My job is to ensure as few of them as possible give up their lives to put David on the throne. Your secrecy bludgeoned me, love. But I forgive you because no mistake is too great for Yahweh to overcome." He kissed her and walked away. Vered covered a sob and fell to her knees.

I'd never seen the woman shed a tear.

Raya and Dalit hurried toward town, but I couldn't bear to leave Vered alone and grieving. Crossing the ten paces and an enormous relational chasm, I knelt beside her. "I know little about marriage, but Joab's love for you bridled his violence. His concern muzzled anger. Though neither you nor Joab are likable people, you love each other as no one else could. Take solace in the gift of your husband's love, and find strength to right the wrongs you've committed."

Her head jerked up. "How dare you—"

I dashed away, having no time for a debate. The interchange I'd witnessed between Joab and his wife had been revelatory. Truly, Joab ben Ahitub showed tenderness to only one person—the one-flesh covenant partner given to him by Yahweh. There was a softness that could only be described as otherworldly between those two impossibly hard people.

And during our year in Keilah, David ben Jesse had shared the deepest parts of his heart with only me. No matter how frustrated he was after meetings with the elders, he said only I had the words that encouraged. When he experienced a milestone in training with the men of Keilah, he shared the good news with me first.

But the realization that struck me like a boulder in the chest was that David's surly nephew, who had disliked me from the moment we'd met, seemed to know David would need me at his side when he heard of Keilah's betrayal. I was confident his captains, too, would allow my presence in their midst. After a year of teaching them rudimentary sharpening skills, they valued my opinions, if not my heart.

My feet carried me to the city almost as quickly as my thoughts moved toward our future. *Yahweh, could I truly be the one You've chosen as David's wife?*

FOURTEEN

DAVID

When David learned that Saul was plotting against him, he said to Abiathar the priest, "Bring the ephod."

1 Samuel 23:9

The shearers had worked in the shade of Keilah's southwest wall for most of the morning. My forearms ached as I rolled my twentieth ram this way then that, quickly and cautiously snipping wool around his curled horns. The dirty, matted wool fell to the ground in a single slab, exposing the pure-white softness beneath. With a final cut, I released the ram. Both he and I bleated joyful triumph. The animal leapt in the air, and I lifted my fist. "That's twenty, Abishai!"

"Someone better check King David's tally." Abishai's head remained bent over his ewe. "We all know how he inflates his count."

"Not true!" I shouted over the heckling.

Abishai rolled the wide-eyed ewe onto her back like a child's toy and gave a final snip. "Go, you beauty." She skittered away, and Abishai swung his long black braid over his shoulder, stretching his massive frame to the sky.

"Aww, little Abishai is getting tired." My single taunt earned my nephew's grin and more good-natured goading. We each grabbed another sheep, but I caught a glimpse of Ahinoam running toward me and shoved my animal at a shepherd.

All levity gone, I started toward her. "What is it?"

Her expression said something was terribly wrong. "Joab is gathering the captains at our house."

"Why—"

"Not here." She glanced at the shearers, my men as well as a few from Keilah who had joined us. "Abishai and Asahel should come, too," she whispered.

I placed my fingers against my lips and blew the three-toned whistle, calling my childhood friends, then guided Ahinoam through the busy shearers, piles of wool, and crowded sheep pens. When we reached home, Joab waited with my captains, along with Abiathar and Gad. Zerry and Toren had also come, my childhood whistle now like the warning t'ruah to them both.

When Joab moved aside, allowing Ahinoam to stand beside me, foreboding snaked up my spine. He'd never shown her such kindness. "What's happened?" I asked my general.

Joab cleared his throat, looked at Ahinoam, then back at me. "My king," he said, "six days ago, one of Keilah's elders sent a messenger to Gibeah."

"Six days?" I exploded. "Why didn't we know this six days ago?"

Joab stared at his sandals. "I just received the report and have ordered that the women and children prepare to leave Keilah immediately."

I studied my eldest nephew. He hadn't fully answered my questions. And why evacuate the families until we knew Saul's position? "Have our scouts verified Saul's approach?"

"Not yet, but if the messenger was sent six days ago, Saul could have already started mustering Israel's troops."

"The families stay," I said. "We close the city gates and use the walls to protect us."

"The walls imprison us!" Joab's head jerked up with the shout. When I studied him in silence, his features softened to pleading. "David, please. I can't be responsible for the deaths of our army and their families."

My general never contemplated defeat. "What are you not telling me, Joab?"

Ahinoam stepped between us and gently touched my arm. "He's protecting his wife," she whispered, "as any husband would do."

"I don't need you to defend me," Joab grumbled at her.

"Evidently you do," I said. "Or will you tell me what Vered has done?"

Joab clenched his jaw and straightened his shoulders. "She heard gossip six days ago about the messenger. She only told me moments ago because Ahinoam overheard her and my brothers' wives talking."

I turned to Ahinoam. "What else did they say?"

"Only the reason she didn't tell Joab."

"Which was . . ."

"Vered was so confident that Yahweh would fight the battle for us, she didn't bother to mention the elder's betrayal to Joab." Had my beloved, with a single statement, defended hateful Vered and challenged our lagging faith? I was speechless and so, it seemed, was everyone in our crowded main room.

"My lord!" came a voice from the back. "My lord, King David!" I recognized Old Jeremiah's gray head parting the sea of muscle and sweat. He stumbled forward, steadying himself with a hand on my shoulder. "Attai ran through the night to bring us news. Saul has called up his army from every tribe in Israel and is ready to march from Gibeah."

Amasai took a knee. "We await your command, King David." Every warrior knelt and saluted, fist over heart.

The sudden silence felt as if a sirocco wind had swept into the room and taken my breath with it. I turned to Gad the Seer, silently pleading for divine direction.

He also fell to his knees, but weeping. "David, my king, a prophet can only speak when God gives him words, and He gave no inkling that Saul was coming." He looked up. "Even now, I hear no directive or guidance."

"It's all right, my friend." I braced his shoulders and helped him stand. "You are as faithful in silence as you have been in building my men's faith through teaching the Law."

Turning to Abiathar, I said, "Yahweh has given us both prophet and priest to know His will. We'll hear God's direction through the ephod." Without further prompting, he withdrew the Urim and Thummim while I asked the Lord, "Will Saul pursue us here in Keilah?"

Abiathar cast the lots into the small space between our feet. The white Thummim landed propped up against Joab's big toe. I met my nephew's eyes and sensed an unspoken agony on his pinched brow.

"Joab will assign Gadite scouts by region to escort the families back to their hometowns," I said. "We stay in the city with the Keilahite men you've trained and within their walls. When the Philistines hear of Saul's advance this far south, they'll attack his flank. God could use the enemy of our enemy to win the battle for us."

"David, please listen to me." Joab was pleading again? "If the elders betrayed us while living in safety, imagine what the Keilahite citizens will do to us inside their walls when Saul besieges their city."

I didn't want to imagine, and I hoped for the best in Judah's people. We'd bled for them, and they'd shared their winter provisions with us. But too many lives were at stake to depend on hopes or imagination. I needed Yahweh's clear direction.

Again, I looked to Abiathar and asked Yahweh to answer through the stones. "Will the people of Keilah surrender me and my men to Saul?"

He'd already gathered them into his hand and immediately tossed them onto the packed-dirt floor. Again, the white Thummim confirmed my deepest fears.

With a sigh, I nodded at Joab and addressed our captains. "Old Jeremiah will remain with our troops to scout passes as we move south into the wilderness."

"My lord?" Gad remained at my side, visibly shaken. "I've heard from the Lord."

"About our journey to the wilderness?" I asked. "Where should we go?" The prophet's fuller descriptions would be helpful since I could only inquire yes-or-no directives with the ephod.

"I won't be going with you, my friend." Gad lowered his eyes. "The Lord has told me to remain in Keilah and speak Yahweh's judgment *and* mercy on His people."

"No!" Abiathar said. "You can't stay. I saw the consequences in Nob when Saul only suspected my family had helped David. What do you think he'll do in his rage when he arrives in Keilah and discovers they not only helped us but then allowed us to escape?" He hugged the prophet like a lifeline. "I can't lose anyone else to the king's madness."

Gad didn't resist the younger man's embrace or dismiss his fear. He held Abiathar just as tightly and looked over his shoulder at me. "A great dread will fall on Keilah's elders and citizens when you and your men leave their city, David. They'll realize the great sin of choosing allegiance to Saul—the king who ignored their need—rather than being loyal to Yahweh's anointed one and their brother Judean. In their fear at King Saul's impending approach, Keilah's elders and citizens will finally open their hearts to Yahweh and set aside the Philistine gods they've adopted as their own."

"They'll betray King David and get away with it?" Abishai shouted, his fury stirring the ire of my Mighty Men.

I lifted both fists in the air, quieting them so Gad could continue his prophecy. "The people of Keilah will live with the consequences of their sin and learn obedience through suffering—as do we all." His sad smile proved he found no pleasure in prophesying Yahweh's judgment, and then his piercing black eyes locked on me. "'David ben Jesse, you will leave Keilah with your troops and every metal weapon and household tool from the Philistine victory that I, the LORD, have given you. Take also your livestock; your goats and donkeys and your freshly shorn sheep into the wilderness where I will lead you. I will be your Shade by day and your Fire by night, and you will know that I AM the LORD your God who rescues you.'"

Abiathar and my household knelt before God's prophet. Gad took the ram's horn from his belt, removed the leather covering from its wide opening, and emptied the scented oil over my head. I lifted my voice in song and my hands in praise as tears mingled with the sweet aroma. Ahinoam's voice joined Zerry's in perfect harmony, and Toren's bass tones resonated in my chest like Dodo's shepherd drum. Though Samuel's anointing had been overwhelmingly powerful, this moment was more lavish with Yahweh's love because of those sharing it with me.

I stood, wiped the oil from my eyes, and reached for Ahinoam's hand. "You know I'd marry you today if I could, but for now I'm only asking that you remain at my side as we enter the unknown wilderness ahead."

She squeezed my hand and nodded. "I'll never leave you, King David."

Every sinew in my body wanted to take her in my arms and never let her go. Instead, I brushed a stray hair off her forehead and let a single finger trail down her cheek. She shivered under my touch. "A wedding will come later, my love, when we're safe again."

"Let's focus on surviving," she said. It was the first time she didn't flinch or turn away. "Then we'll talk about Yahweh's plan for our marriage."

Her words felt almost as holy as the anointing oil. Though Keilah's betrayal stung and Saul's imminent attack loomed large, Yahweh's presence had never been more real.

Wilderness of Ziph

Dozing on my turn at watch, a clanking rock outside our cave brought me to my feet. Ahinoam and Asahel flanked me at the shadowy opening, daggers in hand, and Toren loomed behind his daughter. Zerry stood three paces away with Asahel's spear in her hand. How long since we'd slept deeply enough to ignore the sound of a falling pebble?

"Anyone?" Asahel hissed.

I scanned the steep, narrow trail outside our cave, but the amethyst-colored eastern sky shrouded the dawn and clouds obscured the moon. I answered my nephew with the military signals every Israelite soldier knew, including Ahinoam and Zerry after seven months of hiding. After pointing to my eyes and shaking my head, I cupped an open hand around my ear: *I can't see, so we listen.* Four eager nods affirmed understanding. My wilderness family leaned forward as one. We'd remain in our shelter with only its narrow path to defend.

I listened so hard, the silence pulsated inside me. *How long, Lord? How long must we live in constant fear, enduring the disdain of Judah's towns and leaders?* Though I'd shared Gad's prophecy with our men before we left Keilah, Joab still had wanted to turn our archers on those who celebrated our departure from the wall. I'd forbidden it, trusting Yahweh's word through Gad that the hearts of Keilah's people would soon turn to regret and repentance. When our scouts brought word that Saul's troops left Keilah undisturbed, they also mentioned a pile of idols burning under a tamarisk tree north of the city. *Thank You, Yahweh.*

The fulfillment of Gad's prophecy had been our only good news in months. When Saul averted his troops from Keilah, he led them south instead, relentlessly pursuing us through Judah's wilderness. Thanks to Yahweh's favor, our Gadites' scouting, and our desert warriors' foraging, we'd remained a day ahead of any fighting. Surprisingly, the worst part of our seven months of hiding hadn't been the rationed water, the constant hunger, or the relentless fear. The crushing came when every Judean village refused to offer so much as water from their well. Every rejection sent me into a deeper wilderness of my own.

This morning's eastern sky became a dusky lavender, and still there was no sign of an intruder. We sheathed our daggers, and Zerry propped her son's spear against the cave wall.

"Can I start a fire?" she asked. "Or should we keep moving?"

I was already rolling my sleeping mat. "The Gadites reported Saul's men still searching Ziphite territory."

Asahel remained at the entrance while Toren and Ahinoam began packing their bags. Zerry packed her bag and Asahel's. Each of us carried a sleeping mat, light blanket, waterskin, bow, and quiver. I carried an additional item—my lyre. It had been more nourishing than water, soaking deeper than any discomfit to heal the inner turmoil of leading the now six hundred men in my care.

As we left the cave, I said to Asahel, "Signal the others that we're on the move."

He mimicked a jackdaw's shrill whistle. Then another. And a third. Our men had learned to copy their squawking; however, the annoying jackdaws seldom cawed three times in succession. So, when another three whistles answered across the canyon, we knew our men had heard the slightly altered call. More signals spread as my faithful warriors awakened to a new day of flight. They were scattered across the wilderness but traveled like a unit using altered nature sounds, which we changed regularly so Saul's scouts couldn't predict or learn our system.

I led the downward climb. Ahinoam followed, then Toren and Zerry. Single file. Asahel provided rear guard. All three of my nephews had become like overprotective abbas when Toren's intention to marry my sister became widely known. If Toren offered his hand to steady Zerry, Asahel often nudged him aside to intervene. Joab plied Toren with questions at every opportunity, and Abishai looked at the Kenite as if he might eat him for a meal.

They needn't have worried. Toren and I had been too exhausted by Saul's pursuit to speak more about marriage since we'd left Keilah. However, surviving the wilderness as a household—Asahel, Toren, Zerry, Ahinoam, and me—had knit our hearts together with a familial love that safety couldn't have cultivated. Toren had become more precious than any abba I'd known, and though Ahinoam still hadn't agreed to marry me, I knew somehow Yahweh would reconcile the matter in her heart.

A familiar clucking sound halted my steps, and Old Jeremiah emerged from the brush barely two paces ahead. I let out a good-natured huff. "You old viper. It was you outside the cave earlier, wasn't it? I could have been dead twenty paces ago."

His grin confirmed it. "To your credit, my lord, you were wise enough not to signal your troops before abandoning shelter."

He and the Gadites had been invaluable trainers. "I'm glad you're on my side. Tell me what you've discovered, my friend."

"Saul and his troops have turned back, my lord."

"Turned back? How many troops has he left to scout near Ziph?"

"We've detected none, my lord. Saul fears winter rains and flooding wadis." Old J's pink gums glistened in dawn's light. "The despot marched back to Gibeah and told his whole army to return to their homes. He'll stay in Gibeah till spring."

"You're sure it's over?" Desperation tinged Ahinoam's tone.

"At least for the winter." His rheumy eyes held hers. "We're safe for a while, mistress."

Safe. I pulled her into my arms. "Be my wife," I said loudly enough for our family to hear.

"David." She pressed against my chest, glancing over her shoulder, clearly embarrassed by their whoops of encouragement. When she returned her gaze to me, I saw only trepidation. "You know this decision is more complex than a wedding contract." The celebration behind her stopped, but Ahinoam continued, "I'm a Kenite—"

"I don't care. I love you."

"But the King of Israel must consider more than his heart alone." She spoke with perfect calm, which was more disarming than her previous excuses.

"You've considered this carefully," I said, observing the fact, not asking a question.

The hint of a smile on her perfect lips made my heart flip. "What else did I have to think about during my night watch?"

"But your answer isn't no." I made another observation. "Your heart has softened since my initial proposal."

A full smile bloomed on her sun-kissed face. "My answer is not no."

"Well, I wish you would hurry and say yes." Toren huffed. "Joab has made it clear he won't allow his ima to marry me until my daughter is wed." He produced the tattered wedding scroll from his shoulder bag and waved it like a banner at Ahinoam and me. "I've waived the betrothal period, so all we need are two signatures."

I offered my hand to the man I would someday call Abba. "You will be the first to know when that day comes, my friend." We locked wrists in pledge, and the mischief in his eyes assured me he would not wait long after my marriage to wed Zerry.

Old J had watched our family business with that toothless grin. He'd not only become our personal scout but also the hub of all camp gossip. No doubt he'd alert our whole army that *two* weddings were in our future.

I cocked my head and lifted a brow. "Have you scouted out a place where the whole army can spend the winter?"

"I had thought the forested area of Horesh would do until I found out we may need two private wedding chambers."

"Stop that!" Ahinoam tried to suppress a giggle, but Old J's cackle lightened the mood for us all.

"I suppose Horesh will still be the best spot," he said. "It's near the city of Ziph, has plenty of springs, a wadi protected by high cliffs, and lush green shoots to sustain our flocks."

Thank You, Yahweh, for these scouts who have been Your eyes, ears, hands, and feet in this test of wits with Saul. I clapped the old man's shoulder. "Lead the way, my friend, and Asahel will alert the men with today's sound." Asahel whistled a slightly amended morning lark's song while I closed my eyes and inhaled the first whiff of freedom, letting relief and joy fill me from head to toe.

"David?" Asahel was beside me, his tone implying he'd asked a question and was waiting for my answer. Thankfully, he was more patient than his brothers. "I said you and Ahinoam can follow at the rear if you'd like." He bounced his eyebrows.

I swatted his head and laughed. "Yes, Asahel. Thank you. You and Old J lead us." The old Gadite started downhill, as sure-footed as an ibex, with Asahel following. I captured Ahinoam's waist and leaned back against the mountain while Toren and Zerry passed. "My bride and I must begin the conversation about our wedding."

"David!" Ahinoam's whole weight fell against me, but with quick reflexes she got to her feet. Eyes averted while she straightened her short robe, I examined the lovely crimson color crawling up her neck and cheeks. When she finally looked up, concern pinched her brows together, forming a deep crease between them. "Please. I have questions for you alone, and I suspect you won't want anyone else to hear some of my questions—or my answers to yours."

"How did you get so wise?" I offered my hand, and she took it, snuggling close to walk beside me on the narrow path.

So, instead of the intimate details of the life I envisioned with Ahinoam, the conversation en route to Horesh included our wilderness family who talked freely about what life would be like when we no longer feared for our next breath. The forested location would provide shelter and wood. We'd have four months to rebuild flocks, refurbish weapons, and regain our strength.

Though our supplies were low, our flocks had dwindled, and a nomadic existence meant no planting or reaping of our own lands, we would use the skills Yahweh gave us to protect the Judean towns Saul ignored during winter. I'd divide my army into three contingents. One division would protect wealthy Judean landowners from foreign raiders in exchange for food to sustain the second group, who would stand watch over our weapons and supplies in Horesh. The third group could return home to visit their families, and each contingent would rotate at the end of a prescribed time. We'd continue rotations until Saul resumed his pursuit of us in the spring. *Yahweh, thank You for stirring a fear in Saul of the winter floods.*

As if in answer to my prayer, the heavens opened and drenched us in rain for the rest of our journey. Old J skirted the edges of overflowing wadis, and we all focused on our footing, avoiding the hill country's dangerous flash floods. I knew we had reached Horesh when I looked up and found my entire army splashing each other like little boys. Soaked to the skin, they released months of fear and angst in an afternoon of joyous laughter, safe in the assurance that Yahweh had chased Saul to Gibeah with leaky skies. A cascading waterfall plummeted into a large pool below. Lush vegetation surrounded the pool and lined both sides of a river flowing from it, proving this long and narrow valley was a year-round oasis safe from flooding. High cliffs flanked both sides with protection as far as the eye could see. It was, as Old J had said, a perfect winter home for my faithful soldiers.

Asahel had already joined the other soldiers at play, so Toren offered his hand to steady Zerry as she descended the slippery slope toward the river.

When I extended my hand to Ahinoam, she giggled and slapped away the chivalry. "I'll race you." She sprinted to the stream and won by a heartbeat.

Skidding to our knees at the water's edge, we slaked our thirst—safety tasting better than Israel's finest wine.

"All right, you two!" My sister snared our attention, then motioned us to join her a few paces away. Toren stood at her side and fell in step behind Ahinoam and me as Zerry led us toward a narrow fork of the stream. She splashed into ankle-deep water and squeezed through a rock-walled tunnel where we emerged into a second clearing. "This is the perfect place."

I turned in a full circle, awed by the peaceful paradise. "It reminds me of the pastures where I tended Abba's flocks."

"Perfect for what?" Ahinoam asked.

"For you to discuss your wedding," Zerry said. "Your abba and I will stand watch so you'll have the privacy you want."

"Zerry! You know it's not that simple."

"It *is* simple, Nomy." Toren placed his arm around Zerry's waist. "But it's not *easy* for you to accept. Yahweh has confirmed His will for you to marry David. Simple. However, Zerry says a woman's heart doesn't easily obey even when her head knows something is true."

Ahinoam planted her hands on her hips. "Since when do you listen to everything Zerry says?"

"Since I realized she was Yahweh's gift to me." His sober reply anointed the moment. "Either Zerry or I will accompany you and David to this clearing every day so you two can talk privately about what you need to become husband and wife."

Ahinoam swallowed audibly, making the silence that followed even more awkward.

"So talk!" Zerry waved us away.

Ahinoam gave a good-natured sigh. When she looked at me, mischief played on her lips, and she pointed to the quiet stream. "Ready for another race?"

"I'll be waiting for you at the shoreline."

"Oh!" She darted toward the stream, and I chased her as if my life depended on it—because it did. *I will capture your heart, Ahinoam bat Toren, no matter how hard you run.*

FIFTEEN

AHINOAM

*While David was at Horesh in the Desert of Ziph, he learned that Saul
had come out to take his life. And Saul's son Jonathan went to David
at Horesh and helped him find strength in God.*

1 Samuel 23:15–16

Aviv (March) 1015 BC

The shevarim sounded, and I raced with others from camp to the
top of Hakilah Hill to greet the contingent returning from their
weeklong assignment. I counted the bodies silhouetted on the horizon. Fifteen? Seventeen had gone to serve as mercenary guards
for a wealthy landowner in Maon.

As the contingent drew nearer, I saw them more clearly, and my
knees weakened when I realized David and Asahel weren't among
them. My deepest fear rose first: I'd waited too long to become
David's wife. *Yahweh, have You punished me for making him wait and
taken David from me before I could become his wife?* I had allowed my
heart to love Israel's next king and almost agreed to our wedding on
the night before he'd left. Almost.

Zerry stood at my side, breathless from running. "Where are
David and Asahel?"

I ignored her and ran toward the returning soldiers to ask those who might know. Amasai lifted both hands, urging calm, and offered the answer before I reached him. "David and Asahel stayed behind to determine if we can move farther south into the desert. They're scouting for springs."

"How long will they be gone?" I asked.

The big Kohathite halted barely a pace in front of me, his understanding smile providing some comfort. "He didn't say, but I'm sure he won't stay away from you long."

He and the other soldiers walked past me, and I turned to find Zerry with her hands fisted at her hips. "I don't like waiting while our men are away any more than you do, but David and Asahel are doing important scouting. They'll likely build goodwill with our Judean neighbors on their way back to camp."

"What goodwill?" I snapped. "Did you see the pittance our men are paid for protecting wealthy landowners?"

"Cultivating Judean favor will be more valuable than gold when David sits on Israel's throne."

I roared my frustration and walked away, knowing she was right but refusing to relinquish my anger. Why wouldn't David allow me to go with him on the protective detail? Hadn't I proved my skills with a dagger?

An idea rattled in my head and propelled my feet into a run. Hadn't Abba once said I was the second-best tracker in Israel—that only Prince Jonathan was better? Perhaps if I found David and Asahel in the Jeshimon, south of Maon, David would take me with him on the next assignment, and I wouldn't have to wait and worry like Zerry foretold. Besides, I needed to see David and tell him I would marry him—today, tomorrow, or any day he chose.

When I reached the tent Zerry and I shared near the river, I grabbed my shoulder bag and filled it with only quick-travel items: a mat, a wooden cup, and a few pieces of dried fish and stale bread.

"Where do you think you're going?" Joab asked from outside the open flap.

Dare I confess? He was David's general, after all. "I intend to track David and Asahel to prove my skill so I can be included in the mercenary assignments."

"I wouldn't send you to track them if you were the only person left in my army."

Angry tears threatened, but crying would only prove me a silly woman. "My tracking skills are second only to Prince Jonathan," I said. "Ask Abba. He'll confirm."

"And Toren will agree with me that warfare tracking isn't merely noticing footprints or broken branches or displaced dust. It also requires awareness of an enemy trained to evade your tracking. You must have eyes in the back of your head—which you don't have." He turned to walk away, mumbling.

Furious, I darted from the tent and shouted, "If you can mumble angry words, you should be brave enough to say them aloud."

Joab halted and turned to me, wearing a smile. "I said David would kill me if I ever sent you tracking for this army. Do you know why?" Without giving me a chance to answer, he said, "Because tracking means you venturing out alone. It's dangerous—especially now, at the beginning of war season when Saul's scouts will be all over this wilderness. Though you may be careless with your life, I won't be."

"Because you're afraid." I aimed for his heart as if wielding a dagger.

He merely scoffed. "No, Ahinoam. Because you're as precious to David as Vered is to me, and I honor the love that binds you to Israel's next king." He lifted one brow. "Did I speak clearly enough for you?"

My answering "yes" erupted on a sob.

Joab heaved a sigh and wrapped his arms around me. "Don't cry." He awkwardly patted my shoulder. "I hate it when women cry."

"Good." I wiped my eyes and shoved him away with a rueful grin. "I'll cry more often just to vex you."

"You vex me plenty." With a hint of a smile, he added, "But you're exactly what King David needs." He inclined his head and strode away.

"Well, now I can't even disobey him," I mumbled.

"If you can mumble angry words," Joab shouted, though he continued walking and waved his hand like a turning wheel, "then you should be brave enough to blah, blah, blah."

I needed to stay busy, or I'd go mad with worry. Reluctantly, I wandered over to the metalworking area Abba and I had built with our ten apprentices. I'd intended to stay away since Abba planned to destroy everything today. He'd said if our next seven months were anything like last war-season's flight, we'd never be able to carry disassembled pieces, and we dare not abandon a working forge in the wilderness for our enemies to use against us.

When I arrived, the mood was somber. Abba and our apprentices were reminiscing about their journey to meet Abba's Edomite friend at the copper mines south of the Dead Sea. They'd returned with enough copper, tin, and smelting supplies to build our lovely forge—a skill known only to the Kenites and Philistines. At first, training our novice pupils had been grueling for both students and teachers. I taught them to judge the temperature of a fire by its color, and Abba taught them to shape and sharpen the blades. Our slag heaps grew with ruined attempts, so we melted the errors and tried again. And again. And again.

Finished with words, Abba slapped his knees and stood with a sigh. He drew the heavy iron sword he'd taken from the Philistines' dead general and walked toward the first of four perfect sandstone forms.

"Wait!" I cried. "Couldn't we carry just one with us?"

"Our lives are more important than stones!" He swung his sword and began smashing the sandstone forms, smelting bowls, and thick walls of the furnace. He roared with every swing. Our dedicated trainees and I watched in silence. When Abba's grief was spent, he turned to our apprentices and divided the irreplaceable tools of our trade among us. Each trainee carried a single rasp, while Abba and I were responsible for the two iron tongs. The naked patch of burnt earth where our forge and workshop once stood made our flight into the wilderness feel even more imminent.

With dusk's descent, my melancholy returned, and with it the need to escape our raucous camp. I couldn't wait in the river valley. I needed to see his approach, so I ran to Hakilah Hill. *Yahweh, please bring David home tonight.*

Perched under a tamarisk tree, I occasionally glimpsed one of our watchmen peeking over the ridge opposite me. No doubt Joab had ordered them to guard me. *Thank You, Yahweh, for the security of this family You've given.* Not only David's blood relatives but the whole army of men who had accepted me as a sister among them. I scanned the full view of our beloved wilderness home. Though the terrain of Horesh was harsher than Hereth, and the sandstone cliffs were steeper, the wadis ran deeper with mountain-fresh water.

We'd lacked provisions to celebrate this year's Passover, but Horesh had become even more meaningful than our first winter shelter in the Forest of Hereth. David had openly praised his Abba Jesse's lavish provisions for our first winter's Passover and thanked Yahweh for the healing of their relationship. Even Zerry had wept with joyful tears at the memory. David gathered our whole camp to listen as Abiathar recited the Law.

However, none of the sweet memories shielded me from the rising fear. What if David and Asahel didn't return before we needed to flee from Saul? I scanned the barren wilderness, its patches of green shrubs and tamarisk trees. Through rising heat waves, I saw two blurred silhouettes like specters in the distance. I bolted to my feet and ran down the hill toward two weary warriors moments before the shevarim blew its welcome blasts.

"They're home!" I shouted as others rushed toward the road between two hills.

David broke into a run when he saw me. From three paces away, I launched into his open arms and wrapped his neck with a strangling embrace. "Don't ever send your men home without you again," I cried. "I thought you were . . ." I tightened my grip on him.

David whirled me around to the sound of our men's howling approval. David laughed with them—until he realized I was sobbing. "Shh, my love. I'm here." He looked up and said, "Zerry!" He jerked his head in silent command.

"Leave them to their reunion!" she shouted and began shooing away the hecklers.

David buried his face in the bend of my neck. "Forgive me," he whispered. "Yahweh is my protector." The chaos faded, leaving us alone on the road. "I'll never leave you."

His warm breath brushed my neck, making me dizzy. I pressed my head against his chest and heard his heart racing as fast as mine. In a haze of yearning, I opened my eyes, barely able to draw breath. Just as I was about to demand he immediately make me his wife, I glimpsed something on the road—no, someone.

A soldier. Israelite. Running toward us.

"David!" I pushed him away and, with one fluid motion, reached for my dagger and threw.

He tipped my arm just in time as recognition flashed across his face. "Nooo! It's Jonathan! Prince. Jonathan."

"What?" I glanced around him.

David turned to look at the royal intruder. The soldier had halted thirty paces away, wide-eyed but unharmed. David pressed his lips against my temple and whispered, "Please don't kill my best friend before I can introduce you to him." He released my arms with a chuckle, but I wanted to run and hide.

I almost killed the crown prince! "I saw his Israelite armor and thought he was a spy."

Prince Jonathan approached with a mischievous smile. "This must be the Kenite woman our scouts have reported."

David tucked me behind him. "Why would scouts concern themselves with a woman?"

"Because you were sure enough of her accuracy to tip her elbow." Jonathan peeked around David to see me. "Might I ask your name?"

He seemed harmless, so I stepped to David's side. "I am Ahinoam bat Toren, my prince."

"Well, Ahinoam bat Toren, I'm not sure which I admire more—your skill with a dagger or your ability to mend my brother's broken heart."

Before I could stutter a response, David stepped between us again. "Did you come alone?" His tone held a thousand more questions. *Have you betrayed me? Why have you come? How long before Saul's army attacks?*

"I'm alone, brother."

David's shoulders relaxed.

Remaining behind him, I stepped aside just enough to glimpse the crown prince. Battle scars and sadness marred Jonathan's features. He was nearly thirty harvests older than David but as powerfully built as any of our Mighty Men and quite handsome. Gray hair with black strands mingled like tares in a wheat field, and he wore the bronze band of Israel's crown prince. Most pleasing of all was his tenderness when he looked at David.

"I've come to reassure you, brother. Our God is with you. Never be afraid. Both Yahweh and Samuel have abandoned Abba."

"I'm sorry, Jonathan. I never intended—"

"*Yahweh* intended you to reign over Israel, and I will be your second. Though I can't openly help you now, our covenant endures forever. I will *never* lift my hand against you or your descendants."

"Nor I against yours." David pulled him into a ferocious embrace.

I felt like an intruder but was too awed to walk away. Against all logic and despite all obstacles, Yahweh had established a profound love and loyalty between Israel's crown prince and the shepherd who would usurp his throne.

Towering over David's shoulder, Jonathan saw me staring and nudged him away. "I've also come to warn you, but—" He nodded my direction. "Should Ahinoam leave us?"

David wrapped his arm around my shoulders, and I stood a little taller. "I tell Ahinoam everything. Yahweh has said she'll someday be my wife."

Jonathan pursed his lips. "Perhaps a wedding will make my news about Michal easier to accept."

David's dream. "Is your sister in danger?" I asked.

Jonathan's brow rose. "Why would you care about Michal?"

"I had a dream." David answered for me. "In it, Michal walked into a rushing wadi. Ahinoam called out for me to save her, but I was too far away."

"It seems Yahweh has prepared you." Jonathan sighed. "Abba nullified your marriage to Michal and gave her to Paltiel."

"Paltiel of Gallim?" David sounded panicked. "How could he give her to his insane bodyguard?"

"Abba hopes you'll try to rescue her, so he can trap you in Benjamite territory."

"I won't let him trap me, but someone must save her from that animal!"

Jonathan stared at him for two long heartbeats. "Is Yahweh capable of protecting you and not Michal?" When David refused to answer, Jonathan turned to me. "The next king of Israel is in need of a wife, Ahinoam, and it appears Yahweh has chosen you."

"How can you be so flippant about Michal's safety?" David ignored Jonathan's diversion and continued with his questions. "Did Michal agree to marry Paltiel, or did Saul force her? Does she realize what a dangerous man he is?"

Jonathan's perceptive gaze remained on me, increasing my humiliation. David's visceral reaction had revealed the awkward truth. I'd been a fool to believe *King* David hadn't loved his first wife—because he obviously still did. Though I wanted to run, my legs shook so violently they barely held me upright.

The prince calmly turned to David. "You're about to ruin your future because of bitterness over your past. I know you feel helpless. Every day, I feel exactly what you're feeling now. My abba stalks you, my covenant brother, and I must rely on Yahweh to protect my life and my family's lives from his unpredictable moods. But it's only in the helplessness that God's power and sovereignty proves bigger than my fear. Bigger than my doubts and worst imaginings."

David's tension drained as the words hit their mark. His eyes slid shut, and he released a deep sigh. "I know you're right. Forgive me, brother."

The prince turned David's shoulders so he could face me. "It's your bride you should ask for forgiveness, and you must reassure her that your outburst was only the reaction of a protective warrior, not the ranting of a scorned husband."

David's eyes widened. "What? No! Ahinoam, I wasn't . . . I don't—"

"Stop," I croaked, then swallowed back the raging emotions. "Warrior or husband, it's obvious you still care deeply about your wife."

"She's no longer my wife, and I'd want to rescue *any* woman from Paltiel. He's never married because no Benjamite would give his daughter to such a man."

"Except my abba," Jonathan added, "because Saul ben Kish would do anything to lure David and his men to Gibeah."

His words tore through my jealousy and penetrated my heart. "You believe Michal is truly in danger, my prince?"

"I will do all I can to protect my sister from the Leviathan known as Paltiel." The foreboding in his tone was shocking. "Life in a king's household requires a level of faith and patience few ever consider, let alone fully comprehend, Ahinoam. You're seeing the underbelly of royal blessing, the worst application of my abba's keen mind."

I met David's eyes and whispered, "You must save her."

"What?"

"Save her, David."

"That's exactly what you said in my dream." He cradled my hand between his. "But just as Michal chose to enter the dream's roaring wadi, she also chose to betray me and trust her abba. I'm unable to save her, bound by the golden chains of Yahweh's anointing and Jonathan's warning that Saul is luring me to Gibeah. Make no mistake, Ahinoam. Today, the dream is fulfilled. I love *you*, not Michal, and I want *you* to become my wife."

I could barely breathe. It was true, everything he'd said. Yahweh had chosen me.

"Yes, David. I will marry you."

A soft breath escaped his lips, and he looked into my eyes with the same awe that captivated me. "Today?"

I nodded.

"Yahweh has chosen a brave and loyal woman to be your wife." Prince Jonathan's voice intruded upon the moment. "Any woman brave enough to hurl a dagger at an Israelite soldier is worthy of my brother."

"Truly, my prince, I didn't know it was you."

"Don't be sorry, dear Ahinoam. I'm proud of you for protecting him." He soothed my guilt with a light kiss on each cheek, but his smile dimmed when he stepped back. "May I give you some advice after watching another Ahinoam try to protect her royal husband?"

I'd forgotten the queen and I shared the same name. "I would be honored to receive your advice."

"My ima was a butcher's daughter who married the tall, shy son of Kish—a donkey farmer. I've watched my parents change from the common yet faithful people they once were to royal, faithless people, and I don't want the same future for you or my dear brother."

I swallowed hard, suddenly terrified of what faults this wise and loyal friend of David's might have already seen in me. "I'm only a Kenite, my prince. David deserves better. I know."

"Lovely Ahinoam, you are Yahweh's choice for David. Let no man—or woman—ever question your position or God's love for you. You have the courage of a warrior. But to live as a royal wife, you must be brave enough to forgive a thousand times simply because your husband wills it. You must have the mettle to let a gentle reply deflect criticism. And, to maintain a peaceful royal house and your self-respect, you must fight the most formidable enemy of all—the other women who will bear David's children."

"Jonathan, that's enough," David said. "Just because Saul took a concubine doesn't mean every king does."

"Is there a king you know who has only one wife?" Jonathan shot back.

David paused, seeming dismayed. "I can be different," he said finally.

"You *are* different." Jonathan grabbed the back of his neck. "Your godly passion drives you to battle. Your tender heart will always rescue, and your boundless love was meant to share. You will forever be a warrior, a savior, and a man who loves deeply. Only Yahweh's wisdom will keep you from the pride that ruined my family." Staring into David's eyes, his lips quivered before he spoke again. "But it's your own passion to serve Yahweh, to seek justice, and to show compassion that will test you more fiercely than any personal suffering."

David answered by hooking his arm around Jonathan's neck and pressing their foreheads together. They looked like rams locking horns while studying each other in silence.

I waited. Watched. And I prayed David would refute Jonathan's awful prophecy—at least the part about women who would bear his children.

Instead, he drew the prince into a tight embrace. "Your warnings are branded on my heart, brother." He looked over Jonathan's shoulder. Our eyes met, and I knew.

The warnings were also meant for me.

David was indeed driven by his passions for Yahweh, justice, and compassion for others. And I loved him for it. I loved David, the man, but how would those passions change when he became David ben Jesse, Israel's king? For months I'd been consumed with my unworthiness but had never considered the sacrifices I must make as a king's wife.

"Thank you for your honest advice, Prince Jonathan." My voice broke the silence and gained their attention. "You said I must be brave. I was brave enough to kill a man, and I've deflected criticism all my life. But on the battlefield of women, I'm inept. I neither understand their rules, nor possess the correct weapons to win a war if I must fight for David's love."

"You have my love." David tried to hold me, but I pushed him away.

"No! Let me speak." I turned to the prince. "What advice do you give to a woman imprisoned both by love and Yahweh's will when a broken heart seems inevitable?"

His tenderness deepened the wrinkles around his eyes. "I give you the same advice I offered David. In your helplessness, let God prove himself bigger than your fear and doubts. Your awe of the

Almighty will salve the wounds to come." He braced my shoulders and leaned forward to whisper, "After seeing the way David looks at you, I don't believe you'll ever have to fight for his love." He kissed my cheek and released me.

"None of that. You may kiss her *after* she's my wife." David playfully nudged his shoulder. "How long can you stay with us?"

"Not long—because of my second warning." His humor faded. "You should ask yourself how I found you."

David tucked me against his side. "You're the best tracker in Israel. You could have found me a dozen times while your abba hunted me."

"Yes, but I didn't need to track you, because the Ziphites came to Gibeah and told Abba precisely where you were hiding. They also told him of your plan to move south to the Jeshimon."

David's arm fell from my shoulders, his features hardening. "How long before Israel's army is upon us?"

"Abba gave me two days to muster Judean troops. I'm to meet him in Carmel at Nabal's estate. My scouts assured me that thousands from your own tribe will march against you."

"Does everyone betray?" David said between clenched teeth.

"I will *never* betray you." Jonathan held his gaze.

"And our covenant stands." David offered his hand, and they locked wrists.

"I've already stayed too long. My men are waiting." Jonathan pulled him closer, bracing David's elbow with his free hand. "My abba will not lay a hand on you. He knows you're Yahweh's anointed king, and it tortures him. Until he accepts the truth, I'll do all I can to draw our troops away. But remember: *Yahweh* is your best Protector, so trust Him." His voice broke as he released David and strode away.

David watched as if waiting for the prince to return or at least wave.

Jonathan kept marching. And Saul would soon come with thousands.

My mind whirred with complications. If we went deep into the Jeshimon—a more barren wilderness than this—where could we trade for grain? Would it be another year before our men saw their families?

I linked my arm with David's and whispered my fears. "Where can we hide if Saul uses Judean soldiers against us? They'll know the Jeshimon as well as our own men."

As Prince Jonathan disappeared below the horizon, David faced me. His expression was surprisingly calm. "Are you brave enough to marry a king? Brave enough to marry *me*?"

"David, didn't you hear me? How can we survive if—"

"I don't know where we'll live or when I'll sit on Israel's throne or when we'll have children. But I do know that all of me loves all of you—exactly as you are—and that Yahweh prepared us for marriage and brought my best friend to confirm the timing of our wedding. Now, Ahinoam bat Toren. Marry me now."

Both enraptured and exasperated, I choked out, "But we must move camp!"

"I'm aware." He pulled me into his arms, his gaze smoldering with barely bridled passion. "But I'm begging you to make your decision in this moment because I am David ben Jesse, and I will become Israel's king. So, tell me now, Ahinoam, if you'll be my wife. Today. As soon as we can find Abiathar and our family to witness our vows." He released a great sigh, then let his hands flop at his sides, looking as vulnerable as I'd ever seen him.

Dark circles proved his lack of sleep during his week of mercenary duty. This man served with his whole heart, loved with his whole being. He seemed to love me because I was different than other women, and I loved him despite his royal future, not because of the status other women might covet. Still, I couldn't imagine sharing his love with others.

"What if you tire of me?" I asked, remembering that Abba said

Ima had grown bored with him. "What if you take other wives and forget the love we share now?"

His forehead creased, pensive before he spoke, then he cradled my hands while answering. "Do you know why the Law forbids Yahweh's people to cook a young goat in its ima's milk?"

"Are you changing the subject?"

A mischievous grin brightened his handsome face. "No, I'm saying God commands our reverence for certain earthly relationships. Whether a goat and her kid, a cow and her calf, or a woman and her newborn, imas are bound to their children from birth."

"What has this to do with us?"

"Consider the even greater emphasis Yahweh placed on the marriage covenant that makes a husband and wife one flesh. The Creator who sparks new life in a womb also breathes life into a newly married couple and they become a single entity. One flesh. United, body and soul." He encircled my waist again, gentle yet possessive. "Jonathan was right when he said I'm passionate about battle and rescue and loving deeply. I can't ever imagine loving another woman as I love you, Ahinoam, but I also never imagined loving another woman after Michal broke my heart. I'm learning never to say never to Yahweh, so my heart tells me that if—and I do mean *if*—I ever marry another woman, it would be for reasons linked to battle or rescue. Even in that, we would trust the Lord to pour enough love into all our hearts so we could feel the same certainty you and I feel right now." It almost sounded possible when he explained it. He brushed my cheek with a kiss. "Give me your answer, Ahinoam bat Toren."

Heart racing, I knew he was the husband Yahweh had chosen for me—even if *King* David would someday marry others. "Yes," I whispered.

He lifted one copper brow. "Yes, what?"

I giggled, then shouted, "Yes, King David, I am brave enough to marry you!"

Suddenly airborne, I laughed in his arms as he twirled in dizzying circles. Our celebration overwhelmed every inhibition and drew the attention of others who must have been waiting close by. Whoops and bawdy comments surrounded us, but I paid little attention in the safety of David's arms. When the twirling stopped, he placed my feet back on the road and slid his hands into my hair.

Finally, his lips met mine with the kiss I'd hoped for.

SIXTEEN

AHINOAM

Until the day breaks and the shadows flee, I will go to the mountain of myrrh and to the hill of incense. You are altogether beautiful, my darling; there is no flaw in you.

Song of Songs 4:6–7

While David's lips lingered on mine, I felt tingling from my scalp to my soles, daring not open my eyes for fear of waking.

David pulled away and shouted, "Abiathar!" He took my hand, and we began rushing toward camp.

Startled to my senses, I could barely keep up. "Are we leaving Horesh today?"

"No, my love," he chuckled. "Today, we marry!"

"Now?" I squeaked.

"Abiathar!"

"Yes, my king?" The priest met us on the path. "Is everything—"

"Today you bless our marriage," David said without breaking stride.

He was being ridiculous. How could we delay when Jonathan had warned us to flee? "David! Saul is coming."

"Not tonight, he's not." He whirled, and momentum carried me into his chest. His arms held me fast. I looked up, breathless from the pace and the startling reality that I'd agreed to marry the next king of Israel. "Tonight, you are mine," he whispered and then kissed me again.

When he smiled down possessively, my knees turned to water, but my mind still tripped over obstacles. "How, David? Where? We live in a camp with six hundred men and your sister!"

He laughed, a deep belly-chuckle that resonated off the rock walls around us, then turned to announce to all nearby, "Ahinoam bat Toren has agreed to become my wife!" He lifted my hand as if we'd won a great battle, and our men's rattling weapons joined their shouts in a celebration that shook the ground beneath my feet. David lifted me into his arms and twirled until I was dizzy with celebration.

By the time the ruckus stilled, Abba, Zerry, and her sons had gathered around us. When attention settled on David, he sobered. "Before Abiathar pronounces Yahweh's blessing over our marriage, I must deliver hard news. The Ziphites have betrayed us to Saul, so the king is recruiting Judeans to pursue us into the wilderness." Indignation rose among our warriors while David delivered the last blow. "We have less than two days to retreat farther into the Jeshimon."

My bridegroom's focus remained on me. He began quietly humming. It was a tune I'd never heard. Then, a little louder, he lifted his voice over our men's fury. "Where can I go from *Your* Spirit? Where can I flee from *Your* presence?" He resumed his humming, and our troops settled into the reverence that often accompanied David's musical prayers. "If I rise on the wings of the dawn, if I settle on the far side of the sea, even there your hand will guide me, your right hand will hold me fast." Every soldier bent to one knee, head bowed.

"After a short rest," David announced, "Asahel will lead a cohort of scouts south to the areas Yahweh showed us yesterday. He has already guided us, and His right hand will hold us fast." Victory shouts affirmed God's faithfulness and set David to pacing. "Tonight, we praise the God of our Fathers. We celebrate a winter of peace. We give thanks to the Creator. And tomorrow, men—tomorrow, we rise on the wings of the dawn!" His shout brought them to their feet with another mighty celebration.

Finally, he returned his attention to me. "You asked how and where. Yahweh is the *how* because He's the only One who could have changed your stubborn heart and can keep us safe. The *where* is our familiar grassy space beyond the rock tunnel."

I covered a delighted gasp as David described his plan to the nephews. "Joab, you'll need to assign Amasai, Eleazar, and Shammah to oversee the army for tonight's worship celebration because you and your brothers have weddings to attend." Before Zerry's sons could ask questions, he snagged my hand, and we darted away.

"Weddings?" I asked, keeping pace now that I knew our destination.

His laughter soaked into me like the warmth of the spring sun, and it felt good to run. My thoughts turned to what was about to happen. We followed the river to the rock-walled tunnel. On the tunnel's other side lay the oasis we'd discovered our first day in Horesh. David and I had met there every day to talk, play, or simply escape—with Abba or Zerry as a chaperone. At the fork of the river, we splashed to the right and halted at the ankle-deep entrance of our private sanctuary.

My bridegroom's hungry gaze sent a stab of panic coursing through me. *Why didn't I ask Zerry what to expect on my wedding night?* I'd spent most of my life insisting I'd never marry, much of our time in Keilah brooding over the pain of marriage, and our winter in Horesh enjoying the company of the man I'd agreed to marry. *Yahweh, I have no idea how to be a wife!*

After Abiathar and our family encircled us, David said to his nephews, "Abiathar could just as easily pronounce a wedding blessing over *two* couples."

Before her sons could protest, Zerry shoved both fists at her hips. "If you boys think you can deny me this happiness, you're wrong. I'll take a leather strap to your backsides if you—"

Joab hugged his blustering ima and dissolved into laughter. Abishai grabbed Abba and lifted him off his feet. "Welcome to our family, Toren."

"All right, all right," David said. "Abiathar, let's begin." He kissed my hand and then tucked it against his heart.

Zerry and I stood in the middle, our bridegrooms at our sides, as Abiathar began the ancient blessing. "So the man gave names to all the livestock, all the birds in the sky, and all the wild animals, but for the man no suitable helper was found." The priest continued the blessing I'd heard dozens of times. "Then the LORD God made a woman from the man's rib, and He brought her to the man. The man said, 'This is now bone of my bones and flesh of my flesh. She will be called woman because she was taken from my side.'"

Taken from my side. The words were like a hammer in my heart. I whispered to David, "The man's helper was taken from his *side*—not his head to direct him, nor his feet to be trampled. A wife is meant to serve with her husband, side by side."

He wrapped my shoulders and held me close while Abiathar shared the final words of blessing. "For this reason, a man leaves his abba and ima, and joins his wife, and the two become one flesh. The man and his wife were naked and felt no shame."

David leaned down, pressing his lips against my temple. "It's time, my love. Come with me." Sheltering me under his arm, he guided me through the ankle-deep water and into the rock-walled tunnel.

Heart racing, my breaths came in shallow gasps, and my mind screamed only one question: *How could I allow David ben Jesse to see me naked and not feel shame?* I pulled the neckline of my robe a little tighter, hoping to stall until after sunset, and prayed that clouds would cloak the moonlight.

As if entering a dream, the noise behind us faded. When we emerged from the tunnel and stepped onto the grassy bank, I heard splashing footsteps behind us. I turned and saw Zerry standing behind me with an armload of blankets and a knowing smile.

She leaned close and whispered, "You'll be fine. My brother adores you. I'll see you at dawn." After a quick kiss on my cheek, she hurried away, waving overhead. "Toren and I have found a small cave in the cliff face!"

My cheeks were instantly on fire. *Abba and Zerry.* A shiver worked its way through me—then David's hands traveled up my arms, and all else was forgotten.

"You're trembling." Standing behind me, he leaned down, touched his lips to the bend of my neck, and then reached for one of the blankets. "Here, let me help."

His scent—a mixture of leather and earth—swept over me, and with it, a whole-body tingling like I'd felt with our kiss. I watched him carefully spread the blanket beside the stream, and my chest started to throb with a strange ache. *Is it longing? Or is this the beginnings of the marriage pains?* I clutched the other blankets against the ache, tighter and tighter as he approached.

He halted a step away and offered his hand. "Ahinoam bat Toren, I love you. I will always love you, protect you, and provide for you. Will you become one flesh with me, sharing our hearts, our lives, and our bodies?"

I swallowed hard. Though I still wasn't sure of all that *one flesh* entailed, I was confident in the man offering his pledge. There would be no stalling until tonight's sunset. I dropped the blankets, rushed into his arms, and would feel no shame.

SEVENTEEN

AHINOAM

Saul and his men began the search, and when David was told about it, he went down to the rock and stayed in the Desert of Maon . . . Saul was going along one side of the mountain, and David and his men were on the other side, hurrying to get away from Saul. As Saul and his forces were closing in on David and his men to capture them, a messenger came to Saul, saying, "Come quickly! The Philistines are raiding the land."

1 Samuel 23:25–27

Jeshimon, Desert of Maon

For over a week, our troops had scurried from cave to cave in an earthbound Sheol called the Jeshimon, where waves of heat rose from sunbaked rocks and distorted our thirst-crazed minds. *Jeshimon* described only two places on earth: the Sinai wilderness, and the wasteland south of Maon.

"I see them." Zerry pointed farther south, where David and our six hundred warriors moved along the west side of a mountain.

"Yahweh save them," I whispered, watching thousands of Saul's troops advance on the opposite side of the same mountain.

Zerry reached for my hand and squeezed. We sat in a mountainside cave, where David had left us with two waterskins and a promise to return in two days' time. Now a deep canyon separated us, along with at least a day's hike, too far for anyone to do anything but pray. *Yahweh, You promised! Prince Jonathan assured us his abba wouldn't lay a hand on David.*

Jonathan's warning had given us time to escape deeper into the wilderness and entrust our goats to the shepherds of a wealthy landowner. Though the owner—Nabal, the Calebite—was a despicable man and hadn't yet paid in gold or grain for our protection services, his shepherds were trustworthy and eager to repay David by kindly guarding our flocks. We'd left Horesh before sunrise, but Saul's numbers proved overwhelming. His troops had come from every direction, and our army quickly realized we were outmatched.

Zerry swallowed audibly. "I was grateful David hid us in a cave where we could see the whole wilderness, but now I can't bear the sight." She squeezed my hand again. "Neither can I look away."

We leaned back against the high cliff of Maon's natural fortress. When we had protested being separated, Joab gruffly told us the men could travel faster without us, but Zerry and I knew they left us behind to draw Saul's men away from us. Why did men always feel the need to protect women? How many times had I wanted to scream at him during the past two days, *Don't you know I'd rather die with you than helplessly sit here and do nothing?*

Zerry and I had watched with appalled awe as Saul's keen battle strategies relentlessly pursued and now converged on our friends and family. Both armies were moving south toward a plateau, where David's troops would march directly into Saul's path. Had the unthinkable become inevitable?

"Zerry, we must believe David will sit on Israel's throne. Yahweh promised it." *Even though it appears Saul will capture or kill them all by midday.* I sounded far more confident than I felt and turned away to hide my doubt.

"My brother will not kill Israelite soldiers."

I looked across the canyon. If Yahweh didn't open the earth and swallow Saul's troops, David would either fight or die. Before leaving me at the cave, he'd whispered, "*I fought with these men against the Philistines. We bled together, protected one another. I know how Saul thinks. He'll place my men—the thousand I once commanded—on his front line because he knows I'll hesitate.*"

"You mustn't hesitate," I whispered now as if he could hear me. Jonathan's prophetic warning to David played incessantly in my mind. "*It's your own passion to serve Yahweh, to seek justice, and to show compassion that will test you more fiercely than any personal suffering.*" Each day, I'd silently instructed my warrior husband from my distant perch. *Use your sling at a distance; throw your daggers at closer range. Your sword last, David. Always your sword last.* As if Israel's greatest warrior needed my instruction, but he was no longer *just* a great warrior. He was my husband!

"A rider!" Zerry shook my shoulders. "On a camel, Nomy! He must be from Gibeah." Few besides the king could afford camels.

The one-humped beast raced past Israel's ranks, its long strides throwing sand and rocks all the way to the front line. The messenger, not taking time to dismount, leaned down to transfer his missive to Israel's officers.

Moments later, Zerry and I heard a distant cry louder than a hyena's howl. The sound halted David's men, and the whole desert seemed to fall silent, waiting.

One of David's scouts summited his side of the mountain at the same moment we also saw movement on the Israelite side. Zerry and I leaned forward as one.

"I think—" Zerry gasped as realization jolted us.

"They're leaving," I whispered, afraid the words might somehow recall Saul's men. Impervious to my fears and, evidently, to David's army so near their reach, the Israelite troops retreated with great haste, contingent by contingent.

"It's a miracle." Zerry's lips parted in wonder.

"Yahweh truly protected him." The hairs on my arms rose at the undeniable proof of His power and presence. Yahweh hadn't opened the earth and swallowed the enemy, but only He could have saved David's army. *You have never been more real than in this moment, my God and our Deliverer.* I could hardly wait to tell David what we'd seen and hear the praise that erupted from his heart and lyre.

Three more of David's scouts scampered to the summit while the rest of our men scattered into nearby caves for shelter. A few other scouts followed Israel's troops at a distance, no doubt with orders to return with a report as soon as possible. Only then would we know and celebrate how the Lord had saved his anointed.

Reaching for our last waterskin, I lifted it in the air toward Zerry. "Let's each have three full gulps to celebrate."

"You rebel." Zerry tipped the skin to my lips. "Take a fourth!"

The tepid two-day-old water was as sweet as wine to my parched lips and throat. After my four gulps, I handed the treasure to my friend and felt immediately revived. Never had I realized the healing qualities of a single sip of water, nor the devastating effects of its lack. David had told me that a body could normally endure three days without it, but in the harsh reality of Judah's Jeshimon, a full day—two, at most—without water would snuff out the light of life.

Zerry tied off the waterskin's spout, then glanced at the now-empty mountainside where our men had taken refuge in caves and behind rock formations to shelter from the punishing desert sun. "Now we wait," she said. "And we pray that whatever took Saul away keeps him away."

EIGHTEEN

DAVID

And David went up from there and lived in the strongholds of En Gedi. After Saul returned from pursuing the Philistines, he was told, "David is in the Desert of En Gedi." So Saul took three thousand able young men from all Israel and set out to look for David and his men near the Crags of the Wild Goats.

1 Samuel 23:29—24:2

En Gedi Oasis

I bolted upright on my sleeping mat, heart pounding and jaw clenched, awakened again from the now-familiar dream. Circling my knees, I shivered in the desert air and pulled a blanket around my shoulders. *What does it mean, Yahweh?*

Our peaceful months at En Gedi had been both a blessing and a curse. Every scout's report of Saul's engagement with Philistine raids in the north brought confirmation of our uninterrupted peace through the year's war season. Rather than fleeing for our lives through the unforgiving Jeshimon during summer's heat, we'd spent the entire season at En Gedi's oasis, protecting Judah's landowners, aiding with their crops, and building our camp's supplies for Saul's next assault.

The overwhelming aroma of acacia blossoms calmed me, and I glanced through the cave entrance at the fascinating woman I loved so completely. After nearly three years of vigilance—night watches and daytime naps—our rest at En Gedi allowed us to relax into deeper sleep. Thoroughly content in each other's arms, we'd started to dream again. Unfortunately, both Ahinoam's dreams and mine had been nightmares. Nearly every night.

I stood to admire the last shimmers of moonlight on the Dead Sea. The eastern horizon stubbornly resisted the dawn with no more than an amethyst glow. I grew anxious for the dawn. *How long, Lord? How long?* Even a sluggish sunrise felt foreboding. Why? We were tucked away in a peaceful oasis, and the next war season was at least three months away.

Yahweh, are these dreams prophetic or simply the emerging terror of our past three years?

The dream replayed in my mind without permission. "Stop it," I whispered. Though the details changed from night to night, the core theme remained the same for each of us. Ahinoam's were always bloody visions of raided villages with innocent victims. My dreams, though less violent, were more perplexing. The same three people played the main roles. I stood on some sort of platform—a cliff, a palace dais, a rooftop—and Saul knelt below, awaiting my judgment. Samuel stood like a herald in the space between, reading the sins of Israel's king against me. The moment I'd open my mouth to declare Saul's punishment, I awoke suddenly, fiercely protesting my unclaimed justice.

"Finally, the seventh day." My wife rose from her mat on the other side of the threshold, a smile brightening her sleepy face. She slipped past me, careful not to make any contact. "I'm ready to feel your touch again. Let's go to the pool before anyone wakes."

I followed her down the mountain toward our favorite spring-fed pool, comforted by the anticipation of holding her again. We'd been careful to observe the Law during each month of her uncleanness. Neither Ahinoam nor Zerry had experienced "red days," as they called it, during our desert existence, and I'd been too distracted at Keilah to notice such things. These peaceful months at En Gedi had changed my wife's body with the rhythm of each moon cycle and shown us what normal could be.

My wife glanced over her shoulder. "I'll race you." She dashed away like a doe, and I followed. Everything was a competition, and I adored her for it.

We raced down the path, past scrub bushes, and discarded our robes at the water's edge, plunging into the cleansing pool. I swam to her, stopping short of where she floated, head tilted back and eyes closed in prayer. Was she asking Yahweh to fill her womb with a child? I'd always assumed she wanted children. Didn't all women? But she hadn't seemed disappointed when proof came each month that her womb remained bare. *Yahweh, if I'm to be a king, I need heirs.* Of course He knew. As did Ahinoam.

She opened her eyes and caught me staring. "What?" A spark of defiance lifted one brow.

I pulled her into my arms, thanking Yahweh that the cleansing of her body was complete. "Yahweh opens and closes the womb," I said. "Will you be pleased when He opens yours, my warrior bride? Or will you mourn your carefree days at my side?"

"How can you know me so thoroughly and still love me?" Her eyes never left mine. "It will be my great joy to bear your child, my love, but I'm in no hurry to conceive. I was created to be at your side, remember?"

Her honesty was like a barb in my sandal, but I expected nothing less and wanted nothing more. "As long as we agree to leave that timing in Yahweh's hands."

"Agreed." She teased me with a gentle kiss, then rewarded me with deeper passion to quench seven days of longing. The sunrise came. My foreboding passed. We played like children and loved like feasting beggars until the morning sun sparkled on the water.

Migrating birds overhead called us to duty. We dressed, ate a quick meal of dried fish and day-old bread, then found Toren and Zerry watching Joab working our En Gedi contingent on weaponry drills.

"My ima can throw a dagger better!" Joab shouted at his men.

Toren glanced at me, then back at the two hundred men under Joab's command. "My stepson is right," he said. "Under Nomy's instruction, Zerry has become quite handy with her dagger. Your men need a better instructor, King David."

"Then go teach them, Toren." He'd already refused Joab's request, but the Kenite was by far the best dagger man among us.

"Let Ahinoam teach them." Toren's usual humor was gone.

I sobered, too, glancing at my wife before answering. She focused on Joab and his men, obviously avoiding the conversation. "You know my men respect Nomy, but they would never allow a woman to train them or fight beside them in battle."

"They'll obey your command, will they not?" Toren offered his challenge with a grin. "Let Ahinoam compete for the *chance* to train them. If she can best you with her skill, perhaps she'll win their respect."

Zerry leapt to her feet. "Surely my brother isn't afraid his wife will best him in a competition."

The whole troop turned our way, clearly amused. Joab and his lieutenants walked toward us, and I shot an accusing glance at my wife. "Did you put your abba up to this?"

She lifted both hands in surrender. "I knew nothing." Though she'd stopped asking to train alongside my soldiers, she still practiced throwing every day.

"Accept the challenge." Joab bumped my shoulder when he arrived, then turned to Toren. "But best skill against best skill. If David wins, he teaches the sling to every contingent." My general had been nagging me to train the men that particular skill for months.

Toren shrugged and looked to me for approval. I'd been too busy enjoying my wife to practice, but I was confident I could win with my sling. I offered a hand to my wife. "Best against best?"

She adjusted her dagger belt. "Winner instructs all three companies as they rotate through En Gedi sentry duty."

My nephews commanded each of three companies in two-week rotations. Abishai oversaw those who traveled to their hometowns for family visits. Joab remained at En Gedi to supervise the watchmen and practice drills. Asahel used his charisma with wealthy Judeans to barter our warriors' farming and protective services in exchange for much-needed camp supplies. Because the companies shifted duties every two weeks, the winner of our little competition would train every warrior within six weeks' time.

"Agreed." I grabbed my wife's waist and kissed her soundly.

When wild shouts of approval erupted, she pushed me away. "Are you trying to rattle me, King David?" The lovely blush on her cheeks was already a victory.

"I fear it's the only way I'll win." I winked at my bride.

She immediately pulled me into a heady kiss, inciting more raucous applause. When her lips left mine, I felt the abandonment acutely—until I saw her impish grin. "I'll use every advantage to beat you."

"Enough, you two!" Toren nudged his daughter toward Zerry, then instructed Joab to crisscross two lines on the acacia's trunk as the target. He stepped off thirty paces, Zerry and Nomy trailing behind him.

Joab leaned close. "You'd better win. Our men won't take battle instruction from a woman."

I shoved him away, hoping my wife hadn't heard him. "What do you mean?" I kept my voice low. "She's been giving the men throwing tips since Keilah."

"Tips, yes. Training for battle is different." He stomped toward Toren, who was about to explain the rules. How many other men would be as bullheaded as Joab about Nomy training them?

"David and Ahinoam each have one throw," Toren began. "Whoever lands a deep gash nearest the tree's target with stone or blade will instruct all three rotations of warriors on his—or her—particular skill." Upon his last word, most of the men began cheering for me.

My wife's countenance clouded but only until she squared her shoulders and lifted her chin. It was then I realized what a grave error accepting this challenge had been. If I won, would Ahinoam be humiliated? And if I lost—or let her win—would she endure a different kind of humiliation when six hundred men begrudgingly obeyed my command and patronized her exceptional skill? My mouth was suddenly as dry as the Jeshimon. I wanted nothing more than to return to our cave for a quiet afternoon.

However, with more than two hundred eyes watching, I had no choice.

Reaching for my sling, I took a smooth stone from the bag at my belt and turned to my wife. "Do you want to throw first, or—"

I saw the glint of bronze, her quick release, and the dagger fly. With a solid thunk, it sunk into the tree. My soldiers' "ooohhh" punctuated the expert throw. Eve had landed dead center in the target.

"Your turn," Ahinoam said.

Zerry let out a whoop. Toren guffawed. Every soldier joined in riotous congratulations. Even Joab grinned.

My wife triumphantly stared at me, and I was as proud of her as I'd ever been. "You are a worthy opponent, Ahinoam bat Toren."

Grinning, she said, "No more stalling, my king."

Perhaps I need not have worried about my brave wife. I placed the smooth stone in the leather pocket and began twirling my sling. The celebration stilled as I turned to face the target.

"David, wait!" Joab said at the same time I saw Old J running toward us.

I caught my sling with the other hand and ran to meet him. Ahinoam and Joab kept pace beside me. As we drew nearer, I realized a large group of people followed him, including women and children. "Who are they?" I pondered aloud.

Joab shielded his eyes from the glaring sun. "It's hard to tell, but—is that Abishai?" A gasp and then, "Vered and the children!" Joab ran as if a lion chased him.

"Abishai would never—"

"I know," Nomy said, running faster. We were all tragically aware that Abishai would never bring Joab's troublesome wife to En Gedi unless bigger troubles had chased them from Bethlehem.

Old J reached Ahinoam and me at the same time terrible wailing rent the air. Joab comforted his wife, and Abishai held Raya and his children close.

"Where is Dalit?" I asked the old scout. "Is Ima all right?"

Tears filled his rheumy eyes. "I'm sorry, my king. Both Dalit and Mistress Nitzevet were killed in a raid. Their homes were hit first."

"First? How many others?"

Attai fell at my feet. "Forgive us, my king. We saw no indication of a raiding party until we heard screams. Dalit's was the first house targeted."

A chill raced through my veins. "Targeted?"

"They wore Amalekite armor but fought like Benjamites, wielding sword and dagger both left-handed and right."

"Saul's relatives!" one of the survivors shouted.

"Saul killed my brother's wife," Joab said in a menacing growl.

"We don't know that." I scanned the frightened Bethlehem survivors huddled around Abishai, who was like a mighty oak in a storm. I'd send Abishai to tell Asahel about Dalit and—*Oh Yahweh, no!*

"What about the boy? Asahel's son?"

"He was saved, my king." Attai stood, pointing toward the Bethlehem survivors. "Before the bandits attacked, Dalit's best friend, Abital, had taken Zebadiah for a morning walk to her family's vineyard. There she is."

I hadn't recognized the vintner's daughter. We'd pestered each other as children, and our abbas were good friends. The wine Abba provided for our Passover at Hereth had likely come from her family's vineyard. With empty eyes, Abital stared into the hills and balanced Asahel's three-year-old on her hip. What horrors had they endured together?

"After killing Dalit," Attai continued, "the bandits crossed the street to your ima's home. It seemed they knew exactly where to find her. By the time Mistress Nitzevet's maid screamed, Abishai was too late."

"What about the Moabite maid and her daughter?" Ahinoam asked.

Attai shook his head. "Abishai said the maid probably stepped in front of Mistress Nitzevet and took the first blow. Her daughter was gone, likely taken captive."

Ahinoam hid her tears against my chest. "Just like my nightmares," she said between broken sobs. "If only I could have seen faces or locations, we could have protected them or prevented the attack."

While comforting my wife, I saw another Gadite running toward us. Shouting and waving, Ezer was the fastest of my scouts—and normally as coolheaded as Abishai. *Lord God, help us.*

"My king!" Ezer braced his hands on his knees, panting but rushing to speak. "Thousands of Israelite soldiers . . . from all directions . . . converged at dawn in Carmel. Saul came, too . . . disguised in shepherd's clothing with only a five-man escort." He stood, exhaled a short huff, and said, "Now Saul is leading an army of three thousand toward us. They could attack En Gedi before dusk."

Bethlehem's women and children cried out in fear. I could only breathe out, "How?"

Ezer shook his head, shoulders slumped.

"Speak! How could expert scouts allow my family to be slaughtered and an army to advance with less than a day's notice?"

All three Gadites fell to their knees. "We are at your mercy, my lord," Ezer said. "The raiders walked into Bethlehem as merchants, and Saul's men weren't an army until this morning. Saul kept his regular troops engaged in the north against the Philistines until last month. His three thousand best men were slowly divided into smaller groups and dispatched to our warriors' hometowns."

"I sent runners to *every* soldier's hometown," Attai added, "with orders to lead all family members south to the Jeshimon."

While Abishai and five of our Bethlehem soldiers tried to calm the frightened women and children, I asked Attai, "Were my older brothers and their families also targeted?"

"No, my lord. None of your brothers or their families were touched. Not even threatened." His jaw clenched with unspoken accusation. Had Saul purposely left them undisturbed to heighten family tension? Or had my brothers somehow helped with the king's heinous crime?

"They betrayed us," Joab whispered.

"Stop it!" Zerry glared at her son. "My brothers would never harm Ima, and they would never condone killing women."

Joab and I exchanged a knowing glance. My brothers hadn't helped Saul, but they wouldn't hesitate to betray me or Zerry's sons. Approaching footsteps stole my attention, and I found Abishai's open arms coming toward me. Our family leaned into a circle of sorrow, arms entwined over shoulders, weeping with our heads bowed together. So much emotion made words unnecessary, and looming danger abbreviated our grief.

I straightened with a resolute sigh and met Abishai's swollen red eyes. "You made the courageous choice to rescue those who could be saved and let others bury our dead in Bethlehem. Now we protect the living. You must find Asahel and bear the news and his reaction to it." Abishai pounded his fist against his heart, lifting his chin with the resolve I'd expected.

Scanning the frightened faces of men, women, and children, I'd never felt less equipped or worthy for a task. *In times like these, Yahweh, the weight of Your will is almost crushing.* Even as the truth rose toward the heavens, clarity replaced confusion and faith trampled fear.

"We can only change what is yet to come," I shouted for my army and the Bethlehem survivors to hear. "For nine months, En Gedi has been a respite of peace and safety, and my men know every shrub, pool, ravine, and cave. King Saul is coming with three thousand troops and—"

"We must flee!" a woman shouted.

"I can't survive another raid." An ima pulled two children close.

I lifted my arms, patting the air for quiet, and noticed the same silent objections on my men's expressions. At least they didn't openly resist. I leaned over to Joab. "Get everyone to the large cave. The survivors can see some of the caves along the way, and our men can surround them to maintain order while I speak." To their credit, my men saluted with fists over hearts. Fear swept over the others like a strong wind, blowing the children into their imas' arms. I offered Ahinoam my hand and started toward the cave.

The same angst that tightened her features threatened to tie knots in my belly. I had no courage to console her, only praise for the God who had never failed us. I lifted my voice, hoping the lost sheep of Bethlehem would follow. "Lord, our Lord, how majestic is Your name in all the earth! You have set Your glory in the heavens. Through the praise of children and infants You have established a stronghold against Your enemies, to silence the foe and the avenger."

I sang the simple chorus over and over until we reached the cave of meeting. Ahinoam and I waited at the entrance, listening while the others continued singing, their voices rolling over and over inside the cave. "Lord, our Lord, how majestic is *Your* name . . ."

Humming, I closed my eyes. Ahinoam's hand squeezed mine. "My dreams were fulfilled, and yours will be, too," she whispered. "Saul will not kill you today, tomorrow, or ever. Rather, you will stand in judgment over him. Please let me remain at your side to witness God's miracle." Her declaration felt prophetic, piercing my heart.

I stared into her pleading eyes but couldn't bear to place her in danger. "You must stay with Zerry and Toren. You mean too much—"

"I was created to be at your side."

"Ahinoam." I dropped her hand to drag both of mine through my hair. I didn't want to argue with my wife right now. Stepping away to take a breath, I looked inside the cave. The singing had ceased, and now the tone of high-pitched fear echoed off the walls. My wife stood with her feet planted, her hands loose and better with a dagger than any man among us. Her countenance, though paled moments ago by anxiety, now glowed with faith and determination. If Nomy said there would be no battle, I believed her. So, why couldn't she remain at my side?

I rushed at her and pressed my lips against hers, and without hesitation she responded. When I pulled away, she giggled. "I'll assume that means yes."

Still holding her, I whispered, "You are as fierce as any warrior, my love, and you will be with me when Yahweh proves Himself faithful today." She let out a delighted chirp that made me chuckle. "Let's go reassure the others of God's protection."

The expansive front chamber of En Gedi's main cave was the perfect place for large gatherings. Joab's lieutenants had placed our troops around the perimeter of the Bethlehem survivors as crowd control, while Abishai and Joab remained at the front with their families as respected leaders. The noise settled as Ahinoam and I entered. Only the sounds of children's cries and imas' hushing stirred the tension.

I began with the most important announcement. "No one will die today. You are safe." A great sigh seemed to relieve a measure of angst. "But we still face danger and must be wise to avoid it. Saul's men travel much faster than we can with children. If we tried to flee En Gedi, they would surely overtake us in the wilderness. So, we hide here within small caves. My men will divide you into families and then care for you as a shepherd protects its flock. These men are valiant warriors and will protect you as their own kin."

"What about their families?" one woman shouted. "Who will protect them?" Her tone held more challenge than I'd expected.

"Our scouts have been dispatched to the hometown villages of all our warriors, and their families are even now being relocated to the Jeshimon. After Yahweh saves us, and Saul leaves En Gedi, we'll rejoin the other two-thirds of my army—with their families—and spend the remainder of winter together."

Abishai turned to face those he'd led all night long. "You must listen to King David. It's best to shelter at En Gedi until Yahweh saves us." Dissenting whispers rippled through the survivors.

Joab's jaw began to flex, and Abishai looked at me apologetically. But as I listened to the women of Bethlehem, I was reminded that these weren't soldiers accustomed to following my commands. They were frightened imas who raised their children alone. They made everyday, difficult decisions for their households because their husbands had left them years ago to protect me. They deserved to know more details so they could make an intelligent decision to protect themselves and their children.

"I'm Saul's target," I proclaimed over the murmuring. "I realize how much all of you have sacrificed for me, for the anointing Yahweh has given me, but it's that anointing that keeps us safe today. Does El Shaddai keep His promises?"

No one answered.

"Does He?" I shouted.

"Yes!" My men returned the shout because we did this drill often. The women jumped and children cried, startled by the echo of deep voices in the cave, but they must learn the sacrifice of praise.

"Does Jehovah Jireh always provide?"

"Yes!" A few women joined, and a few less children cried.

"Does Adonai Elohim preside over all creation?"

"Yes!" My men rattled the arrows in their quivers and clanked blade against blade, lifting a joyful noise with their shouts to the Lord. When I finally saw joy on women's faces and children covering their ears without the tears, I lifted both arms, calming the ruckus I'd started.

When silence fell over the gathering, I gave the final instructions. "Only Ahinoam and my Mighty Men will hide with me while the rest of you find caves as far away from me as possible. As soon as it's safe, my men will lead each family south whether I'm with you or not." I glanced at my lieutenants to emphasize my command. "Is that clear? You go as soon as it's safe. I'll follow later." Upon receiving each one's silent affirmation, I turned to Joab. "Instruct your men to divide the family groups and give them details on where we'll meet in the Jeshimon. Ahinoam, you, Abishai, and the Thirty will hide in the deep recesses of this main cave with me."

The meeting had been short. Families were divided, escorts assigned, and the cave emptied quickly. With a torch in hand, Joab led us into the winding belly of En Gedi's largest cave. My wife's grip was like a vise. Working smelted bronze had made her strong, yet Yahweh kept her heart malleable. I held tightly to my treasure through narrow passages, releasing her only when we were forced to crawl through a tunnel into the small innermost chamber of the mountain. Joab's torch continued burning until Attai arrived with news that Saul's men had come to En Gedi.

Then came the darkness. And the waiting. Thick and heavy, dread wrapped me like a shroud. Pressing. Suffocating.

"Breathe." My wife's hand slipped into mine. Her deep, steady breaths became my focus. My only thoughts.

A light shone through the tunnel entrance. My heart thudded. Though I willed it to slow, the beating sped. A familiar tune reached my ears. The voice was unmistakable.

It can't be!

Quiet snickers erupted around me. Every man who'd fought in Israel's ranks had learned the bawdy tunes of bored soldiers and knew Saul sang them loudly and off-key. King Saul's torch on the other side of the tunnel cast enough light for me to see my wife's confusion.

I breathed against her ear, "It's *him*."

"Saul?"

I nodded just as Joab jabbed me with the hilt of his dagger. He motioned me toward the entrance, stabbing at the air with his blade. His intention was clear. My general was ordering me to kill Israel's king.

The thought struck me like lightning. *Yes! Our running could be over today!* My frustrating dream didn't have to end with an unpro-nounced verdict.

"The Lord has given him into your hands," one of my captains whispered.

I shushed him but realized Saul would never hear us. He was singing at the top of his lungs.

"Do with him as you wish," said another of my men.

"Judge him! Like in your dream," Ahinoam whispered. "He sent men to kill your ima."

Didn't the Law say a life for a life? I moved into the tunnel and crawled toward Israel's king. As his singing grew louder, my resolve weakened. How could I kill God's chosen king?

Halting one body length from the tunnel's edge, I glimpsed the back of his head. *Much more gray hair than three years ago.* He paused his song and rubbed his forehead. Did he still suffer pain from tormenting spirits? Who played the lyre to calm his rants?

It felt like a boulder lodged in my throat. This was the man I'd fought with, bled for, and loved like an abba. Would his death end the violence or create more division among Israel's tribes?

The king groaned and sighed. I remembered hearing those sounds only when the king relieved himself behind the partition in his chamber. Could I kill a man in such a vulnerable position? I might have laughed, had my life not been hanging in the balance.

Someone shoved my foot. Joab, no doubt. To delay any longer was to acquit Saul of all wrong, and that was unacceptable.

But hadn't the Lord removed His Spirit from Saul? Yet He hadn't stripped away Saul's authority or taken his life. Was I greater than Yahweh? How dare I take Saul's breath when the Creator gave it? But I couldn't let him leave the cave without knowing I'd shown mercy.

His back was turned, so I crawled forward, reached for the train of Saul's purple robe, and sliced off a corner. I quickly retreated into the tunnel. When his humming abruptly halted, so did I. Half of my body hung in the small chamber with my men, the other half remained in the tunnel.

The outer cave's torchlight danced and then faded with the sound of Saul's footsteps.

"Go!" Joab shoved me forward. "He's getting away!"

Rubbing the expensive cloth between my fingers, a wave of nausea nearly made me retch. What had I done?

Sudden movement jostled me, and someone tried to nudge me aside. "If you won't do it, I will!" Joab hissed.

"No!" I shot into the darkened chamber as a torch blazed to life.

"No one will lay a hand on the Lord's anointed. Not on Saul or his men. Clear?"

Abishai held the torch aloft, his face a mask of confusion. "But Ahinoam told us about your dream. The Lord delivered Saul into your hands. You have every right to judge his sins." His obvious disappointment cut me deeper than Joab's anger.

"You'd better explain," Joab spat, "or you'll have no army left by morning."

The torchlight illuminated approval in Ahinoam's eyes. *Thank You, Yahweh, that she's with me.* "In every dream, I stand over Saul as judge, but Yahweh always wakes me before I pass judgment. When I was in that tunnel and had the chance to mete out justice, I realized the LORD alone will judge Saul. In His time. In His way."

The exchange of disapproving glances fueled my resolve.

"You can remain in this cave or follow me outside to witness God's faithfulness."

Ahinoam gripped my arm. "Shouldn't we wait until Saul and his men leave En Gedi?"

"Do you think the LORD would bring Saul to this cave, fulfill my dream, and *not* complete His miracle?" I held up the scrap of Saul's robe. "When I show this to Saul and his three thousand men, they'll all know I'm not trying to kill him. Saul may be a skilled strategist, but I'm learning that God's strategy reaches beyond anything I can imagine."

NINETEEN

AHINOAM

Now Samuel died, and all Israel assembled and mourned for him; and they buried him at his home in Ramah.

1 Samuel 25:1

Dead Sea Fortress

Since David mercifully spared Saul over a year ago at En Gedi, our lives had become as harsh as the desert fortresses where we sheltered. Even during the milder winter temperatures, the Jeshimon fortress had proven unable to support our six hundred men and their families. So, we begrudgingly split our forces into two camps, both perched atop wilderness plateaus. Though the sheer cliffs of our Dead Sea fortress created the perfect military defense, the abrupt edges and plummeting drops were a constant hazard for the camp's children.

"Zeb, don't go beyond that pile of rocks!" Abital darted toward Asahel's precocious son, ruining the braid Zerry had been weaving into her long brown hair.

Zerry huffed and glared at me. "Will you please watch him while I prepare my son's bride?"

"Gladly." I left Zerry waiting under the goatskin shade and met

Abital in the punishing desert sun to retrieve the little boy who had stolen my heart. "Come to your *doda* Nomy's chamber, and we'll find something fun to play with."

Abital mouthed a silent thank-you, and I winked at the nervous bride-to-be. Though everything else atop our towering plateau was gritty and uncomfortable, I'd found another dear friend in the woman who saved Asahel's son.

Desert life had even more clearly defined the character of our men and their wives. For some, food and water became horded treasures rather than gifts to be freely shared. The other two neph-ews and their wives were assigned to the Maon fortress and took many of the troublemakers with them. Asahel built his one-room chamber beside Abba and Zerry. Abital's was on the other side of them, and ours was next in line. We were family, and the Mighty remained with us, as well.

On the day David spared Saul, something had shifted between my husband and his men. When David stood at the cave's opening and lifted the scrap of Saul's robe over his head—much like I'd imag-ined him doing with Goliath's head—Saul had instantly recognized David's voice.

"Is that you, David, my son?"

My son? I wanted to vomit.

Israel's three thousand troops likely felt the same—but for dif-ferent reason. Such utter failure to protect their king usually meant execution. But there was nothing *usual* about that day's encounter. If only Saul had admitted Yahweh's intervention or acknowledged David's integrity. Perhaps then we could have remained at En Gedi.

Instead, the king begged David's forgiveness and wept like a woman. Then he screeched, "Swear to me by the LORD you won't kill my descendants and wipe my name from the earth!"

Saul's paranoia was immutable. The king on Israel's throne would never stop hunting David ben Jesse or his loyal followers. Though

Saul and his men retreated to Gibeah that night, our silent march from En Gedi echoed the truth in every heart. Maybe not today or next week or next month or even next year, but someday Saul would attack us. And David would *never* kill him.

As Zebby entered our mudbrick chamber, he reached for David's lyre. "Doda Nomy, can I play with this?"

I snagged it from its corner in our single room. "No, no, no!" Though coated with a thick layer of neglect, I held out hope that my husband would someday regain his passion for praise. *Please, Yahweh, stir my husband's embers to a flame for You again.*

"Let's look in a basket for one of Dohd David's smaller slings." I opened a lovely basket that one of the wives had given me in exchange for teaching her to throw a knife. After she had bragged about her new skill, several more women searched me out at the mountaintop forge and asked to learn the skill, as well. Zerry assisted me with the lessons since she was now proficient in the basics.

So, wilderness living had been harsh and demanding but also surprisingly kind to my heart. Most of our women now greeted me by name and even smiled as if they genuinely liked me.

"What's this, Doda?" Zeb dragged out my light-blue linen robe.

"It's just something a mean old king gave me."

"Well, it's sure prettier than the old robe you wear every day." He wrinkled his nose. "This one smells better, too."

I giggled and pinched his crinkled nose. Leave it to a child to tell you the truth. Shaking the dust from the Moabite gift, I pressed the luxurious fabric against my waist and only then realized how thin I'd become. "Well, if there was ever an occasion to wear a pretty robe, it's your abba and Abital's wedding day."

I looked down at the little boy who had single-handedly made me long for a child of my own. Was it proper to change clothes in front of a four-year-old boy? Uncertain, I asked him to turn his back while I undressed and slipped the blue linen over my head. "Okay, you can look now."

His awe was worth the extra propriety. "Doe-dah! You are bee-yew-tee-full!" He wrapped my waist and squeezed tighter than my cinched dagger belt.

I would have thanked him had my love for this little one not formed a lump in my throat.

When the sounds of bickering and high-pitched complaints drifted through my curtained door, Zeb released me and looked up with wide eyes. "Dohd Joab and Doda Vered are here." He was right, and with them came the other half of David's army.

I belted the robe and smoothed the fine material over my protruding hip bones, then donned my dagger belt—still my preferred and only ornamentation—to mask more of my imperfections.

Angry shouting drew us outside. I held Zeb's hand tightly, weaving through the now-crowded plateau. Already one of Abishai's men was complaining about the food we'd acquired for the wedding feast. "How much of the camps' resources did you barter for this extravagance?"

Vered was in the middle of the fray, defending the family's right to celebrate Asahel's happiness after Dalit's tragic death. She was as fierce as any man among us.

When her victory was won, I walked toward Zerry's tent with Zeb, smiling at Vered as I passed. She ducked her head and turned away, still refusing to speak to or even acknowledge me. Raya, too, ignored me, as did all the wives of the second fortress. But it didn't hurt as much since I'd found my place among the Dead Sea wives.

Our warriors' relationships had also become as gritty as the sand between our teeth. Though they'd born hardships as fugitives without complaint for years, their loyalties were divided when their families moved from comfortable villages to the dry and barren Jeshimon.

Atop separate plateaus, two armies built rows of stacked-stone homes like honeycomb—side by side, with narrow alleyways between the one-room dwellings. The men of each plateau were split into three divisions, but this time their duties left little room for rest. Some chiseled cisterns into mountain bedrock, hoping to catch the winter rains. A second group bartered with nearby landowners for food, water, and building supplies, while the third division maintained a constant train of donkeys that carried those supplies up a single serpentine path leading to the top of each plateau.

Abba and I, along with our apprentices, had built a forge at the Dead Sea fortress and shifted our production to picks and axes to tame our mountaintop home. Even the choice to build only one forge had been seen by some as a slight. *Oh, Yahweh, create in us clean hearts, and restore steadfast spirits within us.* The men worked from dawn till dark. Women and children, too. Everyone needed the break today's wedding would provide.

Zeb broke from my grasp and ran into Zerry's arms. "There you are, my little man. Savta saved a candied date just for you." He'd been the only grandchild she could utterly spoil. She'd quickly won Abital's friendship and Asahel's gratitude the day she declared their betrothal . . . though Zerry had neglected to inform either bride or groom. Though Asahel still grieved Dalit's brutal death, his friendship for Abital quickly grew to affection with her diligent care for Zeb. Abital's courageous rescue had proven the fire in her veins that made her the perfect friend for Zerry and me.

Our brave friend, however, currently cowered in the corner of Zerry's chamber, looking as if she'd rather face Saul's troops than her bridegroom.

"Zerry, I'll wait with Abital. You can go ahead and take your place with Abba and Zeb near the wedding canopy."

Without a backward glance, the ima of the groom pulled back the curtain, chattering with her grandson in the singsong voice she used only with him. Abital's eyes widened at the sounds of flutes, lyres, and drums. The crowded plateau erupted with applause when Zerry emerged, likely thinking it was the bride herself. I quickly closed the curtained doorway to calm my friend.

"You look stunning," I said and meant it.

She lowered her head. "Why couldn't Abiathar simply speak the blessing over us privately, quickly, like Asahel said he did for you and David? I've known Vered all my life, and she'll find a way to humiliate me in front of David's entire army."

Furious that one woman wielded so much control with so little integrity, I grasped Abital's hands and demanded, "Look at me." She knew today was important because it was the first time David's army had joined to celebrate anything since leaving En Gedi, but she needed to remember the *most* important thing happening today.

When our eyes met, I said, "Today, you and Asahel will give little Zebby a real home. Focus on the two men in your life, and you'll be fine."

She hugged me. "Will you walk with me?"

"I, uh . . ."

The bride's eyes narrowed. "Ahinoam bat Toren, I'm about to become a member of your family. Don't you dare say no."

We emerged from the chamber arm-in-arm and parted the sea of wedding guests. I was especially grateful Zeb had suggested I change into the blue linen robe. When we arrived at the wedding canopy, Asahel stared at his bride with a similar awe as that with which Zebby had looked at me. I grinned, imagining the bridegroom thinking in his son's words. *You are bee-yew-tee-full, Abby-tall!*

Zerry had stitched their goatskin wedding canopy and painted myriad stars on its underside as a testament to Abraham's promises. Asahel's brothers and their childhood friends Elhanan and Uriah supported its four posts, and David stood at Asahel's side as friend of the bridegroom. My husband had drawn up the marriage contract and ensured proper gifts were exchanged. However, since Abital's family had been killed in Bethlehem's raid, and Asahel was part of David's army, the couple's only gift exchange was the promise of loyalty and protection.

Abiathar began the official blessing, "Then the Lord God made a woman from the rib he had taken out of the man. . . ."

My husband winked at me, sending an almost-forgotten warmth through my veins. How long had it been since we'd shared more than a weary kiss? How long since our intimacy felt more than compulsory? Though our love still felt solid and true, our passion had become as dry as the wilderness around us. Was David's zeal for Yahweh withering with the same weariness that sapped our marriage? Were other women experiencing the same feelings with their husbands? The distance? The disappointment?

I glanced at Zerry and Abba beside me, their hands hidden and likely clasped between the folds of their robes. Thoughts of their intimacy still made me uncomfortable, but they seemed passionate enough. I furtively scanned left and right—Joab and Vered, Abishai and Raya. What about the hundreds of soldiers and their wives? Most were smiling, but all looked weary. Had we been too busy surviving to seek God's abundance? *Yahweh, only You know whether one flesh is whole or has been torn apart.*

"Adam and his wife were both naked, and they felt no shame," Abiathar declared, "and so shall you—Asahel and Abital—share your hearts without shame. Though Dalit was beloved by you both, Yahweh has brought you together to provide a loving home for Zeb and for each other as long as you both live. The Lord gives and takes away."

"The LORD gives and takes away. Blessed be the name of the LORD." Everyone repeated what had been Job's response after he'd lost his wealth and children. As the words escaped my lips, Zebby waved at me from his safe place between the bride and groom. My heart constricted at the thought of Job's praise moments after losing all ten of his children. *Yahweh, I will praise You in this desert place.*

A shofar startled us all with nine short warning blasts.

Zeb hurtled into Abital's arms. "No! They're coming again!" Asahel stood paralyzed for a moment, torn between his duty to follow David to the lookout and his need to comfort his wife and son. With a single embrace, he whispered something to his new family and dashed away with the other captains.

"No, Abba! Don't leave. Don't leave us!" Zeb flailed in Abital's arms.

Zerry rushed to help. "Savta's here, Zebby. Your abba will be back. He's a brave, important soldier. He must protect Yahweh's king." But he pushed Zerry away and clung to Abital. Zerry didn't even flinch. Both women stroked the little boy's hair and whispered calm assurance. In that moment, my whole being screamed for a child. I needed to give David a family.

"Camels!" someone shouted. As if waking from a dream, I noticed women's terrified faces and joined the men rushing toward the plateau's only path. Skirting the cliff's edge, I passed some slower soldiers and glimpsed two riders approaching with a third camel—saddled and no baggage. They intended to return to Gibeah with a third person.

"It's a trap," someone mumbled as I shoved through the press of bodies and reached David's side.

"Or Saul is dead," Joab said. He grinned at my husband. "Perhaps they've come to make you king."

David had learned to ignore many things since forgoing his opportunity to kill Saul. Several men had deserted us, accusing David of cowardice. But Yahweh had replaced the troublemakers with better warriors, men with more integrity who trusted not only David's anointing but also Yahweh's timing.

"Put the messengers on our donkeys and escort them up the

path," David commanded, "while someone waters their camels below. Until they arrive, we coordinate building efforts and protection plans to sustain both fortresses for the coming spring." The camelback messengers were a stark reminder that Saul's wealth and paranoia could change the remorse he'd shown at En Gedi at any moment. We needed to be ready.

I searched for Abba among the captains, but he wasn't there. I stood on a waist-high rock wall to scan the plateau. Women and children congregated in smaller groups, settling their families with a subdued feast while a few musicians still played. Abba and Zerry sat alone at the entrance of their one-room chamber in our family district. While David and Joab engaged in a heated discussion, I hurried over to ask why Abba wasn't at the meeting. From ten paces away, I realized his pallor was enough reason for Zerry to forbid it.

Trying to hide my concern, I approached them, saying, "If you've seen one messenger on a camel, you've seen them all."

Abba offered a wan smile but didn't speak. Zerry knelt at his side, a waterskin in her left hand. She didn't speak, either.

I ducked under the goatskin shade of their small courtyard and knelt opposite Abba. Sweat beaded on his brow. "You look awful." I lifted my hand to his forehead.

"I'm as handsome as the day I married Zeruiah." He brushed away my hand. "It's nothing."

Zerry's sharp look told me otherwise. "He's dizzy. I had to help him walk home." Her voice broke. Then she glared at him. "Don't you dare die, Toren. I let myself love you."

"I said I'm fine, woman." He kissed her gently, lingering too long.

"Enough of that." I chuckled awkwardly. Tempting Abba with messengers' news would reveal if he was truly *fine*. "Will my report of the king's riders suffice?"

"I'm going." Abba rocked to his feet, groaning.

Zerry and I flanked him all the way to where David waited with his captains at the top of the path. I settled Abba and Zerry in the patchy shade of a terebinth and hurried to my husband's side. Before I could ask the dozen questions racing through my mind, two of our men appeared, leading the donkeys up the path with Saul's messengers. The royal visitors' faces were nearly as pale as Abba's. Their news couldn't be good.

"Welcome." David's tone was tense.

Both men slid off the donkeys and fell to their knees. "Forgive us, my lord, but we bring terrible news. The prophet Samuel is dead."

"No." David ripped the neckline of his wedding robe and stumbled back. I reached out to embrace him at the same time a sudden shriek rent the air behind us.

As I turned, the whole world seemed to slow. Sounds and faces distorted. Abba lay across Zerry's lap. She shook his shoulders, but he only stared at the sky. More screaming. Weeping. Abba kept staring. No. He stared at nothing. Abba was gone. Those eyes were empty. Like the ones in my nightmares.

"Toren, no!" Zerry leaned over the body, clutching at Abba's robe. "Don't leave me! I need you!"

I couldn't move. A deafening moan rose to a wail. Someone grabbed me. Strong arms turned me. Surrounded me. Muffled the wailing—my wailing.

"He's gone, love." David's voice. "Hearing of Samuel's death was too much."

Samuel is dead. Abba is dead.

Zerry was still screaming. "Don't touch me!" she shouted as people began to come closer. "Leave me alone!" Zerry fought everyone but Abba.

"My king." Joab's voice. "King Saul requests your presence at Samuel's burial. . . ."

"Of course," David said. "We should leave immediately. Nomy, I'll take Joab and Abishai with me. We'll return as quickly as poss—"

"What?" When he reached for me, I stepped back. "You're leaving? You would honor Samuel above Abba?"

The silence was deafening. Zerry now stood with me. "And you're taking my sons with you into a trap?"

"Please understand," he said to his sister, then turned back at me. "Saul has offered an olive branch. If I honor the prophet we both respected, it could mean unity for Israel. This one time, I must choose duty over family."

When David offered his hand, I slapped it away. "Go, then!" Every sound stilled. "Go bury your prophet, but don't be surprised when Saul's olive branch becomes a spear, and he stabs you with it." I gathered Zerry and knelt with her beside Abba, discouraging more of David's golden-tongued excuses.

Zerry laid her head on my shoulder. "I want to bury Toren in Bethlehem," she whispered, "in my family's tomb."

"Abba would be honored." *Despite the dishonor David ben Jesse showed him.*

I glanced over my shoulder and watched David lead Joab, Abishai, and Saul's messengers down the path. Mourners surrounded us, blocking my view and making any concerns futile. I joined the wailing.

Zerry and I both lost our husbands today.

TWENTY

DAVID

Hear me, my God, as I voice my complaint; protect my life from the threat of the enemy. Hide me from the conspiracy of the wicked, from the plots of evildoers.

Psalm 64:1–2

Jebus to Ramah

Joab, Abishai, and I had ridden the king's camels as quickly as their long strides would carry us over desert roads and hills, leaving Saul's two messengers far behind on our camp's trotting donkeys. I followed Joab, and Abishai was rear guard, which left me with too much time to think.

Toren was dead. My army was crumbling. I heard Zerry's tormented wails in every jackal's howl. I saw Nomy's twisted grief in every barren tree branch. Samuel—God's voice to Israel—was gone, and Yahweh hadn't spoken to me for months.

Yahweh, have You left me as You left Saul?

Silence answered, yet somehow I knew God hadn't abandoned me. *Then why do You remain silent?* The now-familiar anger rose inside. His miraculous protection felt short-lived when we'd left

En Gedi's oasis of blessing and entered the Dead Sea's fortress of suffering.

I wrapped my *keffiyeh* around my nose and mouth to filter the desert's dust. How long since I'd felt clean—inside and out? How long since I'd felt Yahweh's comfort or had the confidence to comfort others? How long since I'd held my wife and whispered or sung of my love for her or we together lifted our praise to Yahweh for His goodness? The truth of my neglect pierced me. I'd abandoned her long before I chose to negotiate peace with Saul at Samuel's burial. *Forgive me, Lord.*

Just before dawn, we passed the impenetrable Jebusite fortress. Their ornate pagan temple shone in the moonlight, mocking Yahweh's faithful. Though Jebus had once been ruled by the mysterious Melchizedek, a high priest during Abraham's time who worshiped God Most High, the Jebusites had succumbed to idolatry by the time of Joshua's conquest but held firm to their fortress in God's Promised Land. Their towering city, naturally guarded by valleys on three sides, was a blight in Israel's kingdom. Saul's clan maintained a begrudging peace, however, since they lived less than a morning's walk from his palace.

"Halt, in the name of King Saul!" I recognized Paltiel's voice. Joab had rounded a mountain path's bend and now faced at least twenty royal guards, arrows nocked and pointing at me.

Abishai rode around me and reined his mount to a halt, becoming my human shield. I slipped my hand toward my dagger, but Paltiel shouted, "If my men and I are harmed, Michal dies. Would Prince Jonathan remain loyal to you, David ben Jesse, if your foolishness cost his sister her life?"

I swatted my camel forward, breaking through my protectors to meet Leviathan face-to-face. "Jonathan knows who is loyal to his family and who seeks only glory and bloodshed."

"Well then," the beast said, grinning, "let's see who proves loyal and whose blood is spilled." His shrill whistle caused more men to emerge from behind rocky cliffs. "You made good time," Paltiel continued. "We scheduled Samuel's burial procession for dusk. The king has saved a place for you and your men at his table. You'll play your lyre for him as you did before."

And he'll try to pin me to the wall with his spear—as he did before. Nomy's warning raced through my mind. *"Don't be surprised when Saul's olive branch becomes a spear."* I looked over my shoulder, and my nephews' battle-ready faces bore the same understanding. I'd led them into a trap, though Jonathan had cautioned me his abba would do *anything* to lure me to Gibeah.

Saul was waiting at Ramah's city gates to greet us, Jonathan on his right, and the wife who had betrayed me—then been betrayed—on Saul's left. The king was the only one smiling. "Welcome, David ben Jesse! I've anticipated this reunion for months."

No longer did he call me *my son* as he had during En Gedi's repentant speech. No longer did my heart skip at the sight of the beautiful princess. No longer would I mourn the family I'd lost in Gibeah. The only things God preserved for me in Ramah were Jonathan's unwavering gaze and the prophets' kind welcome.

Gad led a troop of students to greet me, their heads covered in dust and robes torn from grieving. "We're honored you came, my lord." Gad and his students encircled my nephews and me, an effective shield against Saul's guard. "We've prepared a humble meal for you and your captains in Naioth and rooms for you to rest before the procession."

Saul's features clouded. "I had planned—"

"Of course you are welcome to join us," Gad added. "You and your guardians may partake of our broth and bread—though it's likely a meal too simple for a king." The prophet bowed, as did his students, their implication quite clear. I was *not* a king—yet.

Saul alternated an outraged glare from me to the prophet and then said, "My men will guard your camp to be sure our *guests* don't wander away before the burial. Paltiel and his men will come at dusk to escort all of you to the front of the processional." He grabbed Michal's reins, leading her white donkey away. She didn't protest or look back.

Jonathan, however, remained with us, accompanied by a small contingent of men I recognized as soldiers who had faithfully served under my command. We followed the prophets to their camp in Naioth, ate together, and prayed together.

Gad even coaxed me to sing by forcing a lyre into my hands. "Sometimes we need to worship God even more than God needs our worship."

At first my words were as demanding as my heart. I strummed the lyre strings as if each strike was the stab of a blade. "Contend, LORD, with those who contend with me; fight against those who fight against me." Humming as other voices echoed the words, the calluses on my heart began to soften. "Take up shield and armor; come to my aid." Again the echo of my friends' voices soothed and healed—prophets, soldiers, and prince in supplication. "Say to my soul, 'You are my salvation!'" Midday passed into afternoon, and still we sang, resting in worship that refreshed the soul more deeply than sleep.

When the shevarim blast announced dusk had come and Paltiel's arrival was imminent, Jonathan embraced me and proved his loyalty by whispering, "As soon as Abba, the prophets, and I enter the burial cave, you and your nephews must slip through the mourners to the rear of the hillside. My men will be waiting with three camels."

When he released me, he pulled Joab and Abishai into our circle of trust. "My men will stall Paltiel and his guards. You must get as far away from Abba as you can. Ride fast, and ride far."

"What about you?" I asked. "Won't he know you've helped me?"

Jonathan glanced around us, grinning at the prophets who still hummed the lingering tunes of our afternoon worship. "Surely you know by now, my brother, that it's only Yahweh who saves any of us." His countenance glowed when his gaze returned to mine. "Abba will remember what happened the last time he sent assassins to Naioth to kill you, and he knows Yahweh's favor rests on me through Gad, the prophets, and Israel's troops. Though Abba will pursue you, he won't harm me. He's tried to rebuild favor by choosing a new High Priest, but the imitation ephod has proven void of God's power." With a final squeeze of my shoulder, he warned, "Still, we must all remain vigilant."

Paltiel's guard met us outside, and we followed every detail of Jonathan's plan. The moment Saul, his guards, and the prophets disappeared into Samuel's burial cave, I turned to slip through the crowd, my nephews on my heels.

Michal blocked my path. Her eyes full of unshed tears, she whispered, "I'm so sorry." Then she stepped aside.

Stunned, I couldn't move or speak. Scanning the length of her, she looked more like a peasant in the sackcloth mourning robe. What I saw at her torn neckline stole my breath. Bruises. Two thumbprints in front, four longer marks on each side. Fire raced through my veins.

"Go!" Joab pushed me from behind. He and Abishai linked my arms and dragged me between them, weaving through the endless mourners. Thousands had gathered to honor Israel's last judge, faithful priest, and great prophet. But my mind was consumed with the dream I'd had in Keilah, the golden chains that restrained me from helping the wife who chose to betray.

When we reached the other side of the hill, Jonathan's men were waiting with the camels, as promised. "Thank you," I said, but quickly turned to Joab. "If we ride hard, we might reach Bethlehem in time for Toren's burial."

My nephew looked at me as if I'd asked him to ride into the heart of Philistia. "Duty before family—you said so yourself. We must take the fastest route to the fortress and move everyone before Saul can rally his troops to pursue us."

"My lord," Jonathan's captain interjected, "the prince believes King Saul will wait to pursue until after the thirty days of Samuel's mourning are over, but there are no guarantees. Prince Jonathan suggests you go directly east, across the Benjamin Plateau, and all the way to the Jordan Valley before turning south toward your fortress. He'll direct our army south along the trade routes."

"He'll lead them right to us!" Joab hissed.

Jonathan's man sneered at my general. "That's exactly what we hope King Saul will believe. In truth, the trade routes are a more direct route to your fortress, but they're clogged in winter with merchant traffic trying to avoid mountain floods."

Joab grunted his approval, and I bowed to offer thanks. "Your prince—as always—has proven shrewd in his loyalty, and you've risked your life to help me. I'm in your debt." I returned my attention to Joab and Abishai. "But we're going to Bethlehem first. It's not far out of our way, and it's the honorable thing to do."

"Saul knows the location of our fortress!" Joab insisted. "Are you willing to gamble the lives of our six hundred men and their families that Saul will obey the laws of grieving?"

"I trust Jonathan to delay him." I mounted my camel and turned to Abishai, the reasonable one. "Saul won't pursue us in the winter."

"He came to En Gedi in winter," he shot back, voice trembling. Zerry's middle son was rattled. Abishai was never rattled.

I studied him. "The burial caravan will require at least two days to travel from the fortress to Bethlehem, so we could arrive *before* them. We could comfort our women, honor Toren, and only delay our return to the fortress a few days. Why not honor Toren *and* keep our people safe?"

"We'll honor Toren best by keeping our people safe," Joab said from atop his camel.

"Please, David. Let me ride alone to our fortress." Abishai held my camel's reins, determination hardening his features. "I'll lead everyone to Maon." Unlike his older brother, Abishai seldom challenged me.

My heartbeat raced, fully aware of the urgency and the weight of this decision. If Saul attacked our unsuspecting fortress, Saul's ruse would become more tragic than my dashed hopes for peace. But what my nephews couldn't grasp was the depth of pain I'd seen in my wife's eyes.

"All right, go," I said to Abishai. "Move everyone to Maon. They'll be crowded, but we'll trust Yahweh for a new location where Saul won't find us." I'd barely finished speaking by the time he'd already hurdled onto the third camel. Abishai clucked his tongue, and the beast was on its feet and at a full gallop in record time.

"Well, men." Joab heaved an exaggerated sigh. "It would appear I'm going to Bethlehem."

"There's still time to catch up to your brother." I wished he would.

"What sort of bodyguard would I be if I let you face two angry women alone?" His smirk assured me he held no grudge.

"May Yahweh-Nissi go before you in battle!" The soldier pronouncing the blessing gave a wry grin as I reached for my riding crop and tapped the camel into a gallop. Abishai had followed Jonathan's suggested route, east over the plateau. Joab and I would go southeast, using the shepherds' paths through the Judean wilderness.

We rode until the night covered us like a wet woolen blanket, and our second sleepless night took its toll. Our camels slowed to a rhythmic pace, lulling me like a babe in its ima's arms. Startled awake by Joab's shout, I saw him grip his saddle's pommel and pull himself upright after nearly falling off his one-humped beast. I was too tired to laugh. We needed to rest. Bethlehem wasn't far, and we now traveled the same path the burial caravan would follow.

"Let's stop here." I tapped my camel's shoulder to dismount. Joab didn't need coaxing. He was off his camel and snoring before I laid my head on a smooth stone. I, on the other hand, could only doze. I counted stars and thought of all I should have said to my wife, my sister, and my troops before rushing away to negotiate peace with Saul after ignoring the true Peace-Giver for months.

"Lord, do not rebuke me in Your anger or discipline me in Your wrath. Have mercy on me. I'm so weary. Save me because of *Your* unfailing love, Lord. I'm worn out from groaning." Calm settled over me, as it had when we'd praised Yahweh with Gad and the prophets. "Lord, *You have* heard my cry for mercy; You have heard my prayer."

I woke to the breaking dawn and nudged Joab's sandal with mine. "If we leave now, we can reach Bethlehem before sunrise."

"The gates don't open till dawn." He rolled over, once again ignoring my urgency. If my men carried Toren's bier on their shoulders and traveled through the night, they may have already arrived within the city. If we could arrive before the caravan, which was likely if they carried Toren's bier with a donkey-drawn cart, I could argue the case for the Kenite's burial in my family's tomb. And knowing my brothers, there would most certainly be an argument.

We'd delayed long enough. I removed a bronze-tipped arrow from my quiver and gave Joab an encouraging poke to his backside. He bolted to his feet, huffing and rubbing the offended body part. I ignored his offense and rolled up his sleeping mat and mine.

We rode in silence until we approached Bethlehem. "I told you," he said, nodding toward the closed gates. "It's barely past sunrise." The city had always been closed to me, but memories of our childhood antics lightened my mood.

"Gates never stopped us before." We'd scaled Bethlehem's walls a hundred times as shepherd boys.

Joab groaned. "I'm getting too old for this." But I knew he loved the challenge.

As our camels lowered themselves for our dismount, a twig snapped behind me. I leapt from my saddle and whirled, dagger drawn.

Abba's chief shepherd, Dodo, stood three paces away, grinning like a jackal after a good meal. "The conquering hero finally comes home." I sheathed my dagger and embraced the man who had raised me alongside his son in Abba's pastures. He patted my back with the strength of a young warrior. "I see you're still sneaking around the city wall." His booming laugh sent morning larks to flight.

I released him and only partly feigned annoyance. "If the watch-men opened the gates at dawn as they should . . ."

"*Should* seldom reigns in Bethlehem. Nothing has changed." He held my gaze, and I knew he had more to tell.

"Has Zerry already arrived?" His confused expression told me we'd reached Bethlehem before the burial procession. "Let me start with good news," I said to my old friend. "Your son is one of my Mighty Men. Elhanan has trained a hundred of my men to be skilled warriors while shepherding our flocks."

Pride swelled Dodo's chest. "I taught all you boys to be warrior-shepherds. People are not so different than sheep and need just as much protection with a king like Saul ben Kish." He sobered. "What brings you to Bethlehem?"

"I wish I was here only to reminisce, but I bring sad news. Do you remember Toren the Kenite, the man who helped Abba rescue Ima from the Ammonites?"

"Of course. Your abba and I helped him plan the rescue. Abishai told me he married Zeruiah." He grinned knowingly. "She evidently found a man equal to Ahitub's character."

"Toren was the best of men," Joab said, "but Ima now grieves her second husband."

"I'm sorry, son."

"Toren was also my wife's abba," I said, "and Zerry plans to bury him in our family's tomb."

Dodo's eyes widened. "Eliab has taken your abba's place among the city elders." What he really meant was Eliab would never allow a Kenite's bones to sully the tomb of Jesse's clan.

"Then I'll speak to Eliab before Zerry arrives." I exchanged a determined look with Joab. He nodded, equally resolute.

"I'll care for your animals while you two make arrangements for your sister." He paused, scrubbing his bearded chin, then said, "You should probably visit your brother Shimea before you speak to the elders. He and his eldest son's family have taken possession of Abishai's home."

"What?" Joab shouted. "How dare—"

Dodo whirled his staff and whacked Joab's arm. "Think before you speak, boy. Shimea and Ozem are the only two sons of Jesse's who ever treated David with kindness." He shifted his intense gaze to me. "I don't know why Shimea is living in Abishai's home, but he's the shrewdest merchant in Bethlehem, and he's the only reason Clan Jesse continues to prosper. I suspect he has a good reason for commandeering the home where Zerry raised her sons. Now, off with you both!" He turned and walked away, as he often did when our lesson was finished.

"Should we wait until the gates open?" I called after the old shepherd.

"We're not waiting." Joab stomped toward the section of wall we climbed as children and found a thorn bush blocking it, one as tall as a giant. I imagined it as Goliath and drew the dead Philistine's sword to hack away the obstacle. With every blow, logic succumbed to anger. The old wounds of rejection and humiliation opened wide, and by the time the thorn bush was gone, my heart was also in pieces. Joab cleared the debris from beside the wall and bent to one knee. I anchored one foot on his knee, climbed to his shoulder, and then vaulted from his upraised hand to grip the vertical arrowslit in the wall. I slid my other hand into the same narrow opening, walked up the wall, and then hoisted myself over. Bethlehem's watchmen were doing their rounds on the other side of the city, giving me plenty of time to lower my rope for Joab.

Though I merely provided an anchor for his climb, Joab's muscle and bulk felt like a full-grown bull dangling from my rope. He pulled himself over the wall, sweat dripping from his brow. "That was harder than I remembered."

The exertion had quelled my fury enough to regain reason. "Dodo is right," I whispered. "We must treat Shimea with respect and discover his motive for moving into Zerry's home."

"We'd better discover it before Ima arrives because she'll see it as simply another slight."

"Nothing is *simple* in Bethlehem." We jumped off the wall onto a pile of straw and hurried across the deserted street. The eastern sky was streaked with lavender, orange, and gold, and roosters alerted the whole town to a new day.

Joab and I slipped through the familiar back gate. I saw no lamps lit in the house, so I quietly pushed open the door on its leather hinges. Allowing my eyes to adjust to the darkness, I scanned the main room and found it largely unchanged since I'd last visited Bethlehem a decade ago. A loom sat in one corner with a garment started. A few pillows were arranged around a leather table mat in the center of the room, and several food baskets lined the inner wall. Why would Shimea's family commandeer Abishai's home yet maintain everything as Raya—and Zerry before her—had wanted it?

"It's like they never left." Joab whispered, close behind me.

Hallways led left and right. The right hall had been sufficient to house Zerry's family, but the left had been built for more sleeping rooms when Abishai's family moved in and grew. I motioned Joab left and tiptoed into the right-side hall, hoping to find Shimea in Zerry's largest chamber. Halting at the first door on the left, I reached for the latch.

"Why are you skulking into my bedroom?" Shimea's whisper came with the sting of his blade at my ribs.

Careful to turn only my head to face him, I grinned. "You've become a much lighter sleeper."

The dagger bit into flesh. "Are you here to hurt my family?" The pain in his tone was startling—and felt too familiar.

"I would not harm my own blood." In the gathering light of dawn, our eyes communicated more than words. Perhaps we'd both added bricks in the wall built between us. "Toren the Kenite is dead," I said bluntly. "He rescued Ima. He was Abba's best friend, our sister's husband, and my wife's abba. Zerry wants to bury him in the tomb of Clan Jesse."

"Oh, David." He lowered his dagger and shook his head. "Eliab is one of the elders now."

"I know, but I'd hoped you would help me convince the other elders and our brothers why Toren deserves to be entombed with our family."

"I'll do it."

"You—" I'd been ready to argue but said instead, "I'm not sure when they'll arrive with his body. Maybe today."

Brow furrowed, he asked, "You didn't accompany them?"

A fresh wave of shame rolled over me. "Samuel is dead. Saul used his burial to lure me to Ramah. Joab and Abishai were with me, and we're safe only because Jonathan provided camels for our escape. Joab and I came here before—"

"Will Saul chase you here?" Panic tinged his tone.

"No. We'll stay only long enough to bury Toren and go."

"Go where?" He placed a hand on my shoulder.

"I don't know." The words came on a strangled whisper.

With a deep sigh, my brother pulled me into his arms. "I believe there are some things I should tell you, little brother. Maybe in addition to a burial, Yahweh brought you to Bethlehem for a resurrection."

TWENTY-ONE

AHINOAM

Jesse was the father of Eliab his firstborn; the second son was Abinadab, the third Shimea, the fourth Nethanel, the fifth Raddai, the sixth Ozem and the seventh David.

1 Chronicles 2:13–15

"Uriah, help Zerry!" She'd started sliding off her donkey when we halted a stone's throw from Bethlehem's gate. Uriah and Ahimelek gently righted her, and she patted their cheeks as if they were still the young Hittite boys her sons had befriended as children. Though her initial grief had been unbridled and vocal, while preparing Abba's body she'd assumed an almost eerie calm and had refused to speak to anyone during the arduous journey, except the Hittites and me. I realized now the silence was sheer exhaustion.

Determined to know if my friend was all right, I prodded my donkey forward. He wouldn't budge, so I considered a careful dismount. Since I'd stubbornly insisted on walking most of the journey, my feet were badly blistered.

Elhanan appeared at my side. "Please remain on your donkey, mistress. Otherwise I'll be forced to carry you, which I suspect will be as uncomfortable for you as it would be for me." The man's face was the color of pomegranates, and it wasn't because of the weather.

"Then go check on Zerry," I said more harshly than intended, and the tenderhearted shepherd looked wounded. "Forgive me, Elhanan. I only meant . . ."

Tears burned my eyes, and I lowered my head. Abba would have called me a silly woman—and I would have overlooked the insult if only he'd still been here to give it.

"It's all right, mistress, but please let me go alone to speak to the elders about the burial." He strode away, and I glanced at the ten men in the judges' seats at the city gate. My heart withered when I recognized Eliab, David's oldest brother, among them.

Ahimelek led Zerry's mount steadily toward the gate, and Uriah flanked the donkey, carefully watching Zerry. My little gray mule was next, and sixteen of our thirty Mighty Men followed. They'd rotated in shifts, carrying Abba's bier all the way from the Dead Sea. We had traveled for two days, stopping only twice to refill our waterskins along the way. Our strength spent, two hundred chosen warriors approached Bethlehem's elders with a request burning more like a demand in their hearts. Every soldier in David's army had volunteered to escort Abba's bier to Clan Jesse's tomb.

Everyone except Joab, Abishai, and my husband.

For two days, I'd done nothing but walk, grieve, and think. I knew marriage would mean pain. Crushing, consuming, debilitating pain. Death took Abba from me, but David chose to leave. He claimed leaving was noble. His duty. But my husband went to Ramah seeking more than peace for Israel. David ben Jesse wanted to regain his place in the royal family. I glanced over my shoulder at the misfits and rebels who had become dearer to me than I could have imagined. David hadn't chosen duty over family. He'd chosen royalty over *true* family.

When he'd abruptly taken two of his top three soldiers, Asahel was left to manage the army and establish his new household. Zebby had been traumatized by the shofar blast, the messengers' arrival, and his Saba Toren's sudden death. Though he'd been too young to recall details of his ima's murder in Bethlehem, the events had stirred deep emotions that he didn't understand.

Asahel had comforted him while Abital helped Zerry and me wrap Abba's body with extra cloth and what few spices we had on hand; however, the meager spices meant we must travel hard to Bethlehem to avoid the degrading stench of death. Zerry forbade her youngest son and his new bride from accompanying us, so Asahel chose two hundred of our six hundred men for the procession and Elhanan to lead them.

Elhanan was already speaking with Eliab when Ahimelek halted the procession five paces from the city gate. The other nine elders looked rather alarmed while quietly assessing the number of soldiers. "He was your abba's best friend," I heard Elhanan say.

Curious townsfolk began streaming out of the city; at first, only women and children. Then came the men. I recognized Jesse's sons among them—Abinadab, Nethanel, Raddai, and Ozem. Only Shimea, the one who had been kindest to Zerry, was missing.

Ozem stood beside Elhanan in a surprising show of support as the conversation with elders grew heated. "Need I remind you that Toren the Kenite saved your ima from the Ammonite king?" Elhanan shouted as a hush settled over the gathering. I'd only known the big shepherd for three years, but I'd never seen him lose his temper.

"Need I remind *you*," Eliab sneered, "that you gave up all rights as a citizen of Bethlehem when you shirked your responsibilities as under-shepherd of my family's flocks?"

"Elhanan is now chief shepherd of *my* flock." The voice was unmistakable, but I couldn't believe it until I saw David emerge from inside the city. "Elhanan has managed the goats you chose from our family's flock when Abba left them in my care at our parting after returning from Moab. Elhanan and the under-shepherds he trained have protected our flock through impossible circumstances. I'd say Elhanan has every right to be heard—as does our sister and my wife." His eyes only grazed Zerry before he focused on me and closed the distance between us. His hands were around my waist before I could resist, and he slid me off the donkey's back.

As my blistered feet touched the ground, my knees buckled, and I whimpered.

"What's happened?" He stared so intently, yet tenderly. "Are you injured?"

I wanted to say, *Yes, you've injured me,* but said instead, "I tried to march with the soldiers all the way here." Leaning against my donkey, I lifted one of my feet to show the dust-caked open wounds.

"Oh, Nomy." Without warning or hesitation, he swept me into his arms and held me close. "I'm sorry, my love. I shouldn't have left you." He looked into my eyes and leaned down for a kiss.

I turned away.

After a slight pause, he whispered, "I've made many mistakes, and after your abba's burial, we'll take a long journey together and share all Yahweh has done during our two days apart. For now, however, will you allow me to grieve with you and honor your abba—a man I also loved?"

The sorrow in his tone drew my gaze. "How did you arrive in Bethlehem before us?"

His lips pursed into a sad smile. "After your abba's burial, I'll tell you about a miraculous resurrection." Then he toted me, like a sack of grain, to the front row of spectators, where Shimea was presenting Zerry's case before the elders.

"Four of Jesse's sons wouldn't be standing here today," he shouted over the crowd, "if Toren the Kenite hadn't rescued our ima from the Ammonite king. The Kenites have long been Israel's allies, and Toren was a hero among them. Toren's metalwork provided weapons for Judah's rebels, and he used that same skill to defend my brother against King Saul's unfair and unfounded accusations. Clan Jesse should be honored to add his bones to our family's tomb." He turned his attention to the judges seated at the city gate. "Which elder among you will cast the first vote to honor my family?" Shimea's emotional plea sent a shiver through me, and the crowd began to clamor, prodding the judges to rule in Zerry's favor.

"Aye!" came the first official vote, quickly followed by another. All nine elders gave affirmative verdicts, then turned to Eliab to make it unanimous. He looked like a man fighting a swarm of locusts with a stick.

"Aye" came Eliab's final vote.

A cheer rose, and Zerry fell into Shimea's arms, weeping. Ozem cast a victorious glance at David. Ozem had voiced his support when he delivered Jesse's gift of Passover provisions to the Forest of Hereth, but how had my husband won Shimea's obvious favor? What had Yahweh done during our days apart? I laid my head against David's chest, listening to the steady thrumming of his heart as he carried me to the front of the processional.

"Where are we going?" I asked without looking at him.

"Clan Jesse's tomb is in one of our family's pastures." He pressed a kiss to the top of my head, and I relaxed into his strong arms.

The cave was hewn into a rocky hill tucked between two oaks. Our Mighty Men rolled an enormous stone from the entrance and carried the bier inside. It was a simple ceremony. No paid mourners. The wailing and rending of garments had already been done. An old shepherd offered David a lyre, but he refused, choosing instead to hold me in his arms and use his strong voice as the only instrument. "Though I walk through the valley of the shadow of death, your rod and staff comfort me." Zerry and I sang harmony. The familiar words brought comfort, even as our faithful warriors sealed my abba's body all alone into a cave.

I held tighter to David's neck and buried my face against his chest. Though I'd seen the emptiness in Abba's eyes and knew he no longer dwelt in his earthly shell, the mysteries of life beyond still left me unsettled. Zerry's low groan proved I wasn't the only one struggling with the final good-bye.

When the town's curious onlookers had dispersed, leaving only those who truly supported us at the tomb, David placed me on a large rock beside his sister. Shimea was already seated on her other side. Ozem stood behind us, and David knelt in front, cradling his sister's hands. "Zerry, when I arrived in Bethlehem this morning, I found Shimea and his son Jonadab living with their families in Abishai's house." She gasped, but before she could accuse their older brother, David added, "He told me that our sister Abigal isn't dead after all—that she lives among the Ishmaelites, and you've been exchanging messages with her for years."

Zerry looked more frightened now than angry. "I couldn't tell Abba," she said to Shimea, then turned to David. "And I didn't dare burden you—Israel's champion—with a sister living among a tribe of raiders."

David placed both hands on Zerry's knees. "A resurrected sister isn't a burden, Zerry, and after what happened at Ramah, Abigal may be Yahweh's gift of life to my army, as well."

"I don't understand," Zerry said, alternating glances between her brothers.

"Let me explain," Shimea said. "When our family returned from Moab, I regularly checked on your sons' homes and discovered the large amphora inside Abishai's courtyard was stuffed full of unopened scrolls. Because they bore an unfamiliar seal, I opened the messages and realized they were intended for you, from our sister Abigal. The tone of each missive became increasingly alarmed at the length of time since you'd answered her. I understood that the messenger who delivered them must have usually returned your correspondences, so to establish contact, I moved into Abishai's house—the home where you raised your sons—and wrote my first message to the sister I hadn't seen since she was ten years old."

Tears rolled down Zerry's cheeks, but this time with a smile. "Did she know it was you?"

Shimea, too, shed happy tears. "Yes, and Ozem and I have been corresponding through her husband's messenger for nearly three years. I moved my son's family into Abishai's house with me and told our brothers it was because he needed a larger home for his growing family—but it was really to appear as though I was as antagonistic toward you and David as the older three brothers." He glanced at David. "Ozem would have joined your army at Keilah, but we feared any show of support might have stirred Eliab's anger. Our silence was the best way we knew to protect both you *and* Abigal."

"You've done well." David lifted his eyes to Ozem. "Thank you."

"And thank you for protecting Abigal." Zerry hugged Shimea fiercely.

I focused on my husband. "What did you mean when you said Abigal may be Yahweh's gift of life to our army?"

"Saul used Samuel's burial to lure me to Ramah. We only escaped because Jonathan gave us camels and told us to ride far and fast. Abishai is moving our troops to the Maon fortress as we speak, but I don't believe that's far enough to escape Saul's anger. Yahweh brought me to Bethlehem to bury your abba and to celebrate the resurrection of a sister I thought long dead." David gained Zerry's attention. "You can introduce me to Abigal and her husband, Jether. We leave for the Ishmaelites' Desert of Paran at dawn."

The joy drained from her features. "David, I can't go to Paran."

Joab rushed forward. "What do you mean? Of course you can."

Zeruiah bat Jesse turned to me, shoulders slumped. "Make them understand, Nomy. I let myself love Toren, and now . . ." She shook her head, fighting for control and losing. She leaned into Shimea's embrace and buried her sobs against his chest. "I need someone to take care of me for a while."

He looked up at Joab. "Your ima will be protected and well cared for in her own home, nephew. She needs to rest." Looking at David, he added, "Would our sister forfeit a reunion with Abigal if she thought she could survive the journey?"

The answer was obvious—as was Zerry's complete collapse. Joab pushed David and Shimea aside, scooping his ima gently into his arms, then began a slow walk back to the city. Shimea, Ozem, and David followed. I stood alone, wrapping both arms around my waist for fear I'd completely fall apart without Abba or Zerry in my new world. I was King David's wife, but he'd hurt me more deeply than anyone ever had.

The echo of Zerry's words haunted me. *"I let myself love Toren, and now . . ."* Was I brave enough to open my heart to David again?

TWENTY-TWO

DAVID

Then David moved down into the Desert of Paran.

1 Samuel 25:1

Desert of Paran

My warrior bride had barely spoken since we left Bethlehem three days ago. We'd traveled directly to the Maon fortress and met Abishai's caravan on the way. At our first oasis, we dismounted my camel, and Nomy ran straight into Abital's arms, then clung to Zeb, weeping as if she'd never let go.

Continuing south through Judah's Jeshimon, we passed Mount Sodom and the legendary salt formation thought to be Lot's wife. "Yahweh might as well do the same to me," she'd mumbled.

Appalled, I turned in the saddle and pulled her into my arms. "That's not true. Why would you say that?"

"She was ungrateful." Her tone was flat. Lifeless. "Yahweh sent angels to rescue her, Lot, and their daughters before He destroyed the sinful city, but she looked back at loss instead of looking up with praise."

I cradled her, laying her back in my arms to search her eyes.

"God doesn't punish us for grieving, Nomy. Yahweh gave us grief to draw us closer to himself, just like I'm holding you closer right now. Sometimes, especially after losing dear friends in battle, I felt as if the cords of death entangled me. I've been overcome by distress and sorrow, but it drove me to God. I cried out, 'Save me!' and He heard me. He always hears our desperation, love."

She ducked her chin and said nothing. Had I overwhelmed her with words? Though I tried to be silent, our surroundings reminded me of another story to share about a woman in a desert place. "Hagar also grieved, Nomy. Remember the story about Abram's slave wife who bore him a son, but his wife Sarai demanded she be put out of their camp. Hagar wandered, centuries ago, dying of thirst with her son, Ishmael, in the very wilderness we're about to enter. She cried out to Yahweh, and He *saw* her, saving both her and the boy. She was an Egyptian slave. You are Kenite, married to God's anointed, and we're in the very same desert. Cry out to Him, my love, right here in my arms."

Her quiet sniffling said she was listening, but her silence proved I hadn't yet won back her trust. I held her in my arms for the remainder of our journey. Coaxing. Prodding. Pleading for a glimpse of the spirited woman I'd so carelessly left behind when I chose to hope for a man's promise rather than trust in God's plan. Though I'd sincerely apologized and she'd forgiven me, rebuilding the relationship meant she took on the far more difficult task of choosing to resist bitterness whenever memories rekindled the hurt. *Yahweh, please give her a heaping measure of Your grace to forgive my decision.*

The farther we traveled, the more desolate my whole company became. Heaven's wrath was a plausible explanation for Judah's Jeshimon south of the Dead Sea, but our desert was like a well-watered garden compared to Ishmael's wilderness. Occasional underground springs were only notable by the brown scrub bushes growing above them. We had only a dozen goats left. They panted the hot air, their tongues hanging pathetically out of their mouths. Everyone was covered, head to toe, with some sort of clothing to protect from the punishing sun. Children carried little brothers and sisters. Imas wrapped babies around their chests and leaned hard on walking sticks.

Yahweh, we need more water! Again, my thoughts turned to Hagar, whose desperate cry rose to Yahweh because her young son was dying of thirst. *You are still El Roi—the God Who Sees.* How much longer would we wander in Paran's wilderness to find the sister I'd thought dead? Did Jether even know we were searching for his tribe? He was a Bedouin chieftain who moved his camp wherever the desert could sustain them. Shimea had sent word to Abigal through the messenger, but we couldn't wait for an answer. What if Abigal hadn't received word that we were coming? My Gadite scouts had seen no trace of Jether's tribe. *But You see us, El Roi. Show us the way.*

I glanced down at my wife, asleep in my arms. Her lips were swollen and cracked. We'd rationed water for the past two days. How much longer could my people survive in these relentless conditions? *I will trust You, Lord, and we won't grumble as did our ancestors.* The Israelites had survived in Paran's wilderness for forty years. Called Sinai by our forefathers, the ancient stories came alive as we shivered in cold desert nights and rubbed animal fat on cracked lips and feet.

A gnat landed on my forehead. Then another. And another. I swiped and felt dampness on my fingers. It wasn't gnats. Lifting my face to heaven, I felt a light rain begin to fall. All around me, laughing turned to dancing.

"David?" Nomy stirred, and I helped her sit up.

"Rain, my love."

She tried to smile but winced and placed her finger against her bottom lip, where it was bleeding.

"Lift your face," I coaxed, "and let Yahweh give you a drink."

She nodded but lingered in a tender gaze before tilting her head back and receiving heaven's gift. Her lingering look was my first inkling that perhaps her strength was merely lying fallow during a season of sorrow. I, too, opened my mouth to capture raindrops and felt truly hopeful for the first time since leaving Ramah.

The rain continued through the night, chilling us to the bone and then reviving our whole company the next day. We continued our southerly route, hoping our scouts would return with word from Jether. Nomy seemed content in my arms, especially when Zeb joined us for frequent camel rides and settled into Nomy's lap for afternoon naps. Women's delighted chatter replaced the four-day solemn march we'd endured before the rain turned our weeping to dancing.

By midmorning, Attai raced toward us, shouting wildly. "Nahal Arabah! Nahal Arabah!" Joab followed on his camel and arrived to hear the scout's report. "Nahal Arabah has overflowed its banks." I'd only heard legends but hadn't realized we were so far into Ishmaelite territory.

"What is Nahal Arabah?" Nomy asked.

"The ravine's name means *secret river*," Attai explained, "and it's guarded on both banks by tar pits, quicksand, and sinkholes. We must wait until the rain slows before proceeding."

Joab released a frustrated howl.

"No, no, no!" the Gadite shouted over him. "We are blessed! Few people ever see Nahal Arabah because it only flows after a very heavy rain."

Heavy rain? Paran's rain had been gentle drops compared to Judah's winter downpours. Again, our ancient ancestors' wilderness wandering became very real to me. They braved tar pits, quicksand, and sinkholes through forty years of waiting for their loved ones to die. How they must have grieved a full generation left in Sinai's caves and crevices. I'd seen the agony on Nomy's face when we'd left Toren's earthly shell behind in Bethlehem. There was a cleaving of the heart at that tomb, and again when we left the city.

I couldn't risk losing anyone at Nahal Arabah. "We make camp here until morning." Joab made no attempt to hide his displeasure, nor did Attai temper his enthusiasm. Joab took the news to the captains and scouts at the front of our caravan. Like the tip of a sword, they would lead the strike if any trouble arose on the journey. Attai took my order toward soldiers and shepherds tending our meager flock. They were our rear guard, protection from ambush. Nomy and I had remained in the center of the caravan, mainly because I felt she needed the encouragement of Abital, Zebby, and the other families who had rallied around her after Toren's death and Zerry's absence.

As I tapped the camel's shoulder for dismount, sudden screams and a shofar's blast shattered our peace. "Hyah!" I swatted our camel and raced toward sounds of war. Joab and our soldiers had formed a barrier in front of the women and children. Arrows pierced the earth, the shafts at identical angles with uniform black fletching, no more than a finger-width from my soldiers' sandals. The arrows stood like ghastly flowers in a perfect arc. I traced the angle of flight to their origin and found hundreds of Ishmaelite warriors on a mountain cliff above. Bows raised and arrows nocked, they were ready to fire again.

"You've certainly proven your reputation as great archers," I shouted at their chieftain. He was an enormous man.

"David ben Jesse, I presume." Dark-skinned and fierce-looking, their leader wore a red-and-white-checkered keffiyeh and a large curved sword at his belt.

"Shalom, Jether." I inclined my head but maintained eye contact. The man also nodded.

"However, my friend, I must say you've disproved all I've ever heard about Ishmaelite hospitality."

A slow, dangerous smile spread across his face. "We show hospitality to traveling merchants who carry expensive goods and are accompanied by a few attendants. To a powerful army with hundreds of warriors, we show strength." Another warrior stepped to Jether's side. Slight in build, he wore a scarf that covered everything except his eyes. He was half Jether's size, barely reaching the chieftain's armpit, but he carried a bow nearly matching his height and bowed to me as if introducing a challenge.

"Will David ben Jesse accept an Ishmaelite welcome?" Jether asked.

Surely blind acceptance of Ishmaelite custom was a bad idea. I glanced at Joab, who furtively shook his head. Then I returned my attention to Jether. "I'd like to see my sister first. Then I'll accept whatever welcome you and your tribe offer."

"Proof of your courage and trust is the gateway to meeting my wife, Hebrew." Jether folded his arms across his broad chest. Our conversation seemed to be over.

"Then let the welcome begin." I tapped our camel's shoulder to dismount and started toward the chieftain's mountain.

Amid the deafening sound of the Ishmaelites' ululating, I heard Nomy say, "No, wait!" Before my wife could draw Eve, the spindly warrior had planted three arrows in a tight circle between my sandals.

"Nooo!" Nomy leapt between me and the next arrow.

I caught her waist and pressed her behind me, fury replacing calm. "No more!" I shouted. "You torment my wife to welcome me? You've proven your skill and we, our courage. Now, show me Abigal, or let us retreat!" Had Jether not been surrounded by four hundred archers, he would have been a dead man.

The slender warrior unwound the headscarf from his face—or rather *her* face. "You have Jesse's red hair and our ima's handsome features," said Abigal.

Nomy gasped, peeked around me, and won a coy smile from my sister. "And Zerry was right about you, Ahinoam. Any woman willing to take an arrow for her husband is worthy of my little brother."

Two more slender warriors stepped from behind Jether and un-masked their lovely faces. "My wives and I welcome you," Jether declared. "Now we'll show you *real* Ishmaelite hospitality so you know why our friends remain loyal and our enemies—" He chuckled. "Our enemies are dead!" Jether's men raised an uproarious shout while he led his tribe single-file down the winding path toward us.

Joab glanced from Jether to Nomy, then to me. "Perhaps Yahweh brought us to Paran for more than one purpose."

I lifted one eyebrow, uncertain if I wanted to hear the reason for Joab's wry grin.

He must have thought it an invitation. "Perhaps Yahweh will keep us safe here but also use Jether's multiple wives to convince Ahinoam that royalty must take more than one wife to build a legacy."

"Shut up, Joab," Nomy and I said at the same time, then looked at each other and laughed. My nephew walked away, and my wife walked into my arms. *Thank You, Yahweh, for whatever the wilderness will teach us.*

TWENTY-THREE

AHINOAM

The Lord is my shepherd, I lack nothing. He makes me lie down in
green pastures, he leads me beside quiet waters, he refreshes my soul.

Psalm 23:1–3

Ziv (April) 1013 BC
Three Months Later
Jether's Camp, Desert of Paran

"Will you take this to Zerry?" Abigal handed me a tattered headscarf
bearing the sky-blue and crimson stripes of Jesse's family weave. "I
was wearing it when Jether took me from Bethlehem. I've saved it all
these years, but after hearing the way our brothers have mistreated
David, I no longer wish to be counted among Clan Jesse. Shimea
and Ozem seem the only men of integrity in their number."

Though I agreed with her opinion of David's brothers and appreciated her support, I dreaded delivering such news to Zerry.
"I'm not sure when or even if I'll see your sister again. Our camp
will return to Judah's desert fortresses for war season, and Zerry
seemed content to remain in Bethlehem indefinitely."

"Please, Nomy." She pressed the tattered cloth into my hand.
"Jether and I consider David as true in kinship as Zerry and her

sons who share my blood. When David sits on Israel's throne, Jether will defend him against any who betray."

How could I explain that though her heart was sincere, her vow was impractical? Israel's politics were more complex than the Ishmaelite eye-for-an-eye mentality. The mad king who now sat on Israel's throne had sacrificed his own daughter to a brute beast only to prove David powerless. Yet Jether, an Ishmaelite chieftain who married a sister David had long thought dead, would risk his family and tribe to save his adopted brother that he'd met only three months ago.

All excuses died with my rising emotion. I tucked Abigal's tattered headscarf into my travel bag and hugged her tight. "I will miss you, precious sister."

She apologized again that Paran couldn't sustain both Jether's clan and ours and recounted the imminent hardships of summer in the Sinai. I nodded occasionally but kept packing, working hard to hide the roiling inside me. Along with the fears of returning to Judah's harsh existence, I was already grieving the loss of my first true sister.

Abigal, more warrior than maiden, understood me in a way Zerry never had. David had also found both challenge and comfort in Jether's friendship. The Ishmaelite chieftain ruled his tribe with authority and compassion and his home in much the same ways. Though Jether openly showed Abigal affection, he was also kind and thoughtful toward his two younger wives.

I once asked Abigal why Jether had taken other wives when he so obviously adored her. "He hasn't always loved me," she said with a grin. "I was a child when he took me from Bethlehem to become his first wife's tent slave."

"You were a slave?"

She shrugged and nocked an arrow, continuing her practice while I threw my daggers at a nearby tree. "I loved my mistress," she continued, "and mourned each month her womb remained empty. I was fifteen when she finally carried a baby to delivery. The master was too nervous to wait in camp, but I was excited to attend the birth. Mistress labored for three days. Though I didn't understand the midwife's concern that the baby was coming backward, I knew exactly when the spark of life left Mistress's eyes. Jether was inconsolable and refused when the midwife asked to save the child by cutting Mistress's belly."

Abigal fell silent, loosing three more arrows before she spoke again. "Jether and I grieved for months while I continued my regular duties. Our love grew slowly, naturally, as we began to console each other. One night, he planned a great feast and took me hunting that day while the women in camp prepared the meal. At the feast, he declared us wed. I remained childless for nine years. Because he needed heirs, he married Jamila and Safiya—sisters who became his brides a month apart. A year later, I gave him Amasa, my only child and Jether's first son. Amasa's birth earned me the title of favored wife." She gave a quick wink. "The title to match my place in his heart."

Though three women shared one man, Abigal was undeniably favored with Jether's attention, and her son the undisputed heir. Jamila and Safiya seemed embroiled in their own competition. Each had borne four girls, and then each gave Jether a son as their latest gift.

"Are Jamila and Safiya coming to say good-bye?" I asked, closing my shoulder bag. Though I hadn't spent much time with them, I still hoped to see them before we left Paran.

"They're waiting for my invitation." Abigal stepped to my tent opening and gave permission with a wave. Jamila came first, her son propped on one hip. The eight girls followed—Jamila's four, then Safiya's. Safiya entered last, her little prince toddling beside her with a firm grip on her finger.

"What a wonderful surprise!" My heart was as full as my tent.

"We don't want you to go," Jamila pouted. "You've been such a good friend to Abigal."

"What she really means," Abigal said, "is that I've been less demanding of my sister wives since you've been here to distract me."

"Exactly!" Safiya admitted. "Though we'll miss you, Ahinoam, we'll miss Raya and Abital more."

We laughed together at their unabashed honesty that had been as refreshing as the desert oasis. Even Raya had ventured from Vered's control to befriend Abital and women of Jether's tribe. As the adults of our camp formed friendships among the Ishmaelites, the little ones from David's camp learned desert life from the Bedouin children as they all spoke the language of play. Our soldiers' wives also learned much from their Ishmaelite friends. Besides teaching us to find and collect water from underground springs, they shared easy yet delicious recipes with newfound spices to make the simplest of fare taste like a dish from a well-stocked kitchen.

Perhaps the most important lesson I'd learned came from Abigal. *"Every woman has been wounded,"* she said one day while cleaning our dishes with sand. Then she pointed at an old woman with only one arm, who was braiding a little girl's hair using one hand and the toes of one foot. *"Yamam is the best kind of friend—a friend who neither hides her wounds nor overly laments her scars."*

The laughter had quieted, and Jamila nudged her oldest daughter forward. The twelve-year-old bowed while offering a sackcloth-wrapped package. "For you, Mistress Ahinoam. From your Ishmaelite sisters."

"Thank you, precious girl." I returned her polite bow and untied the string. As the wrapping fell away, I squealed with delight. "I've envied your garments since I arrived!"

"It's called a *saknati,*" Abigal explained. "It means *residence* because we live in them." Giggles filled the tent as she instructed me in how to wear the red garment. I removed my dagger belt and robe. Wearing only my tunic, I stepped into the circular opening at the top of the mountain-shaped cloth, then poked each foot through its opposite corners.

"Now, put your weapon belt on and cinch it tight to hold the saknati in place." Abigal helped secure the loose-fitting cloth at my waist.

With my legs separated by the cloth but completely covered, I leapt, twirled, and lunged, testing the modesty and mobility. I squealed again, hugging each giggling little girl, their imas, and finally Abigal. "Thank you for everything."

And thank You, Yahweh, for my friends.

"What's this?" David appeared at the tent entrance, wearing his own new black saknati.

Jether followed, and upon seeing his entire household crowding my tent, he shouted, "Back to your tasks. Out! Out!" He bowed to one knee and tapped his cheek. "But first kisses." His children swarmed him with delighted obedience. Jamila and Safiya waited until their children had gone before offering more lingering affection.

Abigal reached for David's arm and escorted him inside. "So, brother, were you as pleased with your saknati as your wife was with hers?" She continued glancing at the two women who fawned over her husband—*their* husband.

Though Jether's wives lived in relative harmony and would even call themselves friends, could any woman share the man she loved with another? David cast an awkward glance at me, noting his sister's predicament. Jether seemed oblivious to our discomfort.

"Will our saknatis improve our archery skills, Jether?" My voice was overly loud.

David did a poor job of hiding his smile while Abigal mouthed a silent thank-you. Jether shooed away his young wives, who then hurried after their children.

The chieftain joined us but first gathered Abigal under one arm. Whispering something privately, he kissed her forehead. Turning to us, he grinned and said, "A saknati won't improve your archery skills, but riding a camel is certainly more pleasant."

Laughter again filled my tent, and I etched the moment into my memory. As happiness settled into our final good-bye, I wondered if I'd ever see Jether and Abigal again. *Take good care of them, Yahweh.* My chest suddenly tightened, and I saw the same emotions mirrored on Abigal's quivering lips.

Jether clamped a meaty hand on David's shoulder. "If only Paran was the Garden of God, brother. Or you could change your mind and join our summer raids. It's how we survive, and your men and their families would be well cared for."

"Thank you for your gracious offer, Jether, but if I can provide for my people without raiding, then I must." The two men locked wrists. They'd debated the moral grounds of raiding for over a month and finally agreed to disagree. "I can never repay the debt I owe you, my brother." David sniffed back emotion.

Jether pulled him into a fierce embrace. Abigal and I lifted our chins and blinked away tears, refusing to let the parting defeat us.

"A single act would repay the debt," Abigal said.

Our husbands released each other, and David chuckled. "If you think I'll allow you to shoot arrows at my feet again, you're mistaken." He hadn't noticed Abigal's seriousness.

"Take Amasa to Judah with you," she said, expressionless. Jether slipped his arm around her shoulder.

"He's only thirteen," David said with a tinge of panic.

"Amasa is among my best archers." Jether straightened, seeming offended. "He's better than any of your men."

"But we can't guarantee his safety," I said to Jether, then turned to Abigal. "And he's your only son."

"He's a warrior." Abigal, too, seemed defensive. "Amasa must learn the tactics of other nations and return someday to be a wiser chieftain of his tribe."

How could an ima release her only son to life-threatening danger?

David offered his hand in pledge. "I would be honored to count Amasa among my warriors."

"What?" I started to protest but paused at the warning glances of three people I loved. Instead, I asked Jether, "Help me understand why you've entrusted Amasa to our care."

"Entrusted him to your care?" Jether scoffed. "My son is an Ishmaelite warrior. He's fought and killed in battle. He's raided enemy villages. He's performed every tribal requirement from shoveling camel dung to planning raids."

Folding his arms over his chest, he pinned David with a stare. "I'm not entrusting Amasa to your care, brother. I'm sending my son to protect you."

PART III

David said to Abigail, "Praise be to the Lord, the God of Israel, who has sent you today to meet me."

1 Samuel 25:32

TWENTY-FOUR

DAVID

While David was in the wilderness, he heard that Nabal was shearing sheep. So he sent ten young men and said . . . "Please give your servants and your son David whatever you can find for them."

1 Samuel 25:4–5, 8

Elul (August)
Four Months Later
Dead Sea Fortress, Judean Wilderness

I paced along the northwest edge of the Dead Sea fortress, watching the horizon for my messengers' return while the children's hungry cries grew weaker. *My God, my God, why have You forsaken me?* My people were starving and dying of thirst, and Yahweh hadn't spoken to me since we left Paran.

"Come out of the sun," Ahinoam said absently, focused on the blade she was sharpening. "Perhaps if you took your lyre and found a quiet place to be alone . . ."

She let her words fade while the avalanche of guilt piled higher on my shoulders. I'd stopped singing when we returned to find Judah in the iron grip of drought. I found no reason for praise when our fortress cisterns were nearly empty, having captured too little winter rain to sustain us for the summer. How long since I'd felt the breath of God revive my spirit? How long since I'd felt His favor or the confidence of His direction?

Judah's sparse winter rains meant rock-hard soil, difficult sowing, and light harvests. My army was once again split between two fortresses, enduring summer temperatures that made stones hot enough to bake bread, but we had no grain or water to make dough. Word had spread that we'd left Judah to live among the "filthy Ishmaelites." Many of our own people refused to trade with us because of it, and Nabal still hadn't paid his long-overdue debt. Though he was known as a loudmouthed fool, he was also well-connected to many wealthy Judeans. If my messengers returned with Nabal's so-called "gifts," the other landowners might lift their silent ban.

"I shouldn't have sent Amasa with the young messengers," I mumbled. Abigal's son was volatile. "He draws his bow before he thinks."

"Shammah's son will settle him like Shammah calms Joab—and Abishai and Asahel." She chuckled. "Come to think of it, your whole family is a little impulsive."

"This is serious!" I whirled on her. "Our cisterns are dry. Our flocks are gone, and we've thinned the wild game by overhunting. We should never have gone to Paran. I failed—"

"Stop!" She leapt from her stool and framed my face with her hands. "Our time in Paran was a balm for everyone. Now we move forward." Her lingering kiss helped me relax into her embrace. But when my wife stepped back, she crossed her arms like Zerry did before a scolding. "How long since you've spent time alone with Yahweh—just listening?"

"How long since our camp has eaten more than broom-tree roots in our soup? How long since we've roasted anything but a bony bird or fish over our campfires?" I turned away, trying to bridle my frustration. "Saul need not kill us. The Jeshimon will do it for him."

I needed to find a way to provide for those depending on me. *My God, why haven't you saved me? Why haven't you heard my cries of anguish?*

Nomy's soft humming broke through my thoughts, and I recognized the tune as the one that bubbled out of me while prodding her to call out to Yahweh when she grieved so deeply for Toren. "The cords of death encompassed me," she sang. "The waves of destruction tossed me; the cords of Sheol tangled 'round me; the snares of death captured me. Yet in my distress I called on Yahweh; I cried to my God for help—"

"He didn't answer," I said flatly. "And I don't have water inside me for tears."

She looked as if I'd slapped her. Before she could condemn me further, a shofar sounded. I shaded my eyes, looked toward the horizon, and saw our ten young messengers returning from Nabal's estate.

Their donkeys carried no supplies. Nabal had refused.

Despair met desperation, and fury blazed to rage. "Sound the t'ruah," I shouted at the nearest watchman. "Today, we destroy a fool!"

"David, wait!" Ahinoam trailed behind me. "At least hear the boys' report."

Ignoring her, I found Joab already briefing his brothers. My eldest nephew greeted me with a scowl. "I told you we should have sent warriors, not boys."

I wanted to pound him but held my temper, waiting until the Three and half of my Mighty had gathered. Then I confronted my cocky general. "To what tribe of Israel was I born, Joab?"

Seeming confused, he answered, "Judah?"

"And in which tribal lands have we hidden for so many years?" His features hardened into belligerence, so I answered for him.

"Judah. And Yahweh has anointed me to become their shepherd to protect and guide them. I refuse to be like Saul, who bullies and ignores them."

"Forgive me, my lord." Joab inclined his head.

"So you won't attack Nabal's household?" Ahinoam's question irritated like sackcloth.

I wouldn't dignify it by turning to address her. "A shepherd doesn't allow a witless sheep like Nabal to gore ailing lambs," I announced to my gathered captains. "If our ten couriers bring the news I anticipate, Nabal has proven himself a witless sheep."

Joab raised his fist and bellowed, rousing their fury, then followed me to await the messengers at the head of the narrow serpentine trail. As the young warriors approached, their weary, defeated faces confirmed my fears.

Shammah's son, Jonathan, led the group and halted before me. He slammed his fist over his heart. "We delivered your message, my lord."

"Tell me."

"These were Master Nabal's exact words: 'Who is this David, son of Jesse? Isn't he only a servant leading other servants who have escaped their masters? Why should I give bread, water, and meat, which I've saved for my men, to rebels and fugitives?'" Jonathan spit on the ground, as if repeating Nabal's words left a bitter taste.

Amasa stepped to Jonathan's side. "Dohd, Jonathan wouldn't let me put an arrow in him."

Jonathan shrugged. "I almost let him, but we couldn't have fought off his entire household. Besides, didn't you command no violence? Deliver the message and return?"

I ruffled both boys' hair. "You are men of honor, and the time for talk is over. Both of you, strap on your swords." Turning to my captains, I outlined the plan. "Joab, choose two hundred of our best men to start south as soon as possible. We'll leave one hundred here to guard our families. Asahel, ride one of the camels to the other fortress, and tell Abishai we'll join forces south of Maon and march at dawn to attack Nabal's household tomorrow before midday."

The ground shook with a war cry, proving my men would rather die fighting than succumb to helplessness and shame. Only one warrior wasn't shouting.

Ahinoam.

I never slept well before a battle, but having left my wife at the fortress, angry and sullen, was sheer torment. Why had Ahinoam asked to join the war on Nabal's household when she was so obviously opposed to it? Why ask to fight beside me in battle when I'd repeatedly and unequivocally refused every time? After denying her yet again, I bent to kiss her, and she turned away. Without question, I'd married the most stubborn woman Yahweh ever created. Heaving a sigh, I lay on my back and stared at the stars to consider their Maker.

My God, I cry out by day, but you do not answer, by night, but I find no rest.

I waited for more words to come. None did. My arms felt cold and empty in the desert chill. For the first time in months, I longed to hold my lyre, but only my sword and dagger comforted me tonight. Our Dead Sea troops had traveled hard with little water to meet Abishai's Maon troops in the Jeshimon south of Carmel. We'd scattered to sleep in the caves we once called home, hoping sleep would revive our strength.

But the familiar surroundings had the opposite effect on me. Remembering the happier days of my marriage that started here, I recounted every cross word that had turned our sweet water bitter. How often had I made excuses to help Joab train our men when she begged me to spend time with her? When had our days together become altogether functional, having lost all sense of oneness and adoration?

And was nagging a rite of passage for every wife? Sort of like how all children lost their front teeth at a certain age, did all wives believe their husbands lost their hearing or their ability to make decisions without a woman's constant guidance? Perhaps Nomy's increased time with the other camp women—teaching them to throw, to sharpen their own kitchen knives, and to knap flint blades— caused her to treat me like a child. She'd always freely shared her opinions, but now she intruded on my relationship with Yahweh. Did she think I hadn't noticed His silence?

She'd even presumed to instruct me on military strategy, which instigated our parting argument. *"Judah will hear that you attacked Nabal's household and think you're just like Saul."*

Just like Saul? She might as well have stabbed me with Eve. Worse, she continued her rant, comparing my attack to recover Nabal's overdue debt with the way Saul began his reign with intimidation and sent bloody pieces of oxen to all twelve tribes with a threat that he'd do the same to any Israelite male who refused to fight.

"I'm not King Saul!" I'd shouted, loud enough for everyone on our side of the plateau to hear.

"Not yet," she'd whispered. *"But didn't you say Saul's decline began when he stopped inquiring of the Lord?"*

The implication left me speechless. I'd avoided Abiathar for weeks and hadn't inquired with the ephod since before I went to Ramah. Who else had noticed my avoidance? I didn't even want to admit to myself the terror that Yahweh might refuse to speak to me, let alone risk God's priest publicly declaring God's displeasure.

"You wanted to be a different kind of king." Ahinoam had placed her hand on my cheek. *"Trust the Lord, David. Be different."*

I'd run from our stacked-stone chamber like a frightened rabbit, but her words tormented me still. *Be different. Be different.*

How could I be different when over a thousand people's lives depended on me—six hundred trained warriors *plus* their wives and children?

"Aahh!" I clutched at my hair. My heart was too full of anger and fear to pray.

"You shouldn't scream into the night." Joab appeared ten paces away. "Our men might think all kings are mad."

"Not funny."

He chuckled anyway and joined me on the rock ledge. We sat side by side, legs dangling over a desert canyon, and watched the eastern horizon brighten.

"Perhaps Jether was right," Joab said. "A desert tribe's only survival is raiding enemy villages. We're a desert tribe. Nabal openly recruits Judean support for Saul. He is our enemy."

"We aren't raiding Nabal's household. Our men earned everything we'll take today. Safeguarding wealthy landowners from enemy raids is an honest way to live. Our warriors protected Nabal, his household, and his shepherds for weeks, but he never paid us for services rendered." We could easily survive this wilderness if it weren't for dishonest landowners like Nabal. "So, we make an example of the Carmelite and reinforce our expectation of fair trade." Saying it aloud made my skin crawl. *Make an example of the Carmelite.* Was I being as vindictive as it sounded?

"Wouldn't it be easier—and more heroic," Joab said, wiggling his brows, "to raid Geshurites, Girzites, and Amalekites and take back what they've stolen from our Judean brethren?"

"No." I heaved a weary sigh and focused on the horizon. "If we become raiders on any villages, we become criminals, which gives Saul an excuse to hunt me again."

"Saul never stopped hunting us, David. He'll come for us whether we raid our enemies or not." He released a huff and looked away. "*If* the warrior priests of Hebron bring us more provisions—as they promised—we might survive the rest of this year's war season. And *if* the coming winter rains replenish both our fortress cisterns, we *might* avoid raiding one more year. After that, my king, we raid or die."

I knew he was right. *Yahweh, my Good Shepherd. Please, please, hear my prayer. My people need still waters and green pastures.* Would He hear a silent request, or must I speak aloud? "I must establish both authority and goodwill with Judah's landowners," I whispered, part prayer, part explanation to Joab. "I lost their confidence when I abandoned them to visit Abigal."

"You did not abandon Judah." Joab abruptly stood and offered his hand. I gripped his wrist, and he jerked me to my feet, locking eyes with me. "You made a strategic decision and gained lasting peace with an Ishmaelite chieftain. Has Saul ever brokered such a deal with any Ishmaelite clan? No. His only treaty is with King Talmai in the north, yet Saul allows Geshur's southern clans to harass Judean land and villages as if no treaty were ever signed."

"Where did you hear that? Our Gadite scouts?"

Joab offered a solemn nod.

My insecurities faded with the revelation of Saul's injustice. Because Israel's king lived with loved ones in peace with northern Geshurite clans, he ignored Talmai's treachery in Israel's southern lands. Unlike Jether, my Ishmaelite brother-in-law who, despite sparse resources, provided graciously all winter for my thousand-person camp and asked only one thing in return. And the wealthy fool named Nabal, who refused to settle his debt with the ten least-threatening boys in my camp, would now feel the wrath I dared not pour out on Saul.

"Rouse the men," I said through clenched teeth. "We march on Carmel."

"Lead those donkeys to the rear!" I shouted at my swift-footed Gadites when more of Nabal's gifts trotted past me. "Elhanan's contingent will tend the livestock."

Someone from the rich man's house thought themselves clever. In the ravine south of Carmel, hidden from Nabal's estate watchmen, they met my two hundred angry warriors with a caravan of heavy-laden pack animals carrying bread, wine, and a multitude of much-needed supplies.

But my anger wasn't so easily appeased.

Marching backward, I lifted my sword and shouted to rouse my men, "May God deal with me severely if there's one man still breathing in Nabal's household by morning!" Their war cry echoed off the ravine walls, sounding as if the whole Israelite army would soon descend on Carmel.

When I faced forward again, two more packed donkeys trotted past me, and a third approached. On the last one rode a stunning woman. A man I recognized as Nabal's head steward led the donkey. Perhaps he'd brought his pretty wife, hoping to play on my sympathy. While still twenty paces away, the woman slid from her mount, closed the distance between us, and fell at my feet.

"Forgive your servant, my lord." She kissed my dirt-caked sandals. "Please let my words replace those of that wicked man Nabal. He's just like his name—he is a fool—and trouble regularly finds him. But the fault is mine," she said, barely taking a breath. "I didn't see the men my lord sent. And now, my lord, as surely as Yahweh lives and as you stand here safe and sound, and because the Lord kept you from avenging yourself with your own hands, may your enemies and all who are intent on harming you be as foolish as Nabal."

She looked up, eyes clear as the desert sky. Frightened but no tears . . . *"Because the Lord kept you from avenging yourself with your own hands . . ."* With these meticulously chosen words, this woman had gently reminded me of Yahweh's perspective. If I'd trusted God to judge the king who wanted to kill me, why not also trust Him to condemn one Carmelite fool?

I offered my hand, and she stood. Nearly my height, she was slender, but an inner strength radiated from her dark eyes. "Who are—"

"Please forgive your servant's presumption," she whispered, holding my gaze. "Let the gifts I offered to my lord be shared with your brave men. I'm certain Yahweh will make a lasting dynasty for you because you fight the Lord's battles, and no wrongdoing will be found in you as long as you live. Even though someone is pursuing you to take your life, you will be bound securely in the bundle of the living by the Lord your God. But Yahweh will hurl away the lives of your enemies as from the pocket of a sling."

My breath caught, warmth spreading through me. *The pocket of a sling.* In a single reassuring address, she'd referenced Saul's pursuit and my clash with Goliath. Was she a prophetess? Who else could speak with such boldness?

"When Yahweh has fulfilled for my lord every good thing He promised," she continued, "and He's appointed you ruler over Israel, you won't bear on your conscience the burden of needless bloodshed or having avenged yourself today." She bowed to one knee. "And when the Lord your God has brought you success, please remember me, your faithful servant."

I gaped at her. Was she an angel? Sent to stop me from making another error? Joab cleared his throat loudly. Startled to action, I offered my hand again. She stood and offered me a shy glance, her lips quaking with a tentative smile.

Desperate to reassure her, I said, "Praise the God of Israel, who sent you today. Yahweh has blessed you with discernment and wisdom to help me see that I was trying to save with my own hands rather than trusting Him to avenge inequities. Had you not spoken so eloquently, my anger might have done great harm. Your tact and wisdom have saved every male in your master's household."

"Thank you, my lord. Accept the gifts from my husband's house-hold with our humble thanks."

"Your husband?"

Her cheeks flushed, and she removed her hand from mine. Its absence left me wanting—not a physical yearning, as for my wife. Something more mysterious—a divine curiosity.

"I should return," she said but still held my gaze. Did she feel it, too?

"Tell me your name," I said.

She looked over her shoulder at the steward who waited with her donkey. Only then did I notice the bruises on her neck. Two thumbprints at the base of her throat and four long, narrow lines on each side.

The same marks I'd seen on Michal's neck.

"Abigail," she said, then pulled her collar tighter when she saw me examining her throat.

"Abigail," I whispered, resisting the urge to comfort her. "I pray for the LORD's vengeance to visit your husband for all his wrongs, but I'm also leaving one of my men as your personal guardian to secure your safety from this day forward."

She stepped back with a soft gasp. "My lord, I can't. Nabal would—"

"This meeting has refreshed my spirit, Abigail, and I believe Yahweh is at work on my behalf—and yours."

"May it be as you say." She offered a smile worth more than Nabal's full debt. "I'll pray without ceasing for your safety, as well, my lord, and that someday we might meet again." After a slight bow, she turned and hurried away.

As I was explaining to Amasai his assignment as her protector, a perimeter scout's whistle drew my attention. "I see evidence of a single spy," Attai shouted from a cliff above. "Fresh tracks. Retreating."

"Follow them!" I ordered. Was Saul planning to return to the Jeshimon so late in summer?

Joab appeared at my side. "Saul has had two years to rebuild his troops after the last Philistine skirmish. We must return to our fortress." He leaned closer. "Quickly!"

I watched Abigail's retreat, recounted her prophetic words, and marveled at the miraculous calm permeating my being.

"Let Saul come, Joab. Yahweh is with us." I couldn't wait to tell Nomy what God had done.

TWENTY-FIVE

AHINOAM

*When the messengers returned to Jacob, they said, "We went to your
brother Esau, and now he is coming to meet you, and four hundred
men are with him."*

Genesis 32:6

I'd followed David's army at a distance and undetected, now watching from a promontory perch while they approached the city of Carmel through a wide ravine. Not even the Gadites had spotted me on their overnight rounds. I'd used every trick Old J taught me and a few I'd learned from Abigal in Paran.

Perhaps David's scouts never expected anyone to follow. If Saul should discover David meant to kill innocent Judeans, wouldn't he be pleased to convict my husband of a real crime? Why had no one else in our camp stopped him?

Only after our troops marched away did Abiathar and Abital admit they agreed with me. "Why didn't you protest?" I'd demanded.

"David is God's anointed," Abiathar said, as if the single truth gave my husband irrefutable sanction.

Abital scoffed. "That's a dangerous precedent for the boy who used to pull my hair in Jesse's pastures."

"Yes!" I said, moving to her side, certain she'd help me chase our misguided husbands. "God's anointing doesn't preclude the need to seek him."

Then she looked down at her son. Zeb gripped her waist in silent plea and buried his face against her middle. Abital combed his hair with her fingers and looked at me with an apologetic crease between her brows.

Shaking my head, I reassured her that she must stay with her son, but my heart cried, *Yahweh, how can I follow David alone?* Though he didn't answer audibly, determination hardened into resignation while I packed a shoulder bag. And as I tracked our army through the night, old skills reawakened and settled into peace. *Thank You, Yahweh, for guiding me.*

I crawled on my belly to the edge of the cliff overlooking Carmel's ravine. Parading toward my husband from the city came a caravan of heavily laden donkeys. Though I couldn't be certain, the man sending the animals appeared to be the same servant Abba and I met while traveling from Jezreel to the Adullam Cave—the one I threatened with my dagger. He held the reins of a pure-white donkey on which a woman was seated, erect and elegant. She was likely Nabal's wife, the woman who had secretly given Abba and me a donkey to atone for Nabal's affront.

Was she trying to make similar reparations for her husband's offense to David? Today's gifts were more like the lavish offerings Jacob paraded before Esau when Jacob discovered his brother came to meet him with four hundred men.

My breath hitched. *Four hundred men.* The exact number David brought to attack Nabal's household. A chill crawled across the back of my neck. Perhaps the woman's gifts weren't secret reparations. Had Nabal heard of the approaching army and, like Jacob, sent gifts to avert violence and his wife to gain sympathy?

I stared at the beautiful woman, and my blood ran cold. *Surely David wouldn't kill an innocent woman.* Watching our soldiers march toward her, I realized how foolish I'd been to press David to join his army. David would never place me in danger like the coward Nabal—or as our patriarch Jacob did by presenting his four wives before he met Esau face-to-face. Jether had allowed his wives to disguise themselves as warriors but only trained them as archers to protect the camp when their men went raiding.

"May God deal with me severely," my husband shouted, "if there's one man still breathing in Nabal's household by morning!"

Yahweh, please save my husband from himself. David could justify the violence, and men would follow him—for a while. But he knew killing Nabal's whole household was wrong. I'd seen him flinch when I challenged him to be a different kind of king. Hadn't Saul's debacle started with a single rash act—a quick sacrifice followed by excuses?

When a strange silence fell over the ravine and then a rhythmic clip-clopping of a single donkey's slow pace, I lifted my head and watched the little beast carry the beautiful woman toward my husband. Before the donkey halted completely, the woman cascaded off its back and glided toward David like a wave. When she bent to kiss his feet, my husband's whole body tensed.

The woman's words echoed off the stone walls. I couldn't decipher them, but I read my husband's reaction like a scroll. He was intrigued, his head slightly cocked. Then his shoulders and jaw slackened as anger gave way to awe. As if watching a dream, a sudden rush of memories bombarded my mind, mixing with the scene below.

During our last day in Paran, I stood beside Abigal and watched as her sister wives fawned over Jether. I'd seen helplessness on Abigal's features, the same feeling that pierced me now as I watched David open his heart to that woman in the ravine. I silently begged David to reject her lavish gifts and send her away—but I knew he wouldn't. Forgiveness was written in his gaze.

Yahweh, couldn't You have intervened in some other way?

Her words flooded the ravine like winter rains. She knelt again. I knew the trick. She wanted to feel his hand in hers once more. When her words finally fell silent, it was as if four hundred warriors held their breath with me, waiting for my husband's response.

David offered his hand, and even before his eyes roamed the length of her, I knew he wanted Nabal's wife. Had my nagging driven him away? He now had even more reason to attack Nabal's household. If the fool's wife became a widow, David could claim her as his own. I dropped my head on my forearm. *Yahweh, please prevent him from making a mistake that would cost him Your favor, even if it means . . .*

Could I share him with another wife? Could I share him with *that* beautiful woman?

"Praise the God of Israel," David's clear voice reverberated in the ravine, "who sent you today. Yahweh has blessed you with discernment and wisdom to help me see that I was trying to save with my own hands rather than trusting Him to avenge inequities. Had you not spoken so eloquently, my anger might have done great harm. Your tact and wisdom have saved every male in your master's household."

I rolled onto my back, biting my fist to keep from wailing. Why hadn't *my* wisdom convinced him? Hadn't *I* warned him not to avenge himself? The pain of betrayal told me to flee, but fear of my future forced me to witness the present.

David leaned close to the beauty. I held my breath. He whispered something. She whispered, too. Would he find a way to marry the woman? *Ridiculous! They'd just met.* Though I tried to push away the thought, a bitter realization came. *King* David could do anything he pleased. If he could justify murdering Nabal's household, couldn't he also find an excuse to marry the man's wife?

My control was waning. I wanted to scream, to empty my dagger belt into a tree. Instead, I bolted to my feet and raced into the wilderness without a plan or path. Abba had been right. I was a silly woman who dared marry a king. *I'm not brave enough to be his wife,* LORD! David ben Jesse had stolen my heart and crushed it beneath his heel. *No more, Yahweh. No more!*

I ran, blinded by tears, until dusk brought the gloom to match my mood. I stumbled toward a cave and fell at its entrance. Tossing a stone inside, and hearing no growls or shuffling from current occupants, I spread my reed mat at the cave's entrance. I pulled my headscarf around my shoulders. Though exhausted, dread tortured me.

How can I share him with another, Yahweh? I'd declared my courage to marry King David *before* we were one flesh. How could he now tear himself from me and knit himself to another?

"I don't even know who that woman is or if David wants to marry her." The logical whisper was quickly silenced by the more insistent voice inside that I'd learned to recognize as Yahweh's rod and staff.

The woman will become David's wife.

The same Voice made me sure enough to follow David to Paran. I'd recognized it with the same certainty and followed his army to Carmel's ravine. Yahweh wanted me to see the woman whose beauty, grace, and eloquence transformed my husband from an unyielding warrior to a sensible king. Yahweh wanted me to see that she was everything a royal wife should be. Everything I wasn't.

Can I at least hate her, LORD? It's only fair.

I pillowed my head on bended arm, drew my knees to my chest, and whispered into the night. "I'd rather die than share my husband with a woman like her."

Please, LORD, hear my prayer. My decision made, I felt more settled and slept like the dead.

The warm sun shone bright on my face. I heard the desert larks of En Gedi twittering their morning songs, and David's arms tightened around me. Drawing in his familiar musky scent, I reveled in his nearness, feeling his warm breath on my cheek. How long had it been since I'd dreamed of life in our oasis? The aromas of earth, vegetation. The feel of my husband's arms around me. The cool air of a cave yawning at our backs. A jackdaw's caw nudged me further into wakefulness. The ground beneath me seemed harder. My shoulder and hip ached. David's lingering musky scent made my heart ache, too.

"Ahinoam?" David's arms tightened around me.

My eyes popped open, heart beating wildly. Part of me wanted to turn into his embrace and demand he never look at another woman. The other part wanted to run away and never see him again.

"Why did you venture into the wilderness alone?" His voice broke, and he held me tighter. "Attai found you because a pack of jackals was stalking this cave. If he hadn't been tracking Saul's spy who watched us at Carmel—"

"It wasn't a spy," I whispered. "I watched from the cliff and saw the way you looked at the woman in the ravine." Silence fell between us, so I turned to face him. "Have you already made her your wife?"

His eyes widened. "Of course not. She's Nabal's wife—though he doesn't deserve her. She had bruises on her neck, Nomy, identical to Michal's."

The tenderness in his voice overwhelmed me. I broke from his embrace and leapt to my feet. *My heart will shatter if he loves another!*

He was instantly on his feet, blocking the exit. "I would have killed Nabal's whole household had she not—"

"Had she not kept you from avenging yourself. She had the words to transform your heart, David. Not me." My voice broke.

He couldn't deny it, and when he tried to embrace me, I pushed him away. Snatching the blue-and-crimson scarf from my head, I shoved it into his hands. "You'll need to present this to your new wife at the wedding."

"Stop it!" he huffed. "Why are you insisting I marry Nabal's wife?

I only spoke to her one time." He paused, searching my gaze. "But she said things only Yahweh Himself could have spoken through her. I was drawn to Yahweh in her and awed that He'd finally broken His silence—and used a fool's wife to do it."

Given David's expression, I knew I probably sounded like a ranting, jealous wife. Abba would have been ashamed. But last night's certainty had only been confirmed by everything David had just said. Silly or not, my heart would continue its breaking. "You will someday marry Nabal's wife," I said, then tried to rush past him.

"Wait." He stepped into my path, his chest like a brick wall that stopped me. When his strong arms enfolded me, I was defenseless against my tears. "*You* are my wife, Ahinoam bat Toren," he whispered, then gently laid the blue-and-crimson scarf over my head again. "I don't know what our future holds, but I love you more today than yesterday and will love you more tomorrow. You will always be my wife, my lover, and my friend." He tipped my chin up, searched my eyes, and then kissed me. Softly at first, then his passion deepened. There, in a cave of reckoning between Carmel and the Dead Sea, my husband reassured me with a tenderness we hadn't shared in many months.

Lying in each other's arms, drenched in the sweat of sated pleasure and desert heat, my husband lifted his voice to Yahweh, anointing the moment with praise. "How precious is your steadfast love, O LORD; *we* take refuge in the shadow *of Your wings.*" More words flowed from his lips. Like a mountain spring, they came without pause or scarcity until he pursed his lips into a hum to engrave the tune upon our hearts—as he'd done so many times before.

Thank You, Yahweh, for restoring my husband's soul. It was almost worth seeing his introduction to another woman to see his heart restored. Almost.

"We must pray for safety during the remaining months of war season," David whispered as if thinking aloud. "And winter rains to fill the stronghold cisterns." After a slight pause, he added, "If Saul pursues us again or if our cisterns run dry, we must raid to survive."

I lay quiet in his arms for several moments and then lifted onto one elbow to meet his gaze. "Let's return to the stronghold. Yahweh is with you, King David. He's clearly spoken."

Clearly spoken to you and me. But I'd rather raid an enemy village than see my husband married to another.

TWENTY-SIX

DAVID

Abigail quickly got on a donkey and, attended by her five female servants, went with David's messengers and became his wife.

1 Samuel 25:42

Eleven Days Later
Dead Sea Fortress

Another new day was beginning, and though we were still fugitives with dwindling supplies on a giant rock in the desert, I was content with Nomy in my arms and praise in my heart.

"I'll see you at midday," I said, then kissed her good-bye, as had become our custom since returning from the cave.

When we'd arrived back at the fortress, Attai had already assured Joab that the "spy" was Nomy and not Saul's scout. My general divided the provisions from Nabal's household and sent half the supplies to Maon with word that he'd remain at the Dead Sea fortress. Within a day, we'd seen our children's health improve. Their rosy cheeks and endless giggles were as nourishing as food and wine to replenish the adults' strength.

Yesterday, while sharing our midday meal with Joab, Asahel, and their wives, my general suggested returning to ask Abigail for more provisions, since Nabal's debt still wasn't fully paid.

"Why poke the jackal?" I'd replied. "Since we've heard nothing from Amasai, I suspect Nabal knows nothing of Abigail's generosity. Why risk Nabal's wrath until the supplies run low?"

"Her name is Abigal?" Nomy asked. "Like your sister's name?"

Was this the first time I'd mentioned Nabal's wife by name in her presence? "No," I quickly clarified. "Her name is Abi*gail*."

Still, my wife considered the similarity more than coincidental and saw it as confirmation that she should begin moving a few of her personal belongings to a one-room chamber on the other side of the plateau.

I was furious. "What will my men think when they see you've left me?"

"I'm not leaving you," she'd said, blinking away moisture gathering in her eyes. "And I'll remain in our chamber until you marry Abigail. But when that day comes, David, I can't bear to live in the chamber beside yours and try *not* to hear your whispered conversations and intimate sounds."

"I don't even want to marry Abigail," I'd said, yet I'd thought of little else. Nabal's wife had been beautiful and wise, but I hadn't felt the same ache of desire for her as I did now when Nomy ended our morning kiss.

A glimmer of mischief sparked in her eyes. "Maybe we won't *rest* at midday."

I threw back my head and laughed with my feisty, beautiful wife, then returned my gaze to meet hers. I loved Ahinoam bat Toren with every fiber of my being. Even our thorny disagreements and her nagging were rooted in a love as deep as a willow tree far from any stream. Nomy's insistence about Abigail felt very different than her previous nagging. She remained steady, not panicked. She cared little about the other women's opinions, our soldiers' questions, or even Abiathar's comments. Her unshakeable resolve mingled with my softening perspective proved our roots could be nourished together no matter where the Lord planted us.

My wife's brows furrowed in silent question, so I finally voiced a thought. "If Yahweh has indeed determined that Abigail will someday be my wife, it could still be years before—"

She pressed two fingers against my lips. "Just like the years that have passed since Samuel anointed you, and we're still waiting to see you rightfully placed on Israel's throne." She replaced her fingers with another gentle kiss and said, "I understand, but I still believe Abigail will soon be part of our lives. Now go. Instruct our men on how to use their slings in battle while I instruct our women on sharpening kitchen knives."

With a groan, I left her. Our partings had become increasingly difficult since returning from the cave. Thankfully, our whole camp had experienced a similar rebirth of body, soul, and spirit with the abundant provisions and had returned to a semblance of normal. Morning and evening, the men engaged in weaponry drills, and women tended to children and household chores. At midday, everyone rested in chambers or under shaded courtyards. We had also resumed our camp's nightly worship. I played my lyre and encouraged others to join with their instruments and voices. The words of the most recent tune flowed out of my grateful heart. *We feast on the abundance of Your house, Yahweh, and drink from the river of Your delights.*

The t'ruah's nine quick blasts intruded on the moment. Was it Saul? Had I let my guard down and placed my people in danger again? Racing toward the nearest watchtower, I reached the ladder at the same time Attai shouted down his report. "A single donkey approaching at a trot. The rider looks like Amasai in bulk and carriage, but I can't be sure until he's closer."

I turned to run toward the trailhead and nearly trampled my

wife. Catching her before she landed on the rocky plateau, I stared into Nomy's hardened features.

"Under what circumstances did you instruct Amasai to return?" she asked.

Before answering, I made sure she stood on solid ground and gave myself time to craft a quick yet complete answer. "He was to remain in Carmel until his replacement arrived on our regular two-week rotations. Or he would return with Abigail if Nabal attempted violence against her." If it was Amasai on that donkey, neither condition had been met.

Questions shimmered in my wife's eyes, reflecting my own fears. "Amasai could fight off fifty of Nabal's men. Why—"

"We're not even sure it's Amasai."

"It's him!" Attai shouted.

Without another word, I grasped Nomy's hand and started toward the trailhead to await his arrival. Joab and Asahel were already there; the musical priests who had come with Amasai to Moab had also gathered. They had led in prayer for Amasai's safety, the chief of my Mighty Men, every evening during our worship together. Ahinoam was right—my strongest warrior could fight off fifty of Nabal's men, but a shrewd fool in his own household was as dangerous as an army.

Our waiting ended when, instead of a donkey and its rider, we greeted Amasai alone running up the serpentine trail. Though his face was crimson, and sweat soaked his hair and armor, my joyful captain raised his fists like he'd won a great battle; and a welcoming cheer shook the mountain beneath us. His safety and glee were themselves a victory, since neither would be likely if he'd failed to protect Nabal's wife.

The realization quickly turned my relief to anger. "Why did you leave her?" I jerked his breastplate to gain his full attention.

The celebration died, but Amasai's smile never dimmed. "The Lord struck Nabal dead."

I released him, choking on disbelief. "How?"

"The day our men left Carmel, Nabal was too drunk to remember anything, so Mistress Abigail waited until daybreak to tell him that David ben Jesse's army had come to annihilate his whole household. Upon hearing the news, he grabbed his chest and fell like a toppled cedar, then turned gray as a stone for ten days until he gasped his final breath." The Kohathite's meaty hand landed on my shoulder as he shouted, "Let all Israel praise Elohim Adonai, who Himself takes vengeance on King David's enemies!"

Another loud cheer rose, and I joined the raucous celebration— until I glimpsed my wife's enigmatic stare. She stood like a statue amid the rejoicing, looking grief-stricken. Didn't she understand? Nabal was an enemy whom Yahweh struck down. She turned away. Was she crying? Did she think me heartless? I suppose someone might have mourned the man named Fool. Perhaps . . . *Abigail*.

As if Nomy heard my thought, she lifted her head and shouted above the noise, "What happens to his widow?" With her eyes locked on mine, she spoke again while voices quieted. "Isn't a wealthy man's wife treated no better than a servant after he dies? Won't Nabal's nearest kin inherit his wealth but also be forced to assume the burden of the fool's debts, his livestock, his servants—and his wife?"

"Yes, of course," Amasai said. "By Levirate law, Mistress Abigail will be given to Nabal's nearest relative with the land, buildings, livestock, servants, and other possessions."

At *other possessions*, Ahinoam's eyes squeezed shut, and I felt her cringe all the way to the pit of my stomach.

Looking away from her, I asked the Kohathite, "Do you know the kinsman redeemer?"

For the first time since his return, his smile disappeared. "The kinsman is crueler than Nabal and already has three wives."

"No! Stop him." Hushed concern rippled through the gathering like waves on the sea. "You must stop him."

When I looked at Nomy again, tears were streaming down her cheeks, and her lips were pursed into a thin white line. Nodding ever so slightly, she whispered, "You must make her *your* wife."

I reached out to her, but she darted away through the crowd. All eyes fell on me, waiting. I looked for Abiathar but didn't see him. "Where is the ephod?" I needed to inquire with the Urim and Thummim.

"The priest left at dawn with his cohort," someone answered.

"To trade some supplies for more grain," added another.

Joab stood beside Amasai and said, "You're Israel's rightful king, David, and you need a wife who can give you children."

"Levirate law says the firstborn of the dead man's wife will be attributed as the dead man's son," Amasai said. "Do you think it wise, General, for King David to acknowledge Mistress Abigail's firstborn son as a member of the Calebite clan? Wouldn't such a claim blur the lines of succession?"

"Make sure your lines aren't blurred," Joab sneered. "We follow *King* David, who Yahweh has allowed to set aside the Law of Moses when necessary to save lives. When he went to Nob after fleeing Gibeah, the High Priest gave him the Tabernacle's sacred bread to save our king's life. If David marries Abigail, it will be to save her life and produce an heir. Why would he be condemned for counting her son as his heir when he received no judgment for eating the Tabernacle's bread?"

"Wouldn't you consider the deaths of eighty priests and their families judgment?" Amasai's retort felt like a dagger in my belly.

Did everyone believe taking that bread was a sin and the deaths at Nob were Yahweh's judgment against me because of it? A roiling pot of dissension began to stir. Women argued. Children cried. Warriors' blood ran hot, and the shoving would quickly turn violent.

"That's enough!" I shouted. "Silence!" I lunged atop a stacked-stone platform to ensure everyone in every direction could see me.

The grumbling faded as I scanned the people who had given up everything to follow and defend me.

On the farthest southern edge of camp, my wife stood at the doorway of her one-room chamber where she'd moved her personal belongings. She placed a fist over her heart—a warrior's salute—gave me a confident nod, and then disappeared inside her new home.

If Ahinoam bat Toren was brave enough to marry a king, I must be brave enough to marry another wife.

TWENTY-SEVEN

AHINOAM

The LORD is my rock, my fortress and my deliverer; my God is my rock, in whom I take refuge.

Psalm 18:2

I examined the four walls of my self-imposed exile, and my legs turned to water. Though I'd promised to be courageous and understood that my husband would likely marry another . . .

"Not her, Yahweh." The whisper came out on a sob. "Please, not an elegant, capable woman who will steal David's love from me."

My body convulsed with a groan. Drawing knees to my chest, I curled into a ball to brace against the ache inside. Weeping shook me. I turned my face into the packed dirt and released years of weariness and pain. *I can't go on, Lord. I'm not brave. I'm not worthy. I'm not fit for a king.*

When I felt gentle hands rub my back, I hadn't the strength to resist or respond. I had no pride left. Weeping ebbed only with numbness. Still, I kept my face buried in the dirt to hide my despair.

"You and I have the unfortunate blessing of husbands who care for others." At the sound of Abital's voice, I lifted my head. Her eyebrows rose. "Well, aren't you a sight." She pulled a cloth from her belt and wiped mud from my face.

Her tenderness was too much for me, and the tears came again.

"Well done," she whispered. "That extra moisture makes the mud easier to remove."

We laughed together, despite my desperation, and then my friend sat back on her heels. "David loves you, Nomy. This woman—Abigail—has only known cruelty from a husband. David is marrying her because of his integrity and a strong sense of justice and compassion. But he *loves* you."

Justice and compassion. "Prince Jonathan once told David it would be his passions to serve Yahweh, to seek justice, and to show compassion that would test him more fiercely than suffering. But I feel like I'm the one being tested. I'm the one bearing the weight of David's royal calling."

"Doesn't every wife bear her husband's burdens?" Abital's gentle question broke through my pity. "When we're one flesh, isn't his pain your pain and your pain his?"

"Are you sure we'll still be one flesh?" I swallowed another lump of emotion that had formed in my throat. "Won't David be torn away from me when he becomes one flesh with Nabal's widow?"

"I don't know." The crease between Abital's brows deepened with her pause. "What if David needs more than one wife to help him carry his burdens as Israel's king? What if Yahweh provided you for David's needs during these early years as a fugitive, and the Lord knows Abigail can provide something David will need in days to come?"

"Then she'll replace me," I said, voicing my greatest fear.

"Never."

Then came the second greatest fear. "Without David, I have no one."

"That's a lie." Abital gripped both my hands. "I could remind you that I'm your friend. I could remind you that every woman outside this chamber respects and loves you. Our fortress is a close-knit family that would lay down their lives for you, Ahinoam bat Toren. But anyone can be taken from you in the blink of an eye—as Dalit was taken from Asahel and me, as your abba was taken from you. So, remember the only One who never leaves you, never betrays, never abandons, never dies." She smiled, leaving the Name unspoken.

I closed my eyes and whispered, "Yahweh."

Abital began softly singing. "You are my rock, my fortress and my deliverer; my God is my rock, in whom I take refuge."

David had led us in the same song after he'd spared Saul's life. We'd marched out of En Gedi into the wilderness, so certain of God's faithfulness—before we'd experienced the Dead Sea fortress with its unbearable heat, rocks hotter than ovens, and a refuge that felt more like prison.

While I listened to Abital's repeated chorus, I felt a chill. A breeze. *In the desert?* Prickly flesh raised the hairs on my arms, and I glanced around my small room. Abital and I were alone—but for the first time in my life, I knew I'd never be alone again. With clarity born from within, I felt Yahweh's imposing presence and knew He would forever be my Rock, my Fortress, my Refuge and Deliverer no matter what circumstance held me prisoner.

When I joined my friend's song, she looked up, startled, and continued to the end with a smile. "So, you'll accept a sister wife?"

The term *sister wife* pierced me anew. Evidently, Yahweh's presence wouldn't shield me from hurt, only from bearing it alone. "The bigger question," I said, "is will David accept the consequences of this decision on all our lives? With Yahweh's presence, I'm brave enough to be David's wife, but I don't want to meet his new wife until Yahweh heals my heart."

I saw the disapproval in my friend's eyes as she stood to leave, then paused at the doorway. "I understand, but the women in camp look to us as their leaders. I hope you'll welcome Abigail with the hospitality Zerry and Abigal showed us, rather than the shameful behavior Vered displays to newcomers."

Before I could present excuses, she walked away. No discussion. No argument. *"With the hospitality Zerry and Abigal showed us."* How dare she ask the impossible?

My sorrow turned to fury, and I emptied my dagger belt, all six blades sinking into my wooden doorframe.

Abigail would learn that my hospitality included daggers.

Two Days Later

I stood beside my husband at the serpentine trailhead, having agreed to model the hospitality I'd been shown by my dearest friends. But Zerry and Abigal did not welcome a woman who would become one flesh with their husbands. Trembling with pent-up fury, I shifted from one foot to the other while six white donkeys plodded up the path.

When David reached for my hand between the folds of our robes, I pulled away. "Don't." My throat constricted around more words. After a deep breath, I whispered, "We agreed. No affection in public view or where the other wife might see. I hope for the same courtesy when you and Abigail—" The dread of the future and memories of Abigal's tortured existence of sharing Jether nearly sent me running to my private chamber.

"Joab!" David growled. "Why do I see six women approaching on donkeys when I invited one woman, Nabal's widow, to be my bride? One woman, Joab, not six."

Joab met him nose to nose, voice low. "Ask your new wife when she arrives, my king. Remember, however, that when you negotiated with the shifty Calebite kinsman, forgiving Nabal's remaining debt to pay Abigail's bride price, we lost our leverage to gain more supplies from him or any other Judean landowner. And the supplies Abigail gave us before Nabal's death are almost gone."

David nudged his general aside without a response. His neck and face were crimson. Though I wanted to give comfort or encouragement, fear of my own unruly emotions held me captive. I'd remained in my chamber since Abital's visit. David had come once, but I'd sent him away, too afraid my swollen eyes and uncontrolled grief would permanently condemn me as his *silly wife*. Abigail was, after all, the one whose proven wisdom had saved him.

When Amasai crested the fortress trail, and I saw Nabal's widow on the lead donkey, sitting as regal as a queen, an uncontrolled whimper escaped. David's arms engulfed me, and he pressed a kiss to my forehead. "I love you, Ahinoam."

Then, just as quickly, he released me and marched toward Amasai and the other five women on their donkeys. "I see you've returned with more guests than expected." His tone was tight, words clipped.

Amasai bent to one knee and bowed his head. "My king, Mistress Abigail believed her maids—"

"It's my fault." The widow slid off her donkey and knelt before David. "I couldn't leave my maids to be abused by Nabal's wicked cousin." She pressed her forehead against his sandals. "I come as your willing servant. My maids and I will wash the feet of everyone in your camp. No task is too menial for us, my lord. We serve you— Yahweh's anointed—with gratitude and no complaint, trusting that even the smallest service to you is a way of honoring the Lord."

I'd forgotten how relentlessly she used words. David glanced at Amasai as if pleading for help and then at Joab. His eldest nephew replied with a smirk.

She'd been brave to rescue her maids. Would Joab mock her for it? "We wash our own feet here." I grasped the widow's arm and hoisted her to her feet. "But you've brought five extra mouths to feed into a camp that's already low on provisions and five unwed maidens into an army of . . ." I was at a loss for the uncomfortable word to describe our single men in want of a wife, so I turned to David. "*You* must choose five men to marry her maids. Our warriors must not fight over them."

"How do I know your men are worthy of my friends?" Abigail glanced at me, then back at David. "I'm terribly sorry your mountaintop is overcrowded, but my friends and I can be of great help to you in managing the provisions you have."

Several men snickered, but David silenced them with a ferocious glare. Nabal's widow grew pale while he examined the five women behind her. "Was my messenger unclear when he offered a marriage contract to *one* woman?"

"I had no other dowry to bring into this marriage, my lord." She straightened her shoulders and met his hard stare. "My personal maids were the only treasure Nabal's cousin couldn't claim. They'll bring great value to your camp with varied skills and diligent hands. If your majesty would like to suggest an honorable man for each of my friends to wed—a man beyond reproach—I'll consider the betrothal petitions and interview the men individually." She closed her eyes and winced as if preparing for a slap.

"You'll *consider* . . ." David's clenched jaw relaxed into a grin.

The widow opened her eyes and returned his smile. "Of course, I'll consider only single men. I don't want my friends fighting for their husband's affection." When soft gasps echoed through the gathering, and all eyes turned to me, the widow realized her affront too late. "I didn't mean . . . what I meant to say was—"

"You've said quite enough." David's voice quaked, his hands flexing at his sides. "Amasai, show Nabal's widow to her chamber. Her maids will share the space until we find their perfect husbands."

He turned to walk away, but I caught his hand. "David, one chamber is too small for six women."

"Let the widow deal with the consequences of her careless words. I'm not a fool like her first husband, and I won't be manipulated as he was." He lifted my hand to his lips and whispered, "You never need fight for my love, Ahinoam bat Toren, but this is the last time I'll show any affection to any woman in public." He dropped my hand, inclined his head, and stalked away—as angry as I'd ever seen him.

I stood among our whispering friends and watched Abigail's maids comfort her as Amasai escorted them to the family's side of the plateau. *Hospitality like Zerry and Abigal showed us.* I groaned at Abital's haunting challenge and let compassion stoke my imagination.

What had Abigail expected when she came here today? The David she'd met in the ravine had been angry but quickly soothed. The bridegroom she'd met today had likely been less welcoming than anticipated. How disappointed she must have been. Did she doubt David's kindness? His gentleness? His honor?

He'll show you his heart someday. The thought came without permission, traitorous and disturbingly sincere. I didn't want to like Nabal's widow. I didn't want to admire the way she protected her maids with honesty, pragmatism, and a pinch of shrewdness. Bringing them as her dowry? *Brilliant.* And it had been a defense David couldn't oppose, which probably stoked his frustration. When Amasai deposited the six women in the chamber next to David's, my feet moved without permission.

When I reached Abigail's shaded courtyard, Abital blocked my path. "Perhaps you should calm down before you speak with her."

"I only want to welcome her as Zerry and Abigal would."

"Nomy." She released a heavy sigh. "I feel sorry for her. Don't cause trouble."

One of the maids yanked back their doorway curtain. "Our mistress is quite upset. She's not—"

"It's all right, Orpah." The widow nudged her aside. "Would you both like to come inside? Though I'm not sure there's room for two more people." Even with red-rimmed eyes and a forced smile, she was stunning.

"I'll visit later," Abital said. "Our family's chamber is on the other side of David's. We'll have plenty of time to get acquainted." She gave me a warning look and left me to welcome the newcomers alone.

Before I stepped over the threshold, the widow began talking. "I never intended to offend anyone," she said. "My concern was—and still is—that my maids never need fight for their husband's affection, but let me assure you, Mistress Ahinoam, I stopped fighting for affection years ago. Nabal shared his bed with many women. David is Yahweh's chosen king and will likely have many wives. I'll never expect him to love me. I can only hope—" Her lips quivered, and she cleared her throat. "I have prayed since the first time I met David ben Jesse that I could earn his respect. Mutual respect is my only goal for our union, but I can learn to live without it. I assure you, even the disdain of a righteous husband is more appealing than the attention of a wicked one."

I released a weary sigh. "You talk a lot."

She covered a smile. "Yes, so I've been told."

We stood there, staring at each other, and I suddenly felt like the misfit Kenite girl again. I turned to leave, but she grabbed my arm. Instinctively, my hand reached for Eve, but this time I stopped before an impulsive decision caused trouble.

"I'd heard you were a warrior." Abigail stepped back. "Forgive me. I shouldn't have touched you. I merely wanted to talk with you a little longer." She bowed to one knee and motioned her maids to do the same.

"Stop it! Stand up," I said. "Don't ever do that again."

They obeyed. The maids exchanged uneasy glances, but Abigail held my gaze. "What does King David want from me? Why did he ask me to be his wife when he has you?"

"He wants a son," I blurted.

She looked as shocked as I was by my honesty, then her features hardened into resolve. "For my first three years as Nabal's wife, I prayed Yahweh would open my womb. For the last seven years, I took every precaution to ensure I wouldn't bear a fool's child. Now I'm nearly thirty harvests old and unsure if I can give King David an heir." Her eyes glistened. "Would you like to tell him, or shall I?" She raised her chin, displaying the same courage that defended her maids, despite personal risk.

"You were right to bring them," I said, motioning to the women. "But when David says he'll find worthy husbands for them, you must accept his word as true. He doesn't lie, and you must never deceive him." I locked onto her dark brown eyes. "Your friends will be well cared for—as will you."

"Thank you." She blinked a stream of tears down her cheeks but offered no more words.

The moment felt too intimate, far above compulsory hospitality. I had no intention of becoming her friend or confidante. "I'll stay on the south side of the plateau. You remain among the family chambers on the north side. It's the only way we'll dwell in peace." Without another word, I fled.

"Ahinoam! Ahinoam, come back!"

Hurrying through the crowded plateau, I ignored the widow's persistent shouts and ran past curious friends and family. When I reached the trailhead, impulse took me down the serpentine path toward the barren wilderness.

Yahweh, You are my Rock, my Fortress, and my Deliverer. In You I take refuge. Adonai Elohim was more than sufficient, but a mountaintop was entirely too small to house Nabal's widow and me.

TWENTY-EIGHT

DAVID

Place me like a seal over your heart, like a seal on your arm; for love is as strong as death, its jealousy unyielding as the grave. It burns like blazing fire, like a mighty flame. Many waters cannot quench love; rivers cannot sweep it away.

Song of Songs 8:6–7

I stood alone on our eastern watchtower and watched Nomy run like a frightened desert hare into the wilderness. My soul ached for her.

"Attai! Take five men and follow." I pointed toward my scampering wife. "At a distance, so she doesn't see you."

"Shouldn't we bring her back?"

"No. Leave a trail so I can find her."

With a quick salute, he was off to obey my command. *Yahweh, protect her until I can hold her in my arms again.* She would find a cave for shelter, and we would find shelter in each other's arms. If only I could stay in a cave with her forever. If it weren't for my calling, the anointing, I could live like any other man. I could tend Abba's flocks on Bethlehem's hills and—

No, I couldn't even finish the thought. *Forgive me, Lord.* The pain I'd caused Nomy and Abigail wasn't because of duty or even our circumstance. I'd hurt Nomy because I'd been a coward. Knowing I'd caused her tears, I'd left her alone to grieve for the last two days. And I'd lost my temper with Abigail when I should have confronted her privately. Apologizing to one wife was difficult, but tending two marriages felt impossible.

Yahweh, I know You've given both Nomy and Abigail to be my wives. I need Your wisdom to love them well. The simple prayer struck me like a slinged stone. *I'm called to* love *Nabal's widow?* If I believed Yahweh had truly ordained our marriage—and I did believe it—then Abigail was intended to become as much a part of me as Eve was Adam's own rib. Ahinoam and Abigail. Life and breath. Sun and moon.

I could no longer reassure Ahinoam that I loved her and felt only compassion for Nabal's widow. "Oh, Lord." I dropped my head in my hands, continuing my prayer in silence. *How can I convince my warrior bride that love is meant to multiply, not divide? That my love for her will never diminish because You pour an unquenchable stream of it into our hearts?*

"I've been looking for you!" Joab shouted from below. "You'd better decide which of my five soldiers will marry your new wife's maids. I've already broken up ten fights." He started to walk away but turned and added, "And if you choose any of our Bethlehem friends as the bridegrooms, you'd better invite Ima to the celebration."

Zerry! Zerry could come from Bethlehem—at least for a visit—and help me explain to Nomy what the Lord intended for our marriage.

"Send for your ima now!" I shouted at my nephew. "We'll have all six wedding ceremonies in one week." He saluted, bowed, and strode away with a smile. Zerry's sons would be as happy as Nomy when their ima arrived.

I slid down the watchtower ladder, my sandals hugging the sides, hands slowing my descent by grabbing every other rung. Hitting the ground with a thud, I jogged toward the family chambers. I'd first apologize to Nabal's widow and then follow the Gadites' markers to find my wife in the wilderness and spend the night proving I was brave enough to face her tears.

When I neared the family compound, Abital marched toward me, looking very much like the angry little girl I teased in Bethlehem's fields. "You've placed six women in a human-sized oven, and they're quickly becoming overbaked bread. I've given them their full ration of today's water, and it's not even dusk."

"We'll split them three and three between Abigail's chamber and mine," I said. "I'll sleep among my men for the next week until Abiathar pronounces the wedding blessings. Then the maids can move into their husband's chambers."

Abital blinked rapidly, her indignation momentarily paused.

"Now, if you'll excuse me, I was about to apologize to Nabal's widow and inform her of the direction I've received from the Lord."

She stepped aside and extended her hand toward the chamber, lifting her brows in the same stubborn way she'd done when refusing to admit I'd won a race or beaten her at sling practice. Resisting the urge to torment her further, I proceeded to Abigail's chamber.

"May I come in?"

The curtain jerked aside, and one of the maids looked as fierce as any warrior. "Forgive us, my king, but we are unable to entertain visitors at this time." Her face was as red as a ripened grape and dry as the desert floor.

"You need water." I barged past her and found the others huddled around their mistress, who was lying on the single sleeping mat. *My temper did this.* "The five of you may leave Abigail in my care. You'll find a woman named Abital in the second chamber to your right. She's the wife of my youngest nephew, Asahel, and she helps my wife manage the camp's women. Tell her I've approved more water for you and Abigail today."

Nabal's widow tried to sit up as her maids left us. I knelt beside her and noticed the one who had opened the curtain remained. She lifted her chin. "I assume that you, my lord, being the honorable man you are, would appreciate a chaperone until you've officially wed my mistress."

Was every Carmelite woman so opinionated? "Of course," I said, then returned my attention to Abigail. She was now sitting, her back propped against the wall, probably lightheaded from thirst. "I've come to apologize," I began, "and to reaffirm my intentions of making you my wife—if you'll still have me after my shameful display of temper."

The fog cleared from her eyes. "I would walk across a field of scorpions to marry you." She gasped and covered her mouth as if trying to recapture the words, but I found her honesty delightful.

"Thankfully, there's no need for that." We held each other's gaze, studying the one with whom we'd soon share our lives. "I have in mind the five honorable, *single* men your maids will marry. Your insistence seemed to suggest your own concern that you must fight for my affection."

"No, I—"

"Let me assure you," I said, laying her back on the mat when her face drained of color, "I believe we are a gift to each other from Yahweh, and He'll pour His love into our hearts. With His help and through His power, I promise to love you with every drop of blood in my veins—just as I love Ahinoam. Never more and never less. As the sun and moon are essential yet distinct, so will be my love for my wives. I also vow never to speak of our relationship to Nomy or of the relationship I share with her to you. I will have separate lives with each of you, yet Yahweh will bind us together as one flesh—all three of us—in unity of heart and purpose. Do you understand?"

She nodded, her brow pinched and drawn together. "I'm afraid I've offended Ahinoam somehow. I thought we were getting along well, but then she left so abruptly."

Nomy's escape made sense now. "My wife doesn't easily reveal

her heart, Abigail. I'm guessing she likes you more than she wishes."
I felt the urge to touch her cheek but resisted. "You and I will be
betrothed for a week, as will your maids. During that time, I will
sleep on the south side of the fortress and use that time to reassure
Ahinoam that I need not love her less to love you more."

When I started to leave, Abigail sat up and grasped my hand. "I
must tell you something." Her eyes flitted every direction, the sudden uncertainty making her seem vulnerable. "I was married for
ten years, my lord, and never produced a child. I know a king must
marry many wives to establish a lasting lineage, but—"

I slid both hands behind her head and tipped her chin up with
my thumbs to capture her gaze. "I'm not marrying you so you can
give me children, Abigail—though a son or two would be welcome."
I meant to lighten the mood, but she tried to look away. I brushed
her cheek with my thumb. "Look at me," I whispered.

"Yes, my lord." Her eyes were too dry for tears, but the sorrow
was no less poignant.

"I'm marrying you because both Ahinoam and I are convinced
you are God's choice to become my wife." When I saw the hint of a
smile, I added, "And since you'll be my wife in seven days, perhaps
you should call me David."

Four days ago, I'd found Old J guarding a wilderness cave and
Nomy inside, curled into a ball, weeping. This time, my words
couldn't penetrate the wall she'd built around her heart. From dusk
until dawn, I held her. Praying silently and aloud, I pleaded with the
God who had joined us with another to comfort my wife and prove
to her the secure place she held in my heart. Still, she wept—until
her features turned to stone.

"We must return," she said when dawn brightened the cave's
entrance. "You've been away from the fortress too long."

Her detachment was worse than tears. I'd visited her chamber every day since, but she'd maintained her stoic distance. "Let me stay with you," I'd begged. "Why not enjoy this time we have together before—"

"Before you take another woman to your bed?" Yesterday's anger had been worst of all.

I woke this morning on the eastern tower before dawn. My watchman stood twenty paces away, alert and scanning the desert floor. I stretched and looked to the horizon with hope of a better day. Zerry would likely arrive. She'd be pleased that two of the chosen bridegrooms were men she'd helped raise: Elhanan, the son of Abba's chief shepherd, and Ahimelek, the Hittite. I couldn't in good conscience suggest his brother, Uriah, since the largest man among all my soldiers hadn't yet professed faith in the one true God.

I'd chosen the other three grooms because they were men of integrity and my top soldiers: Amasai, chief of my Mighty Men; and Eleazar and Shammah, two of the Three sent with Abishai on the most dangerous missions. I'd chosen all five because they shared one common deficit: Each needed a wife to prove his life was more important than his next great victory. They needed the love and purpose only a wife could give.

The t'ruah sounded from a distance, then another from our north tower. My camp sprang to life, and three hundred men formed ranks at the center of the plateau. I ran to meet Joab and my captains at the tower.

"There!" Joab pointed at a single runner, who blew his shofar again, then gave another warning blast before he started up the winding path to our mountaintop fortress.

"Get the families and livestock ready to travel," I said to Elhanan. "None of our scouts would blow two warnings unless we needed to move quickly."

I turned to Joab. "Prepare the troops to move to Maon as soon as we hear the Gadite's report."

My captains scattered to their tasks, but I remained on the tower to watch the sunrise and await the scout's ascent. *Yahweh, protect Zerry and her escort.* We couldn't wait for their arrival if danger was coming our way. The first rays of dawn showed a quiet horizon, so I joined my captains at the trailhead as the scout dashed to the top, huffing and panting.

"Saul . . . coming." Ezer, chief of the Gadite scouts, braced his hands on his knees, took several deep breaths, then faced me. "The Ziphites went to Gibeah. Told Saul the location of our second fortress. The Hill of Hakilah."

Outrage exploded from my faithful troops. Angry threats rose, begging for revenge against another Judean town that betrayed us. I was too dejected to be angry. Why did my own tribesmen prefer a king who repeatedly ignored and threatened them over one of their own who had offered them protection and fair trade? *If we're not safe in Judah, Yahweh, where can we go to escape Saul's grasp?*

"My lord, may I speak?" said Eliphelet the Philistine, nephew of King Achish, who had helped me escape Gath when I'd foolishly sought sanctuary among Israel's greatest enemy.

"Of course," I said. "Your counsel is always welcome."

Joab leaned closer to hear Eliphelet's whispers. "May I return to Gath, to my Dohd Achish, and request sanctuary for our troops and their families?"

"He'll kill you on sight." Joab gave the same answer I would have.

"You helped me escape," I said. "You betrayed your own people by rescuing the man Israel's maidens touted in songs. I suspect Achish now despises you more than he hates me."

"My ima is his only sister, and he adores her." Eliphelet grinned. "I'll make Achish an offer too sweet to refuse."

I glared at Joab. "Have you and Eliphelet been conspiring?"

My nephew lifted both hands, asserting innocence.

"What offer?" I asked the Philistine.

"I'll say David ben Jesse has been betrayed by his own people and is now ready to raid the Judean villages to have his vengeance."

"But I would never—"

"Dohd Achish doesn't know that." Eliphelet's hard stare silenced me. "My lord, please consider my proposal. If we move your whole army and their families to Gath, we would be beyond Saul's reach. We could raid foreign villages within Israel's borders and make Achish believe you had turned against your own people."

Joab quickly turned to me. "It could work, David." He dug into his beard, scratching his chin. "Can we wait to see Ima before we leave?" My general had two weaknesses: his wife and his ima.

Lifting my head from the private conversation, I asked the Gadite scout for more details. "How many troops is Saul bringing and how long before they come?"

"Saul chose General Abner and three thousand of his best men to march into the Desert of Ziph. They could arrive here by tomorrow."

"And Prince Jonathan?" I asked.

"He remains in the north, commanding Israel's regular army against a Philistine confrontation."

Saul had left an active battle to pursue me? I exchanged a concerned glance with Joab and then examined the men, women, and children whose lives were as tightly woven as fine linen. Nomy stood among my captains like a blossom among acacia thorns, while Abigail and her maids waited with Abital and the other wives. If we gathered the other half of my army from Maon, we'd march toward Gath with six hundred soldiers and at least that many more women and children. Achish would see us as easy prey. I couldn't risk their lives on the hope that the Philistine king loved his sister as much as I loved Zerry.

"We must abandon our mountaintop fortresses and march toward

Maon. However, we'll wait until midday to give my sister and her escort a little more time to join us. During the wait, my captains and lieutenants will divide our cohorts of twenty into smaller groups of ten. Those groups will hide together in wilderness caves as we draw nearer to Maon. But first—"

I scanned the crowd for Abiathar and found him standing among the Kohathites that joined us at Moab. "Before my officers divide the groups, Abiathar will pronounce the wedding blessing over the six women who joined us a few days ago and their bridegrooms. Today, we must all be reminded that family is the reason we fight to stay alive."

Murmurs fluttered through the gathering. The women began preparing the six brides for the impromptu ceremony. The five men looked like birds stunned by a fowler's snare. I walked toward them and slid my arm around Nomy's waist before she could escape.

"Abiathar will recite the simple blessing," I explained to the men. "You may then spend the morning in your private chamber with your brides." All five fierce warriors exchanged uneasy glances. Every man's bluster was tested on his wedding day, faced with the woman he must please for the rest of his days. "Might I suggest you go now and tidy your chambers before your brides arrive?"

During their hurried departure, I swept Nomy behind a storage chamber to steal a moment of privacy. "I had hoped Zerry would have been here to be your support while—"

"It doesn't matter, David." She pushed me away, avoiding my gaze. "Yahweh is always with me. He's my support."

Surrendering with a sigh, I leaned against the mudbrick wall. "What else can I do, Nomy? How can I convince you of my love and make things right again?"

She shook her head, and I thought she might walk away. Instead, she looked up at me, her brows knit together. "You can do nothing, David. I know you love me, and I know Yahweh has chosen Abigail to be your wife. So even I can't force myself to stop feeling angry, jealous, and sad. I've tried and can't stop, which makes me even angrier." She choked out a mirthless laugh.

"I'm sorry, my love." Offering my hand in consolation, I added, "Thank you for telling me. At least now I don't feel responsible to fix you."

She placed her hand in mine, and I drew her into my arms. She came willingly, resting her full weight against me, and laid her head on my chest. "It's harder to hate Abigail after I spoke with her." My suspicions were correct. Nomy had fled into the wilderness after they'd met because she'd liked Abigail. Though I couldn't see her expression, I could tell she was deep in thought. Finally, she said, "I don't understand how you and I can remain one flesh once you join your body with Abigail's."

I braced her shoulders to monitor her reaction as I spoke. "Once we are joined as husband and wife, not even death separates us, my love. And you know our union is not physical alone. Yahweh gave man and woman the physical expression of our love, but that's not the only thing that makes us one flesh. We are adding Abigail to our one-flesh relationship—not physically, of course—but in the unity of our hearts and Yahweh's purpose."

She'd already started shaking her head. "I'll never feel unity with a woman who—"

"You will." I gently framed her face, looking through the windows of her soul. "Will you marry me again, Ahinoam bat Toren, because you trust Yahweh has given Nabal's widow to join us in one heart and one purpose?"

A silent battle raged behind her eyes, but finally peace came with surrender. "I will marry you again, David ben Jesse, because Yahweh has also chosen Abigail to be your wife."

TWENTY-NINE

AHINOAM

Abigail . . . became his wife. David had also married Ahinoam of Jezreel,
and they both were his wives.

1 Samuel 25:42–43

I was a bride in my second wedding ceremony with David ben Jesse. The moment was surreal in both its strangeness and dread.

David, Abigail, and I stood, holding hands, in our small circle of three, lined up beside the widow's maids and the five bridegrooms David had chosen for them. I hadn't learned the women's names yet. At the moment, I could barely remember my own. We were surrounded by the entire population of our mountaintop fortress. Children fussed in the rising heat, and sweaty bodies crowded close to see the six couples wed.

Nauseous with nerves and roiling emotions, I kept my head bowed and swallowed back the insistent protest in my throat. *Yahweh, please don't let me vomit on my husband's sandals.* I would aim at Abigail's if the urge grew overwhelming.

"Adam and his wife were naked," Abiathar declared, "and they felt no shame."

With a slight gasp, my head shot up. David's eyes met mine with the same panicked look. I turned to Abigail, who appeared equally unsettled. Without thinking, I whispered, "May the Lord bless your union," then fled through the mass of family and friends.

Pity marred every face along the way to my southern chamber, and I burst through my curtain and buried my tears in my lamb's-wool headrest. How could I bear the images in my mind of my husband with another wife? *Even if I know she's a gift from You, Yahweh! How could You?*

"Well, that was the most courageous thing I've ever seen."

I bolted to my feet. "Zerry!"

She opened her arms, and I flew into the comfort of my first-ever friend. "Uriah told me all about these weddings and how my witless brother decided to marry that widow."

"David isn't witless," I said, pushing her away. I may have been distraught by the public humiliation of sharing my husband, but no one would criticize him—not even Zerry. "Yahweh made it clear to David *and* me that Abigail was meant to be his wife. She'll be an important addition to our household."

Zerry stepped back. "They've broken you, Ahinoam. How much of yourself will you sacrifice to keep David's love? No man is worth dismantling the person Yahweh created you to be."

I studied her in silence and realized David had never asked me to be anyone but Ahinoam bat Toren. And I'd loved him because of his passion to obey Yahweh. Wasn't he obeying Yahweh when he married Abigail? If I truly loved David ben Jesse, I must obey Yahweh with the same passion—even when it hurt.

"I've changed during our year apart, Zerry. Though I understand why you think I might sacrifice myself for others' approval, I assure you that I've never been more fully me or entirely loved. You know I would forgive you for anything because you made Abba's last years the happiest of his life, but never again speak a demeaning word against my husband." She couldn't have looked more shocked if I'd sprouted an acacia tree from my head.

"Then why were you sobbing when I followed you into your chamber?"

Her question came as a gentle reprimand from the Lord. "I was as embarrassed by the marriage as I was furious about sharing my husband." The confession warmed my cheeks, proving a root of pride still needed more attention. Perhaps humiliation had been the only path my stubborn heart would walk toward obedience.

Zerry still studied me. "What do you do all day without—" She sniffed back tears. "Without your abba to help you at the forge?"

I led her to my cushions so we could be more comfortable. "I've trained a dozen more apprentices with the skills Abba taught me. At midday, the women assigned to weekly cooking duty serve our meals and—"

"Women are *assigned* cooking duties?" Her eyes bulged.

I grinned, eager to compliment Abital. "Your daughter-in-law has organized our women into the tasks they enjoy: cooking, weaving, mending, laundry."

She rolled her eyes. "No one enjoys laundry."

"You're wrong."

Her spine stiffened. How long since anyone told Zerry she was wrong? "So now you're the expert on women in David's camp?"

"I'm not an expert, but I care about them."

"When did that happen?"

I glimpsed my reflection in her eyes and was startled by how much had changed during our time apart. How much I'd changed. "I saw honest conflict confronted with kindness when we visited Paran, and Abigal's genuine—Oh!" I startled us both. "I almost forgot the gift Abigal sent for you."

She looked down at my saknati. "Please tell me she didn't send one of those dreadful-looking things for me."

I chuckled. "Abigal only gives a saknati to sisters who visit Jether's camp."

Zerry grunted her disapproval. "I stayed in Bethlehem because I thought I could fix things with the family."

"Have you mended relationships?"

She looked away with a cynical laugh. "Perhaps Abital should return to Bethlehem with me and organize our family because I don't know what to do with them."

"Why not stay with us?"

"I'm needed in Bethlehem." She looked down, fiddling with her hands, which meant she didn't want to talk about it anymore.

I rummaged in a small basket of treasures and produced the tattered family headscarf Abigal told me to return. I placed it in Zerry's hands. "Abigal no longer wishes to be a part of Jesse's clan."

Color drained from her cheeks as the rejection dawned. "No!" Zerry tossed it back at me. "Abigal can't refuse her birthright. She'll always be my sister, the daughter of Jesse ben Obed."

I sat across from her and caught her hands, trapping the scarf within our grip. "Abigal will always be your sister, Zerry. She isn't rejecting you, but she'll have no connection with anyone who rejects David as Yahweh's anointed king."

"Our family will accept him when he becomes king." Her expression dissolved into pleading. "They'll soften someday. Shimea, his family, and Ozem support David, but the others haven't yet relented. Eliab says our brother—"

"Your *witless* brother?" I asked. "Who is influencing whom, Zerry?" She looked down without answering. "David is already our king," I said. "Don't allow your brothers to poison your heart against the only brother who loves you for the person God created you to be."

When she looked up, a tear slid down her cheek. "I miss Toren. His love made me a better person."

"Love makes us all better people." Still gripping the tattered scarf, I pressed it against her heart. "Abigal is happy, Zerry. Jether adores her. They're united in vision for their people. They even sent their only son, Amasa, to serve among David's warriors."

"Their only son? He could be killed! He must come home with me."

"Zerry, stop!" I saw the fathomless fear beneath her bluster. "You can't fix everything. You can't protect everyone. There is one God, and you're not Him."

"How dare you—"

"My ima didn't love me, and Jesse didn't love you. But it's not our fault."

A soft gasp parted her lips. Stole her words. Our wounds were laid bare. How had I not seen them before? So similar, our pain. "And it wasn't your fault Abigal was taken from Bethlehem. It wasn't your fault that Nitzevet tricked Jesse into conceiving David. You shouldn't have been forced to care for seven little boys and a household in her absence. It wasn't your fault Jesse never accepted David as his own. You loved and cared for David when Nitzevet couldn't, and you did a remarkable job."

Tears streamed down her cheeks. I wiped them away with Abigal's scarf and finished with what I hoped would relieve a lifelong burden. "David isn't your son, Zerry. He's God's anointed king, and your responsibility is simply to love him. Love makes us all better people."

She took the scarf and sheltered me in a hug. We wept cleansing tears together, and when our hearts had room for joy, I sat back and saw a clarity in my friend's eyes like an En Gedi spring. My soul felt it, too—with a little mischief. "I'm sure one of David's unmarried soldiers would be honored to wed his feisty sister."

She swatted me with the scarf. "I'm not looking for another husband."

"You weren't looking for Abba, but Yahweh surprised you."

"If I marry again, the man will be a gift from Yahweh, as Toren was."

"As Abigail and I are to David."

She lifted her chin and declared, "Your abba would be proud that you're not a silly woman."

"Oh, Zerry," I whispered past the knot in my throat. "No one has ever said anything sweeter."

"May we come in?" Abital called from outside my curtain.

Zerry squealed. "Only if you've brought my adorable grandson!"

But it wasn't Zeb who followed Abital inside. When David's new wife appeared, Zerry was on her feet and ready for battle. "How dare you—"

"Zerry!" I nudged her aside. Abital stood like a shield in front of Abigail, so I peered around her, trying to show the humility I'd lacked for days. "Both of you, forgive us for that welcome. Please, sit with us."

They looked at me with more suspicion than relief, but we found four cushions to make ourselves comfortable in my small space. I kept staring at Abigail, aching to know why she was here instead of enjoying her first intimate moments with our husband.

Finally, I lowered my head, praying against the returning sorrow. *Yahweh, it's not only pride at the core. This is real pain. My covenant marriage is being thrown into a forge. Melting completely, then being poured into a completely different shape. I don't know how—*

"Ahinoam," Abigail whispered, "I can't pretend to understand what you're feeling. I've never known a husband's love, so I don't know what it means to share it with another." Her voice broke, and I looked up to face her. "David was kind enough to agree when I suggested we postpone our . . . our union until after we tend to more pressing matters."

"What could be so pressing?"

She shrugged and swiped at her cheeks. "Things like rationing our supplies and escaping before Saul attacks us."

I laughed, which seemed to loosen her smile. Zerry elbowed me, so I said, "Abigail, this is David's sister, Zeruiah."

"It's an honor, Mistress Zeruiah." Abigail nodded an elegant bow. "I've spent a lot of time with Abital and Zeb—and your son, Asahel, has been very kind. I've briefly met your eldest, General Joab."

"You should stay away from him," Zerry said. "He's too much like his ima." She paused with a stony expression and then winked. We all chuckled, still a little tense, but at least amiable.

"David is meeting with the captains," Abigail said. "He wanted the women to get an accurate count of the supplies and prepare a rationing plan, should the whole camp need to move to Gath."

"Gath?" Zerry said. "You must have heard wrong."

I'd heard David's whispered conversation with Eliphelet and Joab. He'd already sent Eliphelet to talk with King Achish, though my husband wasn't yet certain life with the Philistines was safer than life in the Jeshimon.

"Saul is coming for us," I said to Zerry. "I'm sure fleeing to Gath would be a last possible option for us."

"Don't be ridiculous, Nomy! The Philistines remembered him six years ago, and they'll remember him still. David killed their giant. He paid Michal's dowry with two hundred Philistine foreskins. They'll never forget that silly song about Saul killing thousands but David killing tens of thousands. And wasn't it King Achish's nephew who made David pretend to be a slobbering madman so they could both escape Gath? If David goes back there, he might as well deliver Eliphelet into Achish's prison for treason!"

Yahweh, give me patience. "I'm sure David will make the right decision, Zer—"

"Do you think Achish will provide food and shelter for our six hundred men and their families? Even the cities in Judah refused to feed you! The Philistines will chop David to pieces, and who knows what they'll do to my grandchildr—" Her voice broke.

I pulled her into my arms and let her grieve. Zerry had changed in our year apart, as well. Losing Abba had left her vulnerable. She was as opinionated as ever, but the hard shell she'd worn as armor was much thinner now. *Lord, heal her heart.*

Abital and I exchanged a concerned glance. What could we do? The stress of our fugitive lifestyle might be too difficult for our new Zerry, but she needed us—her real family—to comfort her.

Abigail left her cushion and knelt beside Zerry. Cradling Zerry's hand, Abigail gently pressed it against her forehead.

Startled, Zerry pulled away. "You're not a slave, and I'm not royalty. Why did you do that?"

"I'm not a slave," Abigail said, "but I'm determined to serve King David's household. I would be honored to serve you, Mistress Zeruiah."

Zerry's lips quivered. "No one serves me," she whispered.

Abigail tilted her head and smiled tenderly. "I'd like to change that. Will you allow me to help you love and care for your grandchildren on our way to Gath? I have no children of my own, and Zeb is a delight. I'm eager to meet your other sons' wives and their children. If they're even half as wonderful as—"

"You talk as much as David." Zerry turned to me with a wry grin. "She'll drive you mad with all that chatter. I'm staying, if only to watch her torment you." Then she sobered. "I'm also staying to convince David he'd be a fool to lead his faithful followers into a Philistine city."

"You're wrong, Zeruiah." Abigail's tone was no longer gentle. "Every day I lived in fear of a wealthy fool in Judah. Yahweh delivered me into David's care, as He did every soldier and his family on this mountain. We're safer under Yahweh's protection in Gath than fearfully staying in Judah to protect ourselves."

"Hmph." Zerry looked from Abigail to Abital and back to me. "Sometimes her words are almost palatable." It was as close to a compliment as Zerry would offer Abigail until they were better acquainted.

I offered Abigail an affirming nod and felt the first hope of friendship with a woman who could love those dearest to me.

THIRTY

DAVID

So Saul went down to the Desert of Ziph, with his three thousand select Israelite troops, to search there for David.

1 Samuel 26:2

Hill of Hakilah

The Jeshimon surrounded us, a yawning wasteland that proved our utter dependence on nature's fickle provision. I stared into the weary faces of my fifty best men who were waiting for answers I didn't have.

"Eliphelet returned. King Achish accepted our proposal to shelter at Gath under the condition that we raid Judean villages under his Philistine banner." Their expressions hardened, but none openly protested. "We've received reports that Saul's troops are nearby, so stay alert. Make sure the children are quiet and our women know the escape routes."

"Which escape routes?" Joab asked.

I'd chosen my eldest nephew as my general because he always spoke truth, no matter how hard or who was listening. Right now, I wished for more discretion.

"West."

My general and I locked eyes. We'd barely spoken since leaving the

Dead Sea fortress a week ago. We followed the trade route through Maon, Carmel, and Ziph, still offering protective services against raids on the coming harvest. Unfortunately, our emaciated warriors inspired little confidence. Elders at all three cities turned us away, so we traded the last of our flocks for grain and marched into the Desert of Ziph. Our camp met Abishai's three hundred troops and their families at the dwindling Brook of Maon. We divided all six hundred men into cohorts and family groups, then sought shelter in caves like the animals I'd made them.

"West takes us toward Judah's country and more cities that will betray us," Joab said.

He was baiting me with the obvious. "And toward Gath, if seeking sanctuary there becomes our only option."

My general exhaled a long breath through his nostrils, resembling a bull ready to charge. Before he could speak, I glimpsed a runner approaching and jogged toward him.

Ezer, the captain of our Gadites, met me before I descended the hillside. "King Saul and his men are making camp on the other side of this hill, across the road on the Hill of Hakilah."

I shouted at Joab in a coarse whisper, "Muster everyone at the Jeshimon main cave!" Then I turned to Ezer. "Prepare the men to flee so they'll draw Saul's troops away from our women and children."

Joab rushed at me, his eyes ablaze. "You must end this, David. If the LORD gives Saul into your hand, you must kill him!"

I grabbed his robe and ground out the words. "I. Will. Never. Kill. God's. Anointed. King."

"You must! He won't stop!"

"We're going to Gath." I shoved him away, earning disapproving looks from my bravest men. "Go. That's an order. Abishai and Ahimelek, stay with me."

Slowly, deliberately, Joab pressed his fist against his breastplate with a sneer before stalking away. Abishai and Ahimelek remained. They were my most skilled spies and best friends since childhood.

They slammed their fists to their chests. "We follow you, my king," Ahimelek whispered. Though a Canaanite and Hittite by descent, his faith in Yahweh was strong—strong enough that I'd entrusted Abigail's maid Miriam as his bride. Was the men's faith strong enough to believe Yahweh could rescue us from our current trap?

Was mine?

"Follow me." I began climbing back up the hill to assess Saul's army.

Without hesitation, they followed. No yammering. No unnecessary inquiries. We climbed boulders, skirted rocky cliffs, and crawled on our bellies to the edge of an outcropping at least ten camel heights above Israel's army, encamped across the road on another hilltop. In the descending darkness, Saul's men settled onto their mats around small fires, preparing to rest before tomorrow's killing. King Saul was heavily guarded by three thousand bodies and encircled in the center of camp by a double ring of his royal guards. I'd been captain of that elite squad before Saul's paranoia poisoned his heart against me.

Abishai's loud stomach growl interrupted my musing. I shot him a chastising glare. His eyes bulged with silent apology, and we barely stifled our laughter. Danger made warriors a little giddy. A few good-natured shoves settled us into serious nods and resumed focus. These men were my brothers. Closer than family. And they were about to risk their lives for me.

"Which of you will go with me into Saul's camp?"

"I will," Abishai said.

"Aww," Ahimelek grumbled. "I'll miss all the fun."

"If the fun starts . . ." All lightheartedness fled. "It means Yahweh decided not to rescue us, and you must get to the cave and save the others."

"Yahweh will save you, my lord." Ahimelek offered his hand, and we locked wrists. One side of his mouth lifted in a wry grin. "Perhaps the Lord could use Abishai to kill Saul so you wouldn't have his blood on your hands."

"No!" I turned to Abishai. "No one touches the Lord's anointed." I hurried away, hoping neither of them saw my fear. *Yahweh, I know You can deliver us, but will You?*

Abishai and I found a spot closer to Saul's camp and hid until the moon was bright. To make sure all was quiet before our approach, I threw a small rock near one of the perimeter watchmen. He didn't flinch. Abishai shrugged as if to say, *What sort of watchman is he?*

We crept forward, daggers in one hand, swords in the other. But every watchman was sound asleep. Propped against boulders. Slumped in the sand. We tiptoed past them, weaving our way through Saul's contingents. Some of them even snored. We reached the first circle of royal guards and they, too, were sleeping. *Impossible.* Israel's soldiers never slept so deeply—especially the night before a battle.

Abishai and I stepped over the second row of Saul's guards, and I was suddenly looming over the man who had trained me for war—Abner, Saul's cousin and general. He, too, was sleeping!

King Saul lay beside Abner, and between them was the king's spear and water jug. I looked up at Abishai with as much wonder as relief.

He whispered, "This is Yahweh's miracle! He delivered Saul into your hands." Reaching for the king's spear, he said, "Let me pin him to the ground with one strike. He won't feel anything."

"No!" I grabbed the spear.

Abner released a loud snort. Abishai and I froze, our arms arched over the general, hands locked on Saul's spear. Heart pounding in my ears, I waited for Abner to resume his snoring—or wake and begin the slaughter. In those intervening moments, two things became clearer than a mountain stream.

One, only Yahweh could make trained soldiers sleep this deeply. *Thank You, Yahweh. You haven't abandoned me.* But as encouraging as was the first realization, the second was equally devastating. Abner's presence meant Saul had convinced his general that I was worthy of his full attention.

This three-thousand-man troop wasn't the same as En Gedi's army. These were Abner's special force. They were here to scout the Jeshimon, to learn wilderness warfare, and to kill me, my men, and their families, no matter how long it took. The first lesson Abner son of Ner taught me was that a true soldier never abandoned his mission. The wisest military move was to kill *both* Abner and Saul, but to honor my vow and let Saul live, we must escape to Gath.

When Abner began snoring again, Abishai's eyes met mine. I jerked the spear from his hand and whispered, "Saul will die by the Lord's hand or in battle but not by my hand or yours." I nodded toward the water jug. "Take that, too." Abishai's jaw set, resembling his older brother, but he took the waterskin, and we fled their camp.

Ahimelek waited at the overlook and met us with a strangled "How did they not wake up?"

"El Shaddai made Saul and his army sleep so deeply that I'll be able to prove my innocence with these." I displayed the king's spear and water jug like war prizes.

"Your innocence?" Ahimelek's features hardened. "It won't matter! They'll never stop chasing us!" His shout echoed into the stillness.

Abner's voice rose in a chilling command, stirring the Israelite army across the road.

We crouched low, taking cover behind desert scrub. Perimeter guards woke from a death-sentence violation, sheepishly glancing around them. Abner marched through camp, crowing like a rooster to cover his own shame. When he returned to the king's side, he paced with a vigilance born of confusion. No one would sleep again tonight.

We watched in silence until dawn. Then I nudged Abishai. "It's time."

"Don't." He gripped Saul's spear in my right hand, halting me, pleading. "I know he was like an abba to you, but now Abner is involved. He'll pierce your heart with an arrow when he sees you."

I held his gaze. "Yahweh will deliver us. We're going to Gath."

"No!" he spat. "The men won't follow you, David. Especially after you've refused to kill Saul a second time." He paused for less than a heartbeat. "I won't follow you."

My bravest nephew, the leader of the Three, had reached his limit. *The Lord is my rock, my fortress and my deliverer; my God is my rock, in whom I take refuge.* The song came to mind, and prickly flesh covered my body. Yahweh's presence surged through me with an otherworldly peace. I drew my nephew's forehead close, kissed him, and then met his terrified gaze. "You must follow where Yahweh leads you, Abishai—as will I."

Wrenching Saul's spear from his grasp, I strode to the precipice edge. Highlighted in the dawn, I shouted to Saul's army across the chasm, "Aren't you going to answer me, Abner?"

The whole camp scurried to attention, while Abner stood like a shield in front of his king. "Who dares address Israel's general?"

"What kind of warrior are you, Abner, that you didn't protect the Lord's anointed? Shouldn't you and all your men die for your negligence? Where is King Saul's spear and water jug?"

While Abner searched around his feet, I held them aloft.

Saul nudged him aside. "David, my son, is that you?"

"It is, my lord king. Why are you pursuing your servant again? What have I done?"

Abner lunged toward Saul, giving quiet counsel.

"No!" I shouted. "Let the king listen to *my* words!"

Saul shrugged off his general's pawing. "Then speak, David."

"If the Lord has incited you against me, then may He graciously accept my offering. But if others have corrupted your heart against me, may those men be cursed before the Lord! They have now driven me from my share in the Lord's inheritance and have said, 'Let him go serve other gods.' Please, my lord, don't let my blood fall on ground far from the Lord's presence."

"David, don't do this," Ahimelek hissed.

I ignored him and offered a final plea. "The king of Israel has come out here to chase a flea, a partridge in these mountains."

Saul's telltale shriek signaled his mania. Then came an eerie shout. "Come back, David, my son. I know I've sinned. Today, you considered my life precious. Surely, I've acted foolishly and been terribly wrong. I won't try to harm you again."

"He's lying, David." Abishai gripped my arm. "Don't listen."

Ignoring him, I placed Saul's spear and water on the precipice, then gave a final reply to Israel's king. "You may send one of your young men to retrieve your water and weapon. Know this: The LORD rewards us for our righteousness and faithfulness. Yahweh delivered you into my hands today, but I didn't lay a hand on the Lord's anointed. As surely as I valued your life today, so may Yahweh value my life and deliver me from all trouble."

I climbed down from the precipice and pinned my nephew with a hard stare. "Not only will I never return to Gibeah, Abishai, but the next time Saul pursues me, he'll have to breach the Philistine gates of Gath to do so."

Saul's weepy voice wafted over the chasm. "May you be blessed, David, my son. You will do great things and surely triumph."

I faced my two most trusted spies and said, "Let's get to the cave and see if anyone will follow me to Gath."

THIRTY-ONE

AHINOAM

But David thought to himself, "One of these days I will be destroyed by the hand of Saul."

1 Samuel 27:1

Wilderness of Ziph

As the seemingly endless night twisted the tension in my belly, more and more soldiers came with their families to the giant cave David had claimed for our family's small cohort. He'd invited Zerry to join us with Asahel's family and three Gadites. Old J, my favorite among the scouts, remained as our constant guardian while Attai and Ezer had executed special missions for three days without sleeping. At least now that we knew exactly where Saul and his assassins were camped, our faithful Gadites slept soundly, despite the noise of over a thousand terrified people in our large but confined space.

I was seated against a wall near the cave entrance with Zebby sprawled across my lap. He still loved to cuddle and had finally fallen asleep while cradled in my arms. Though a gangly five-year-old, he'd become as weak as the other children without proper food or water. Fear had become our daily bread and despair our ever-flowing fountain.

The Lord is my rock, my fortress and my deliverer; my God is my rock, in whom I take refuge. I hummed the tune aloud but silently repeated the words, trying to engrave them on my heart and replace the doubts in my mind.

Zerry, Abital, and Abigail managed their anxiety differently. They'd stayed busy since Joab arrived with the news that David had ordered everyone to the main cave. At first, all four of us welcomed every man, woman, and child with a warm smile, trying to reassure them as dusk turned into darkness. When I needed silence and Zebby needed sleep, I was more than happy to spend time with my favorite little human and watch as the other three women served our faithful friends. Abigail and her maids had served our whole camp, as they'd promised, and done it with such kindness. Though Abigail wouldn't dare waste precious water to wash feet as she'd offered, she'd massaged many tired women's shoulders and soothed their crying children.

Zerry plopped down beside me, exhaling a weary breath. "I think I fell asleep while standing up." She laid her head on my shoulder. Abital sat on my other side and wrestled her boy off my lap, wrapping his arms and legs around her like a blanket and squeezing her eyes closed in utter rapture.

Yes, someday I wanted to be an ima.

"He should be back." Abigail stood over us, tears gathering on her lashes. "What could be happening? It's well after dawn. If there was a battle, we would have heard the t'ruah blast. Joab is still pacing." She pointed to the other side of the entrance, where the general met with David's captains—minus Abishai and Ahimelek. "Why haven't they gone to help David? Why are they waiting? Why are *we* waiting?"

Zerry released a huff and pushed to her feet. "Good questions." She marched toward her son and the Mighty.

I exchanged a wary glance with Abigail and Abital. Zerry was the only one Joab would listen to, but she was also as volatile as her eldest son. "Should we join her?" I asked Abital.

"You two go," she whispered, trying not to wake Zeb.

By the time we were ten paces from the group, I heard Zerry's raised voice. "If Yahweh delivers David from Saul as he did at En Gedi, we should sing His praises and follow Yahweh's anointed wherever he leads."

"You know nothing about what we've endured since you left. David has lost the confidence of his men, and—"

"Not David," she shouted. The whole cave fell silent. The captains moved aside so Abigail and I could stand beside Zerry. She didn't seem to notice, remaining wholly focused on her son. "If what you say is true, Joab—that some of these warriors will refuse to follow David to Gath or that they'll abandon him if he was given another chance to kill Saul and didn't—then they haven't lost faith in my brother. They've lost faith in the God who chose my brother as Israel's next king."

Zerry shoved past Amasai, Elhanan, and other captains to address those gathered in the cave. "The decision you make right now may divide our camp." Her voice echoed off the walls, reaching to the farthest reaches of every offshoot. "Opinions may pit brother against brother and wife against husband, but know the foundation on which your opinion stands. Do you believe Yahweh's protection is more effective than your own strategies and strength? Do you trust God's anointed leader with the authority to make decisions that differ from your own will and judgment?"

"But my children!" a woman cried out. "They need food."

"And water!" another woman shouted.

"Of course," Zerry said, "but we're alive, and we have rations to last us until we reach Gath—if that's where David leads us."

"Why not kill Saul so we can live in peace?" A man's voice, barely audible, also came from the back.

Zerry turned to me, lifting her brows as my invitation to answer. Heart pounding against my ribs, I walked to Zerry's side and said, "I was in the cave at En Gedi when David could have killed Saul the first time. He wanted to. He'd planned to do it. But when he returned to our hiding place with only a corner of the royal robe he'd cut off, I saw more than guilt on his features. I saw empathy.

"Only two men in Israel know the burden that flows with the oil from Samuel's horn. The prophets say Yahweh's presence comes with the heavy weight of anointing, but because of Saul's disobedience, Yahweh no longer abides with Israel's king. Now Saul bears the burden without power to carry it—and only David can fully comprehend such a desperate state. That was the empathy I saw at En Gedi. Who are we to remove the burden God gave to Saul? Who are we to steal the air God breathed into his lungs?"

"Why not return to Paran?" The question came from behind me, from among the captains.

I turned and found Zerry glaring at Uriah the Hittite, hands fisted on her hips. Before she could berate him, Joab stepped between them. "Jether raids Judean villages, and he'd expect us to do the same."

Arms crossed over his broad chest, Uriah said, "And why shouldn't we? What has Judah done for us?"

"Bethlehem of Judah gave you and your brother a home, you big ox." Zerry marched over and grabbed his arms, pulling him down for a surprisingly gentle hug. "And before I'm done with you, we're going to show you that Yahweh is the only true God."

Quiet settled over the cave as dawn's rays fought back the night. I glimpsed Abigail standing among the captains, beside Asahel whom she knew best, and I remembered Zerry's challenge. *Do you trust God's anointed leader with the authority to make decisions that differ from your own will and judgment?* David had complied with God's will in both action and heart when he married Abigail. I admitted

God's truth with my mind, but my heart and actions were still sluggish to embrace it—and her.

Our soldiers and their families knew we couldn't stay in Judah. They knew Saul would eventually find us, and his tortured mind would likely show no mercy. Their minds knew we must obey David's direction—whatever it may be—but their hearts and wills wanted to rule their own futures. If only each one of us could feel the smooth flow of Samuel's anointing oil dripping down our heads and experience that moment when Yahweh's presence comes to live inside us. *Oh, El Roi, the God Who Sees, see me now and interpret my words to those who hear them.*

I walked over to Abigail, took her hand, and led her to the center of the cave. "I've known many of you since Abba and I joined David's camp at Adullam Cave. I didn't adjust easily to life in David's camp and found it especially difficult to find my place as a woman when I had so few womanly skills." Joab's wife, Vered, looked as stern as usual, but a few smiles softened other grim faces and gave me courage to continue. "Many of you were kind to me and even asked to learn about daggers. Some of you can now throw better than your husbands." With that, my audience came alive. The men shouted insults, the women bold challenge.

Abigail squeezed my hand and whispered, "Maybe I should talk less so you would talk more."

Thank You, Yahweh, for my sister wife. Without responding, I returned my attention to those who had become family and lifted Abigail's hand with mine. "David chose to marry a second wife," I shouted, and the cave fell silent again. "Will it be easy for us to live in harmony and share the attention of a single man? No. But we trust Yahweh's anointed and his authority and decision even when they differ from our desire. For the same reason, Abigail and I are leaving this cave to find and follow David ben Jesse—wherever he leads us."

A battle roar echoed off the cave walls. Abigail's eyes widened, and her mouth gaped. She tried to hug me. I grabbed her hand instead, and we hurried out of the cave for fear of being trampled. Once David's army was on the move, we dared not linger. Zerry appeared with Joab beside us, David's captains not far behind. Women and children mingled with warriors, revival coming with the dawn.

"It's David!" Abigail shouted.

"They're safe." Zerry stopped and covered a sob.

I could only run. Stumbling, nearly falling, I ran toward the only man I could ever love. The only man who could love me as I was and as I would become. He caught my waist as I leapt into his arms and whirled me in a dizzying circle.

His eyes, full of fire and determination, looked at me with more love than I could fathom. "How did you get everyone to come and say good-bye?"

"Good-bye?" I wriggled from his grasp. "We're ready to follow you anywhere, David ben Jesse."

A slow, adoring smile curved his lips. Then he nodded toward our army. "It appears my sister is convincing Abishai and Ahimelek they, too, should join us." I realized they had walked ahead to meet the other captains, and Zerry was wagging her finger at them.

That's when I saw Abigail.

She stood ten paces from us, in the chasm that separated David's army from where he'd publicly embraced his first wife. In my overwhelming relief, I'd broken the rule I asked David to keep and displayed affection for David in Abigail's presence.

I recognized Abigail's expression. It wasn't the jealousy of a loving wife. It wasn't even the humiliation of a second spouse. But my heart ached for her with everything I'd felt so deeply. The loneliness. The sorrow. I knew exactly what she was thinking: *I don't belong anywhere.* But she did belong.

I slid my arm around David's waist and extended my hand toward

Abigail. Lips parted, brows lifted, she hurried to join us as surprise mingled with a little hope. I hugged David's left side, turning my head away to focus on him, while my husband held us tight.

Abigail's hand pressed against my back, and she whispered, "Thank you, Ahinoam. You're the bravest woman I know."

AHINOAM

David and his men settled in Gath with Achish. Each man had his family with him, and David had his two wives: Ahinoam of Jezreel and Abigail of Carmel, the widow of Nabal.

1 Samuel 27:3

Two Weeks Later
Gath

Something tickled my cheek. Rancid city odors seeped into my consciousness. I brushed another tickle from my cheek. When I opened my eyes, I saw David sweeping a small piece of cloth over my face. "I've been waiting since dawn. Today we gash figs!" He kissed my nose and leapt to his feet, offering a hand to help me up.

"Can't I sleep a little longer?" I rolled over, trying to ignore him.

"Not today!" He hoisted me into his arms, twirling and dancing in spontaneous song. "Fig trees await. New life is here. Pick in four days. And eat for a year."

"Uhhh! Stick with praise songs."

Undeterred, my joyful husband repeated the jingle while placing my feet on the floor. He then grabbed my hand and swung me in a circle until the room began to spin and gorge rose in my throat.

"Oh, David, no!" I lunged for the waste pot, barely reaching my target before losing the contents of my stomach. Though grateful for the little house King Achish had bestowed on the "Israelite champion and his wives," we weren't yet accustomed to living so near the city's waste drain or to the rich foods shared from the king's table. Each morning, my evening meal had reemerged in the same demoralizing way. David only slept in my room every other night to witness my morning humiliation.

"Please let me send Eliphelet to find a healer." He handed me the cloth he kept tucked in his belt.

I wiped my mouth and nudged him away. "I'm sure it's only the rich food and awful smell."

"What smell?"

I was in no mood for teasing. "I know I should be grateful that we have two fig trees ready for gashing. I should be relieved to sleep in a house, not a cave or on a rock ledge. I'm thankful Abigail and I have separate rooms to spend time alone with you, but—"

Tears came suddenly, as they had since we'd arrived in Gath. I was happy, truly, so why was I crying? Why so tired all the time? I buried my face in the lamb's-wool headrest and cried, "I'm just a silly woman."

"Abigail!" My husband sounded panicked as he called for my sister wife.

I was too weary to protest, but when I heard them whispering, annoyance overcame fatigue. "Stop it." I sat up but closed my eyes to fight another wave of nausea. "Tell me what you're saying."

David sat on my right and Abigail on my left. When I opened my eyes, I saw the same strange expression on both of their faces. David spoke first. "Do you want to hear the good news first or the bad?"

Dread skittered up my spine, raising the hair at the nape of my neck. "Start with the bad."

"You're not gashing figs today."

Why was he smiling? Indignation warred with relief. If I was too tired to walk into the main room, I probably shouldn't strap on a leather belt and climb a tree with two sharp blades in my hands. "What's the good news?"

David looked at Abigail and back at me. "Abigail said she's been talking with Zerry about your symptoms."

Annoyed, I shot a glare at my sister. "They're not *symptoms*. I'm just—"

"Nomy," David said, demanding my attention. "We think you're with child."

Surely I'd misunderstood. I couldn't be. "Why would Yahweh give us a child in Gath when we've been married three years in Judah?"

Abigail reached for my hand. "Maybe because the Lord will give us rest here and time to enjoy a child."

David kissed my hand and Abigail's. "You can come outside and tell me how to gash figs. I haven't climbed a tree since I was a boy. We'll make a good life here, Nomy, until the Lord fulfills His will for me in Israel."

"Next year, I'll race you up those fig trees."

"And I'll tend the baby," Abigail said.

David pulled us into his arms, his laughter deep and resonant, pouring over me like warm oil. I held my breath. Could we truly be happy in a Philistine city?

Yahweh, let it be so.

AUTHOR'S NOTE

I hope you've enjoyed reading about the first two of King David's brides. My goal for every biblical novel is to present the immutable truth of God's Word as the story's foundation, add building blocks of historical research, and then apply the mortar of creative fiction to develop a warm and inviting world in which readers imagine what biblical characters *might have* experienced. In the following note, I'll explain some of the biblical and historical research that formed the fiction for Ahinoam's ancient world.

Who Was Ahinoam?

The Bible names two women as Ahinoam: King Saul's wife, and one of David's wives. Some commentaries propose David may have married Saul's wife, but I found no biblical evidence, and common sense made this hard to believe, since Saul's wife would have likely been Michal's mother and Levitical law prescribed a death penalty for a man who married both a woman and her mother (Leviticus 20:14).

David's Ahinoam is always defined in Scripture by her hometown of Jezreel, likely referring to a small village in the hill country of Judah (Joshua 15:56) rather than the northern city of Jezreel or Jezreel Valley. Because David's first "wilderness wife" needed to be tough, I concocted a dagger-wielding woman to match the bravery of Jael, a Kenite woman who killed a Canaanite general during the time of Israel's judges (Judges 4). Though Ahinoam's heritage is completely fictional, the *Holman Illustrated Bible Dictionary* confirms that ancient Kenites were a Bedouin people who lived in the southeastern hill country of Judah. Fun fact: I didn't discover Kenite meant *smith* or *metalworker* until I'd written almost half of the first draft. That's when I knew God was at work on this story!

Was David's Mother Really Captured by King Nahash?

Second Samuel 17:25 ESV affirms that an Ishmaelite named Jether married Abigal, who was the sister of Zeruiah, Joab's mother. The same verse also tells us that Jether and Abigal had a son, Amasa, who David later named as general over his troops, but Joab killed Amasa before he could replace him as David's general (2 Samuel 19:13—20:10).

The Bible is silent about David's mother. The Talmud, sometimes referred to as "the encyclopedia of Jewish life," gives her name, Nitzevet; includes the story of her capture by the Ammonite king, Nahash; and says she bore him two daughters, Zeruiah and Abigal (*Bava Batra* 91a). The Talmud also includes the strange story about Jesse, who set aside his wife, was tricked by Nitzevet and her maid, and then disapproved of his youngest son, David. The truth of David's anointing in 1 Samuel 16 seems to confirm at least some animosity between Jesse and his youngest son.

When Did David Write the Psalms Quoted in the Story?

David is credited with writing the following psalms: 1–41, 51–71, and 138–150. We know the occasion of some because they've been titled to give us their context.

Psalm 18—David is delivered from his enemies and Saul

Psalm 34—David feigns madness and is delivered from King Achish at Gath

Psalm 52—David learns Saul killed the Nob priests because Doeg the Edomite saw David at the Tabernacle

Psalm 54—The Ziphites told Saul where David was hiding

Psalm 56—The Philistines seized David in Gath

Psalm 57—David flees from Saul into a cave

Psalm 59—Saul sent men to watch David's house in order to kill him

Psalm 63—David in the desert of Judah

Some scholars suggest David was perhaps leading his troops through the current-day Wadi Qelt, experiencing this deep ravine of dark shadows and quiet waters, when he heard about the horrifying slaughter of Nob's priests and wrote Psalm 23. The other quotes were borne from my personal devotional study in the Psalms as I wrote the manuscript and revisions.

Fig-Gashing, Anyone?

"Gashing" figs was a real thing in ancient horticulture, used as a harvest-control mechanism (Theophrastus, Enquiry Into Plants, trans. A. Hart [W. Heinemann: London, 1961]). When a fig is scraped (or gashed) with the appropriate tool and in the right climate, it can be predicted to ripen within four days. Ancient fig farmers could plan their harvests around Sabbaths, special feast days, Aunt Bertha's visit—whatever!

Wouldn't life be simpler if more of our tasks were as predictable as harvesting figs?

Why David's Brides?

In *Brave: The Story of Ahinoam*, you've met David, a valiant warrior who's not perfect, but he passionately pursues God because his life and many others depend on it. The Bible gives us a detailed account of the circumstances surrounding his marriage to Abigail and adds, "David *had also married* Ahinoam of Jezreel" (1 Samuel 25:43), implying he married Ahinoam *before* he married Abigail.

Whenever the Bible mentions David's first two wilderness wives, each is always associated with a label: "Ahinoam the Jezreelite," implying she was from a small and probably poor Judean village; and "Abigail, the widow of Nabal of Carmel," whose first husband was slain by Yahweh, which left her in need of a husband/provider. These are clues I gleaned from biblical truth and ancient culture to craft what I hope is believable fiction.

But why would David, the man after God's own heart, marry multiple wives when he likely knew the Law forbade it (Deuteronomy 17:17)? First, David has broken the Law before, when he flees from Saul with no food, no weapons, and nowhere to turn except his friend, the High Priest at the Tabernacle in Nob (1 Samuel 21:1–9). David breaks God's Law when he eats the sacred bread reserved only for priests (Leviticus 24:5, 9). Centuries later, however, when Jesus picks grain and eats it on the Sabbath (also breaking Mosaic law), he earns the Jewish leaders' rebuke and uses David's eating of the sacred bread to prove that Yahweh desires mercy over sacrifice (Matthew 12:1–8; Mark 2:23–28; Luke 6:1–5). According to Jesus, God is more concerned with meeting people's needs than meeting their expectations.

Studying Jesus's teaching about David and the sacred bread helped me grapple with David's decision to marry multiple wives. What if marrying each woman was necessary to satisfy some practical need—and the sacred, one-flesh bond was the only way to do it? In *Brave*, he protects Ahinoam and Abigail. Continue the journey with KING DAVID'S BRIDES and discover why David must marry Maakah, the daughter of Geshur's King Talmai.

Discover the true-life stories of Samuel, Saul, Jonathan, and David in 1 and 2 Samuel. I write fiction in hopes that you'll run to the Bible for truth! If you have questions or comments about Ahinoam's story or how I built her fictional world, I'd love to hear from you at mesu@mesuandrews.com.

Happy reading, dear friends!

DISCUSSION QUESTIONS

1. Like many children today, Ahinoam was raised by a single parent. She, however, was raised by a single dad, which presented unique challenges in an ancient culture. Other than her external appearance and skills, what long-term struggles did Nomy face because she had only Old Miriam's Sabbath-meal influence during her formative years? How did her childhood with a single father uniquely prepare her to become David's wife?

2. David and his family remain at odds throughout the book, but he comes to the following realization early in the story: *I must change how I respond even if my family never changes.* In what ways did David successfully change his responses to family? Can you think of examples of when he reverted to unhealthy reactions prompted by past wounds? Is there someone in your life to whom you might change a specific response regardless of his or her continued behavior?

3. Early in the story, Ahinoam has a difficult time cultivating friendships with women. What traits do she and Zerry share that allow their friendship to blossom? How does

Ahinoam grow beyond Zerry's circle of trust and open her heart to women with a variety of interests, temperaments, and life experiences?

4. The first time Ahinoam happens upon David while he's singing and playing his lyre, she misunderstands his words and is frightened about where he might lead his army. David explains that he, like Yahweh, will sometimes lead his soldiers into hard, wilderness places to avoid what seems easy—but is truly dangerous. Can you describe a circumstance when you understood, perhaps only in hindsight, that God led you into a narrow wilderness to avoid a dangerously easy path?

5. David discovers Saul sent Doeg the Edomite to kill Abiathar's priestly family at Nob. Though David had the benefit of using the high priest's Urim and Thummim to determine death for the Edomite assassin, I imagined David wishing those stones could have given him more than a mere yes or no from Yahweh. David prays silently, *Why do you so seldom give long-term plans, Lord?* Have you ever wished God would reveal the long-term plan for your life? Or are you grateful you don't know the future? Explain your answer.

6. When Jonathan meets Ahinoam, he shares that it's through the helplessness of leaning on God's power alone, while living with his father's mania, that his faith has grown bigger than his fear. Later in the story, David battles fear and despair after hearing of his mother's death in Bethlehem but leans on Yahweh in silent prayer to regain calm and to encourage those who survived Bethlehem's raid. Can you cite other examples from *Brave* in which characters' faith journeys were strengthened? Have you experienced fear or

despair recently in which your faith in God has been made stronger by leaning into him?

7. As a biblical fiction author, I must set aside my twenty-first-century, Western-civilization mindset to immerse myself in whatever biblical era I'm writing. I'll confess, however, writing about David's polygamy has been one of my greatest challenges. David is my favorite Old Testament hero, so I've presented him as believing his heart was big enough to love multiple wives. Do you believe Ahinoam or Abigail could ever feel *fully* loved by a husband they shared?

8. Both David and Ahinoam teach us much about forgiveness, a process David describes early in the book: *The decision to forgive took only a moment, but healing from the pain would require Yahweh's constant help.* Ahinoam chooses to forgive David after he attended Samuel's burial instead of her father's, but restoring the relationship requires time and perseverance. Why do you think their journey to the Desert of Paran might have been helpful to rebuild their relationship? What steps toward forgiveness have you found helpful in your life?

9. After David and Ahinoam are married, the hardships of wilderness living drain their passion, and Ahinoam wonders if they've been too busy surviving to seek God's abundance. Could the same question apply to your modern "wilderness"? If so, what steps can you take to move beyond survival and seek the abundant life Jesus promises in John 10:10?

10. Through much of the story, David endures ongoing challenges by relying on Yahweh's constant presence. In the beginning, Ahinoam attempts to avoid pain and hardship. By

the end of the story, she knows Yahweh's presence doesn't shield her from hurt, but she never bears hardships alone. If you've experienced the same comfort, would you be willing to share how God's demonstrated presence made you *Brave* during a difficult time?

Read on for a sneak peek of

The Story
of Maakah

Book Two of the
KING DAVID'S BRIDES series

Available August 2025.

MAAKAH

Ner was the father of Kish, Kish the father of Saul, and Saul the father of Jonathan, Malki-Shua, Abinadab and Esh-Baal.

1 Chronicles 8:33

Sivan (May) 1010 BC
Geshur, King Talmai's Palace

The girl in the mirror wasn't fit for a prince, not even King Saul's fourth-born. Staring at my drab reflection in the body-length polished bronze, the future of our Geshurite kingdom weighed heavy on my shoulders.

"What if Prince Esh-Baal rejects me, Zulat?"

My maid stopped humming and looked up from packing our wooden trunk. "Prince Esh-Baal likely had no more choice than you did in the betrothal. Kings make those decisions to secure peace and power. A woman's power is strengthened when she brings pleasure to her husband, and you've been well-trained to do so by Inana's priestesses."

I examined my reflection again. "The high priestess said, 'Women love with their hearts and men with their eyes.' Esh-Baal's eyes will not love a dowdy princess devoid of cosmetics who wears peasant clothing."

"We must appear as peasants to keep you safe as we travel," Zulat said, then gently framed my cheeks. "And remember your ima's words: 'Royalty is born, not worn.' Your prince will see your beauty soon enough, and then you'll do as every shrewd wife does. Allow him to believe he's in control, then slip a gold ring in his nose so you can lead him wherever you desire." With a tap on my nose, she added, "Focus on our new adventure. In five days, our caravan will reach Gibeah, and you'll sit at King Saul's table as his honored guest."

Or I'll skulk back to Geshur after his son rejects me, causing the kind of shame that could damage Abba's kingdom more than a defeat in battle.

Though Abba had never spoken of previous negotiations, I was certain he'd sought betrothals among the other four Aramean kingdoms after my body declared me a woman. I'd waited month after month for the news of a royal match. Then year after year. As the only offspring of Geshur's royal couple, the whole kingdom knew I was the only political bargaining power. The decaying hope for my future hung on me like the stench of a decomposing camel. When the announcement finally came of my betrothal to Israel's fourth-born prince, it was like piercing the camel's bloated carcass. Perhaps the peasant's robe and no cosmetics was perfect for meeting Prince Esh-Baal.

"Prin!" Zulat's raised voice meant she'd said my name more than once. The use of my pet name and the crease in her brow proved her concern. "You can feign courage for your parents, but don't pretend with me. I know you're frightened to leave Geshur for the first time, and every bride is nervous about—"

"I'm not afraid." I rushed past her toward the door, tamping down my swirling emotions. "It's well past sunrise, and I'm tired of waiting for Abba's summons to say good-bye." Flinging open my door, I surprised both chamber guards, nodded curtly, and marched past them through the harem hallway.

"Princess Maakah!" Zulat only used my title when she was angry.

"You will not enter the throne room uninvited!" Sometimes she forgot I was no longer a little girl in her charge.

I whirled, abruptly halting Zulat and my lifelong chamber guards. "We've already wasted valuable daylight for an already long journey. Abba will understand my urgency and would be more perturbed if his only child left the city without a farewell."

Flustered, Zulat seemed at a loss. "But he—"

"Is anything more important to Geshur than this betrothal?" I glared at the woman who had taught me reading, writing, and the intricacies of national politics. "Well? Can you think of anything more important?"

"Yes." She lifted her chin. "You."

"Uhhh!" I groaned and strode away to hide the tears burning my eyes. Then why did Abba secure a treaty with King Saul's son—a second-generation donkey farmer? Humiliation drove me toward the throne room regardless of royal etiquette. Abba's guards tensed as I approached, their stance widening to the breadth of their shoulders.

"Princess Maakah," said the ranking officer, "King Talmai has ordered that we allow no one to enter until he and the queen resolve a difficult matter."

With a regal calm like a snake's rattle, I explained, "My caravan is ready to leave for Gibeah and is waiting for me outside the palace. I won't leave without a parting farewell to my parents. If you're the reason my arrival in Israel is delayed, our peace treaty is quashed, and my betrothal is canceled, how do you suppose King Talmai will respond?" I paused only long enough to awaken the guard's fear, then added, "My abba keeps no secrets from me. Now, open those doors."

"Yes, Your Highness." The guard nodded to his partner, and together they swung open the heavy cedar doors.

Victorious, I crossed the threshold and only then noticed Abba shouting. He'd descended the dais, his back to the doors, and stood face-to-face with a dust-covered messenger. The man spoke Hebrew, a language I'd learned in order to rule and trade, and the language of my soon-to-be husband. Before I could interpret the words, everything around me seemed to slow.

Abba reached for his sword and swung. The glint of bronze approached the messenger's neck. His eyes widened. A terrible whoosh echoed in the nearly empty room, then a thud when his head hit the floor. The body slumped at Abba's feet. Blood poured out—a river of it—flowing over and between mosaic tiles.

Abba spit on the dead man, then turned, only then seeing me. His right forearm and royal robe were splattered with blood. I covered a sob. He flung his sword across the floor and opened his arms. "Maakah, come to me."

My feet felt rooted to the floor. I glanced at Ima, who was seated on her smaller throne on the elevated dais. Our eyes met, and though she remained silent, her raised brow was like a shout. *Remember your training.* How many times had she stanched my tears or calmed my tantrums with that singular reminder? Royalty may have been a birthright, but it was maintained by a will of iron.

"Maakah." Abba's tone commanded my attention. "We have much to discuss." He walked toward me, hands extended as if approaching a skittish colt.

He looked like a monster with the blood dripping from his beard. "Wipe your face!" I said, stepping back and bumping into Zulat.

"You must obey," she whispered. The arms she placed around my shoulders both comforted and held me captive.

Abba stopped two paces from me, looked down at his bloodstained right hand and robe, then pulled a cloth from his belt and wiped his face and beard. Tossing the soiled cloth aside, he focused on me again. The slight crease between his brows forecast the gentleness in his voice. "I can see you trembling. Let me hold you, love."

There he was. My protector. King Talmai of Geshur. My champion. I ran into his arms and nestled against his muscular chest, the safest place on earth.

"Azam." He called over my head for his captain.

"Yes, my king?"

"Didn't I specifically say no one was to enter this room until my business with Saul's messenger was concluded?"

"You did, my king."

"You will execute the guards who allowed my daughter to enter."

"Consider it done, my king."

"Abba, no!" I pushed him away. "It was my fault. I—"

"My guards chose to disobey me. It cannot be your fault."

"But I—"

"Show your strength, Princess." He waited, his fingers digging into my upper arms as his eyes bored into my soul.

I glanced at Zulat, but she reflected Abba's hardness. Of course. My maid followed my parents' commands—as did Azam. I watched him march toward the exit and close the heavy door behind him. No one could save the guards I'd convinced to disobey my abba. My regret bowed to birthright, and I swallowed down the guilt to embrace Abba's acquittal. *"My guards chose to disobey me. It cannot be your fault."*

A commotion near the dais stole my attention. Two royal guards were dragging the dead messenger toward the throne room's side door, and four maids entered with buckets and rags to clean up the mess. Everyone seemed quite proficient at the task. I suddenly remembered other days when I was denied entry into Abba's throne room until certain matters were finished. How many times had King Talmai kept his violence secret from his daughter? *"My abba keeps no secrets from me."* How naïve I'd been. No more.

Stiffening my resolve, I focused my full attention on Geshur's king. "Should I assume my betrothal to Prince Esh-Baal is canceled since you've beheaded King Saul's messenger?"

"Indeed." A slight grin curved his lips before he extended his hand toward the dais. "We should join your ima to discuss the matter."

Zulat followed as we walked past the freshly cleaned floor toward the dais. My maid remained on the main floor when I ascended the three steps to the platform where Ima waited.

"Come, Prin." Geshur's queen beckoned with an outstretched hand, wiggling her fingers as if I were a toddler learning to walk. Her perfectly applied cosmetics starkly contrasted her pallor. Was she ill? Or had her face involuntarily paled with horror though she'd mastered all controllable responses?

I sat on the plush tapestry between my parents' two thrones and took Ima's hand. "Are you well, Ima?"

"As well as any ima whose daughter is leaving today."

"I'm still going to Gibeah?" I turned to Abba. "I thought you said the betrothal contract was canceled."

"King Saul reneged on your betrothal, and I'm sure he sent a disposable courier to deliver the news." Abba waved a dismissive hand toward the maids now leaving the throne hall, then handed me a small scroll he retrieved from his belt. "To avoid a delay of your departure, I'll summarize Saul's message. The Philistines will engage Israel in battle at Jezreel. King Saul has already marched his troops there under the leadership of his three oldest sons—the courageous ones—and left the coward Esh-Baal to rule at Gibeah in his stead. The scroll says King Saul broke the betrothal out of concern for your safety during Israel's tumultuous time, but my spies tell a vastly different story. Saul fears offending his Hebrew god, its priests, and a dead prophet named Samuel. Yahweh priests warned him that marrying a *pagan* Geshurite princess would offend their god. In hopes of appeasing this god, Saul removed Baal from Prince Esh-Baal's name and now calls him, Ish-bosheth." Abba sneered. "Saul should have feared offending *me* because soon his fourth-born son will be called dead."

My mouth went dry. I now knew Abba was capable of such violence.

"You deserve a warrior, my beautiful girl." He leaned back but his focus remained intense. "You will marry a man favored by all gods and many nations. A man who fights with the Philistines against Saul's weak leadership. You will marry David ben Jesse, the next king of Israel."

"You want me to marry an outlaw?" My contempt displeased him.

"A warrior," he said sternly. "David ben Jesse is shrewd and worthy of a throne. He's avoided Saul's capture for years and won the favor of King Achish even after killing the Philistines' champion, Goliath. This David has the courage and charisma to win the heart of his enemy." He cradled my chin with his bloodstained hand. "Perhaps he'll even win your heart. I've already sent a messenger with a betrothal contract."

"Without my consent?" I pulled away and looked to Ima for support. "David ben Jesse has no royal blood—and worse, no loyalty. He fights with the Philistines and betrays his homeland."

She still looked gray. "A betrothal to Israel's next king is better than a marriage to a royal coward."

"It's decided," Abba said. "Fifty of my best guards will escort the caravan to one of our Geshurite villages south of Philistia. David has likely already marched north with the Philistine army, so I've sent my messenger to wait south of Jezreel and negotiate the betrothal immediately after the Philistines destroy King Saul and his successors. My spies say the Philistines will place David on Israel's throne, and you'll be waiting in a nearby Geshurite village to become his queen."

Become his queen. More hopeful, I glanced at Ima again. She was smiling now but still pale. "Are you sure you're all right?"

She exchanged another unreadable look with Abba. He nodded

what seemed like permission, and she turned back to me. "I'm with child, love."

"You're . . ." Fear shot through me like a flaming arrow. Ima had endured four miscarriages, and the last one nearly took her life. "I can't leave until I know you'll be—"

"You will leave as planned," Ima said forcefully. "Your marriage to David ben Jesse will secure Geshur's future, and Geshur is always most important."

Abba reached for Ima's hand, giving it an affectionate squeeze before refocusing on me. "If your ima gives me a son, I'll have an heir to the throne. If I have a second daughter, you and David ben Jesse will inherit Geshur to rule someday."

More unknowns. And Ima's pregnancy had been another secret kept from me. I stood and bowed, etching my parents' hopeful faces into my memory, then turned to join the caravan to an unknown south Geshurite village.

My past and my future felt as if I were grasping at smoke, but by the gods, I would make Geshur proud.

MESU ANDREWS is a Christy Award–winning, best-selling author of biblical novels and devotional studies, whose deep understanding of and love for God's Word brings the Bible alive for readers. Her heritage as a "spiritual mutt" has given her a strong yearning to both understand and communicate biblical truths in powerful stories that touch the heart, challenge the mind, and transform lives. Mesu lives in Indiana with her husband, Roy, where she stays connected with her readers through newsie emails, blog posts, and the social media we all love to hate. For more information, visit MesuAndrews.com.

Sign Up for Mesu's Newsletter

Keep up to date with Mesu's latest news on book releases and events by signing up for her email list at the link below.

MesuAndrews.com

FOLLOW MESU ON SOCIAL MEDIA

Mesu Andrews   @MesuAndrews   @MesuAndrews